To
Bob
Your contribution
to my writing skills
has been invaluable. Best
of luck with your books.
Terry Wright 9-01

THE 13th POWER

Terry Wright

© 2001 Gardenia Press

The 13th Power
Copyright © 2001 by Terry Wright

Library of Congress Number: 2001092250
ISBN Number Softcover: 0-9678895-4-5

This is a work of fiction. Names, characters, places and incidents are either the product of the author's imagination or are used fictitiously, and any resemblance to any actual persons, living or dead, events, or locales is entirely coincidental.

This book was printed in the USA.

For inquiries or to order additional copies of this book, contact:

Gardenia Press
P. O. Box 18601
Milwaukee, WI 53218-0601 USA
1-866-861-9443 www.gardeniapress.com
orders@gardeniapress.com

With Special Thanks To
Glen Garry

Chapter One
BORNEO

With white knuckles, Fred Jenkins worked the stick. "What the hell do they want?" he yelled as he skimmed his copter over the rainforest canopy. White tracers streaked past the glass bubble. Faint gunfire rattled in the distance. "They're gonna kill us!"

Melvin balled a fist. "Just fly this damn thing," he shouted over the clattering engine and slapping rotor blades. Heart pounding, he twisted in his seat and looked behind them. Three Malaysian Federation patrol choppers were flying a wedge formation several hundred yards back—and closing. "Damn!"

The radio crackled. "Control. Victor Eagle One. We have visual contact," a chopper pilot reported.

Melvin shuddered. "Those bastards never give up."

"Give up? Good idea," Fred said. "Before they blow us out of the sky."

"Not that easy…"

"Jesus! I've got kids at home."

"Hope you kissed 'em goodbye this morning."

"Damn it, man! We don't stand a chance against these guys."

Melvin gulped. Fred was right. This little two-seater was no match for those military choppers. Sure—it was risky chartering this copter to Ketapang, but there was no other way. The Malaysian authorities were watching every transportation hub. He had to catch a fishing trawler to Jakarta. He had to get away.

The copter banked left and descended sharply. His stomach floated for an instant. He glanced at Fred. Beads of sweat trickled down the pilot's weathered face. Little had he known his high-dollar passenger would cause him so much trouble. Bad luck for Fred. "Hope you're a better pilot than a hero—watch out!"

Fred veered left, just missing a tree branch. "Think you can fly this thing any better?"

"Damn right! I was flying copters between Java and Sumatra back when your mommy was packing you off to kindergarten."

Gunfire rattled again. "What do they want with you?"

"Ah—they're just a bunch of sore losers."

"I didn't ask for none of this military shit and I don't want in the middle of your squabble. I'm just running a flying service, for God's sake."

"You'll be flying with wings on your back if you don't shake these guys." Melvin turned around to check the squadron's position. Another volley of tracers streamed past, closer this time. There had to be a way out of this mess. He searched the leafy canopy whizzing by below. Maybe over there. "Go right! Go right, damn it!"

Copter blades strained in the turn.

"Down there!" Melvin pointed to the river that snaked below them, peeking out from under the forest canopy here and there. "Go! Go!"

"You gotta be nuts!"

Melvin grabbed the stick and pushed it forward. The copter dove toward the river.

"Shit!" Fred pulled out of the dive and skimmed over the frothy surface.

Jungle closed in around them, darkening the riverbed. Blinding bursts of sunlight flashed through scattered gaps in the canopy. Melvin swallowed hard. He really screwed up this time.

Fred flipped the landing light switch, lighting the eerily forested tunnel. His skids clipped riverbank ferns as the rotors nicked low-hanging branches. One wrong move—they'd be swimming with the fish.

Streams of white tracers flashed by.

Melvin whipped his head around. Damn! The Federation choppers were flying single-file right behind them, their spinning rotor blades clipping tree branches as they rocked side to side in the air. Another burst of gunfire erupted. "Ha! They missed again!"

"Warning shots," Fred shouted as he dodged a fallen tree. "They could've shot us down already. Don't you see? They're giving you a chance to surrender."

"No way in hell!" Melvin snarled. "I'm not gonna spend the rest of my life in a Sumatra prison. I'd rather die—so keep this bird in the air."

"Sore losers, huh?" Fred banked his copter through a sharp bend in the riverbed. Ahead, another large opening in the canopy appeared. "We're getting out of this deathtrap, right now."

"No, don't!"

The copter nosed up and broke out into sunlight. Melvin clenched his jaw. What a stupid move. Now they were in the open. "God damn you, Fred!"

The Federation choppers flared out and flanked the copter on both sides. Rotor tip to rotor tip, Melvin looked at the chopper on the left. The officer bared his teeth and pointed his finger down.

Melvin sneered and turned to the chopper on the right, locking eyes with the pilot and flipping him a finger. "Bastards! You'll never take me alive!"

The radio crackled. "Hail Delta-Four-Niner-Echo. Melvin Anderson—you're under arrest."

Wide-eyed, Fred said, "Now what am I supposed to do?"

Melvin pulled up the pant leg of his jungle fatigues and reached into his boot. He fingered the smooth steel of his .44 Magnum. *Risk nothing, gain nothing.* There'd be no prison in his future, even if he had to fly this damn thing himself—or die. He snapped back the breach and pressed the muzzle against Fred's temple in plain view of the flanking officers.

"Say goodbye, Fred."

Melvin squeezed the trigger.

Chapter Two
THE MATHEMATICIAN

Janis Mackey, sweltering in his suit coat, stood on the bandstand and scanned rows of gold and black banners hanging limp in the hot, still air. The CU Buffs had a great stadium. They were a great football team. But today was *his* day for glory—a day he'd worked toward for a long time.

Pride welled up inside as he looked over the crowd gathered for his induction ceremony: faculty, friends, and students, familiar faces, all smiling. They sat in bleachers on the fifty-yard line. Classes were out; the semester was over. Summertime had come to the Rockies. He pushed his wire-framed glasses up the bridge of his nose, wishing his mother could have been here. But she didn't even know him anymore.

He hooked a finger under his collar, gave it a tug, and looked west to the foothills. This heat wouldn't last much longer. A gray cloud hung over Flagstaff Mountain. Silent forks of lightning streaked to the ground. It would be a typical summer afternoon in Colorado: thunderstorms, wind, and hail. But he loved it here—the peaceful university life of Boulder.

Dan Billings gave him a nod and stepped to the microphone. Sunshine glinted off the top of his head and his tie looked too tight. "A-hum." His voice reverberated around the stadium.

"As you all know, Dr. Mackey has been on the faculty here for twenty-two years. He's been a credit to the University of Colorado and an excellent teacher. Today he takes the big step up to administration."

The crowd applauded.

Janis showed them a big smile. Had it really been twenty-two years? Teaching and researching the awesome power of numbers and the rules by which they existed had made him well revered in a small group of elite men. But it didn't pay enough—just a notch above the poverty level—after Mother's expenses: medications, doctors, and the nursing home. Like leaches, they'd sucked her savings dry—and then his. After the money ran out, Medicaid kicked in, which helped some, but not enough. He couldn't let her wilt away in some low-dollar nursing home. She deserved the best care his money could buy.

"As head of the Mathematics Department, he'll oversee the faculty and counsel students on their career goals."

Janis ran his fingers through pepper-gray hair. How many hundreds had he seen graduate? He enjoyed working with the kids, especially at the annual seminar. Accelerated students from other colleges came to match wits with him and try out new theories on each other. It turned out to be a big event for the Mathematics Department and one of his favorite projects. But like all the projects around here, it took up more of his time and didn't pay any extra.

"Dr. Mackey and I have been best of friends for a long time. I'm proud of his achievements and honored to have him on my staff."

Again, applause echoed around the stadium. Janis waved. Finally, a promotion and a raise. Now, after taking care of Mother, there'd be money left over. He could junk that old Subaru and buy a new car. And that little house just off the turnpike—that would be nice.

Dan tapped the microphone. "And by the way, he's still single—in case any of you ladies might be interested."

Janis frowned. Did he look like he needed any help finding the wrong women? He was doing just fine on his own—like with Donna. She was a nice gal but complained he didn't have enough time for her. She wasn't really mad when she left. She just left.

And then there was Jill—what a babe. But her cats stunk up the apartment. He told her she had to make a choice, him or the cats. She *was* mad when she left. Would he ever find the right woman?

"Ladies and gentlemen, Dr. Janis Mackey."

Chapter Three
NO SURVIVORS

The muzzle blast was deafening. Fred's skull blew apart. Bullet and bone fragments shattered the copter's glass bubble and blood gushed across the instrument panel as Fred fell on the controls and sent the copter into a spinning dive. Trying to pull back on the stick, Melvin struggled against centrifugal force and Fred's dead weight. But the forest canopy was there too quickly.

Belly first, the copter slammed into the treetops, its rotors ripping branches into splinters and sending leaves flying through the air. With a reverberating twang, the blades twisted, snapped, and whipped off into the foliage. As the copter rolled on cracking tree limbs, Melvin jumped out, grabbing at thin air as he plummeted down with the copter. Sticks and leaves stung his face. His mouth hit a branch—hard. Everything went by in a whirl. Something snagged his legs. Pain shot through his body but the falling had suddenly stopped. With blood spilling down his chin, he spit red. What a rush.

Sucking air, Melvin watched the copter crash down through the branches below him. It hit black swamp water with a horrendous splash.

Damn!

Howler monkeys sounded an alarm from above as the hot engine sizzled in the water below. A hissing geyser of steam shot up from the wreckage. Melvin spit out a broken front tooth. His mouth burned. But he was okay. It could have been worse.

Suddenly, the air thumping sound of chopper blades thudded overhead, sending a blast of air whipping down through the trees. Shit! It had just gotten worse.

He scrambled down the rickety limb toward a massive, worm-riddled tree trunk. The downdrafts pelted him with stinging splinters of wood and leaves that flew through the air like razor blades. He turned his face down and away from the blast.

Through the patchwork of sun and shadows below, he spotted crocodiles swimming toward the wrecked copter. Three, four, five of them, their lumpy tails swaying in the water with a deadly grace.

Holding his breath, he watched in horror as the crocs broke into the copter and grabbed Fred in their toothy jaws. They yanked him out of the wreck and, twisting and thrashing, ripped his body apart. Pink and white strands of intestines floated in churning, red-stained water. The beasts snapped and quarreled over the gruesome remains.

Melvin shut his eyes and fought off nausea now throbbing in his guts. But maybe the officers hovering overhead had seen the bloody carnage and would think he had suffered the same fate. Several minutes passed before the hammering from above drifted away.

"Control. Victor-Eagle-One. Delta-Four-Niner-Echo has crashed. No survivors."

Chapter Four
THE PROMOTION

Lightning forked to the ground from a rolling gray sky. A clap of thunder rattled the old Subaru's windows. Pushing the mushy clutch pedal down, Janis wrestled the gearshift into second. The engine revved and knocked. Skip third gear—go to fourth. Third made a lot of noise anyway. Heavy raindrops pelted the car as his wipers streaked the windshield.

Thunk, screech. Thunk, screech.

Janis shivered. After a couple of paychecks, he'd get a new car. A Lexus would be nice, but he'd probably settle for a Camry.

Mailboxes cluttered the corner up ahead. Just beyond them, an entrance to a parking lot went off to the right. He'd driven this route most of his adult life—thought he could find it with his eyes shut. Pea-sized hail clattered on the roof as worn CV joints rattled in the turn. He was home.

Mission Meadows Apartments. Luxury living. Well—maybe twenty years ago. Now, wind-driven litter entangled in untrimmed hedges fluttered violently and busted toys strewn about a weed-infested lawn dripped rain. Three stories up, laundry flapped from open windows. He parked his Subaru next to a rusted Ford, sitting on flat tires. Things were going to change, after a couple of pay-checks.

He shut off the engine. It backfired. Well—maybe after *one* paycheck.

Dodging hailstones the size of marbles, he ran for the front doors. Rain angled to the ground. Hail bounced, thunder clapped. He bounded into the lobby and stomped water off his shoes. Colorado weather—don't like it—just hang around ten minutes. It'll change.

He could hear the phone ringing as he keyed the lock to his apartment. Pushing through the door, he rushed to answer. "Hello?"

Thunder boomed.

"Janis," came Dan Billing's voice. "You there?"

"Dripping wet. What's up?"

Dan coughed. "I didn't want to spoil your ceremony this

morning, thought it best to save this 'til later. Bad news I'm afraid."

Janis' stomach tightened. Bad news? Mother?

"If there was anything I could do about it, you know I would."

Confused, Janis said, "Give it to me straight, Dan," expecting the worst.

"Those damn budget cuts—the Board of Trustees has been giving me fits."

"What's that got to do with me?"

"It's about your promotion."

"What?" Janis felt like he'd been hit with a board. His head began to throb. "My promotion? What about my promotion?"

"Don't get all excited. You're still heading up the math department. But, well, your salary, Janis. It's been frozen. Six months—maybe a year—tops. You can hang in there that long—right?"

Chapter Five
A VILLAGE IN THE JUNGLE

Melvin struggled to catch his breath as he clung to the tree. Silence returned to the jungle. His body trembled, his broken tooth ached. The coppery taste of blood lingered in his mouth.

He ripped off a piece of his shirttail, shoved it into the space where his tooth had been, and bit down hard. Pain shot up to his temples. He peered across the sun-speckled darkness under the canopy. A bird cawed from somewhere. Crocodiles slithered into the shadows. What kind of mess had he gotten himself into this time? Did a violent death await him down there? Maybe. But for the moment, he was satisfied to be in a tree—alive.

He forced air through clenched teeth. Now how was he going to reach Ketapang? The Malaysian authorities had ruined everything. Sure—stealing their ancient artifacts and selling them on the black market had been a profitable endeavor. He'd made a fortune as the world's most notorious grave robber, a reputation that suited him well. But how was he to know those crazy bastards would go to war over that junk? Why was it *his* fault they'd killed each other by the hundreds? Guessing the fools had to have somebody to blame, Melvin shook his head. He needed a new occupation.

Looking down from his sanctuary to the murky pool below, he thought about crocs, snakes, and quicksand. How much fun could one guy have? He spit out the bloody rag and began to negotiate the treacherous way down.

Now he missed his .44. Sometime during the crash it had slipped from his hand. He felt almost naked, defenseless. What could he do to protect himself from the vermin that lurked about? A dead branch forking off from the tree trunk gave him an idea. He broke it with a sharp crack: a good poker, three foot long or so, and sturdy. Something was better than nothing. Straddling the last woody knot above the water, he carefully studied the swamp. Nothing stirred.

Quietly, he slipped into the water, which rose to his waist and felt surprisingly warm. A fuel slick from the copter floated on the surface in rainbow-colored swirls.

He tried to take a step away from the tree but his boot stuck in the mud. Curling his toes, he strained harder, trying to pull his boot free. But it seemed as though the swamp wanted to suck it right off his foot. He struggled with this new dilemma—but the bottom didn't yield a single step. "Damn!" What else could go wrong?

Suddenly, the water surged upward. From under the black surface came the shining throat of a monster croc, a million dagger-like teeth glistening in the boil. Melvin let out a yell and thrust the poker between its gaping jaws. Writhing in the water, the croc bellowed and thrashed. The stick cracked and snapped.

"Oh, shit!" Melvin grabbed the tree trunk, pulled his feet out of his boots, and climbed to safety. The angry croc roiled the water. Melvin hung on to the tree and shook from adrenaline burning in his bloodstream.

Gasping, he scouted the swamp again. There had to be another way out of here. He'd been in worse jams than this before, though he couldn't remember when. But traversing this swamp wasn't an option—he'd surely die. He looked up to the canopy where irate Howlers clambered from tree to tree, complaining. Vines dangled down like the wavy tentacles of jellyfish. His spirits lifted. The way through the rainforest was up there.

*　　*　　*

The sun cast long shadows by the time Melvin had worked his way through the trees to the edge of the swamp. He slid down a vine to solid ground, a narrow dirt path, and looked left and right. Which way should he go? Did it matter? He chose right.

Between the copter crash and the jungle trees, his clothes were shredded to rags and soaked with sweat. Stinging scratches and aching bruises covered his body. His mouth hurt more than his muscles, which tortured him with every step. Darkness began to envelop the jungle. His tattered socks flopped in the dirt as he plodded onward.

From the eerie shadows of nightfall, birds chirped and cawed. And other strange noises filled the night air—grunts of a wart hog family foraging in the bush, shrieks from a troop of monkeys swinging in the treetops, the faint strains of music. He cocked his head. What? Could there be civilization in the midst of these wilds? He picked up his pace.

A few minutes later, the jungle opened into a clearing. Light glowed from the windows of huts lining the path. Scattered campfires dotted the meadow and wordless voices reached his ears. As he strained to listen, the heady aroma of food drifted to his nostrils. He took in a deep breath of it. "Ahhh." He couldn't remember the last time he'd eaten. Warily, he made his way down the path and into a little village.

A barking dog announced his arrival but no one paid it any mind. Music was coming from a large hut with colorful lanterns flickering from the porch. A makeshift boardwalk stretched across a mud puddle and led to the doorway where an "OPEN" sign hung canted. The smell of food wafted from inside. He put on a stern face, threw his shoulders back, and pushed through swinging doors. Every head turned toward him.

He stopped and looked around the hut. Small wooden tables cluttered the room. Most were vacant but all had a small candle burning in the center. Shadows danced on the thatched walls. Stout wooden beams supported a rope net ceiling from which beer signs and banners hung. Behind the bar, a cassette recorder was playing an old Australian tune and a chubby-faced man wearing a white apron looked surprised. "What duh hell happened ta you, mate?"

Melvin didn't reply. He walked to a corner table and pulled out a chair, which thudded on the wood-planked floor. Finally, he could sit down. What a relief. Through shredded socks, he rubbed his aching feet. The roomful of staring eyes made him nervous. With a sneer and a sharp jerk of his head, he motioned the curious onlookers to go about their business. Some did. Some didn't.

"Martha," the bartender called. "We've another guest for dinner."

A moment later, the kitchen curtain parted and a short overweight woman waddled out carrying a heaping plate of food. She looked at the bartender. He pointed. "Over there."

Smiling, she made her way across the hut, her blue flower-print dress dragging along the floor. She put the plate down in front of Melvin and handed him a big spoon. "Care for a spot of tea—or somethin' a bit stronger, sir?"

He didn't answer. He ate. Stew of some kind. But it smelled like prime rib, the meat melting in his mouth, the potatoes fat and soft, peas firm and fresh, all drowned in thick brown gravy. The pain of his broken tooth was numbed by the joy of eating.

When his plate was empty, he pushed it aside and called to the bartender. "Bring a bottle of whisky and a glass." From a tattered pocket, he pulled out a wad of soggy cash and tossed it on the table. The bartender was quick to respond.

Chapter Six

BORIS DAGLOSKOFF

Melvin's whiskey and money attracted the attention of a patron sitting alone. Peering out from under bushy gray eyebrows, Boris ran his callused fingers across weather-cracked lips and stared at the stranger. "Hmm." Though his initial interest in the haggard man wasn't compelling, the thought of a free drink was. His heart beat a little faster. Should he? Why not? He stood, and slightly hunched over, shuffled across the hut with a discernible limp. Though his frizzy gray hair hadn't seen a comb in a month and his old wrinkled clothes smelled bad, he truly believed he was in better shape than the well-to-do stranger.

Grabbing a chair, Boris sat down without an invitation. "So, vhat happen to you?" he asked in a broken Slavic accent and cast an obvious glance at the whiskey bottle. At least he hoped it was obvious.

Melvin eyed him warily for a moment, then picked up the whiskey bottle and filled the glass. Nose-stinging vapor rose in the air. He lifted his drink, inspected the fill. "I just fell off the turnip truck."

"Ha!" The stranger was a smart ass. Boris licked his lips. "Look like mighty fine vhiskey you got."

Melvin threw down a gulp. "Where can I get some boots around here?" He grabbed the bottle and poured again.

"Tell bartender to bring another glass."

Glaring, Melvin stopped pouring.

Boris gulped. Was he pushing his luck? Undaunted, he extended his hand to Melvin, who just stared at him with gray eyes that had no soul.

"Name Boris Dagloskoff."

Chapter Seven
THE ULTIMATE DIG

Melvin hesitated to shake Boris' hand. His breath stunk of booze and his clothes smelled like cat piss. "Go away!"

"Only try to be friendly."

"You're a beggar!"

"Things not always vhat they look," Boris said, his hand still offered.

"Be off with you!"

"You want boots or not?"

Melvin thought about that as he finished filling his glass. Maybe the old man could be of some help after all. A little whiskey would be a small price to pay for a pair of boots. Without smiling, Melvin shook Boris' leathery hand and called, "Barkeep—another glass for my friend."

Boris showed a smile full of half-rotten teeth. "Vhat name you?"

"Call me Melvin." He pried his hand from the old man's robust handshake.

The bartender brought a glass, set it on the table and said, "Be careful of old Boris. He glows in the dark."

Patrons started laughing.

Melvin wondered what he meant by that. Before he could ask, Boris said, "My old job, nuclear scientist in Mother Russia. They always make a joke."

"Kind of far from home, aren't you?" Melvin said, not seeing any humor.

"Long story. But you, I will tell." Boris reached for the glass and placed it where Melvin could easily pour from the bottle. "But first, we drink."

And they did. With the help of the old man, the booze was soon gone. "Barkeep—another bottle." Melvin started to relax, the whiskey numbing the ills of his day.

The bartender clunked a new bottle down, and as he sorted through the soggy cash for his fee, Melvin looked Boris up and down. How did a Russian scientist end up here in the middle of nowhere? The old man must be smarter than he was acting. Was it a sympathy ploy for free booze—was he really down on his luck? He looked harmless enough. One way to find out, get him talking. "I fell out of a helicopter," Melvin said and took a slug of whisky right from the bottle.

Boris laughed. "Turnip truck—hic—better bullshit."

"No really—and—a big croc about bit my damn head off." He gave the bottle to Boris. "In all my years of searching for treasure, I've never come that close to dying."

Boris cracked an ugly smile. "Ah! You search for treasure? I too, search for treasure. We do same thing." He slapped Melvin on the shoulder. "Comrades! Yes?"

"If you're an archeologist."

"Scientist. In Russia we search for 13th Power—hic—deep inside atom." He guzzled from the bottle and handed it to Melvin.

Bottleneck in hand, Melvin's interest spiked. "What kind of treasure is that?"

"Find Higgs boson, key to unlock atom, key to unlock universe. Very much power—very much money. With Higgs you can alter reality. Think of possibilities of 13th Power. Be possible you change lead to gold, water to petro, or maybe if you like, salt to cocaine." He stared at Melvin and twitched his bushy eyebrows. "Make very famous man who finds it."

Melvin glared at the Russian. Had the booze loosened his tongue? Was he telling the truth or just bragging through his whisky? Melvin's head felt woozy. The 13th Power couldn't exist anyway. "Turn lead into gold? I think you're full of shit, old man."

Boris' eyes widened. "Oh yeah?" He sounded as though he'd been challenged to a duel. "Boris not full of shit."

"Yes you are, Boris," the bartender put in. "When the hell you gonna get off that old rag tale of yours?"

The other patrons howled and jeered, "Too dangerous. Too dangerous."

Boris scowled at the bartender. "You I tell. Now him I tell. Search for 13th Power very dangerous."

His mockers roared. "Too dangerous. Too dangerous."

Melvin thought Boris must've told this story many times. Didn't anybody believe him? What if there was something to it? With the right amount of money, personnel, and equipment invested, there'd be a fortune for the taking, unlike any other.

"Enough!" Melvin slapped the table with the palm of his hand, silencing the ridicule and laughter. "What's too dangerous, Boris?"

"One time I was prominent Russian citizen 'til lure of Higgs screwed up my life. Moscow stopped our experiments with 13th Power. Arrest scientists. I almost not escape. Five years now I hide in jungle—no caviar, no fine Russian Vodka. Only eat mangos and snake stew and drink this cheap Aussie bootleg whisky. Some life I have now—huh!"

Melvin swallowed. Snake stew? He looked at his empty plate. "This Higgs boson—does it explode?"

"No. No—it make things disappear. Fourteen reactor probes disintegrated, gone into black void. Lost whole particle accelerator one time. Leave big hole in ground. Moscow have a fit." Boris shook his head as if he didn't believe his own story. He grabbed the whisky bottle from Melvin and took a face-contorting slug. "Better to leave 13th Power alone. Too dangerous."

Too dangerous? Melvin tongued the space where his tooth had been, recalling how he'd lost it. Talk about dangerous. Risk nothing—gain nothing. His father had always told him that. Nothing worth having was too risky to get. Could the 13th Power be the ultimate dig, an excavation deep into an atom to pluck out a key to the universe—the Higgs? Could he really create his own riches? The possibilities were endless. He looked Boris in the eyes. "Tell me how to find this 13th Power."

"You don't want to know."

"Bet me."

Boris stared a moment, thinking really hard. "How about you stay here in village, be guest of mine. I will tell you about Russian experiments and 13th Power. Then you will see why I say too dangerous. You will change your mind."

Melvin put his hand on the old man's shoulder. "That's more like it." If Boris were lying about the 13th Power, a knife through his gut would be his reward. If not, then he'd bragged to the wrong man. *Too dangerous* didn't mean shit to Melvin. Besides, he needed a new occupation. Smiling, he downed the last of the whisky. "Let's go get them boots."

Chapter Eight
DIRECTIVE NUMBER 119

John Nathan walked into the Oval Office. Sunshine beamed through the windows and the whole place smelled of fine leather and polished wood. His official title gave him access to this office, Deputy Director of the White House Chief of Staff. Only the President had any knowledge of his real title, his real job, and the reason he was here today.

Under his arm, he carried a red file folder, thick and heavy with *Directive Number 119* stamped on the jacket in bold black ink. The silver-haired President looked up from the papers on his desk and spoke with a Southern accent. "Is it all there?"

"Everything you need against General Brigham."

"Let's have a look."

Nathan placed the file in front of the President and flipped it open.

"Just as I thought," the President said.

Nathan looked it over. The first report read:

From: Dr. Tracy McClarence, Cambridge, UK. Laser Physicist.

To: The Department of Defense, Ballistic Missile Defense Organization, Orbiting Laser Research Division.

Re: The latest series of particle beam tests failed. Request more funding.

"They're out of money again. Same old story." The President leaned back in his chair and folded his arms across his chest. "Reagan's Directive Number 119, the Strategic Defense Initiative, fell to the budget ax in '93. Seems the Department of Defense spent everything Congress gave them. Star Wars didn't have a chance with those crooks running the show." He pointed to the second report on the facing page. "Looks like history is repeating itself with the BMDO."

Congressional Report. Particle Beam Funding. Denied.

"All this bureaucratic bickering and the United States still sits vulnerable to a nuclear strike from anywhere around the globe. General Brigham and his cronies get away with grand larceny while the rest of us scramble for disarmament treaties."

"They've been working, so far," Nathan put in.

The President leaned forward. "Did penned words on a piece of paper ever insure peace? Hell no! Ask the American Indians—they know only too well. Treaties aren't worth the ink they're written with." He stood and walked to the window. "Besides, there are too many crazies in this world. All it would take is one lunatic in Iraq or Pakistan to push a button. We're sitting ducks."

"But they're not nuclear capable, Sir."

"To hear your boys at the CIA tell it."

"We're on top of it."

"Why am I not relieved?" The President walked back to his desk and closed the file. "As of this afternoon, General Brigham and his boys are out of business. I'm giving Directive Number 119 to *The Ark*. I want you to handle it."

"Are you sure?"

"Find another way to get the particle beam working." The President sat down and clasped his hands on the desk. "This is your chance to be a hero, John."

"And just how do you expect me to work this miracle?"

Pointing to the file, the President said, "Get a line on this Dr. Tracy McClarence for starters. Maybe she can help."

Nathan back-stepped toward the door. "Right away, Mr. President." When he walked out of the Oval Office a chill went up his spine. *The Ark?*

Chapter Nine

DR. FRANK CURTIS

Biting into a chunk of mango, Melvin looked out the window of Boris' hut. Searching the jungle path and the muddy Jeep trail, he hoped for any sign of the old man. Wispy rolls of fog bumped the treetops as cattle and goats grazed in the meadow. Black-skinned children played in puddles left by the last downpour. But no Boris.

The air hung still as death, hot and muggy. Buzzing, a fly landed on his ear and he swiped at it in irritation. The time had come to leave. Finally. He'd been stuck in this shit hole for the last three weeks and Boris' negative attitude was driving him crazy. *Too dangerous. Too dangerous.*

Cutting off another chunk of mango, he sat at the table, thinking. Boris had told him about the rules of physics and the power of the Higgs, how the Russians had opened holes into the universe and risked global disintegration. Just the kind of story Melvin loved—danger, adventure, and riches beyond his wildest imagination.

Boris appeared in the doorway, kicking mud from his boots. He clunked into the hut and tossed a manila packet on the table. Melvin looked at it—felt a chill.

"Your new papers," Boris said. "Melvin Anderson officially missing and presumed dead. Got that from Singapore office. Now you are Dr. Frank Curtis. Congratulations."

Melvin thumbed through the papers. Everything was there—passport, California driver's license, Social Security card, and even some credit references. "Smitty did fine job."

Boris plucked a mango from a bowl on the table. "He told me to tell you—no more favors."

"He's a crybaby. But he's damn good at his craft. Got me in and out of a lot of countries." Melvin sorted the documents and slipped them back into the packet. "When's the Jeep gonna be here?"

"Soon," Boris said sullenly. He seemed distant, worried—had the long face of a man whose mother had just died.

Melvin squinted. "What's your problem?"

"How you think you pull this off?" Boris said and bit into his mango. "Need money, equipment, scientists. Where you find these things?"

"I've amassed a fortune over the last thirty years—enough to buy all the equipment and scientists I need. In California, I have a friend, Jonathan Kyles. He will help me with everything else. The 13th Power *will* be mine."

Boris looked at the floor. "You go to USA and find the 13th Power. Say not I didn't warn you." He walked out of the hut and didn't look back.

Chapter Ten
JAKARTA

A foghorn blared as a fishing trawler docked in a slip at the Port of Tanjung, Jakarta. Melvin was home at last. The Java Sea crossing had been rough, the boat pitching and yawing over wind-driven swells. But it was more comfortable than that mud-slinging Jeep ride through the jungle to Ketapang. His body ached; his eyelids felt like boat anchors. But he had a plan, places to go and things to be done.

Seawater rose up against the concrete harbor walls and slipped back down to crusty barnacles. Timing his jump, he leaped to the dock. Wooden planks creaked under his boots as he ran toward a cab idling at the end of the pier. Pelicans that were perched on the posts took flight. As seagulls sawed back and forth in the wind, cawing, he climbed into a dilapidated Toyota van and said, "Rangkayo Rasuna."

"Buckle your seat belt," the driver replied.

Melvin clutched the window frame as the cab clunked along a rutted road toward the inner city. A seemingly endless clutter of shanties with red-tiled roofs closed in around him. He slouched in his seat. Poverty. In the distance, skyscrapers towered above the greenery. He smiled. Wealth.

On the Gunung Expressway, the cab weaved through heavy traffic, past Merkado Palace, Parliament, and the University of Indonesia. Melvin took in all the sights. At Rangkayo Rasuna, the cab slowed and turned a corner. His heart fell into his stomach. Military Jeeps surrounded his bungalow. Barbed wire curled across his front yard and armed soldiers stood at his door, eyeing the cab as it approached. He ducked behind the seat. "Drive on! Drive on!"

A sweat broke out on his brow. The Malaysian government had seized his property. Had they found his secret bank accounts—stripped him of his wealth, his hoarded loot, and his prized possessions? What a rotten homecoming that would be. He tapped the driver's shoulder. "Bank National Indonesia." The cab turned right and headed toward the skyscrapers.

In the bank lobby, Melvin's fingers trembled as he typed at a computer terminal. His list of accounts scrolled down the monitor. They were safe. He thought he would faint from relief. Working the keys again, he transferred several hundred million dollars to banks in the United States. He picked three that sounded good—First Industrial, United Bank and Trust, Empire. *TRANSFERS COMPLETED* scrolled across the screen. Now for the toys.

The bank manager unlocked Melvin's safety-deposit vault. He stepped into the room and switched on a light. A musty odor assailed his nostrils but everything was still there—gold from Egypt, ivory from India, rubies and gems from the ancient kingdoms of Kediri and Mataram.

He looked over his treasures—it had to be here somewhere. Ah. His prized golden staff leaned in a corner, alone. An eagle's head of gold, with green emerald eyes, adorned the top of a four-foot golden shaft. Ramses III, King of Egypt, must have been proud of this walking staff. Melvin took it in his hands, savored its weight, and caressed the cold and shiny gold, its beauty only eclipsed by its deadly secret.

Looking around the room, he spotted the black wide-brimmed hat and long black coat once worn by an evil eighteenth century Count of Portugal. History had said he was beheaded for his crimes against women. Melvin grabbed the old clothes. The Count was a fool. He got caught.

In a box of gold jewelry, Melvin spotted a bracelet once worn by a Queen of Ethiopia. Because he didn't know exactly which Queen wore it, the World Society of Archeologists claimed it was just another gold bracelet. What did they know? He darted his tongue across the gap left from his missing tooth and thought of Sahib, his dentist. Bracelet in hand, he locked his vault and left.

*   *   *

Melvin stashed the packet of fake documents under his long black coat and boarded a 747 at Halim International Airport, bound for Los Angeles. In his first-class seat, he set the golden staff across his lap and laughed aloud for the joy of his new adventure.

"I'm glad you're having a good time, Dr. Curtis," the flight attendant said. Her voice floated in the air like classical music.

"Would you like a drink to go with that?"

Dr. Frank Curtis smiled, showing her the bright shine of his new gold tooth.

Chapter Eleven
THE MISSION

Nathan pushed through the double doors at Andrews Air Force Base and quickstepped down the concourse toward gate #7, the hard soles of his patent leather shoes clicking on the tile floor. He hadn't bothered to shave, change into a clean shirt, or even button up his black suit coat. Not enough time. The briefcase he clutched in his right hand was all he really needed. This was the break he'd been hoping for. One phone call from Singapore had changed everything. Hell—he'd take luck over skill any day.

He glanced around the concourse. Where the hell was Lawrence? He should've been here by now. The CIA Chief of Internal Affairs had better not be late. Dr. McClarence was waiting for them in Atlanta. They had no time to lose.

"Nathan."

His name echoed through the terminal. He looked left and saw Lawrence running down a corridor, his long overcoat flapping behind him. His bald head shined and his tie whipped back and forth with each stride. "This is never going to work, I tell yah."

"You let me worry about that," Nathan said.

Breathing hard, Lawrence ran up beside Nathan and matched his stride. "Let's just arrest the son of a bitch and be done with it."

"I want to hear what the Russian has to say, first. Tracy tells me it'll blow the lid off Star Wars."

"We're all gonna end up with our necks on the chopping block."

"You worry too much."

"Only when *The Ark* is involved."

"I can handle it," Nathan said, picking up speed when he saw an attendant waving them on at gate #7. He ran outside to a shiny Falcon jet, its turbine engines whining. Strobe lights flashed on the wingtips and a blue and silver CIA insignia glistened on the tail.

A flight attendant stood in the doorway, waiting for them to board. Dressed in a sharply-pressed blue uniform, her smile shined as bright as the silver bars on her collars.

"Evening, Lieutenant," Nathan said, handing her his briefcase. "Sorry to drag you out like this."

"Glad to be of service, sir." Her smile didn't waver.

He ducked inside the plane. Perfume lingered lightly in the air. Taking the executive seat halfway down the cabin, he cinched his seatbelt. Higgins buckled up in a seat across the aisle.

The intercom crackled. "Ready when you are, sir."

Nathan said, "Let's go."

Ceiling lights dimmed as engines revved and the jet began to roll. Nathan bit his lower lip. Takeoffs and landings—can't have one without the other.

He looked out the window. Strobe lights pierced the darkness with an eerie rhythm as the aircraft rocked and thumped along a taxiway lined with blue lights. The jet turned, stopped. Green lights edged the concrete now. He looked at Lawrence who was pulling on his seat belt, sweat beading his forehead.

A chime echoed through the cabin. Nathan shifted his eyes to the Lieutenant as she strapped herself into the first seat behind the cockpit.

The engines revved to a thunderous roar. Nathan turned his eyes to the window again. The aircraft started down the runway—slowly at first, then faster and faster, inertia pushing him against the back of his seat. Green lights streaked by the window at a dizzying pace. As the nose pitched up, the runway lights dropped away and landing gears banged into their compartments. Inertia subsided into the floating sensation of flight.

Washington, DC glowed below him like a carpet of Christmas tree lights, the city of his boyhood dreams. The President, the White House, the most powerful city in the world. His home. The only place *The Ark* could ever function—and get away with it.

Rolling left, the Falcon climbed into the night sky. Nathan turned his attention to Lawrence who still looked nervous. Was it because of the Russian or because of *The Ark*? Nathan glanced at his watch. Atlanta was more than an hour away. They had a lot to talk about. "Tell me what you've got on the Russian."

Lawrence wiped his brow. "Boris Dagloskoff," he said over the whining engines. "A Russian nuclear physicist. He's clearing customs in Atlanta, in about an hour. Agent Stevens will have to run him through INS before Dr. McClarence can see him."

"I hear he's not cooperating," Nathan said, reclining his seat.

"He wants the 13th Power experiments stopped—says

they're too dangerous."

"Offer him a permanent resident visa if he helps us out."

"Political asylum in exchange for his story—that's all he wants. We stop Dr. Curtis—he stays out of prison in Russia."

"Not good enough," Nathan said, rubbing his chin. "Give him a choice—the visa or deportation."

"But what if he's right?"

Nathan frowned. "The end of the world? Not likely."

"But he was right about Solartech Labs in Simi Valley, California. Dr. Curtis took control of the corporation, just like he said."

"That's why I'm sending in a team to cover the operation."

"Oh? And who'd you get to lead this team?"

Nathan grinned. "Alex."

Lawrence raised an eyebrow. "Alex Gibson?"

"Only the best for *The Ark*." The jet rolled right and continued to climb. Nathan examined his fingernails. "What did Boris say about Curtis?"

"He's an impostor, some grave-robbing ex-archeologist named Melvin Anderson. Seems he invited Boris to join him in California, illegally of course, to help him on the project. The old man said he never thought Curtis would go through with the 13th Power experiments. Boris got scared, turned himself in to our agents in Singapore. Curtis doesn't have a clue that we're on to him."

"And we're going to keep it that way."

"For how long?"

"No telling," Nathan said, the thought of a lengthy operation settling in his stomach like a rock. "Dr. McClarence is due in Simi Valley tomorrow night. Curtis is looking to hire a top mathematician to work with his nuclear physicist—some guy by the name of Ray Crawford. Nobody's ever heard of him."

"And what about this disintegration Boris keeps talking about? These guys could screw up everything."

"Dr. McClarence doesn't think so," Nathan said as the jet's nose pitched down to level flight. "She says Crawford won't have any better luck than the Russians. The 13th Power is unattainable. But the particle beam is all we want. When it's working, we'll move in, steal the technology, and arrest Curtis for his past crimes."

Lawrence balled a fist. "It's too risky. We should nail the bastard right now, before it's too late."

Nathan scowled. "We're not walking away from this, Lawrence. Directive Number 119 is at stake, the security of the nation. Besides, history is going to show that we got the job done. Hell—everyone else failed. They didn't go about it right. This time we're doing things differently, ruthlessly if necessary. Failure is not an option."

Lawrence gave him a sour look. "Failure is always an option."

"Not this time. I'm counting on you to support the mission in any way you can. Do your job—we'll get through this without a scratch."

"You're asking for trouble."

Nathan shrugged. "Would *The Ark* have it any other way?"

Chapter Twelve
SIMI VALLEY RAIN

Los Angeles Boulevard. Simi Valley. And rain. Tonight it was pouring. Tracy McClarence stood inside the door of Bennie's coffee shop and peered down the rain-slicked street. Headlights reflected off the wet pavement. Cars sloshed by in an endless rhythm, like the rain in the streetlights, an unending drizzle. Her eyes searched the shadows. Was he still out there—somewhere—watching?

Door glass reflected the fear in her eyes. She pulled the scarf over her head and tied it under her chin. Why had she let the cabbie drive away? Now she had to wait for another. It seemed like a good idea when she left Solartech Labs, a magazine and a cup of coffee. She couldn't sleep anyway, worrying about the project. But she didn't know she was going to be followed. Didn't Dr. Curtis trust her? Or was he suspicious of every new technician on the team?

Her breath fogged the glass. She wiped it away with the palm of her hand and stared out into the night. It was unnerving—Curtis' bodyguard spying on her. Judas gave her the creeps. She'd heard stories about him. Horrible stories. They couldn't be true. Could they? Why was he tailing her? Did he know about *The Ark*? Oh, God. He'd kill her for sure.

"We're closin' up, lady." Ceiling lights went out. "Yah can't stay here all night."

"I was hoping for a cab."

"It's almost midnight."

She zipped her jacket and tucked the magazine under her arm. "Well—goodnight then." She pushed through the door and into the rain. Her hair was going to be a mess.

A horn honked. Was it a cab? She looked toward the street—saw some drunk hanging out the window of a red T-Bird, waving at her to come to the car. Sure—she'd been told her legs were destined for stardom in nylons commercials. But did she look like a hooker? Pretty and slim—yes. But sexy? Not tonight—not with her long red hair tucked under a scarf and fatigue lines etched under her eyes. She ignored him and rushed around the corner. Her heart clutched. Bad move. Judas!

Leaning against the building, his ashen and pockmarked face shined eerily under the streetlight. His hands were thrust deep into the pockets of his trench coat, the collar turned up against the rain, which dripped from the brim of his hat. He stared at her with cold eyes. What did he want? Why was he here? If he knew about *The Ark*, it would ruin everything.

Judas pushed himself upright and slowly walked toward her, his breath wisping from his nostrils. Her eyes shifted to his hidden hands. Did he have a gun? A knife? Her feet wanted to run. She told them *no*. Her knees trembled. "W-what do you want?"

Judas kept walking. The rain kept coming down.

*   *   *

"He's getting closer. We gotta do something."

Rain trickled down the windshield. "Give her a chance."

"He's gonna kill her."

Alex glanced at his partner. Craig Stevens was a good agent. He seemed to have a sixth sense—knew when somebody was going to die. This time he was wrong. Alex felt it in his gut. "There's no way Judas can know. He's trying to scare her, see if she has anything to hide."

"Look at her face—she's going to crack." Craig pulled a rifle from the back seat.

"No! She's tough. She can do this."

"I'm going to be ready." Stevens rolled the window down an inch and pushed the barrel through the crack.

Alex held his arm. "Shoot and the mission is over. Curtis will know we're on to him."

"I can't let her die."

"*The Ark* said she's expendable. No one is more important than the 13th Power project."

"But… "

"Hold your fire, agent. That's an order."

*   *   *

Tracy clenched her fists at her side. Judas was getting too close. Her knees felt like rubber, her head faint.

Judas glowered in her face. "What are you doin' sneakin' around this time of night?"

She tried to get a breath of air. Why hadn't he tried to kill her? Why...? Hell, he didn't know a damn thing. Come on, Trace. Think. "Look who's talking. You scared the shit out of me, damn it."

"I think you're meetin' up with someone tonight." His eyes narrowed. "Who is it?"

"Are you nuts? I went to Bennie's for an espresso. Cleared it with Security first. They even called the cab. So don't start on me with this cloak and dagger stuff." She sidestepped.

He checked her move.

Her magazine fell to the sidewalk, landing in a big puddle. "Now look what you've done."

"Klutz," Judas said.

She glared at him. "What's with you?"

"What are you doin' on this project—comin' in late and all. Somethin' don't seem right."

Tracy blinked raindrops from her eyelashes. "Lasers have been my life. That's what I'm good at. When Curtis called the Russian, he called me at Cambridge."

"Why did Ted call you?"

She looked away, tapping her foot. Ted Benning, Boris Dagloskoff—one in the same thanks to some phony ID work by a guy in Singapore. She heard he wouldn't be seeing daylight for a long time. Sumatra prisons were unforgiving—much like Judas and this damn rain.

"We worked together in Russia, before Moscow shut us down. Curtis needed help with his laser problems. Ted told him I was the best." She stared at Judas now, hoping he wouldn't detect a lie in her eyes. Truth was, she hadn't met Boris before Atlanta. But the story wasn't so hard to believe. Curtis bought it, just like *The Ark* said he would.

Judas stuck out his chin, pools of water spilling from the brim of his hat. His eyes got big around. "I'll be watching you." He turned and walked away.

"Wait. Give me a ride back."

"Find your own ride."

She put her hands on her hips and watched him disappear

into the drizzle. What a jerk.

A car pulled up to the curb, honking.

"Forget it, Buster!" She turned, thinking it was the fool in the red T-Bird again. Instead, a black four-door Ford idled in the rain—a staff car from Solartech Labs. She recognized the silhouettes of two men sitting inside.

The rear door swung open. "Get in."

She grabbed the doorframe and slid onto the seat. The dome light lit Alex's handsome face. His square jaw and high cheekbones were sexy and fearsome. She heard he'd done a lot of killing in Vietnam. But he didn't look fifty and his smile was the most beautiful thing she'd seen all night.

"Are you all right?"

"I'm soaking wet." She shifted her eyes to Agent Stevens. He had that country boy look—blonde hair combed down over his forehead and freckles scattered across his nose and cheeks. She thought he'd look more in character with a pitchfork in his hand instead of that big rifle.

"You did great," Stevens said.

She pulled the door shut. "No thanks to you guys."

"We were backing you." Alex accelerated the car into traffic.

"We shouldn't have let you go," Stevens said. "But we had to find out if Curtis was suspicious. When Judas followed your cab, we knew you were in trouble."

Tracy shivered, the cold rain soaking through to her bones. "They don't know anything. Tell *The Ark* we're in the clear."

Chapter Thirteen

CAPTAIN BEN

Must meet with you at once. URGENT!
The Balli Club. San Francisco, noon
Friday. Tickets at United counter,
Denver International Airport, 8:45 A.M.

Janis stashed the note in his coat pocket, drank the last splash of orange juice, and rinsed the glass. Why did Ray Crawford send the note "Special Delivery"? Hadn't he heard of telephones or e-mail? What was he up to? Or had he been working at that secret company in Nevada too long? The hot sun must've fried his brain.

Walking to the picture window, he pushed his glasses up the bridge of his nose. The summer sun shined high above the horizon. What did Ray need that was so urgent? Was he in some kind of trouble?

A mustard-yellow cab pulled into the parking lot, glistening in the early morning rays. *About time.* The horn blared as he pushed through the front doors of Mission Meadows and, dodging busted toys on the sidewalk, headed toward the cab.

"Beautiful day," the burley black cabby said, holding the rear door open for his fare.

"Yes, it is." Janis looked at a clear blue sky. "Too bad I won't be here to enjoy it." He slid into the car. "I have one hour to get to the airport. Can we make it?"

"If I can't get around the traffic, I'll go over it. They don't call me Captain Ben for nothin'."

As the door closed him in, Janis groaned. Just great. Another manic cab driver.

Settling into the back seat, Janis noticed the lack of odors that usually linger in a taxi. Instead of stale cigar smoke, sour beer, and cheap perfume, the interior had that new car smell. He buckled his seat belt. "How long have you had this car?"

Captain Ben dropped the gearshift into reverse. "Since yesterday. Ain't she a beauty?" He twisted around, put his elbow over the seatback, and released the brake. "The old one was a wreck. I swear I keep my body shop boys stocked with beer and loose women."

"How's that?"

"Don't know what it is about my luck. Momma says I was born with none. Somethin' always happens to tear my shit up. But not with this one. No, sir." His wide smile showed off a mouthful of white teeth. "This one's not gonna get a scratch."

"Would be a shame," Janis assured him.

*　　*　　*

Captain Ben backed out of the parking lot and drove south on Rogers Lane. When he turned east on Baseline Road, a blue van pulled away from the curb, made a reckless U-turn, and raced up behind him. Captain Ben paid it no mind and made a tire-squealing turn onto the freeway ramp. He merged the cab effortlessly onto the Boulder Turnpike. When he checked his rearview mirror to make a lane change, he saw the blue van speeding up alongside him. It slowed and didn't pass.

"Idiot," he grumbled under his breath and released the throttle. The van slowed. He accelerated. The van sped up. Ben shot the driver a frown. The driver flipped him a finger. What? Suddenly, the side door of the van slid open and he found himself looking down the black barrel of a 50-caliber machine gun attended by two masked men.

"Holy shit!" He slammed on the brakes. The tires squealed as the machine gun began its deadly report. Lethal rounds pummeled the fender and hood.

"Get down!"

Shards of metal, ricocheting at random, shattered the windshield and spewed a crystalline mist into Ben's face. He spit.

"Hang on!"

Stomping on the emergency brake, he yanked the steering wheel to the right. His pulverized cab spun in a circle and careened into the lane directly behind the van. Slamming the throttle to the floor, he released the brake and rammed the van's rear bumper. The jolt sent the hood ripping over the roof.

"You guys wanna play tough?" He kept his foot on the gas, hard to the floor. Engine roaring, he plowed the van into the guardrail. Sparks cascaded across the median as the railing chewed up the van. Crunching metal and breaking glass filled the air. But he kept the throttle down, bouncing and jerking, pushing the van along the ragged guardrail. Chunks of smoldering rubber slapped his shattered windshield. Ben gritted his teeth. Sons of bitches! He gave the steering wheel a quick jerk left, sending the van into a right-hand skid. Blue tire smoke pumped from the undercarriage as it careened across the highway and smashed into a sign pillar, head-on. The van crumpled and exploded into a yellow ball of fire.

"Take that, you morons!" After slamming on the brakes, he turned to watch the fury of smoke and flame rise from the highway. Stinking rubber and gunpowder permeated the air.

He looked down at his passenger sprawled on the back seat. His face looked ghostly white as he sat up, staring over the frames of his crooked glasses.

"I'm alive!" Janis exclaimed. "We're okay!" Wide-eyed, he looked around the car. "Oh shit—your cab is a mess!"

"Damn! My body man is gonna be pissed."

Sirens sounded in the distance.

"Here come the cops."

Janis pushed his glasses up and looked out the rear window. Distorted through the heat waves emanating from the burning van, he saw the flashing overheads of approaching emergency vehicles. "I don't have time to deal with them. I've gotta make that flight. Let's get out of here."

Captain Ben shrugged. "You're the boss." Returning his attention to the front he added, "Tell yah the truth. I've had more than my share of cops." He floored the accelerator.

Janis watched the smoking carnage fade away in the distance. It was a miracle they'd survived, thanks to Captain Ben's driving. "How did you spin around like that?"

"Easy," Captain Ben said, cocking his head toward the back seat. "Just lock the emergency brake and crank the wheel. Rear end 'll slide right around. Trick is to hit the brake release and the gas when you're pointed where you want to go. In this case, right up that damn van's ass."

"Doesn't sound very easy to me," Janis said, wiping glass dust from his slacks. "Sorry about your cab."

Captain Ben grunted. "Never fails."

The rest of the trip was uneventful, even reverently quiet. As the cab rambled down Pena Boulevard toward the airport, questions whirled through Janis' mind. Who had targeted him? And why? Was the meeting with Ray connected somehow? One thing was for sure, the answers were in California.

Captain Ben swung into a "No Parking" zone at Departures. Janis fumbled for his wallet.

"Never mind that," Ben said. "It's on me. Good luck. You're going to need it."

"You think?" Janis closed the door and backed away from the wrecked cab. He couldn't help but notice the smile on Captain Ben's face as he drove away.

Chapter Fourteen
RAY CRAWFORD

Ray stood under a stone archway and looked into the empty dining room of the Balli Club. A bearded man in tan coveralls appeared to be cleaning up around the tables. Ray noticed a hearing aid in his ear, an older model, much bigger than newer styles.

The kitchen doors swung open and Jimmy rushed out. The tuxedo he wore fit his lanky frame perfectly. "Mr. Crawford—this way, please."

Ray followed him to a reserved table against the back wall. "This should do nicely."

The janitor wandered out, as if onto other chores. Jimmy disappeared through the swinging kitchen doors. Alone in the dining hall, Ray gathered his thoughts for the up-coming meeting. Would Janis even show?

Checking his view of the entrance, Ray adjusted his tie and flicked a piece of lint from the sleeve of his suit coat. He kept every detail of his appearance as neatly organized as his laboratory—his jet-black hair nicely cropped and combed and his thick mustache pruned to look like his mentor's, Albert Einstein. Satisfied nothing was out of place, he reached into his pocket and pulled out three folded newspaper clippings. The papers crackled with age as he laid them on the table.

Crawford-Mackey Team Up On 13, headlined the first article from the University Press. A surge of pride welled up inside as he read the text:

Ray Crawford's physics team joined forces today with Janis Mackey's mathematics team in an attempt to find the 13th Power. Professor Yeager VanBlought predicts these students can do it. However, the University Board of Trustees has limited funding to the project, casting a shadow over all hopes of success.

His jaw set as he turned to the next clipping:

Crawford-Mackey Fail On 13.

"Damn it!" He slapped the table. What did they expect with junk equipment and no money from the budget? The damn fools hadn't given them a fair chance. The memory rekindled his anger—an anger he had carried with him for twenty-seven years.

His stomach churned as he recalled what happened after that. Disgusted with the penny-pinching Board of Trustees, he dropped out of college and never achieved his degree. Working at Atomtech, an atomic research and development company in Nevada, gave him little satisfaction. He had tried to persuade Walter Devin to take on the challenge of finding the 13th Power. But that proved to be a fantasy, as his boss handed him one disappointing rejection after another. Through it all, his obsession for the 13th Power only grew, his drive becoming more resolved. He justified his struggle by surmising that this was the price truly great scientists must pay to grasp their place in history. A price *he* must pay.

He turned to the next clipping: *Dr. Janis Mackey Takes Top University Seat.*

Envy sliced through his guts like the blade of a knife. Twenty-seven years in the private sector had not brought him the fame he deserved for his dedication in the field of nuclear physics. What he wanted most eluded him. Recognition for the 13th Power could be his reward for all those years of obscurity. And now, with this meeting, he had reached a turning point. If Janis joined the team, Ray had a chance. If not, he was finished.

"May I get something for you, sir?" Jimmy asked.

Ray quickly glanced around. Patrons had already begun to arrive before the lunch hour rush. A wave of anxiety rolled in his stomach. "Not yet, Jimmy. Keep your eyes sharp for Dr. Mackey." He pointed to the picture in the third newspaper clipping.

Jimmy gave him a two-fingered salute and walked away.

Ray carefully reorganized the old clippings and returned them to his pocket. He took a deep breath, but it didn't help quell the anticipation.

Chapter Fifteen
SAN FRANCISCO

The 737 streaked toward San Francisco. Janis stared out the window but his mind wasn't on this flight or the sights to see below. Ray was up to something. In college he and Janis were inseparable. Aside from an occasional beer bash or Spring Break, they were immersed in their studies. While Janis spent his spare time boxing and playing chess, Ray hung out in the science labs, always tinkering. He was never satisfied with the normal everyday rules of physics, always looking for a bigger or better solution to problems that already had answers.

"Drink, sir?" the flight attendant said. "Coffee, tea, or maybe something stronger?"

"N-no thanks," Janis replied, his voice still hoarse from his shaken nerves. He removed his glasses, rubbed his eyes, and returned to his thoughts. Ray had aced Atomic Principles and went on to study the theory of relativity and the space-time continuum. He became obsessed—couldn't talk about anything else. The atomic force and the speed of light were making Ray a dull boy. When a company in Nevada offered him a job—*zap*—he was gone. Though his degree was only a few semesters away, he gave it all up and disappeared. Sometime later, just before graduation, he'd called with news of his marriage and birth of a daughter. Her name escaped Janis' memory. It must have been 25 years ago.

And now this. He set his glasses back on and pulled the note from his suit coat pocket. A surge of panic welled up inside, like nausea. The note was shredded, a hole ripped through it, the writing unreadable. He quickly examined his pocket and fingered the path of a bullet. His throat went dry. Why had those men attacked his cab? Who were they? Maybe he should've dealt with the police—but he would've missed this flight. He needed to find out what Ray was up to. Janis looked out the window. Had he done the right thing? Only time would tell.

He called out to the flight attendant. "I'll take that drink now. Coffee, black."

*   *   *

The jet came to a stop at the gate. Passengers jumped up from their seats and grabbed their carryons, jammed the aisle and scrambled for the exit. Janis waited for the melee to subside, then strolled down the gangway.

Walking onto the concourse, he spotted a young woman holding a sign.

Dr. Mackey.

His heart skipped—not because of the written page, but because of the woman, a California girl if he'd ever dreamed of one. Her blonde hair hung straight down past her shoulders like beams of sunshine and the dress she wore, a one-piece yellow miniskirt with white lace, looked a size too small. He tried to stop his eyes from tracking down her body, but they refused to obey, taking in her shapely curves, her long tan legs, and white high heels. Hand in the air, he could hardly spit out the words. "I—I'm Dr. Mackey."

She smiled.

Approaching her, he caught the fragrance of perfume, light and flowery. Her blue eyes sparkled and her glossy red lips begged to be kissed. Beautiful.

"I'm Lisa. Welcome to California."

"I wasn't expecting anyone."

"The Balli Club sent me to escort you. Our limo is out front. Let's get your luggage."

"I'm going home this afternoon, after the meeting. Didn't pack anything."

Lisa's smile disappeared. "How unfortunate. My boss instructed me to show you the town tonight. Guess I'll miss the opportunity to party with you."

Janis gulped. Was California on earth or in heaven? *When in Rome* came to mind. "Well, plans can be changed."

With a wink, Lisa took his hand. "This way," she whispered and led the way out.

The limousine gleamed in the sunshine, a black Lincoln with tinted windows and elegant lines. Lisa opened the rear door to the spacious executive compartment. Janis climbed inside. The air smelled of fresh pine. He picked the right-hand seat, up front, so he could be close to Lisa.

As she walked around the front of the limo, he eyed her fluid motion and confident stride. Thoughts of the meeting started slipping away to thoughts of Lisa and the possibilities. But when she slid into the driver's seat, his eyes went to work sweeping the area around them, looking for anything suspicious—especially blue vans.

When Lisa accelerated away from the airport, he put his elbow over the seatback and peered at the large percentage of thigh exposed by her hiked miniskirt. The sight was inspiring—but why would a chauffeur be wearing something so provocative? She looked more like an executive's assistant than a limo driver. Something wasn't right about that. Adjusting his glasses and hoping not to show any special interest, he said, "Do you live around here?"

"Yes, of course," she replied with a giggle. "Do you?"

"N-no, of course not," he stumbled. "Colorado."

"Oh?" She looked intrigued. "A real cowboy?"

Janis chuckled. "If you like." He had never thought of himself as a cowboy. "How long have you been working for the Balli Club?"

"You sure are full of questions, cowboy. Let's just say I'm a free woman in a free world and I'm into doing a lot of things. I know you're attracted to me—most men are. But they only have one thing on their minds and don't bother taking *my* feelings into consideration. Are you that kind of man, cowboy?"

"I'd like to think not," Janis said, suddenly confused. Did all California women say exactly what was on their minds?

She looked at him for a moment, smiled, and returned her eyes to the road. "No, of course you're not, Dr. Mackey."

"Please, call me Janis."

A few moments passed in silence. Her hair laid lazily over her shoulders, springing this way and that way as she attended to her driving duties. Judging from her figure he thought she must be very athletic, probably did some kind of California aerobics or something. Occasionally she would glance at him, so he didn't want to be caught looking in any one place too long. The evening invitation flashed through his mind. Should he...?

"So, what's your story, cowboy?"

"Ah, well, I'm here for a meeting. An old college buddy needs me for something. I haven't heard from him in more than twenty-five years." Again, the invitation flashed back. "Let's do it tonight," he blurted out, earning an odd glance from Lisa. "I mean the town thing, like you said. I'd like to spend some time with you."

"Great!" A smile lit up her eyes. "Call me on my cell when the meeting's over." She pulled a card from her purse. "Here's my number."

Janis examined the card. It had a phone number on it, hand-written, as if she'd prepared it for just this purpose. "Anytime?" he asked.

"Whenever you're ready."

He slipped the card into his shirt pocket. California—what a great name for heaven.

A few minutes later, the limo stopped under the Balli Club's marquee, its lights flashing *Tango tonight with THE BOB MAN-SON BAND.*

"We're here." She got out, walked around the limo, and opened his door.

Janis stepped out.

"Good luck with your friend," she said. Then kissing her fin-gertip, she placed it on his nose and whispered, "Call me, cowboy."

He blinked. "I will."

She closed the door and dashed around the car. As the limo drove away, he stood there a moment, watching it disappear around a corner. "Whew!" Walking up the steps to the club, he checked his watch. 11:50. Time to get back to reality.

The doorman squared his shoulders. "Good afternoon, sir. Will you be joining us for lunch?"

"Yes—and thanks for sending your limo. Your chauffeur is a doll."

The doorman frowned. "Sorry to say, sir, I've never seen *that* limo before."

Janis quickly looked down the street where the limo had dis-appeared. He clenched his fists. What was Lisa trying to pull? Why had she lied? Damn! The doorman held the door open. After one deep breath, Janis pushed his glasses up and stepped inside.

The Balli Club looked like a rich man's paradise, the foyer adorned with beautiful tapestries and furnishings. He took in the subtle smell of polished wood and waxed floors. The sound of classical music drifted lightly in the air.

A young man in a tuxedo greeted him. "Hello, Dr. Mackey. My name is Jimmy. Please allow me to show you to your table."

Janis started. How many strangers knew he was coming to this meeting? Somewhat reluctantly, he followed Jimmy under an archway and into a dining room skirted by a mahogany bar. The smell of food filled the air—roast beef, fresh bread, and garlic. Silverware clinked and plates clattered among the hubbub of conversation. He scanned the crowd of diners and bar patrons, searching for a familiar face. Ray Crawford, sitting at a table in back, looked up and smiled.

Janis clenched his jaw.

Chapter Sixteen
THE REUNION

Ray stood and embraced his old college pal, patted his shoulders, shook his hand. But Janis seemed distant, his smile restrained, his handshake clammy. Was something bothering him? This wasn't the warm reunion he had expected. Leery to ask what the problem might be, Ray offered Janis a chair. "You look great."

"Nice to see you, Ray," Janis said blandly. "How's the wife?"

He sighed. "I divorced Kate twenty years ago. She was a complainer, always nagging about my long hours at work—you know the type."

"Can't say I do. And your daughter, how is she?"

"Who knows?" Ray twitched his mustache. "She hasn't called in a long time, probably still angry at me for one damn thing or another. Seems to be her favorite pastime."

"Angry?"

"It's a long story. Did you ever settle down? Any wife and family?"

"No. I use the excuse there's no time for anything serious. Truth is, I haven't found her yet. So I bury myself in my work."

"Looks like you're sitting pretty on the Colorado U staff."

Janis shifted in his chair. "It was quiet and peaceful around there, the way I like it. Until this morning, anyway."

"Something happen?"

"That's right, Mr. Top Secret."

Ray gulped. "What are you talking about?"

"I get one note from you in twenty-five years and I'm suddenly up to my neck in trouble." He pulled a shredded piece of paper from his pocket and flipped it on the table. "Recognize this?"

Ray picked up the note he'd sent Janis. A sudden jolt of heat hit his bloodstream.

"Bet you don't know how I got this, either." Janis showed him the hole in his coat pocket.

"What happened, damn it?"

"A couple of goons tried to disassemble my cab with a machine gun this morning. A blue van, a lot of noise, and all hell broke loose on my way to the airport."

Ray couldn't find words. Why would anyone try to stop Janis from reaching this meeting? Was it an organized attempt at sabotage or just some random big-city violence? He struggled to explain it. "Hell if I know," he finally said. "Sure it wasn't a neighborhood gang ritual or something?" He slid the note back toward Janis.

"I doubt it. Those guys were professionals with a deadly interest in stopping me from getting to this meeting." His eyes narrowed. "I want to know why. So let's have it. Right now!"

Ray removed the newspaper clippings from his pocket and unfolded them. He felt Janis' icy stare. Slowly, Ray slid the papers across the table.

Janis sat upright, looked at the clippings. "What's this?"

"Check it out."

As Janis read, Ray watched for any hint of a favorable reaction. He felt light-headed—faint from anticipation, as if he were waiting to hear his name announced as the winner of the Nobel Prize. Each second that ticked by made his blood flow faster. But he let Janis read in silence.

A few heart-pounding moments later, Janis looked over the top of his glasses. "I remember this deal. We had a blast until the money ran out. Came up with a really good hypothesis, too." He pushed his glasses up and glanced over the old papers again. "I give up. What's *this* got to do with anything?"

"Look, Janis—back then, we didn't have the money or the equipment to give this experiment a fair shot."

"Yeah, but... "

"Now I've got everything we need to finish what we started. Everything, Janis. It'll be just like old times, only better."

"Now hold on—hold on one minute, Ray!" Janis glared. "The 13th Power? What are you, out of your mind? That was a college project designed to stimulate our minds to the possibilities. The numbers are worthless, beyond reality. There's nothing to find. Remember? It's not real."

"Bullshit!" Ray stuck out his chin. "The 13th Power is at the center of matter's existence and, as tiny as it is, I aim to find it. But I can't do it alone. I need your help."

"You don't say."

Ray paused, wondered how he could get Janis to listen to reason. *Tell him everything, from the beginning.* "Things are different for me now. My life has changed rather quickly. I quit working at Atomtech—spent twenty-five years there, you know. But they wouldn't listen to me, Janis. They couldn't see the possibilities of the 13th Power. I couldn't get their top mathheads to help me. My boss wasn't interested."

Leaning forward, Ray lowered his voice. "However, a rich man who believes the 13th Power is attainable approached me a few months ago, asked for my help. Like a dream come true, his organization has given me their full support. But their mathematicians keep getting error messages from the computers. We need your expertise to fix the problems."

Janis' jaw muscles started twitching. "You brought me here to finish a stupid school project? Didn't you consider I have a life of my own?"

"Life? What life? No family—hooked on your work. We're two of a kind, you and I. The quest for answers has been our whole life. This is like our Super Bowl, the big cohune, the whole ball of wax. Cut the bullshit and let's figure out how we're going to do it."

"You haven't changed a bit—still trying to make something out of nothing, chasing your silly obsession with nuclear space and time that doesn't exist. When are you going to grow up and get back to the real world?" He slid his chair back and stood.

Ray grabbed Janis' arm. "No—damn it! This is not a school project with no solution. I'd never have brought you here for nothing." Staring into Janis' eyes, Ray had a feeling this was his last chance to convince him to stay. "How does a million dollars sound?"

For several tense moments, Janis' eyes returned a cold stare. Ray felt a chill. If Janis wouldn't do it for money, he wouldn't do it for anything. Unyielding eyes told Ray the 13th Power was slipping away. "A million dollars, Janis. Just think of it."

"Don't play games with me, Ray!"

"This isn't a game," he said, the desperation in his voice rising. "I'm talking about earning a million dollars here."

Janis yanked his arm free. "You're gonna pay me a million dollars? Ha! That's a laugh."

"Not me, Janis. But if you'll just wait, I'll introduce you to my money man. He's on his way, right now."

Again, Janis stared into Ray's eyes as if he were looking for the madman within.

Ray met his gaze with the same intensity. "I'm serious, Janis." Time seemed to stand still.

Janis took a breath, held it for a moment, then exhaled. "Okay, I'll wait—for old time's sake." He sat down. "We'll see what your money man has to say."

Ray smiled, a heavy weight lifting from his shoulders. There was hope after all.

Wearing a fake beard and dressed like a janitor, Steve Raven put his elbows on the bar and adjusted the hearing device in his ear. At 32, he had a reputation as a top-notch private eye. His eavesdropping tools went unnoticed under the table where Ray and Janis held their conversation. Steve didn't know what they were talking about, but he was sure his client would. With a compact tape recorder running silently in his pocket, he swallowed the last swig of beer in his mug and scratched his phony beard. "Barkeep—another beer. And this time don't foam it up so bad." He flung another buck on the bar and turned when the front door suddenly opened with a rush of wind.

A tall man wearing a long black coat appeared under the stone archway. His black wide-brimmed hat partially covered his face, hid his eyes, and created an eerie veil about him. He leaned on a golden staff that glistened. Steve shuddered. What was this, Happy Halloween? He turned back to his beer and the assignment at hand.

Janis spotted a sinister-looking man standing at the entrance. His dark form sent a chill up the back of Janis' neck. He nudged Ray's arm, directing his attention to the stone archway.

"That's him!" Ray said. "Dr. Curtis. He owns Solartech Labs and called on me to conduct the 13th Power experiments. I tell you—this guy's our ticket to the Nobel Prize."

"Just came to you out of the blue?"

"With these newspaper clippings."

Janis drummed his fingers on the table. "This day keeps getting weirder by the minute."

Chapter Seventeen
THE MONEY MAN

An afternoon breeze gusted through the Balli Club as Curtis stood in the doorway. Hanging on his six-foot frame, his long black coat whipped in the swirling wind and attracted the attention of several patrons seated nearby. From under the wide brim of his black hat, he saw the fear in their eyes. He liked that.

Jimmy stepped up. "Good afternoon, Dr. Curtis. Your party is waiting. This way, please."

The golden staff thudded on the marble floor as he walked in, leering at curious patrons who quickly turned away. At a table in back, he saw both his guests were already standing. Excellent. Taking a gold watch from his vest pocket he said, "12:30. Right on schedule."

He looked at Jimmy. "My good lad—fetch me that bottle of wine, the one I've been saving for a special occasion such as this." Jimmy rushed away. Curtis nodded to Ray.

"Janis—I present Dr. Frank Curtis. Dr. Curtis—this is the mathematician I've been telling you about, Dr. Janis Mackey." They shook hands. Curtis smiled. Janis didn't.

"Please, gentlemen—be seated," Curtis said.

Janis whispered to Ray. "So this is your money man, eh?"

Curtis sat down and laid the golden staff across his lap. He noticed an atmosphere of tension surrounding the table and, for now, chose to ignore Janis' remark.

Jimmy returned with a bottle of wine on a golden tray with three crystal glasses, one of which had a golden stem.

"Thank you, Jimmy. Please do the honors with this." Curtis removed a gold corkscrew from his coat pocket.

Jimmy went to work opening the wine bottle.

Curtis handed out the glasses. The crystals he gave to his guests—the golden-stemmed glass he kept for himself. Jimmy poured the wine. Curtis thought these few minutes of wasted time were acceptable. He'd get to the point of this meeting soon enough. Success was close at hand.

Satisfied the drinks were ready, he stood and raised his glass. His guests followed his lead. "Gentlemen. A toast to the 13th Power. I salute you."

The glasses clinked together. Janis didn't drink.

Curtis grumped. "This is no time to be skeptical, Doctor. Drink up."

"What makes you think I'm skeptical?"

"If not skeptical, then you are stalling. May I suggest you are not the type of man to waste your time like that?" He showed Janis a deliberate smile.

"True. I don't like wasting my time," Janis said. "And I *am* skeptical in a calculating sort of way." He tipped his glass and took a sip of wine. "Like a mathematician should be."

"I thought as much." Curtis sipped his wine, eyeing Janis over the rim of his glass. Was the mathematician going to make things difficult? Let him play his silly game. Curtis motioned with one hand. "Sit."

"Ray tells me there's a million dollars in this 13th Power deal," Janis said. "Just how does that work, Mr. Curtis?"

"He's a doctor," Ray corrected him.

Janis lifted his eyebrows. "Oh? A doctor of what?"

Curtis sat upright in the chair, clasping his hands over the top of his staff. "I am a doctor of archaeology, though that occupation is long into the past and best forgotten. Many people around here, including Ray, seem to think I am pleased by the title because I collect priceless artifacts such as this golden Pharaoh's staff I have here. Truth is, I spent decades searching for artifacts only to have them snatched away by fanatic officials. I became disgusted with the whole business. So you see, I have retired from the *Doctor* occupation a long time ago. You may call me *Mister* if you like."

"I see." Janis' voice dripped with sarcasm. "Well, *Mister* Curtis—getting back to the original question—what about the million dollars?"

Staring at Janis, Curtis sipped his wine. "Dr. Mackey—or may I call you Janis?"

"Be my guest."

"Then Janis it is. I have found that money can buy anyone or anything. I have enough to do both. I acquired Solartech Labs because it is the best facility in the world. It's also a money machine, thanks to the government, that is. But its real purpose is to bring in new ideas and develop them through radical technology." He set his wineglass on the table and leaned forward on the golden staff. "The 13th Power is a radical concept, rejected by most because of its impossible dimensions—you know, too big and too small. But as an observer of the past, Janis, I have discovered that history, over and over, has displayed a forsaken lesson of unreality in reality, myth in fact, and delusion in science. The 13th Power is simply another example of this ignored concept. The rewards are hidden within the solution. The solution requires great minds and massive amounts of money. I have the money. You and Ray have the minds. Sounds like a team project to me." He picked up his wineglass and leaned back in his chair. Taking another sip, he kept his eyes keen on Janis, awaiting his reaction.

"Why the 13th Power, *Mister* Curtis? Why not a cure for cancer—or AIDS?"

"Why climb the highest mountain? Why send a man to the moon? Why fly a kite in a thunderstorm? Because it's there, that's why—a new discovery to be made by those men brave enough to take on the challenge."

"Then why us? There are other scientists and mathematicians."

"I have checked on your research in college. You two worked well together and have experience in this. You have already developed a hypothesis as a foundation for your experiments. I know you are the ones that can make this thing happen. So here we are."

"That's all fine and dandy, *Mister* Curtis. But where does the money come in?"

"You confuse me, Dr. Mackey. Here you are, a prominent mathematician, professional and practical. I would expect a man of your caliber to care more about science than money."

"You're asking the impossible. I want to be sure I'm going to get paid."

"Perhaps Ray was wrong about you."

"I'm not one to waste my time—remember?"

"Or you just can't cut it."

Janis' face turned red. He stood, glaring.

"What's the matter, Doctor? The 13th Power too tough for you?"

"You're crazy."

"He believes in us, Janis," Ray said.

"You're both crazy."

"However crazy, I am prepared to pay a million dollars for the 13th Power."

Janis stared at him for a moment, then jotted a number on a napkin. "Transferred to this account." He slid it across the table.

Curtis picked up the napkin. Too easy. He stood quickly and extended his hand, smiling. "Deal!" But Janis didn't accept his handshake.

"Not so fast, *Mister* Curtis! I'm not wasting my time chasing a worthless number unless you guarantee payment, even when the project fails." Janis leaned forward on the table. "And it will fail—I promise you that."

His hand still extended, Curtis said, "I will guarantee payment regardless of the outcome *if* you will not invite failure and open your mind to the possibilities of the 13th Power."

"Transfer the money on Monday?"

"You shall have it."

Janis finally shook his hand.

Curtis smiled, the delight on Janis' face giving him great pleasure. The mathematician would have opened his mind to the *lollipop power* for a million dollars. Some professional *he* was. Pathetic. But his grip was surprisingly solid. He seemed sure of himself. Confident. Had Curtis misjudged Janis' integrity? Was the money really important to him?

Sitting again, Curtis laid the staff across his lap, peering at both men from under the brim of his hat, pleased by the smiles on their faces. They thought they were so smart. He pulled a checkbook from his pocket, and a gold pen. "Let's see now," he said and wrote his new employee a check for $10,000. He placed it on the table in front of Janis. "Here's a little spending money."

Janis, eyes cold, slid the check to the side and set a shredded note in its place. "Any idea who might have wanted to stop me from making this meeting?"

Curtis inspected the paper.

"Someone attacked Janis' cab on his way to the airport this morning," Ray said.

"Would anyone you know do that?" Janis asked.

A lump formed in Curtis' throat. Was someone screwing around with his project? He swallowed hard. "I think not, Janis." Curtis tossed the note down and said to Ray, "Get Dr. Mackey to

Solartech Labs this weekend. I want a meeting of department heads in Tech-Com Control at 9:00 Monday morning. No dallying on this, gentlemen." He rose from his seat. "You have history to make." Turning his back on the scientists, he grinned and strutted toward the exit, his golden staff thudding on the marble floor.

Chapter Eighteen

THE GLADIATORS

Ray broke the silence. "Eh! What do you think of my money man, now?"

Janis didn't answer. "Yo, Jimmy—my good lad," he said, mocking Curtis. "How about a couple of menus." He set aside the wine. "And a tall glass of iced tea."

"One for me too," Ray put in.

"Right away, gentlemen." Jimmy took off.

"What are you going to do with a million dollars?" Ray asked.

Janis folded the check, slipped it into his back pocket, and looked around the room. Was this million-dollar deal a godsend or had he just sold his soul to the devil? Certainly, the money would make things a lot better. The scraps they called raises at the university were never enough. Mother's expenses outpaced his income every time. He looked at Ray. "I'm not going to waste it around here, that's for sure. As long as Curtis comes through with the money."

"Don't worry," Ray said. "He has the money. About two years ago, he bought up the stock in Solartech Labs. Someone said he walked into the stockholders' annual meeting and offered five times the share value to anyone who would sell to him on the spot. He walked away owning the company."

"Why?" Janis skimmed a menu Jimmy had set on the table.

"When you see this place in Simi Valley, you'll figure it like I did. He wanted the labs and the equipment. He canceled the company's commercial contracts—said there'd be no time for them. But the government contracts he kept."

Janis set aside the menu. "Any reason?"

"There are more ways to stuff cost-overruns into billing—more money involved, less work and little quality control. Atomtech is probably the biggest government contractor in the country, racking up tens of millions of dollars per year in cost-over-run billing. Curtis is no dummy. He won't give up his gravy work to Atomtech—or anybody else for that matter."

"So the guy wants to use the labs for his playpen and finance his new toys with government contracts. Atomtech could be in for some stiff competition when new contracts come up for bidding." Janis took a sip of iced tea. "Somebody could lose a lot of money."

"If you're right, Atomtech could be in trouble and Devin will have to fight to protect…"

"Who's Devin?"

"Walter Devin, my ex-boss."

"Could he have ordered the attack on my cab this morning?"

"How could you be any threat to Devin?"

"Maybe he has it in for Curtis."

"I don't see how killing you would resolve anything with Curtis. He's an old archeologist for Christ's sake. He doesn't need to cheat Devin out of his contracts. Curtis is already rich."

"How did he get rich?"

"What difference does it make? Why would Devin give a damn?"

"Maybe he knows something we don't," Janis said as Jimmy approached.

"Take your orders, gentlemen? Lunch is almost over."

"I'll go for the Deli Special Combo," Janis said. "How about you, Ray?"

"I'll have the same." He handed the menus to Jimmy.

Janis leaned back in his chair. "It seems to me there are too many unanswered questions much more important than the 13th Power here. We may be dealing with dangerous people who have suddenly been shoved into an arena together. A couple of scientists like ourselves won't fare too well if they start playing gladiators."

"You may be right," Ray said. "Who knows?"

Who knows? Janis clenched his jaw. Lisa! What did she have to do with this? He looked at Ray who was again studying the ruined note. "Did you send a limo to pick me up at the airport?"

"Not me." He looked puzzled." I figured you'd take a cab."

"Well—somebody did. Somebody knew my name. They had it written on a sign, for Christ's sake. What's going on around here, Ray?"

"Will you relax? After lunch, I'll check with my people—see if I can find out anything. We'll hit my motel room, make some calls."

"What motel?"

"Super 8, what else? Room 214. It's not the penthouse, believe me."

"Got a phone number?"

Ray scribbled it on a napkin. "Why?"

Janis stuffed it in his pocket and removed Lisa's makeshift card. "You go ahead. I'm going to follow a lead of my own."

At the bar, Steve pushed away his empty beer glass, dumbfounded by what he'd just heard. Devin had agreed to pay him a thousand dollars for this information. Now Steve thought it had to be worth much more—say—something with two more zeros.

Chapter Nineteen

TECHNOLOGY AND GOLD

A gold Rolls Royce pulled up to the curb in front of the Balli Club. As sunbeams glistened off the silver lady poised on the hood, Curtis rushed out of the club, his long black coat trailing in the breeze behind him.

The doorman gave him a nod. "Afternoon, sir."

Curtis tipped his hat and hurried toward the waiting car. Standing six foot six, lanky and thin boned, Jonathan Kyles held the rear door open. His big blue eyes stared out from deep sockets, and though he looked a lot like "Lurch," Jonathan was quick on his feet, fast-witted, and never backed down from a fight. After Curtis slid across the leather seat, his hat just clearing the ceiling, Jonathan closed the door gently, swung a salute to the doorman, and climbed into the driver's seat. "All set, sir?"

"Let's be off." Curtis removed his hat. "Call the airport and have my jet prepared for takeoff to Dallas within the hour." He checked his watch. "It's party time."

Jonathan picked up the cell phone and drove away from the Balli Club.

As the Rolls maneuvered through traffic, Curtis cast a sober stare out the window, his mind playing with emotions he dared not reveal. The 13th Power was becoming a reality. The thought of it stirred his imagination. But Boris's warning echoed in his mind: *Too dangerous.* Were they about to make a scientific blunder into the unknown and change the world forever? The consequences could be catastrophic, but the rewards, boundless. He felt like a child playing with fire—frightened, yet bedazzled by the brilliance of it all. Risk nothing, gain nothing. The pieces of the puzzle were coming together. Everything was in place for success.

Suddenly, the foreboding attack on Janis' cab came to mind. Was an anonymous threat hanging over his project? Who was behind it? Was somebody onto him—or did someone have it in for Janis? Curtis huffed. That wouldn't be hard to figure. But he had to consider the threat real even though its source a mystery.

Turning his attention to the car-bar, he poured himself a Peach brandy. The wine had left a foul taste in his mouth, though it had added a nice touch to the meeting. He downed the brandy and pressed a button on the armrest. A black glass divider rose from the seatback, sealing his compartment in privacy. He lifted his briefcase from the floor and opened it in his lap. A green light blinked on the Vidphone panel, which flipped up like a laptop computer.

WAITING scrolled across the display.

The engineers at Solartech Labs had designed this video-phone to be untappable, its voice and video transmissions digitally coded and scrambled. He enjoyed being surrounded by high technology, almost as much as by gold. Almost. He punched a code on the phone pad. A series of tones emitted from the speaker.

"Dallas Central. Hello, Dr. Curtis." The monitor lit up with an image of a young woman peering over her reading glasses.

"Hi, doll," Curtis said. "I'll be out of this town in an hour. Can't wait to see you, baby."

Curly locks of brown hair spilled from her shoulders as she leaned forward and ran her tongue over ruby red lips. "I'm *so* ready," she said breathily.

"Save it, baby! Tell daddy-o you have a hot date in Dallas tonight. When are you gonna dump that husband of yours, anyway?"

"When you promise to marry me, darling." She blew him a kiss.

"Fat chance! Keep it warm for me." He hung up. The monitor went blank. Dumb broad. But that was the way he liked his women. He pressed the intercom button. "Jonathan. We set?"

"It's a go, boss."

"Let's get this show on the road. Sleazy Susie is hot to trot in Dallas and time's a wastin'." Feeling as though the world revolved around him, he settled back into the plush leather seat. The 13th Power would soon be in his grasp.

Chapter Twenty
LISA

Lisa aimed the limo down an alley behind a three-story warehouse, just off the waterfront. Dust swirled into the air as she drove into the dark interior. Tires squealing, she headed up a ramp to the next level, turned into a brightly lit parking area, and stopped in front of a door marked "THIRD LEVEL OFFICES - Authorized Personnel Only." Taking in a quick breath and blowing upward to stir her lofty bangs, she reassured herself. "You can pull this off. Just keep your cool, girl."

Glancing at the sign she had held at the airport, she thought about Dr. Mackey, how she figured he'd be uninteresting, expecting a stuffed shirt kind of professor with the personality of an eraser. Her attraction for him surprised her, even excited her. *Dr. Mackey. Mrs. Lisa Mackey?*

"Wouldn't that be something?" Gabbing her purse, she noticed a blue Corvette parked in a space marked, *Executive 1.* "He's here!" Smiling, she bolted through the door and dashed up the stairs.

"Lo!" she said, rushing into the office.

"How did it go, pretty Miss Lisa?"

She plopped into a chair and propped her feet up on his desk, not caring what might be revealed under her short skirt. "I just know he'll call. What red-blooded American scientist wouldn't want to know what makes this machine tick?" With a wave of her hand, she motioned to her outstretched shapely legs.

Chuckling, Lo returned to his paperwork.

Lisa put her purse on the desk and studied him for a moment. Lo Chin looked to be about 60, had a stout frame and a face glowing with character, handsomely Oriental. Fragile glasses sat low on the bridge of his nose. Lo ran a successful business but she couldn't see any hint of what that might be. On the wall, he'd hung a diploma from UCLA, some kind of certificate from the National Guard, and a variety of photos in which he'd always posed alone.

Lo had been a big help to her in San Francisco—gave her a place to stay and the use of his limo. At first, he thought she wouldn't be able to handle the big Lincoln. But after she told him how she'd driven a tractor-trailer rig in Canada, hauling logs while she worked on her economics degree, he handed her the keys with a smile. Devin was right about Lo. He...

"Oh shit!" she said, jolting Lo from his work. "Devin!" Her feet hit the floor as she grabbed the phone.

"Auto dial 1," Lo said. "It's 1:00 in Nevada. You have time."

After two rings, "Hello," came a voice over the line, gruff and unfriendly.

"D-Devin?"

"How's San Francisco, Lisa? Was it a no-show at the airport?"

"He's in the meeting now... "

"Damn fools!"

She heard glass shattering on the other end of the line. "Did I say something wrong?"

"Never mind. What about the meeting?"

"Dr. Mackey doesn't know anything. I'll find out this evening and get back to you."

"I'll be waiting."

Lisa set the receiver down. "Lo—how long have *you* known this creep?"

"For many years now I've been doing business with Atomtech. Devin always treated me right. Ask for favors sometimes, like now, with you. No need to worry about Devin, Miss Lisa."

Lo's smile wasn't very comforting.

Lisa slumped back in the chair, dropping her floozy façade for her more girlish nature. "It's not fair!" she said with a whimper. "Did he say how this charade was gonna help me get back at my father for ruining my life?"

"I don't know. Devin asked me to help you." Lo took off his glasses and put them on top of his pile of papers. "He also told me about your problem with your father. Not good for child to grow up without mother. Father gave her boot long time ago. Nanny okay, but real mother better. When your father sent you away to private schools in Europe and Japan, you thought he didn't want you. Ah, but things not always what they seem. Maybe father want only what is best for you. After all, college in Canada must be very expensive. But you come back all mixed up, full of blame and hate. Revenge have high price, Miss Lisa. Must sleep with enemy."

"Maybe you're right, Lo. But my path is set before me and I must travel it like a voyager in the dark."

"Maybe Lisa see light at end of voyage."

She managed an uneasy smile. Was he just trying to be helpful? Did he really care? Maybe if Lo had been her father, her childhood wouldn't have been so loveless. Maybe then, she wouldn't be tangled up in Devin's plot in an effort to even the score.

But Devin was part of the problem. He was a powerful man that wielded his empire like a ruthless sword, laying waste to his business rivals as he gorged himself on lucrative government contracts. The meek followed him like some kind of pied piper. And now, she found herself marching in that same parade of fools. For fear of Devin's wrath, she stiffened her resolve and glanced at the purse that held her cell phone. Come on—ring damn it. Let's get this show on the road. Patience was not one of Lisa's many virtues.

Lo stood. "How about we go to the mats? Waste some time and burn up some of that bad energy in you. Beat you bad, I will, this time."

She made him wait for a reply. He meant well.

"What do you say?"

"No thanks, Lo. I gotta save my energy for this evening. Besides, you don't want to sleep with a hot pad again tonight."

Lo took a step back. "Maybe you're right. Not good for old man to get beat up by pretty girl. How did you get so good at karate, little Lisa?"

"Practice, Lo. Every time I kicked that damn bag, I saw my father's face. Blamo! Over, and over again 'til I thought the bag would bleed."

"Your hate... "

An electronic ring came from her purse. Lisa dug out the cell phone, her heart fluttering as she flipped it open. "Hello," she said sweetly.

"I need to see you right away."

"Where are you, cowboy?"

"Meet me in front of the Balli club as fast as you can."

"I'll be right there." She stashed the phone and stood, facing Lo. "It's time to pay the piper. Thanks for everything."

"You go quickly, pretty Miss Lisa. But you go carefully. I need to see you again."

"Don't worry. I've got the tiger by the tail." She pecked him on the cheek.

"Ah, but pretty Miss Lisa—tiger tail have teeth on other end."

*   *   *

Janis paced the Balli Club's front sidewalk. The California sun had stripped him of his suit coat, but slung over his shoulder, the weight was more a burden than a fashion statement. He loosened his tie and undid the top button of his shirt. Sweat trickled down his neck. He had to get some California clothes. Soon.

He stopped pacing and pulled the check from his back pocket. *$10,000.* Curtis' signature was smooth and simple with exaggerated capitals. A rich man, dressed in black, obsessed with gold, and sporting a Pharaoh's walking staff seemed a bit overdone, even creepy. Scarier yet, Curtis wanted the impossible—the 13th Power. But why? Janis made note of the bank, *First Industrial*, and returned the check to his pocket. Come on Lisa!

While waiting for the limo to reappear, he sat on the steps. The doorman eyed him warily. Shade under the awning was comforting. His mind wandered back to the incredible chain of events leading up to meeting Ray, Curtis, and the mysterious Lisa. He tried finding some logical way to explain it all. But like Ray's obsession with the 13th Power, it defied reasoning.

"Looks like I'm in this up to my neck," he said to himself. "How did that go again?" The nucleus of an atom to the 13th Power *negative* was a place so small that the space around it would be as vast as the Milky Way galaxy. And at the other extreme, the 13th Power *positive* was a place so large that the space inside it would be as vast as the Milky Way galaxy, too. Did that mean negative and positive were equal? Made for a good hypothesis.

Janis rubbed his chin. If negative and positive were equal at those extremes, then the laws of math and physics would be nullified. Nothing would function properly—not gravity, not light, not numbers. Because he knew those laws were universal, he believed the 13th Power was unreal—unusable. Or had Curtis found a use for it? What could it be? His mind came up blank. "If nothing else, it's got to be good for a Nobel Prize." He stood and began to pace again.

A stranger walked up, prickly-faced and smelling of sweat. An unlit cigarette dangled from his lower lip. "Do you have a light?"

Sidestepping, Janis said, "Sorry, I don't smoke." Just then he caught the motion of a blue van, tires screeching to the curb. Instantly, the stranger grabbed Janis' arm. Janis spun around in panic and tossed his suit coat over the stranger's head. The thug released him and flailed at the coat. Janis landed a left hook to the bad guy's head, staggering him. Rubbing his knuckles, Janis drew back to throw another punch as the van door flew open, revealing two big goons. The odds were suddenly stacked against him.

The goons jumped out, fists balled.

Janis delivered a swift kick to the stranger's left knee, buckling it backwards with a sharp crack. The thug hit the ground, screaming. Janis gritted his teeth. The odds had just gotten better—one down—two to go.

Taking a step backward with fists clenched like a prizefighter, he awaited the onslaught. Back in his college days, he was pretty good at this boxing thing. The goons must've sensed his expertise and paused for a moment. Or maybe they were concerned about their comrade, writhing on the sidewalk with a coat over his head. Janis' adrenaline level surged. *Come on. Let's get this over with.*

Suddenly, screeching tires filled the air. The goons spun around.

Janis bolted to Lisa's limo. "Go! Go! Go!" he shouted as he flung open the passenger door, preparing to hang on and ride it down the block.

But the limo didn't move.

As he dove into the car, he pulled the door shut and kept an eye on the approaching goons. The driver's door swung open. Lisa got out and stepped to the sidewalk.

Janis couldn't believe it. "What are you doing?"

The goons stopped in their tracks and looked back and forth at Lisa and each other.

Like an exotic dancer, she gracefully discarded one high heel, then the other. Standing in her bare feet, she beckoned to the pair of thugs. "Come on you guys—I wanna play, too."

The ugliest goon responded to her invitation first, launching his assault without warning. Lisa spun with a left kick, high to the bridge of the bad guy's nose, revealing a flash of white panties in the afternoon sunshine. Before the big oaf hit the ground, she recoiled a lovely knee and caught him in the throat on the way down.

Janis grimaced. That had to hurt. His mouth fell open as he watched the second man writhing on the sidewalk. Shifting his eyes to the Balli Club entrance, he noticed the doorman was nowhere in sight. Damn! Janis threw the door open to offer assistance with the last goon left standing. But Lisa motioned him to stay back.

Crouched like a Kung Fu master, her elbows raised, her hands flat, she looked ready, poised for an attack. "Come on, Mr. Tough Guy," she said. "Your turn to see my panties." She took a step toward the scumbag.

Hands raised in surrender, the goon pleaded with her. "Look, lady. We got no beef with you. We'll leave real quiet like. Okay?"

Lisa took another step forward.

"Please, lady," he said, stepping backward. "Give me a break here. Somebody has to be in one piece to drive the damn van."

Standing upright, she blew the coward a kiss, and turned her attention to the big lug hacking on the ground. "Get this garbage off the sidewalk." She pivoted on her toes, stooped to pick up her shoes, and swayed back to the limo.

Stunned, Janis watched her slide in behind the wheel.

She threw her shoes on the floor. "Check the van—Nevada license plate."

The injured goons crawled inside and drove off.

Janis spotted his coat lying on the sidewalk. "Wait." As he started to push the door open, wailing sirens pierced the air. "Damn!" The coat wasn't worth the delay. "Let's go! First Industrial Bank." He gave Lisa a suspicious glare. "Then we're going to have us a little chat, my dear."

Lisa didn't look at him. She bit her lower lip and sped away from the Balli Club.

Chapter Twenty-One
ROOM SERVICE

Ray dug in his pocket for the key to his room. A vacuum cleaner was running somewhere down the hall, unseen. Once inside, he flung his coat on the bed, loosened his tie, and poured a glass of water from a pitcher on the dresser. The air conditioner under the window hummed softly. With drawn curtains, the dimly lit room felt cool. He settled into a recliner in the corner and took a moment to relax. The meeting had been a success—but not without complications. Now he had to solve some problems he hadn't counted on. Though he didn't want to believe the assault on Janis' cab had anything to do with the meeting, he had to be certain. He had too much at stake to let anyone ruin his chances of achieving his goal. Putting down his glass, he reached for the phone and dialed the labs in Simi Valley.

"Solartech..."

"Trish—get me Gibson right away!"

"One moment, Mr. Crawford."

The phone went silent—endlessly silent. What was taking so long? Hurry up, Alex. Ray looked at the ceiling and thought about Alex Gibson. The Chief Security Officer of Solartech Labs had some powerful credentials, even a lengthy stint with the CIA from which he had said he'd retried. He seemed truly concerned about Curtis' quest for the 13th Power and had an uncanny knack of getting anything needed to ensure security for the project. He had turned Solartech Labs into a military-like fortress. To breach his security, one would have to be exceptionally cunning.

"Mr. Crawford," Trish came back. "Alex is with the perimeter patrol at South Gate. Apparently they found some cut barbed wire out there. Can I get a phone number...?"

"Cut wire? What...what's going on?"

"All I know is they caught some guy in the mail room, day before yesterday. Seems he was disguised, dressed in a lab coat and wearing a fake beard. Come to think of it, he had your Special Delivery letter in his hand."

A lump formed in Ray's throat. The letter to Dr. Mackey. "Tell Alex I want that guy under wraps 'til I get there—and no cops."

"Sorry, Mr. Crawford—the wraps didn't hold and Mr. Slippery got away. Alex went ballistic. He's heading up the investigation personally."

"So nobody knows who he was?"

"Nobody."

"Just great. Thanks, Trish." Ray hung up. He paced the floor. Now he was convinced: Janis was targeted. Someone was definitely interested in the 13th Power project. But who?

Knuckles rapped on the door. "Room Service." The voice sounded cold, like a construction worker, unlike the cordial tone of the stewards.

"I didn't order room service."

The knock came again. "Room service."

"I said..."

Suddenly, a rattling machine-gun sent bullets bursting through the door. He dove to the floor as murderous rounds ripped at curtains, walls, and mirrors, destroying everything in their path and turning his room into a death chamber of flying debris. Glass exploded. Lamps threw sparks. The air-conditioner hissed gas. Throwing his hands over his head, he awaited the inevitable end of his life.

As suddenly as the onslaught began, it ended. Silence. Was someone coming in? Would they shoot him execution style? A chunk of mirror fell and shattered on the floor—almost gave him heart failure. He peeked over the bed. No one was in sight. Dust swirled around the room, reflecting in beams of sunlight shining through bullet-riddled curtains. The smell of gunpowder hung thick in the air. Fighting off an urge to panic, he slowly got to his feet and haphazardly brushed himself off.

"Good thing I didn't have a damage deposit on this dump!"

He grabbed his suit coat and pulled open the pulverized door. A wide-eyed maid stood in the hall, her white apron balled in her fists. She peered into the room then looked at him. "I'm not cleanin' up that mess." Shaking her head, she waddled away.

A steward rounded the corner in full stride. "What's going on up here?"

"I need another room!"

In the distance, the wail of sirens filled the California air once again. Ray threw on his dusty jacket, tightened his tie, and prepared for the interrogation to come. He was stuck here, waiting for Janis. A sudden wave of horror crashed over him. Janis really was in danger.

Chapter Twenty-Two
THE INFERNO

Lisa accelerated the limo away from the bank as Janis counted his cash. Curtis' check had paid off like a slot machine jackpot. "I need clothes. Where's a good place?"

"The Executive Man on Vanness," Lisa said and aimed the limo toward the downtown section. "It's a high-class men's wear store..." she paused and winked in his direction, "...for high-class men like you."

Though the compliment was flattering, Janis didn't respond. He just stared at her. Was this woman for real? Not knowing her intentions, he had to be careful. The mystery surrounding her involvement in this affair shot nagging questions through his mind, questions he wanted to confront her with. But if she were playing some kind of game, maybe playing along would get him the answers he sought. But how was he going to do that? An idea came to him. He let a few minutes pass before he asked, "Will you help me pick out something with California flair—you know, cool and comfortable?"

She looked him up and down as if sizing him up. "Sure thing, cowboy," she said with a smile that made his heart race. He hadn't expected to find something like her in California.

Satisfied, he turned his attention to the sights of San Francisco. In the distance, the Golden Gate Bridge spanned the bay, teeming with boats of all sizes. The afternoon sun hung low in the sky, casting shadows across the water. A light sea breeze swept in from the west, cooling the heated city. He reclined his seat and settled back to relax. Lisa seemed to sense his weariness and tuned the radio to a soft music station. He glanced at her. Maybe she wasn't his adversary. Maybe she was his protector. Smiling, he thought, what a beautiful protector, indeed.

Twenty minutes passed before Lisa swung the limo into a parking lot beside the prestigious men's store. Janis didn't want the ride to end. With a yawn, he stretched the sleepiness from his arms and legs.

"Okay, Dr. Mackey. Recess is over. Let's get you dressed up for show." Her smile shined like she meant it.

Walking toward the store entrance, Janis took Lisa's hand and looked around the parking lot for anything that seemed suspicious—especially blue vans. His safety assured, they entered the lavish shop.

A balding clerk greeted them eagerly, like a puppy anticipating a treat. "How may I be of assistance?"

From then on, Lisa took over. She dragged them from one department to another, selecting shirts and pants, belts and ties, a sport coat and a shiny pair of black snakeskin shoes. Socks, underwear, a shaving kit, and a soft-side suitcase rounded off her shopping list.

Janis admired her eye for fashion and her ability to barter with the bewildered clerk. If it wasn't on sale, she insisted he put it on sale, constantly threatening to take their business to K-Mart. He felt a little embarrassed but swallowed his pride and let her carry on with her harmless antics.

As he tried on clothes and paraded around the store in his stocking feet, he had to laugh at her enthusiasm and boundless energy. But in a small fitting room, when she squirmed her way in and pressed her body against his, his laughter fell silent while she playfully gazed into his eyes. Her warmth overwhelmed him, her lips so close, her breath so sweet. He fought the temptation to kiss her and sent her out with a slap to her fanny.

More than two hours had passed before she seemed satisfied that he'd be dressed properly for any occasion. And he was satisfied that Lisa wasn't his adversary. He couldn't bring himself to believe any differently. The explanations he had sought earlier seemed less important to him now. Crossing his arms, he leaned against the counter piled high with his new clothes. Was she the one he'd been looking for all his life? He hoped the answer was yes.

When the clerk finished sacking everything, Lisa winked at Janis. "I'll bring the limo to the front door."

Dusk had settled over San Francisco. The parking lot lights showed faint flickers of life but seemed to resist the end of day. A breeze carried with it the briny scent of seawater.

Lisa skipped toward the limo as Janis stood at the store entrance, watching her hourglass shape move gracefully away. He smiled—the possibilities racing through his mind.

After walking around the limo, she opened the door, and

blew him a kiss. Janis pretended to catch it in midair. She slid in behind the wheel. A moment later, the starter whined but the engine didn't start.

Janis frowned.

When Lisa tried again, white sparks spewed from under the engine and bounced on the ground like hail. A spike of horror cut into his stomach, sharp as a knife.

"LISA!"

With a massive blast, the limo lunged upward. A brilliant red and yellow fireball billowed into the sky, turning dusk to daylight. As the hood ripped off, windows blew out and fire rushed in. Glass and metal debris rained down in every direction. The boom rolled away like thunder. A peaceful California evening had suddenly turned into hell on earth. Janis ran straight toward the inferno.

"LISA!"

As he approached the fiery tomb, he could barely hear himself calling out over the roar of the flames.

"LISA!"

Through searing tongues of fire, he tried to look inside the burning vehicle, the heat whipping him like a wind from hell. With his arms, he shielded his face and ran around the inferno.

The driver's door hung open on bent hinges. Could it be? He turned his search away from the burning car. His chest felt as if it would burst.

"Lisa?"

Several yards away, he saw her lying on the pavement, curled in a fetal position, motionless, her sooty hands covering her head, her blonde hair singed and soiled. He ran to her side and, fighting tears of despair, placed his fingers on the side of her neck. A pulse.

"Yes! Lisa!"

He scooped her up in his arms and carried her farther away from the inferno. As he ran, she opened her eyes and threw her arms around his neck. "Oh, Janis." She held him as if she would never let him go.

He felt his heart beating in his ears. Had he fallen in love? How could that be? So little he knew of her, so strongly he felt for her, and so nearly he had almost lost her. It must've been love, the feeling racing through him like the flames engulfing the limo. He didn't know which fire was hotter.

Through the inferno's roar, he heard wailing sirens. But this time he didn't care. He just held her.

Chapter Twenty-Three

THE CONFESSION

Janis paced back and forth behind the ambulance, occasionally stealing glances into the windows. Paramedics were checking Lisa. He wanted to be with her but they wouldn't let him in. Crowded around her, they went about their work, poking and prodding, their voices coming from the ambulance, but not their words. Lisa only looked to be scraped and singed. She had said her eardrums hurt. He hoped they'd find nothing more.

A chill ran through him as he glanced around the parking lot, the darkness flashing with emergency lights. Firemen, police, and curious onlookers were but silhouettes moving about erratically, like disco dancers under a strobe light. This wasn't his idea of a good time in California.

*   *   *

Chief Driskell watched his firemen douse stubborn flames. Only a blackened shell remained of the limo, twisted and disfigured. Gray smoke swirled from debris and leaned with the breeze. Several men wearing Arson Squad coats were examining the wreckage. Flashes from their cameras lit the scene with an eerie contrast of gray and black shadows. Other investigators searched with flashlights and metal detectors. He hoped they would find some remnants of the bomb.

"Over here," one of his men called out.

Driskell rushed toward the fireman. "What is it?"

He displayed a handful of charred debris. "Crude device. Not very professional." He wiped his chin with a sooty glove. "A pipe bomb with a Swisher fuse. Puts out quite a sparkler show before it rips."

Taking the fragments in cupped hands, Driskell inspected pieces of twisted metal pipe and burnt packing, which were still warm and smelled of sulfur. "Has Michaels seen this yet?"

"No. He's over there." The fireman pointed toward a group of men in suits.

Michaels looked irritated as Driskell approached the detectives, huddled in conversation. They shook hands.

"Never fails," Michaels said without a smile. "Mother's in town and this shit happens."

"Life's a bitch. Take a look at this stuff."

The detective examined the debris then jerked his head toward the ambulance. "What do you know about them?"

"The lady is the limo driver—damn near got killed. The man is a professor from Colorado. She's got to answer some questions when the medical boys are done with her. If we…"

The back doors of the ambulance swung open with a creak. Two paramedics helped Lisa out. Her left elbow was wrapped in a white bandage and she seemed wobbly on her feet.

"Now's as good a time as any." Michaels handed the evidence to one of his partners. "Bag this stuff." He turned to Driskell. "Let's go."

Together, they headed toward the group that had gathered behind the ambulance.

*   *   *

Janis hugged Lisa. "Are you going to be okay?"

"I was almost killed."

Firemen and paramedics clustered around. "Glad you're all right," one said. "Talk about a close call," said another. Some were jabbering among themselves about how lucky she was.

Two approaching officials caught Janis' attention. The taller man wore a helmet, an orange jumpsuit striped with reflective tape, and big brown boots. The other man walked with slouched shoulders and wore a tan trench coat that hung unbuttoned down the front, revealing a white shirt with no tie. Faces pinched, they both looked ready to give someone the third-degree.

In full stride, Michaels pointed to the wreckage being loaded on a tow truck. The cable winch whined as it pulled the twisted hulk up the flat bed, screeching. "Anybody here have a clue what this mess is all about?" He displayed a badge and looked at Lisa.

Janis didn't like his accusatory glare. "Officer—this day's been a disaster from the start so lay off the girl. We don't know anything."

The detective frowned. "Talk about a bad day. First I get a report of a street brawl at the Balli Club. Nobody's around when I get there. Seems the perps split in a limo. Funny thing about that. Now I've got a limo lookin' like Pearl Harbor."

He pointed to the tow truck and stared at Janis.

"An occupant of said limo is some kind of professor scientist or something. Funny thing about that, too. This afternoon some other scientist-type guy gets his hotel room redecorated by a machine gun assault force. Am I patrolling somewhere in the twilight zone or are these things connected?" He glared at Janis as if he were awaiting an enlightening reply.

But Janis was struggling to take his next breath, his mind reeling in the terror of the officer's words. This deadly gauntlet was not computing and Ray's fate became a burning question. "Was...is...Ray...Is Ray all right?"

"Ray?" Lisa said, wide-eyed.

"Ah, so we do know something after all," Michaels said. "He's okay. Room 218. So let's have it." The clever detective eyed them back and forth.

"Ray?" Lisa said again, her voice an octave higher. Janis looked at Lisa, trembling in his arms. Now was the time to ask her *his* questions.

"What's this all about, Lisa. I know you don't work for the Balli Club. You lied to me. Why...?"

She pushed herself out of his arms and turned a full circle, looking for an escape. But officers, firemen, and paramedics were standing all around them. Janis resisted the urge to grab her arm, thinking it best to let her work this dilemma out for herself.

Slowly, she returned to him, and with a look of despair in her eyes, took his hands, her lips quivering. "R-Ray who?"

"Ray Crawford. Why?"

"No! It can't be! It can't be my father!" She threw her arms around Janis' waist and buried her face in his chest. "It was Devin," she sobbed. "He sent me to find out what your meeting was about. I didn't know it was with my father." She looked up, her tear-streaked face contorted with fear. "It's Devin! He's trying to kill us!"

Janis patted her on the back like a father. So *this* was Ray's daughter. He felt suddenly pleased, somehow more connected to her. But how had she gotten mixed up with Devin? "What did you tell him?"

"Nothing," she whimpered. "You haven't said a word about the meeting. But it's obvious he doesn't care anymore. He's just going to kill everybody that's connected to Curtis."

Janis felt a chill. "What does Devin have against Curtis?"

"Who cares?" Lisa turned to Lieutenant Michaels. "Officer. Help us. Devin is a dangerous man."

"Sure, Missy. Just tell me where he is and we'll go arrest his ass—right after you two get an Oscar. Devin! Father! Curtis! Beam me up, Scotty! I should haul you both in right now."

"On what charge?" Janis asked.

"Disturbing the peace and felony littering." He motioned to the mess in the parking lot.

"But Devin is trying to kill us," Lisa said.

Janis thought about that. "Can you put us in jail for the night?"

Driskell said to Michaels, "You can't lock them up. They didn't do anything."

"You're right. It's not worth the paperwork. Besides, Mother's waiting."

"You can't just leave us here," Janis said.

Michaels nudged the Chief. "Let's get out of here. My meat loaf is getting cold."

The disbelievers walked away.

Lisa sat on the back bumper of the ambulance. "They don't get it."

Sitting next to her, Janis looked into her tear-swollen eyes, started to speak but she pressed a finger on his lips.

"Janis, wait. Let me explain. I knew it was Devin when I saw the Nevada plates on that van at the Balli Club. Atomtech is in Nevada and Devin uses a fleet of unmarked blue vans. He's convinced that Curtis is up to something and obsessed with finding out what it is. I thought all he wanted was information."

Her chin quivered as if she were resisting the urge to cry.

"Devin's known me since I was a little girl. He just tried to kill me, Janis. I can't believe he'd do that." Slowly, she removed her finger from his lips. "We need help, and I know just where to find it. I'm going to call him right now."

"Wait," Janis said. Questions ran through his mind, not one more important than the other. If he was going to trust her, he had to know. "How did you get mixed up with this assassin?"

Lisa wiped tears from her cheeks. "I agreed to help him find out what Curtis was doing by pushing myself on some old professor coming for a meeting." A soft smile brightened her eyes. "Some *old professor* you turned out to be."

"So I was set up."

Her gaze dropped. "I know it sounds terrible of me. But Devin knew I'd help him because he knows how I feel about my father. I'd do anything to get back at him for what he did. I hate him."

Janis stroked her arm, feeling goose bumps. "What did Ray do?"

"He ruined my life."

"How?"

"First he got rid of my mother—and then me. He sent me away to school, far away, clear around the world. And he was always moving me around from one school to another. I was never in one place long enough to make any friends, felt like a prisoner in those horrible places. He took away my mom. He took away my home. I was from nowhere, going nowhere. So you see, he ruined my life."

"Why?"

"Because of his job—that's why. I was in the way, like my mother. His career was more important than me. It hurt, Janis. I cried and I cried 'til the hurt turned to hate."

"And Devin took advantage of that."

"When he told me I could help him ruin my father's new career move, I saw my chance to get back at him. So I agreed to find out what Curtis wanted with you. I certainly didn't think Devin would try to kill us."

Janis rubbed her shoulder. "It's not your fault, Lisa. Devin did this on his own. But how did he know we were here?"

"I don't know."

Janis glanced around the parking lot. Except for the ambulance and two cop cars, all the other emergency vehicles had left. If not for the smell of melted asphalt, the darkness would have given no hint of what had happened here. He brushed back a tangle of

Lisa's hair. "What about that help you mentioned?"

She got up from the bumper. "I'll call him right now."

"Who?"

"Lo Chin," she said with a smile. "You'll like him."

As he watched her walk into the store, he wondered how Ray could have been so cruel to his only daughter. Recalling Lisa's version of her childhood, anger boiled up inside. His compassion for Lisa nullified any respect he had for his old friend. Janis gritted his teeth. Ray had some explaining to do.

"Lo—help us," Lisa said when he answered the phone. "Devin is trying to kill us. He just blew up your limo and the cops aren't buying our story."

"Slow down, pretty Miss Lisa. You talk too fast for old man's ears. What did you say is wrong with my limo?"

"It blew up. You know, ka-boom! A lot of fire and smoke, pieces scattered all around."

"Devin destroyed my limo? That no good son of a…" The line fell silent. "Miss Lisa, you okay?"

"I'm banged up some, Lo. I was trying to start the car when I saw sparks flying from underneath. I dove out the door. If I hadn't left it open, I'd be fried Lisa right now. Please come get us. We're at The Executive on Vanness."

"I'll be right there, Miss Lisa. You watch out for more trouble." Lo hung up.

Lisa clutched the phone to her chest. *Please hurry.*

She saw Janis, still sitting on the bumper of the ambulance. Her heart beat faster. He was strong and handsome. Mature. Feelings for him began welling up from deep inside, new emotions she'd never felt before. Were they a little girl's infatuation-with-the-teacher kind of feelings? No. These were *woman* feelings—strong, wanting, and sometimes demanding—feelings that only the right man could bring out in her—that man, the cowboy from Colorado. She smiled and began her sultry walk back to the man she desired.

Chapter Twenty-Four

LO CHIN

A rickety '52 Chevy pickup rattled into the parking lot of The Executive Man. Lo surveyed the scene of his limo's demise. The emergency vehicles were gone. Only a scorched and melted circle of asphalt remained. He put his forehead on the steering wheel, sadness sweeping over him, sadness for the loss of his limo and his friendship with Devin, who could have no excuse for this.

Lo's sadness turned to anger and then to dread. Miss Lisa! He scanned the parking lot. She was nowhere in sight. A big pile of packages by the store entrance caught his attention. He coaxed the old truck, popping and wheezing, to the curb and shut off the noisy engine. The night went silent.

Lisa came out of the store and started running toward him, her arms outstretched, her hair trailing behind her like a silken scarf. Thank goodness. A distinguished-looking gentleman appeared in the doorway.

Lo jumped from the cab, his feet hitting the ground at the same time Lisa threw her arms around his neck.

"Lo!"

"Lisa...now Lisa...it's okay now. Be careful of old man's bones."

"Thank God, you're here."

"And thank old truck, too. Corvette is good for picking up girls but not to carry gentlemen friend and half of store you buy." He waved to the professor. "Come on. Load this stuff up and we go. Hurry. Hurry."

Lisa helped, then took Janis' hand and led him to Lo. Her girlish expression and a glitter in her eyes gave her feelings away.

"Ah, Miss Lisa. What you have here?" He smiled at her gentleman friend.

"Lo—I want you to meet Dr. Janis Mackey from Colorado. Janis—this is my friend Lo Chin from San Francisco." They shook hands, smiling.

"Nice to meet you," Janis said.

Lo bowed.

Janis returned the gesture, though clumsily.

"Good." Lo said. "Now we go before we get killed like sitting duck in barrel...or something like that."

They climbed into the truck, Lisa sitting in the middle. Lo fired up Old Faithful, ground a couple of gears, and rumbled off into the California night.

As he drove the rattletrap along, Lisa took Janis' hand and rested her head on his shoulder. The sight warmed Lo's heart. "You'll be safe at my place tonight."

Lisa snuggled into Janis.

Lo worked the steering wheel back and forth as the old truck lumbered across the Golden Gate Bridge toward Marin County. A full moon hung on the horizon just below the spire of the Transtar Building. Ribbons of high clouds reflected the silver moonbeams and appeared to wrap the city in silk. Even the clunking of the old truck couldn't dent the mood cast over the lovers nestled together on his front seat. As bridge cables streaked above his windshield, Lo sensed that Lisa felt safe again. Her gentle breathing seemed in rhythm with Janis' and she fell asleep in his arms.

*   *   *

The old truck rattled through the gate to Lo's luxurious estate and lumbered along a tree-lined drive that curved around to the front of his mansion, stopping next to a blue Corvette.

Janis yawned, too tired to be impressed. He gathered sleeping beauty in his arms and carried her up granite steps to a door, which Lo held open.

"This way. Upstairs."

Janis followed him to a foyer that went around to a large bedroom.

Lo turned on a light.

In the middle of the room sat a round bed with high wooden posts and a silken canopy. Lo parted sheer pink veils that draped to the floor. Janis laid Lisa on plush bed covers, gently released her, and took a step back. Black soot spotted her dress and face, scratches etched her legs, and the white bandage on her elbow had already become soiled. Her scorched hair lay in tangles on the pillow. She looked beautiful. Could she be the one? It hardly seemed possible. Love at first sight? He had never believed in that before. Why should he now? How could he? She was Ray's daughter. But he couldn't resist the way he felt; he didn't want to ignore what his heart was telling him.

He turned to Lo. "Where's the phone?"

"Kitchen, where else?"

Janis followed him downstairs. A light scent of incense drifted in the air. At the end of a dimly lit hallway, Lo flicked on kitchen lights and headed straight for the refrigerator.

Taking the wadded-up napkin from his pocket, Janis dialed the phone number Ray had scribbled. Waiting, he watched Lo rummage through the refrigerator. A moment later, the front desk answered.

"Do you have a Ray Crawford in 218?"

"One moment."

Lo set out fixings for ham sandwiches, lettuce and cheese, pickles and olives and a big bag of chips.

"What—no Egg Foo Young?" Janis asked.

"You want Chinese food, you go to restaurant. I no like."

A sleepy voice answered the phone. "Janis—that you?"

"In living color."

"Are you all right?" Ray said, his voice rising.

"Tired. Hear your room got shot up."

"How did you know about that?"

"Word gets around."

Ray cleared his throat. "Where have you been?"

"Downtown. My limo got blown up."

"Jesus! We gotta get out of here, Janis. Somebody's going to get killed."

"Pick us up tomorrow morning at 10:00 sharp."

"Us? Who's with you?"

Janis thought telling him wouldn't do any good. It was best he didn't know about Lisa. Not yet, anyway. "A woman I met."

"Come on, Janis. Can't you leave the damn women alone for one day?"

"Not this one."

"Where do I meet you?"

Janis asked Lo, "What's the address?"

"147 Willow Circle," Lo replied loudly, pressing down on the lid of a sandwich.

"Got it," Ray said.

"Don't be late."

"Watch your back, Janis. I called the lab. They had a security breach. A spy got in and found my letter to you. Somebody wants you dead."

"You too, Ray. And worse—Devin is the shooter. But I don't know why."

The line fell silent. "Devin must not want us do the 13th Power experiments," Ray said finally. "He was adamantly against them when I worked for him."

"Why?"

"He thinks the 13th Power can destroy the world."

"What do you think?"

"He's crazy. But I'll bet he's trying to keep us from helping Curtis. Our only safe place is Solartech Labs. He can't get to us there—it's a fortress. Tomorrow we make a run for Simi Valley. It's our only hope."

"The three of us will..."

"We're not taking the damn chick, Janis!"

"Yes, we are!" Janis yelled into the phone, his chest burning. "I think I'm in love with her and I'm not letting her out of my sight!" He slammed the receiver down. "Jerk!"

He looked up. His heart missed a beat. Lisa was standing in the doorway, face cleaned, her hair brushed back into a ponytail, her smile reddened with fresh lipstick. A silky white gown replaced her soiled yellow miniskirt. She stared at him, looking as if she would explode with joy. Oh, no. Had she heard him? Did she know how he felt?

She ran to him and threw her arms around his neck.

She knew.

Holding her in his arms, he kissed her with breathy passion. Her tongue darted in and out of his mouth, sweet as candy, tempting him to play. Her perfume electrified the air. He caught quick breaths, short gasps between long kisses as he savored the taste of her. But his insides churned with a sudden dread. Now she knew how he felt about her, his feelings suddenly exposed before he had a chance to try them on, see how they fit, see how he liked them. Untested feelings tended to be misleading, over-reactive. He tasted strawberry lipstick and touched the softness of her tongue.

Their lips never parted until Lo interrupted.

"Okay, you two—eat first, play later. Make babies when old man not around."

Janis released Lisa and put his hands on her hips. "Lo's right." A twinge of embarrassment warmed his cheeks. Had he lost his head over this woman?

Lisa resisted letting go of him. He kissed her ear and whispered, "Let's eat something." Slowly, she backed away, sat down at the table, and winked at Lo.

"Whew!" Janis said. Must be the way things were in California. Fast. He took a seat and grabbed a ham sandwich, glad he had something else to think about. "Big day tomorrow. I'll pack my stuff tonight." He took a bite of sandwich. "We'll get your things in the morning, Lisa. Where do you live?"

"Right here, cowboy. How did you like my room?"

Janis swallowed. "Loved it."

Lo explained. "When Devin sent Lisa, I agreed to put her up here, for two weeks now."

"My townhouse is in Santa Barbara," Lisa added, taking a napkin. "I love shopping on the pier, sunbathing on the beach, partying in the nightclubs. It's a wonderful place to live."

"California girl that you are," Janis added with a smile.

"And don't you forget it, cowboy."

He thought he'd better keep that in mind. California and Colorado were like two different worlds. After downing the last of his milk, sleep tugged at his eyelids.

Lo cleared the table, shuffling packages of meat and cheese and clinking silverware into the sink. He finished and bowed from the doorway. "Goodnight." His silhouette disappeared down the hall.

Lisa smiled. "We're alone at last."

Janis was speechless. Did she mean what he thought? He should be so lucky. Or should he? *Don't forget, she's Ray's daughter.* He slid his chair back. "It's late."

"Pooh." Her lower lip curled. "Guess that means you get the guest room. It's big and cold and lonely in there."

"It'll do. Where is it?"

"Last door on the left," she said, pointing down the hall. "Enjoy." Blowing him a kiss, she left him standing alone in the kitchen.

Janis turned off the light and made his way to the guest room. Thanks to Lo, his clothes were already laid out on the bed. He sorted through it all and haphazardly packed his suitcase.

The hot shower felt wonderful. Still dripping wet he slipped into a pair of California-style boxer shorts and admired them in the mirror. A tanned and bikini clad surfer-girl rode a yellow board on a big blue wave with a frothy crest, her blond ponytail trailing behind her. He imitated her pose and shifted his hips as if he were surfing. Gotta love California.

He climbed into bed and turned off the light. Lisa was right; the room was big and cold and lonely. But sleeping with her tonight and making love would be as unreal as the 13th Power itself. He folded his glasses on the nightstand and sighed heavily. "Good night, Lisa," he whispered, closed his eyes, and drifted into dreamland.

Chapter Twenty-Five

FINGER IN THE PIE

The phone clicked. Ray slammed the receiver down. Had Janis gone nuts? What woman had made him act like such an idiot? And how did he know Devin was the shooter? A bad feeling dropped into Ray's stomach.

He got out of bed, turned on the table lamp, and paced. Why was Devin so violently opposed to the 13th Power experiments, shooting up cabs and motel rooms and blowing up limos? Did he really believe the fate of the world was at stake? Ray pulled his loose underwear up a little higher as he paced. Would Devin stop at nothing to derail Curtis' project?

Opening the closet door, Ray pulled out his suitcase. He threw it on the bed and took out an electronic box—his Vidphone—an older model but just as secure as the fancy new ones. After setting it on the table, he flipped a power switch. A green light came on. The monitor chirped. Taking the phone from its cradle on the nightstand, he placed the mouthpiece into a groove on the box. A series of tones emitted into the phone. It rang.

"Dallas Central," Jonathan said. "What do you want, Ray?" He looked angry.

"Is Curtis there?"

"This better be important."

"Just get him, Jonathan. It's serious."

A few moments later, Curtis appeared on the monitor. He looked angry, too. "What is your problem?"

Ray glanced at the ceiling, thinking, *Well, hello Ray. And how are you tonight? Oh, I'm fine Dr. Curtis. Thank you for asking.* Did he have to be such a jerk?

"We've got a problem, sir. Looks as though Devin doesn't want us to do the 13th Power experiments. According to Dr. Mackey, Devin is the one responsible for attacking the cab this morning. Since then he's shot up my motel room and bombed Janis' limo."

"How does Janis know it was Devin?"

"He didn't say—but he was certain."

"I wondered if that ex-boss of yours would stick his fat finger into our pie."

"He's going to ruin everything."

"Not if I can help it," Curtis said with a huff.

"Tomorrow morning we're going to make a run for Simi Valley."

"Be careful. In the meantime, I'll take care of Devin."

The phone line went dead, the monitor black.

Ray turned off the lamp and fell back into bed. Devin's *finger in the pie* was not a good thing. The man was powerful, resourceful, and determined—equally as much as Curtis. A chill ran down Ray's spine. Were the gladiators about to do battle?

Chapter Twenty-Six
AN AUTHORIZED ASSAULT

Curtis keyed the Vidphone. Devin had become a dangerous threat to this project and he had to be stopped. The monitor blinked. *Waiting For Answer* scrolled across the screen. The message changed to *Transmitting* as Alex appeared, red-eyed. "What's up?"

"Devin has endangered the lives of Ray and our new employee, Dr. Mackey. We can't afford to lose these people and I'll not tolerate any interference in this highly prioritized project." He saw frustration on Alex's face.

Rubbing his temples, Alex said, "I wonder if Devin sent that spy with the beard the other day. We found a breach in South Gate's perimeter. That's where he got in—jumper-wired the fence alarm circuits before he started cutting. We're going to…"

"Never mind the snoop," Curtis cut in. "I want Devin dead and I don't care how you do it—just get on it right away. Lives depend on it."

"No problem."

Curtis hung up. "Damn Devin! I never did like that son of a bitch."

*   *   *

Alex sat at his desk in Security Central and contemplated Curtis' request. Though a need for sleep weighted his eyelids, the excitement of this new assignment spurred his imagination and kindled a second wind. After the embarrassing breach at South Gate, he needed the morale boost of a precision assault mission, just like in Vietnam. He knew it would take that much firepower to put Atomtech out of commission, to get close enough to Devin to kill him. His security was first-rate. The place was heavily defended. A military operation of that magnitude would require resources beyond those of Solartech Labs. And the use of those resources required authorization from a higher authority.

He went to his computer and typed "The Ark" along with a security code. The monitor beeped and turned bright blue with a silver CIA insignia embedded in the background. He typed, *Request authorization for military operations against Atomtech. Urgent. Mole.*

Leaning back in his chair, Alex knew *The Ark* was serious when he said the 13th Power project was to be protected—at all costs. But would he go so far as ordering the death of American citizens to do it? A few minutes later, a chime signaled a response. *Why? The Ark.*

Alex typed again, *Curtis believes Devin is trying to kill the scientists he has recruited to conduct the 13th Power experiments. The project is in jeopardy. We need to intervene. Mole.*

He clicked on the pulsating *Respond* button. The e-mail window went blank except for the flashing cursor. He stared at the screen, waiting for what seemed like forever.

Devin's interference is not tolerable. Stop him! Authorization granted.

Alex felt a chill.

End Transmission scrolled across the screen.

He knew just the man for the job.

Chapter Twenty-Seven

RED

Alex held the phone in his hand, thinking a moment before dialing James "Red" Colburn, a soldier from Vietnam. He had served twenty years in the Marine Corps and said he loved every minute of it. The nickname, *Red*, he earned with blood, the blood of his enemy—and lots of it. Sometimes killing wasn't enough for Red. He'd go berserk, leaving behind corpses disfigured and mutilated.

Retired with every medal a soldier could pin to his chest, he now commanded a paramilitary unit headquartered somewhere in the Chino Hills. His wife, Virginia, lived the life of suburbia, in comfort and style, while Red roughed it in the wilderness with his troops. Alex had kept in touch with them over the years—mostly because of Virginia.

There was a time, before she even knew Red existed, when she was in love with Alex. But their life together wasn't meant to be. His heart sank with the memory. When Red came home from the war, rugged and tough, Alex had introduced him to Virginia— or more like showed her off. "He saved my life," Alex had told her. Red took her hand. She smiled. From the look in their eyes, Alex knew it was the end for he and Virginia. The pain he felt on the day she married Red burned worse than the bullet he took while wallowing in that stinking rice paddy.

But as the wound healed and painful memories faded, he eventually found solace in the fact that the woman he loved and his best friend were happy. These days, to get to Red he had to go through Virginia. That was okay. It gave him a good excuse to call her. He dialed. The phone rang.

"Hello." Virginia's voice came over the line like ice cream and blueberries.

"How are you, Virginia?"

"Alex! It's late."

"I need to talk to Red."

"He's right here—he'll be delighted."

"I'd rather talk to you."

"One moment—I'll get him." As he waited for Red to come

to the phone, Alex wondered what the old soldier was up to. Being home on a weekend night seemed highly unusual. He should be busy with his men in the field, training for that possible Communist invasion or government insurgency.

"What is it, Alex?" Red's voice blared like an old tuba—heavy, low and loud.

"What are you doing home?"

"We're going out on a training mission tomorrow, me and my men. Spending the last night at home just in case I don't make it back. You know the way it goes."

Alex knew. Red always held to tradition. In 'Nam, before every mission, he and his men went into town for a night of wine, women, and song. For many, it would be their last night on earth, so it was time well spent.

"Why the call?"

Alex shifted the phone to his other ear. "I need you for a dangerous mission."

"What are you talking about?"

"*The Ark.*"

Silence.

Alex knew it had been a long time since Red had heard that name. It must've sent a shiver up the old soldier's spine.

"W-what does he need?" Red asked.

"We can't discuss it over the phone. Be at Solartech Field in Simi Valley tomorrow morning. I'll fill you in then."

"We're flying out of Edwards on a C-130 transport. Be there by 6:00 AM. I've got thirty-nine troops, top notch men, I tell yah, heavily armed." A hint of excitement radiated from his voice.

"Any C-4?"

"Enough to level a town. Will that do?"

"Nicely. Tell Virginia I said goodbye."

"See you at six."

*   *   *

Red set the receiver down slowly, turned to his wife and held her close. If it weren't for Alex, he'd never have met Virginia. Funny thing about love—how it takes its own course. There were winners and losers in war, winners and losers in love. Alex lost on both counts, a bullet knocked him out of the war, and his woman fell in love with another man. Maybe his luck would change. Maybe not. *The Ark* was certainly no guarantee.

Red put his hands on Virginia's shoulders and looked into her eyes. "The mission tomorrow is for real."

He didn't need to say any more. She took his hand and led the way upstairs.

Chapter Twenty-Eight
THE GOOD OLD DAYS

As the early morning sun cast long shadows across Solartech Field, Alex leaned on the fender of a security bus, his eyes on a C-130 Hercules touching down on the rubber-scarred runway. Tires screeched; blue smoke swirled. With full flaps deployed and reverse thrusters roaring, the huge aircraft slowed and taxied to the tarmac. Four turboprop engines droned to a stop, the propellers coasting on their own momentum. The cargo ramp whined to the ground.

Red marched out of the plane, alone. His troops formed a double-file formation inside the fuselage, helmets on, rifles slung from their shoulders. Standing at attention, they were waiting for an order to disembark.

Treading toward the bus, Red didn't smile. The years had been hard on him. Though his stocky frame carried him upright, the wrinkles on his face gave away his age, maybe more than he deserved. His jowls hung lower than Alex remembered. But pride still glowed in the soldier's eyes. He was a strong man, a dangerous man.

Goose bumps climbed up Alex's arms as he remembered the chaos, the rapid fire of machine guns, the fecal smell of the rice paddy, men yelling, men moaning, men dying. Alex had never known fear like that before. It seemed like only yesterday when that AK-47 bullet slammed into his chest and ripped through a lung, which started leaking air like a punctured tire. Moments later, Red had hold of him, cursing, firing his M-16 wildly and dragging him through the muck to cover. Seeing Red brought it all back. Alex thought he'd be sick. He swallowed hard, greeted the old soldier with a salute, and followed him into the bus.

"What does *The Ark* want of me?" Red asked.

On a makeshift table set up across the aisle, Alex laid out a map. "Dr. Curtis, the CEO of Solartech Labs, tells me that Devin, here at Atomtech in Nevada," he pointed to an *X* on the map, "is trying to kill two of our key personnel as they make their way toward Simi Valley." He traced his finger south from San Francisco. "It's our job to stop him."

Red looked over the map.

"Currently, Devin is inside the Atomtech compound directing operations against our people. We need to get in close, infiltrate, and eliminate him."

Red lifted his eyebrows. "A real live bad guy, huh?"

"Bad enough for *The Ark* to want out of commission."

"That's bad enough for me."

Alex folded the map. "I've laid out a model of Atomtech in the main briefing room at C-Wing. We'll put together our mission teams and set a timetable for executing the assault. But we must be ready to go tonight."

"Then let's get started." Red jumped from the bus and headed back to his men. He barked commands. They filed down the cargo ramp and marched across the tarmac as if performing in a Veterans Day parade. The fully armed formation halted on command and stood at attention.

Red approached the pilots, saluted, and talked with them for a moment. After an about-face military turn, he marched back to his men. With a sharp command, the formation paraded toward the bus. Alex, his chest heaving with pride, stepped aside as they boarded and took their seats.

"At ease, men!" Red ordered. "We'll be moving into a briefing room to prepare for tonight's mission. No smoking!"

The bus rumbled toward C-Wing. Smiling, Red looked over the troops under his command and said to Alex, "Just like the good old days."

Alex didn't smile. He just watched the rocky hillside sweep by and wondered if Red could stop Devin—before it was too late.

Chapter Twenty-Nine
THE DELIVERY

In the guest room, Janis stirred to a knocking sound. "Go away," he mumbled in his sleep.

More knocking.

He suddenly remembered Lisa, Lo Chin, the mansion. A dinging chime sounded eight times from somewhere inside the house. Groping for his glasses, he checked the nightstand clock: 8:00 AM. He yawned. The knocking persisted. "Okay! I'm awake!"

Lisa rushed in and threw herself on his bed. "Good morning, cowboy." She kissed him.

He put his arms around her, delighted by the softness of her silky nightgown pressed against his chest. Her body felt warm, smooth, and inviting.

He rolled her onto her side. "Good morning, California girl." He kissed her again. A short kiss, tender and loving, without the passion of last night. He gazed into her blue eyes and took in the flowery scent of her perfume. His body responded. But he had no time to play these lovers games. "Up you go, young lady," he forced himself to say. "Get dressed and packed."

She whimpered like a child being sent to her room. "Can I stay a while longer, please?"

"No." He couldn't believe he'd said that word.

Her smile drooped into a sad puppy-dog face. She sat up on the bed and ran her fingers through her long hair. Through the sheerness of her gown, the light from the window silhouetted her figure. He thought he could see all the way to heaven.

Was she trying to change his mind? He found it hard to resist her charms—she wasn't playing fair. Leaning over him with her blond hair hanging down around his face like a shimmering curtain of sunshine, she kissed him again. A soft hot kiss—the kind that made him want to surrender. Now he was sure he had made the wrong decision. *No* was not a word he used often. But he smiled through his regret. "Git along little doggie." He chuckled. "Cowboy talk."

"Don't dally, cowboy," she said as she slid off the bed and sauntered toward the door, her hips swaying with each step. She looked back, winked, and disappeared down the hall.

Though she was gone, her fragrance still lingered. Janis climbed out of bed and shuffled into the bathroom. Looking in the mirror, he said, "I'm too old for this shit."

*　*　*

Sitting on the patio by the pool, Lo sipped his coffee.

Jeffries put the pot down. "Lovely morning, sir," he said as he scanned the sky. "It's a shame about your limo."

"I already called insurance company," Lo replied bitterly. "Please show Dr. Mackey out here. We need to talk before he goes on trip today."

"Soon as I see him." Jeffries went back to the kitchen.

Lisa bounded onto the patio dressed in blue-jean shorts and a white blouse with the shirttails tied above her navel. Her sandals slapped the slate deck as she skipped around the tables and chairs toward Lo. With a kiss to his cheek and a cheery, "Morning," she helped herself to a chair next to him.

"Pretty Miss Lisa look like cat got mouse this morning. Were you a good girl last night?"

"Oh, Lo, you silly. Of course," she said with a shy smile. "I don't know what's gotten into me. Must be love."

"Ah, yes. About time Lisa find love. Now you must lose hate. Only then will you find real happiness. Today is good day to start. Your father will be here—10:00 sharp."

"No way! He's coming here?"

"I hear doctor tell him on phone last night, before you rush in and get all mushy. He says you go on trip together. Bad time for bad feelings, Miss Lisa."

Lisa pulled her knees up to her chest and hugged her legs. She held no hope for changing her feelings for her father, too many years of hate and anger to erase. But she had to be strong. She had to keep the peace for Janis' sake. Gritting her teeth, she turned her attention to the calm surface of the pool, its crystal water relaxing her mind. She'd deal with her father in her own time, her own way.

"Whoa! Look at this layout," Janis said as he stepped onto the patio. "What do you do to deserve all this?" He took a seat at the table.

"Computers," Lo said. "I program the ones called 'Super.' They're all the same to me. Glad you like."

Janis winked at Lisa. She winked back.

The doorbell rang. Janis glanced at his watch. It was only 8:55, so it couldn't be Ray. That showdown was coming at 10:00, when he planned to confront his old college pal about the way he'd treated his daughter.

"Fed Ex," Jeffries announced as he went to the door.

The courier's voice carried through the house. "Guaranteed delivery by nine AM and it's here with five minutes to spare. Sign right there."

"Have a nice day," Jeffries said. He appeared on the patio, carrying a package, which he set on the table then headed back to the kitchen.

Lo examined the box, wrapped in brown paper. He seemed puzzled, his thin gray eyebrows taut, forehead furrowed. A message stamped in large black letters read *Guaranteed Delivery by 9 AM*. No return address. The chime from the clock in the house began to sound the hour.

Ding...Ding...Ding...

"Say one thing," Lo said. "It's on time. I wonder..."

Ding...Ding...Ding...

Janis caught the look in Lo's eyes. It seemed as if he was locked in the terror of his own thoughts.

Ding...Ding...

Janis grabbed the package and threw it into the pool. Lo flung Lisa to the grass. Janis hit the patio deck, belly first, as a numbing explosion erupted from the pool, blasting water skyward like a Yellowstone geyser. Windows on the back side of the house shattered with a bang. The shock wave echoed into the distance, rolling away like thunder. Water rained down on the back yard.

Ears ringing, Janis scrambled to his feet and ran to the pool. Most of the water was gone, the tiles cracked. He looked up to the twisted patio roof where water cascaded over a buckled eave. Jeffries screamed.

Turning toward the back door, Janis saw him staggering out of the kitchen, blood gushing from his chest.

"Help me!" He fell, his blood now staining the gray patio slate.

Janis rushed to his side. It didn't look good. Hand shaking, Janis positioned it over the gushing wound and pressed down hard. A blast of pain shrieked up his arm. He pulled his hand away and stared at a bloody gash in his palm. Shocked, he suddenly realized a jagged blade of glass was barely protruding from Jeffries' chest, a shard of window that had been turned into deadly shrapnel by the blast. It glistened like a diamond wrapped in a scarlet shroud.

"Damn it!" He squeezed his wrist. How stupid! He should have checked the wound first. "I need a towel!"

Lo pointed to the pool room and Lisa ran.

"I'll Call 911." Lo disappeared inside the house as Lisa brought towels.

Janis pressed one to Jeffries' wound but it quickly became soaked red. He grabbed another. Jeffries' body jerked. His breaths were but short erratic pants now. Janis saw death in his face, which had turned ghostly white, his eyes wide open, pupils fixed and dilated. A moment later, his limbs quivered and he went limp.

Lo ran to his side and knelt. "Hang on, Jeffries!" He shook his aide's shoulder.

Jeffries' last breath gurgled from his mouth.

Janis stood and looked at his blood-soaked hands, not able to tell the difference between Jeffries' blood and his own. A rage swept over him. Devin had to be stopped.

California was again assailed by the wail of sirens approaching in the distance. Janis grabbed another towel, wrapped his hand, and then turned to find Lisa. She was lying on her back in the grass, her eyes staring up into a misty blue sky. Janis kneeled at her side.

"I couldn't bear to watch him die," she said, her lips quivering like a whimpering child.

Janis stroked her shoulder. "He must've been a good man," he said softly. Looking around at the destruction, he suddenly realized that Lo Chin's life was in peril now. The madman had marked him for death, too.

As Lo directed paramedics to the patio, Janis could see sorrow etched deep in his face, his eyes shining from tears that didn't flow. Standing by his side, Janis watched the medical team attempt to revive Jeffries. Hope faded from their faces. All the medical technology in the world couldn't save him.

After homicide detectives took photos of the scene, the Coroner laid Jeffries on a body bag and unceremoniously zipped it around him—then lifted him to a gurney.

Detective Lieutenant Michaels walked out of the house and stood on the bloodied patio, his hair uncombed, his face unshaven. He looked annoyed.

"Where's the owner of this place?" he bellowed.

Lo acknowledged with a finger in the air.

Janis almost panicked when he caught Michael's glare. Had the cop recognized him from last night? Lisa rushed to Janis' side and clung to his arm.

"What's with you two?" Michaels said, striding toward them, the anger in his voice like venom. "How come I see you every time something gets blown up in this town?"

"Just lucky, I guess," Janis said. He didn't care if he sounded sarcastic. "You weren't interested in what we had to say last night, so why should this morning be any different?"

"Last night we didn't have a customer for the morgue," Michaels sneered. He turned a full circle, scanning the wrecked back yard. "What did this?"

"Mail bomb," Lo said.

"Sounds like a job for the Feds."

"That's right," Janis said. "You haven't got enough talent to find a firecracker on the Fourth of July. We told you Devin was a dangerous killer. Have you got that now?"

"Look, Dr. Smart-Guy," Michaels growled, pointing a stiff finger at Janis. "Any more lip out of you and it'll be a night in county jail. Have you got that now?"

Janis stared at the officer, frustrated with his arrogant attitude but electing not to press his anger any further.

Michaels turned to Lo, put a hand on his shoulder. "What's this all about?"

"You guess—me guess. Same thing. I only know we're in trouble. Must find safe place."

"All four of us have to make a break for Simi Valley," Janis said.

Lo looked at Lisa, his eyes heavy with loss. "Now I must pay high price," he said. "For revenge on Devin, I too will sleep with enemy. Don't care no more."

Chapter Thirty

A DAUGHTER'S HATE

As Ray got out of his Jeep Wagoneer, he spotted Detective Michaels walking out of the house on Willow Circle. "What's going on?"

"Your friend is out back," Michaels said. "I can't protect you people, you know." He walked backwards toward his squad car. "You better run for your lives."

Ray stood in the street and watched the police car disappear around the corner. What was that all about? He went into the house and spotted Janis on the patio. Glass littered the floor. A coroner's gurney rattled through the dining room, complete with body bag. Ray shivered. "What happened?"

"Your 13th Power has just claimed another victim," Janis said.

Ray looked around the patio, strewn with broken glass and stained with blood. "How?"

"Devin struck again."

"He bombed the place?" Ray followed Janis out to a pool where a blond woman stood with her back to them, talking to an Oriental man. She suddenly turned around.

"Lisa?" He couldn't believe his eyes. "Lisa? What are you doing here?"

She glared at him for a moment then gave Janis a hug and kissed him on the cheek. Ray set his jaw. Though a hundred questions rushed through his mind, the sight of Janis touching his daughter sent a rage burning through him.

"Oh no you don't!" he yelled, grabbing Janis by the shoulder and spinning him around. "Not with my daughter!" He connected a right hook to Janis' jaw, sending him to the ground. His glasses flew off and clattered across the deck.

Flat on his back, Janis rubbed his jaw. "You son of a bitch."

Ray leaned over him, grabbed his shirt, raised him off the ground, and slugged him in the mouth. Janis' shirt ripped and he hit the ground again.

Before Ray could recoil and strike a third time, Lisa jumped on his back, her forearm cinched across his throat. He tried to get a breath of air, but her hold was strong, stronger than he'd thought possible. He spun around, trying to throw her off, but the pressure on his throat shot a blast of pain up through his eyeballs. He gagged. Through a ringing in his ears he could hear her yelling, "Bastard!"

Struggling to free himself, he caught a glimpse of Janis getting to his feet, approaching with fists balled. Oh, shit! A sudden gush of pain across the bridge of his nose blackened his vision, filled his head with swirling, flashing lights. His knees buckled and he hit the ground. Lisa landed on top of him. Everything was spinning around.

"Lisa! Let him go!" Janis shouted, wrestling with her grip. "Now!" But she wasn't listening—she wouldn't release the chokehold she had on her father. Ray's face was turning blue. "You're going to kill him!"

She finally let him go. "Bastard! You don't own me any more!"

Janis pulled her to her feet. Ray rolled on the ground, coughing, his nose bleeding.

"Did he hurt you?" she asked, looking at Janis' swelling lip.

He rubbed his jaw. "My glasses!"

She found them quickly. "He didn't need to do that," she said, handing Janis his glasses. "He's a jerk. I'm getting out of here." She headed toward the house.

As she walked away, Janis put his glasses on and looked down at Ray. "Are you out of your mind?"

"You're damn right!" Ray stood on wobbly legs. He wiped the back of his hand across his bloody nose and glared at Janis. "Don't ever touch my daughter again. I'll kill you!"

"Take a reality check, Ray. You can go to hell if you think I'm worried about your stupid threats. Professionals have been trying to kill us for two days now—so cram it up your ass."

Ray spit. "You're too damn old for her."

"Since when does love have an age limit?"

"I'm just protecting her from the wrong people. First her mother, and now, you."

"Protect her? Hell—you condemned her. Because of you she was isolated in misery. You call that protecting her? I call it abuse. Where is your heart, man—up your ass?" Janis felt the need to slug him again, but Ray just glared at him—daring him to do it.

"Don't judge me too quickly, Janis. I had good reason."

"Good enough to justify her hate for you now? I saw it in her eyes, Ray. She'd have killed you—just like that." He snapped his fingers.

"I don't think so."

Lo pushed his way between them and handed Ray a towel. "Fix bloody nose," he said. "Playtime's over—kiss and make up. We go now, before somebody else comes to kill us."

Janis backed away from the confrontation and rubbed his swollen lip. Lisa was right. Ray was a jerk.

* * *

Lo watched the coroner's wagon pull away with Jeffries' body inside, the other official vehicles following behind it. Hanging his head as they drove off, he realized it was time to take a stand against Devin, and standing with Janis and Ray seemed the logical place to be. He believed in the old saying, *every dog had its day*. Lo intended to be there when Devin had his.

* * *

Janis changed his ripped shirt and collected his things. A few minutes later, he helped load the Jeep wagon. They were ready to go. He knew the sooner they got to Simi Valley, the sooner they'd be safe. Grabbing his arm, Lisa pulled him into the back seat. Ray climbed in behind the wheel. Janis looked toward the house. They were waiting for Lo.

"Ray—this trip is going to be hard enough with Devin trying to kill us," Janis said. "What do you say to a truce?"

Turning around, Ray looked at his daughter. "You hate me that much?" he asked her.

"That much," she said, her voice icy cold.

Ray looked at Janis, exhaled. "It's going to be a long trip."

The door creaked open and Lo got in. "Let's go. Keep eyes open for more bad guys." He put his elbow on the seatback and said to Lisa, "Teeth on other end of tiger tail sharp."

Lisa said nothing, cuddled into Janis, the Jeep now accelerating down the driveway and into the city.

Chapter Thirty-One
STEVE RAVEN

Steve pitched his Cessna for sixty-five knots, dropped the flaps ten degrees, and reported into the radio mike, "Desert Rock traffic, Cessna niner-four-niner on downwind for two-zero, full stop, Desert Rock."

The wings of his blue and white airplane glistened in the Nevada morning sunshine. He banked left and lined up with the runway. Bumping and yawing in convective air, the plane descended. In the distance, heat waves rose from the brick and concrete compound of Atomtech. A black Cadillac raced down a dirt road toward the airfield, a plume of dust swirling in its wake. Steve grinned. His plan to put the squeeze on Devin for more cash was about to swing into action. Tires barked as the Cessna touched down.

Parking his plane, he recalled the Balli Club meeting. Curtis was passing out millions and Devin was paying peanuts. He shut off the engine. Now it would be a whole new ball game.

The Cadillac pulled up beside him and the front doors flew open. Two heavily armed goons stomped toward the plane. They wore baggy black pants, black shirts, and sour faces.

Steve's throat went dry but he wouldn't give them any hint of anxiety. "What are you guys—the welcome wagon?"

"No funny stuff, Raven," the big goon bellowed, his belly overloading his belt. "Devin is in a bad mood and some of it's rubbed off on us."

Steve locked the plane. "I'm real scared—can't yah tell?" He headed for the Cadillac. "Swing by the fuel shed on our way out."

He helped himself to the back seat and took a last look around the airfield. An eerie calm hung over the desert floor, cacti and sage basking under an intense sun. But the serenity wouldn't last. Afternoon winds would intensify and temperatures were expected to soar over one hundred degrees. Bad conditions for flying. He needed to finish his business with Devin before noon and get out of here.

His escorts piled into the front seat. As the car headed for the fuel shed, the big goon riding shotgun turned around. "You better have the stuff on that meeting or Devin is gonna let *us* take care of you." The bad guy grinned, revealing a mouth full of missing teeth. "Personally, I hope you screwed up—never did like you pretty-boy private eyes."

"Don't take a bite out of something you can't chew, Toothless." Steve pulled his .45 and pointed it at the goon. "Turn that ugly mug around before I blow it off. Get the picture, bean brain?"

The runty driver turned a frightful look to the back seat and Steve switched targets. "You too, Little Man." The goons turned their attention forward as he guarded them from behind.

At the shed, Steve called out to Thompson, an old man dressed in gray coveralls. "Fill up the Cessna and bill it to Devin."

Thompson headed for the fuel truck.

Rumbling down the dirt road toward Atomtech, the Cadillac creaked and rattled. Steve surveyed the vast desert around him. It offered solitude for Devin and his henchmen. The place was bleak and dusty, surrounded by bleak and dusty. A chain-link fence, laced with barbed wire and entangled with tumbleweeds, stretched for miles. Four fifty-foot sentry towers stood guard over a complex of metal sheds and hanger-sized Quonset huts. The main building was constructed of brown brick, stood three stories high, and looked as big as four football fields. A huge array of antenna and satellite dishes decorated the rooftop. Steve chuckled under his breath as the drawbar angled up for the speeding car.

Piece of cake.

Chapter Thirty-Two

WALTER DEVIN

From a window in his third floor office, Devin watched the Cadillac speed toward the main gate. He had known Raven's plane was coming, having tracked its approach on radar. Raven would have a tape of the meeting at the Balli Club. Puffing on a fat Cuban cigar, Devin turned to his intercom.

"Miss Rivers—get Leonard up here."

Devin strutted up to his full-length mirror to admire himself and practice his sinister mannerism. Dressed in drab tan slacks and matching long-sleeve shirt, he never professed to being a fashion statement. Unwilling to turn old gracefully, he had dyed his hair dark brown. He puffed out his chest and pulled in his beer gut. Not bad for sixty.

Returning to the window to check on his approaching guest, he sucked his cigar, the smoke thickening the air. When the Cadillac pulled up in front, the men got out and disappeared through doors below him.

Leonard ran in, breathless, sweat shining the top of his balding head. A rim of brown hair hung down to his collar, uncombed. His white lab coat was stained with coffee. Wearing thick black-framed glasses, he was an aging nerd who often boasted about his position at Atomtech as lead technician in communications, heading up the satellite reconnaissance department. From his eye in the sky, he could win any game of hide-and-seek. "Yes, sir—you called for me?"

"What's the story from San Francisco this morning?"

"They're headed for Simi Valley," he said with a nervous twitch. "We aren't having any luck stopping them."

"No shit! A pack of Boy Scouts could have done better than the boneheads you've been sending. Can't they do anything right?"

"They're trying, sir."

"Like hell! They couldn't manage to delay a stinking cab, detain Dr. Mackey for questioning, or even disable a limo without destroying it."

"At least they didn't turn traitor—like Lisa."

Devin curled his upper lip. "I shouldn't have trusted her."

"You should've left her out of this."

"And *you* should've kept your mouth shut."

"So what should I do now?"

"Track their every move."

Leonard ran out and headed downstairs to his control center. Devin stood in the office doorway and grumbled, "Dumb bastard. Maybe Raven has some answers."

Elevator doors slid open. Raven pushed the goons out, Toothless at gunpoint and Little Man cowering along. Devin could only shake his head as Raven paraded the humbled thugs past Miss Rivers, sitting at her reception desk. Susan lifted a sleek eyebrow. She seemed impressed with the private eye's entrance.

Undaunted by the menacing weapon, Devin waved Raven into the office. Raven wasn't a big man, maybe five-foot-nine, but gutsy for his size. Wavy brown hair hung down over his forehead. His eyes were dark and daring. He wore Dockers, a flight jacket, and a crafty smile. Devin had seen his type before—a sleeper. Didn't look like a bad ass—but he was.

"I certainly hope you didn't rough up my boys too much." Devin puffed on his cigar and motioned toward a chair in front of his massive desk. "Have a seat."

"No thanks," Steve said. "I don't dance sitting down." His voice carried an air of confidence, even malice. "I'm tired of babysitting your bozos. Get rid of 'em."

Devin snapped his fingers. His goons backed out the door and slammed it shut.

After holstering the .45 under his leather flight jacket, Steve walked to the window and looked out. "I don't know what game you're playing with Curtis, but it's time to ante-up." Reaching into his pocket, he turned to Devin. "This tape I have here," he displayed the tiny reel, "is worth more than a lousy thousand bucks. I'd say a hundred thousand would be more like it."

Devin took a step forward, glaring at the greedy private eye.

Raven reached for his .45, but didn't remove it from the holster. "Don't get cheap on me now."

Leering, Devin sat behind his desk, propped his feet up, and puffed on the cigar. He studied Raven for a moment. Did the clever sleuth have more guts than brains? Was he bluffing? Maybe.

But it wouldn't be wise to call him on it—not yet anyway. "Let's hear the tape." He slid a recorder across the desk. "Then I'll decide what it's worth."

"A hundred-thousand, Devin."

"You'll get shit if I don't hear it."

"It's worth a hundred grand, I tell yah."

"What do you know?"

Steve showed teeth, then relented and inserted the tape.

The recorded conversation came through clearly. When it ended, Devin snatched the recorder and threw it against a wall. "Damn it!" He stood and leaned forward, snarling at the astounded private eye. "You fool! Curtis wants the 13th Power. Do you have any idea what that means?" He walked to the window and looked out across the desert. "He has Ray Crawford and Janis Mackey, the best atomic physicist and the best mathematician this country has to offer. And he has the best equipment in the world at Solartech Labs. The 13th Power could be his."

Steve shifted in his chair. "So what's the big deal about Curtis anyway . . .other than the fact his mother dresses him funny?"

"He's a dangerous man—a fraud. His real name is Anderson. Melvin Anderson. He was once a world-renowned archeologist—along with his father. They had many successful digs together, in Mexico mostly, until his father was killed. That's when Melvin turned to stealing, became a goddamned grave robber—made Indonesia his specialty. He stole everything he discovered. Hoarded the good stuff and sold the rest on the black market."

"Jesus! He must be worth a fortune."

"The World Society of Archeologists banned him from digging. He was finished—but the damage was already done. Countries he defrauded tried to retrieve their lost artifacts from the black marketers. Hundreds died in the conflict."

Steve sat up. "What does an archeologist want with the 13th Power?"

Devin didn't look away from the window. "The Higgs boson, most likely—the atomic strong force, the most powerful force in nature, the force that gives matter mass. He wants the power that's hidden deep inside every atom's nucleus. Whoever controls the Higgs will control the universe—like a god." He looked at Raven. "Trust me—Curtis would make a terrible god."

"Maybe you should call the cops in on this."

Devin huffed. "I told Colonel Fallon about Curtis. But the hotshot Air Force Security Police Commander didn't believe the impostor posed a national security risk. He said he didn't give a shit *what* was going on at Solartech Labs. It's a free country. Hell—he even had the nerve to accuse me of whining about my competition getting an upper hand on Atomtech." Devin blew a cloud of cigar smoke into the air. "Fallon is my best friend. If *he* didn't believe me, why would anyone else?" A chill went down Devin's neck. "So you see—Curtis is *my* problem. If I don't stop him, life on earth will never be the same—if at all."

The room fell silent. Steve sat back in his chair, thinking about Devin's last words. Life on earth was a bit heavy. Money was the only thing that interested Steve—and a new plan was already forming. Curtis would probably pay big bucks to keep his little secret quiet. Excited, Steve said, "Let's get back to the price. Sounds like my offer of a hundred thou' is right on."

Padding back to his desk, Devin snuffed the cigar in an ashtray. "It's in a safe, behind that picture on the wall." He pointed to a painting of a lovely young lady dressed in rags. "Go ahead. It's unlocked."

Steve approached the picture cautiously, hesitated, then pulled on the frame. It came away from the wall like a cupboard door. Behind it was a safe, its door slightly ajar. His eyes went wide. He was rich. Piece of cake. He reached for the handle.

Something clanked. A horrifying sinking feeling suddenly engulfed his body. The safe disappeared, the floor swallowed him. His chest tightened with terror. Devin's sinister laughter echoed in the distance as Steve plummeted into darkness.

Devin released a hidden button under his desktop and laughed aloud for his clever dismissal of the troubling private eye. With a clank, the trapdoor closed. Plucking another fat cigar from its case, Devin turned to leave. Life was good.

Miss Rivers appeared in the doorway. "What's so funny?"

Devin lit the cigar with a silver Zippo. "Just another day at the office."

She batted cigar smoke and coughed. "Where's your guest?"

"Gone."

Leaving her with that thought, he headed downstairs to the communications control room and pushed through its double doors. Walking down the center of the room, he passed a row of super computers, humming. Along the walls, lighted consoles with multiple monitors buzzed with activity. Flashing lights: green, yellow, and red, pulsed rhythmically. Technicians in white lab coats nursed the precious hardware like ever-vigilant mothers caring for their young.

Tension filled the air. Working a joystick, Leonard aimed the probing eye of his Sky Spy Satellite—the SSS, Atomtech's hottest government contract. Watching over Leonard's shoulder, Devin could see an image on the monitor, which had been transmitted from space to a dish on the roof—a Jeep Wagoneer speeding through traffic.

"Ah ha!" With a mouse button click, Leonard locked the SSS on target.

"You sure that's them?"

"I'd recognize Ray's Jeep anywhere—the luggage rack is broken." Leonard reached for a headset and put it over his ears. He positioned the mouthpiece and pushed a button on his control panel. "Racer Ten—come in. Sand Trap. Racer Ten."

Devin couldn't hear the reply.

"Target locked on. Coordinates coming to you on one-two-four-point-three. Redirect now." Leonard paused. "Confirmed—Sand Trap." He pulled the headset off and said to Devin, "We'll get 'em this time."

"You better."

Several technicians gathered around Devin and Leonard at the monitor as the SSS tracked the speeding Jeep. Like watching a movie from the top down, they saw it careen onto southbound I-5. No one spoke. The deadly game was on again.

Chapter Thirty-Three
THE PIT OF HORROR

Steve tried to release a scream but it lodged in his throat like the blade of a knife. Cold, dark, emptiness surrounded him. He gritted his teeth. Was he sliding into hell? Was he going to die? He reached out, groping for something, anything to grab. But there was nothing but slimy walls entombing him in a downward sloping tunnel of black.

Suddenly, the sliding stopped and falling began. His mind swelled with horror as he felt the emptiness of nothing around him.

"SHIT!"

A bone-jarring impact knocked the wind from his lungs. The shock of cold water forced him to suck air. Though it was pitch black, he knew he'd landed in a stinking mud puddle. Yuk! He groped the mire like a blind man. Thick slimy muck oozed through his fingers. The air even tasted like mud—and worse—smelled like a sewer. A rat squealed in the darkness. His senses went on full alert. He was alive—but for how long?

Where was he? Was there a way out?

Rolling to his knees in the goo, he struggled to his feet. But his boots stuck in the mud. When he tired to take a step, he tripped and fell face first, back into the slop. He spit. Crawling seemed to have a distinct advantage in this goddamned pit.

On his hands and knees, he slogged his way through the foul darkness and bumped a wall, which crumbled when he ran his hands across it. Dirt? What kind of hellhole was this?

He went right, crawling along the wall. Feeling his way through the mire, he encountered an obstacle in his path. A pile of sticks? He about gagged when he realized his fingers were plying the bones of a human skeleton. Again, a scream surged up from his lungs but stalled in his throat. He gulped stagnant air and feared he'd go insane.

"Where's the damn light switch, Devin?" His words echoed away quickly. "You bastard, Devin!" It felt good to yell, stifled his fear and tightened his resolve to find a way out.

He crawled onwards encountering other skeletons along the

way. What had *they* done to deserve Devin's wrath? His chest heaved with a wave of panic. Had they searched for a way out, too, just as he was doing now? They had obviously failed. Maybe there was no way out. How long had it taken them to die? Probably days of starving, freezing, lying alone in this putrid hell. Must've been a horrible way to go. His future started looking bleak.

Suddenly, a rattling sound shattered the silence and turned the darkness into a terror he'd never known. Chills rippled through his body without restraint. He'd heard that sound before. A rattlesnake. He froze. Where was it coming from? How close? How many? How big? His fears of a long, arduous death had just been nullified.

His old hunting buddy, Ben Reager, flashed through his mind. Bitten by a Diamondback, the poison swelled his leg 'til it split wide open. He died screaming. Steve swallowed the lump in his throat. Did he dare move? If only he had a flashlight. A match. Anything. Ah, his trusty .45.

Slowly, he reached inside his mud-logged jacket and slipped the gun from its holster. The eerie rattling grated his nerves, made his hand shake. He aimed toward the sound. *Give it your best guess, Steve.* Was it in front of him and to the right? He squeezed the trigger. A deafening muzzle blast lit the chamber long enough to reveal the rattler's broad head, looming above him, well within striking range. Its shiny forked tongue slithered back into its mouth as darkness reclaimed the pit of horror.

The rattling got louder, faster. Steve shivered. In the flash he'd seen a ten-footer, maybe twelve, thick gray body, scales laced with a black diamond pattern. Its rattles were stacked on the tip of its tail—a lot of them. He was an old boy and pissed off. But he was alone. Not good odds against Steve's .45.

He fired again and again, counting spent rounds and lighting the pit of horror like flashbulbs at a photo shoot, the reports blasting, echoing, his ears aching. Randomly aiming, he fired wildly. The snake struck, its fangs glistening in the muzzle flashes, its mouth slamming into the sleeve of his leather jacket. Steve rolled in the mud, shaking with fear, waiting for the pain, the sting of poison.

Nothing.

Big boy had missed. Crouching on one knee in the muck, he held his .45 in both hands and locked his elbows. Two rounds left.

He squeezed the trigger, the muzzle flash again revealing the snake's head and flicking tongue. Steve fixed his eyes on that spot in the darkness. Steady. Holding his breath so hard his lungs burned, he aimed on that fix in his mind. Steady...He fired.

The rattling stopped. Mud splattered as the rattler thrashed in its throes of death. Then silence. Devin's pet was dead. A sudden spasm took hold of his guts. Had he just condemned himself to a long and arduous death?

Steve grasped on to what was left of his sanity. He ejected the empty clip from his .45 and slapped in a new one. "I'm going to kill you, Devin!" Yelling made him feel better.

Wiping gunk from his face with a mucky coat sleeve, his stomach knotted from the stench. He thought he was going to throw up, a reflex he resisted mightily; he hated the taste of vomit. His clothes were soaked and caked with muddy slime, which he tried to rinse off with fetid water from a puddle. But it was no use. He leaned his back against a dirt wall, like his other skeletal pit-mates must've done. A slow and soggy death awaited him.

Just then a noise, like footsteps, echoed through the pit, a light now piercing the darkness above cliff-like walls. He heard angry voices yelling. Crouched in the quagmire at the bottom of the pit, he waited, he watched, his .45 again in hand. Was it friend or foe up there?

Chapter Thirty-Four

SUSAN RIVERS AND THE GOONS

Susan watched Devin disappear downstairs to the control room. Sometimes he could be such a jerk. She returned her attention to his office. Where did the stranger go, the handsome man who had single-handedly muzzled the goons? He was her kind of guy.

She spotted an open safe on the wall behind a strangely hung picture. She'd never seen it before. Was there anything in it? As she stepped forward, the floor creaked beneath her feet. She quickly looked down and spotted the telltale edges of a trapdoor in the carpet. Stomach clutching with a sudden fear, she jumped back to safer footing. Had the handsome man been dispatched to his death? *My God.*

She ran to her desk, grabbed the phone, and dialed maintenance. As the phone rang, she looked up and saw Toothless and Little Man coming up the stairwell, machine guns slung over their shoulders, pistols holstered. They eyed her suspiciously, like her brothers had done whenever she tried to sneak a cookie. The goons plopped on the couch, watching her. Calmly, she hung up and sat at her desk as if nothing important was on her mind. What was she going to do now? How was she going to distract them? Hmmm.

"Get you boys some coffee?" She smiled brightly.

They looked at each other and shrugged.

"Be right back—so don't go away." She walked to the elevator with a casual stride. Once inside, the doors slid shut and she hit the first-floor button for maintenance even though the cafeteria was on the second floor. She didn't have time to play musical elevators in order to fool the sentries upstairs. Though she'd been working for Devin ten years, his dopey bodyguards always treated her like an outsider. She guessed they'd needed someone to pick on and she'd been an easy target. The elevator stopped and she rushed down the hall to maintenance.

Pushing through heavy double doors, she called out, "Booie. Booie—where are you?" The cavernous room smelled of coal dust and floor wax. She walked past a furnace room door and headed down a corridor toward the main electrical substation. "Booie."

"Up here," came a raspy voice from a catwalk above. The janitor, black as pitch, had been around when this technical wonder was built and claimed to know every inch of the place. "What's all the fuss about?"

A wave of relief swept over her. "I need your help," she said. "The trapdoor in the floor of Devin's office—where does it lead to?"

"Hold on now, Missy Suzie. Never seen no trap door." He slowly negotiated his way down a metal ladder to the floor. Breathing hard, he hobbled up to her, his thin hair dripping sweat, the whites of his eyes glowing. "No trap door, I tell you."

"Let me put it to you another way." She placed her hand on his bony shoulder. "If I told you to build a trap door in Devin's office, how would you do it—where would it go?" She hoped to spark the old guy's memory of the building.

He scratched the stubble on his chin. "Don't rightly know. Need to check the blueprints." He motioned her to follow him down the corridor. "In here."

The storage room looked like a trash compacter that someone forgot to turn on. There had to be a floor somewhere under the piles of papers, books, and boxes that cluttered the dingy room. And what was that smell?

"'Scuse the mess. Don't come in here much no more."

She didn't want to touch anything for fear a bug might jump out, or worse, a rat.

Dust swirled in the air as he opened a huge cabinet crammed full of important-looking papers. He shuffled from shelf to shelf, analyzing old documents, some bound, some scrolled.

"Ah—here it is." He pulled a cardboard tube from a shelf. On a pile of boxes stacked against the wall, he rolled out the blueprints and pulled the chain on an overhead lamp, which swung back and forth, casting eerie shadows that swayed.

"Let's see. Here's Devin's office on the third floor." He pointed to one plot. "Below that, on the second floor, the cafeteria. See—a lot of air ducts and plumbing here."

She looked over his shoulder as he continued tracing downward with his bony finger. "First floor's the control room for the old particle accelerator that runs under the desert."

He turned to the next plot, pausing as he looked it over.

"Here. Below the control room deep underground—the waste-water holding pit for the accelerator cooling system." He looked up. "'Fraid it hasn't been used in years."

"What's this?" Susan pointed to an area above the pit.

"Stairway, ma'am. Goes down to the upper deck...ah...looks like some thirty feet above pit's bottom. There's water valves up here, too," he pointed. "That's where I'd make my trapdoor go, Miss Suzie. Right there." Pride rang in his sandpaper voice.

"You're my hero, Booie." She kissed his sunken cheek. "Show me how to get down there."

She followed Booie out of maintenance to the other side of the building. The control room doors were locked. He fiddled with a big ring of keys and looked up. "I don't have no key for these doors," he said. "Been closed off for years."

A chime came from the elevator. The door slid open and two goons stepped out. They scowled when they spotted Susan and Booie standing at the locked doors.

"Wait! Hold it right there!" Toothless ordered. "Hands up!" He lowered his machine gun.

"Sorry about the coffee—I got sidetracked." She took a step toward the goons. Little Man stood behind Toothless. He didn't seem anxious to get involved.

"Damn the coffee!" Toothless yelled. "What are you sneaking around here for?"

"Well...ah...Booie thinks the guy you brought here today is hiding in there." She pointed to the locked doors.

The big goon's chest swelled. "Raven? That son of a bitch! Get out of my way!"

Susan pulled Booie to the floor as the crazed killer opened fire on the door, blasting away the locks as if they were papier-mâché. Gun smoke and dust swirled in the air. Both goons ran into the control room and turned on the lights.

"Those guys are dumber than dirt," Susan whispered. "Let's go." She pulled Booie to his feet and they ran in after the goons, who were searching around the equipment, crouching, guns ready as though they expected a surprise attack.

"He ain't in *here*," Booie said. "He's down them stairs!"

The enraged goons clunked down a dark stairwell. Booie flipped switches that lit the upper deck. Susan went down after them. An awful stench hit her like a low punch.

"Whew-wee," Toothless said. "Even Raven don't smell this bad."

The goons tromped over to the edge of a pit and peered into an abyss. "Hey, Raven! You down there?" Toothless fired his machine gun into the darkness.

Chapter Thirty-Five
ESCAPE TO SIMI VALLEY

Steve got the answer he was looking for—more bad guys, Toothless and Little Man, their silhouettes unmistakable. Raising his .45, he took careful aim at Toothless. Tightening his finger on the trigger, Steve suddenly saw a motion behind the goons, someone stepping forward and pushing them over the edge. Screaming, they tumbled into the pit. Steve jumped to the side, again diving into the sludge. The goons hit bottom with a splat, landing somewhere close-by, real close. He could hear them cursing and groaning and flinging mud in the darkness.

"Hey, Raven." A woman's voice rang out from above. "You okay?"

Spitting mud, Steve wondered what a woman was doing up there. The sound of her voice was much too sweet for this sour place. "I've had better days."

"I brought a couple of friends to play with you."

"Thanks, Miss. But now I'm gonna have to kill 'em."

"Behave yourselves, boys. You'll need all your energy for your swimming lesson today."

"What?"

"How long can you tread water?"

Suddenly, rushing water cascaded into the pit of horror with a sound like thunder. "Oh, shit!" Steve barely had time to holster his .45 before the torrent engulfed him. The initial blast of water lasted only a few moments. The pit began to fill. Steve could hear the goons thrashing around in the darkness, but he wasn't worried about them killing him. Right now they were busy swimming for their lives.

Steve shivered in the cold water, his chest tightening with each breath of air. He swam in the rising boil, which began to strip the mud from his body, a relief he welcomed in spite of the chill. The water level finally reached light. He spotted the thugs. They saw him at the same time.

"Raven!" Toothless roared. "I'm gonna kill you!" The goon swam toward him. Steve could see rage in the big man's eyes.

Treading water, Steve greeted him with a quick right hook to the mouth, knocking out another one of his precious few teeth. "Keep it up and you'll be eating baby food, you dumb shit."

The goon backed off, one hand over his mouth. "Damn you, Raven." He thrashed in the water. Little Man kept his distance.

As the water reached the upper deck, Steve swam for it, leaving the goons behind. A beautiful woman reached for his hand and pulled him out of the water. He recognized her from Devin's office.

"Raven? What kind of name is that?" she asked.

"Steve Raven, private eye, at your service and in your debt forever, ma'am," he said with all the charm he could muster for the lady who had just saved his life. "But I don't understand. Devin puts me in here and you get me out?"

"Devin's crazy. I'm Susan Rivers. I just work—or rather *worked* here." Her smile could have lit up the pit of horror.

Steve took her hand. "'Pleased to meet you would be an understatement."

She smiled. "I was very impressed with your entrance."

Dripping wet and shivering, he was unable to take his gaze from her face. Her deep brown eyes bedazzled him and her black hair shined in the lights. His admiration for her went deeper than gratitude.

Booie turned the water valve off and opened the drain valve. The water level in the pit began to fall rapidly.

"Help us!" the goons yelled, dropping away in the swirling water.

Looking down at the goons going around and around, Steve shouted, "Now you know what a turd feels like when you flush it down the toilet."

"Not funny, Raven! Give us a break!"

Booie turned the drain valve off. The water stopped receding. From an emergency cabinet on the platform, he removed a rescue rope and tossed it over the edge. "Can't leave 'em down there to die," he said. " But this'll buy you some time."

"Thanks, Booie." Miss Rivers waved goodbye and ran up the stairs with Steve.

Outside, they climbed into the black Cadillac. Steve grabbed the wheel.

"Where are we going?" Susan asked with a wink.

He twisted the key. "Simi Valley, California." The engine fired.

"What are we going to do there?"

"Get rich." Steve dropped the gearshift into drive.

"How?"

"You just leave that to me," he said. The sour look on her face told him she wasn't satisfied with his answer but he left it at that. She didn't have to know everything—did she?

Accelerating, Steve headed for the main gate where the guard brandished his pistol. Steve floored the gas. "Get down," he told Susan. Engine roaring, he smashed through the drawbar as gunfire banged and bullets pinged.

As the car fishtailed down the dirt road, Susan sat up. "You're going to get us killed before we even get there."

"Not if I can help it."

A moment later, a blue van burst through the main gate. Steve caught a glimpse of the approaching menace in the rearview mirror. "That didn't take long."

He raced across the airfield to his plane. "Quick. Get in and buckle up."

Flipping switches, he started the engine. The propeller buzzed to life. No time for checklists. He pulled the mixture, pushed the throttle, and steered down the taxi ramp. Heat waves shimmered from the runway. Fuel gages read *Full*. Not good for a fast take off.

Gunfire rang out as he swung the Cessna onto the runway and pushed the throttle all the way in. The plane accelerated down the centerline, the blue van careening alongside, weaving back and forth, gunfire popping from open windows. Steve clenched his jaw. The bastards were aiming for his tires.

Hot afternoon air and gusty winds took a toll on his plane's performance. Because of the added weight of a passenger and full fuel tanks, he'd have to lengthen his takeoff roll. It now became a life or death drag race to the end of the runway—only a quarter mile away. He checked the airspeed indicator—45 knots. Not enough. It would take 75 knots to get off the ground under these conditions. His palms felt suddenly sticky as the airspeed needle climbed to 50 knots.

Tires squealing, the van fishtailed. Gunfire banged. A round tore through the fuselage, ripping into the back seat.

"Shit!" 55—

The engine roared, the propeller buzzed loudly —60—

At sixty-five knots now, the van began to fall behind. Steve looked back, saw muzzle flashes but couldn't hear gunshots. Bullets ricocheted, pinged off the plane. It wouldn't take much, one slug through a gas tank or control cable and his plane would go down. Almost there —70—

He glanced at Susan. Her eyes were wide, her fists clenched in her lap. The end of the runway was dead ahead.

75!

Steve pulled back on the yoke. The Cessna sliced into the Nevada sky. He quickly banked left, away from the speeding van, which skidded off the end of the runway and plowed the desert sand.

Susan smiled, her face washed with relief.

Chuckling, Steve thought she seemed impressed with his exit, too.

Chapter Thirty-Six
COBRA

Maneuvering through heavy traffic, Ray glanced at his watch. 11:30. Could they make Simi Valley by nightfall? It seemed an impossible task. He looked at Lo's long face. What a rotten way to start the day. Ray had a bad feeling it wasn't going to get any better.

He checked his speedometer. Seventy-five seemed too slow for the urgency of this journey. In the rear-view mirror, he saw his daughter snuggling up to Janis. Again, rage boiled inside. Ray wasn't about to let her take up with an older man. Resolving to end their love-at-first-sight affair, he returned his attention to the freeway.

Janis lifted the bloodstained towel from his hand. The bleeding had stopped. "Needs stitches," he said as Lisa took a closer look.

"Does it hurt much?"

Forcing his fingers to move, he made a fist a few times. The gash stayed closed but throbbed. "It'll be okay." The fat lip he had gotten from Ray hurt worse.

Lisa hugged him.

He felt better already.

The engine roared.

"We should make Simi Valley by sundown," Ray said, careening the Jeep onto I-5.

Janice glanced at the speedometer. "You better watch your speed, Ray."

"Troopers thick like flies," Lo added. "Best slow down not attract them."

Ray looked at Lo. "Got a fly swatter?"

Janis chuckled at Ray's arrogance. It would be his ticket.

Traffic congestion of the city gradually dwindled to a scattering of vehicles on a country highway. Janis settled back in his seat. The humming engine and whining tires calmed his nerves. Lisa kicked off her sandals and rested her head in his lap, eyes closed. He stroked her shoulder while looking at Lo who seemed nervous, glancing repeatedly between Ray and the rear window. Ray looked edgy too, constantly checking the rearview mirror. Janis caught one of his quick glances. Was Ray watching the road behind them—or him?

As the Jeep roared under a viaduct, Ray spotted a cop car parked in the shadows. But it was too late. He blew by the California Highway Patrol trooper at 90 miles an hour. In the rearview mirror, Ray saw the cruiser light up like a Christmas tree, throw dirt from its rear tires, and speed after them.

"Shit! We have company!" He sat upright, pushed the accelerator to the floor, and grasped the steering wheel with both hands.

"What you do—outrun radio, too?" Lo said. "Just stop, get ticket. Then we go on."

"A police escort may keep Devin off our backs," Ray said. "Just hang on."

But his Jeep Wagoneer was no match for the patrol car. The trooper pulled alongside, motioning Ray to pull over. Ignoring him, Ray pressed the Jeep over 100 miles an hour.

A wailing siren wrenched Lisa up from her nap. She glared at her father. "You're going to get us killed!"

But Ray wasn't listening. He was watching the trooper talk into his radio, probably calling for backup. Ray had to think fast. He had to do something—even if it was wrong.

"Hold on!"

Giving the steering wheel a jerk left, he veered into the trooper's car. Metal crunched. Glass busted. Fish-tailing, the trooper regained control of his car and pulled in behind the Jeep.

Janis pushed Lisa to the seat. "Get down!"

Ray swerved from lane to lane but the patrol car stayed on his rear bumper. This wasn't going to work. He had to—

A helicopter suddenly appeared, hovering above the highway directly in front of him, a Cobra, black and ominous. Bombs, missiles, and machine guns clung to its body like pollen on a honeybee. "What the...?"

The Cobra's undercarriage erupted in smoke as a Sidewinder missile twisted toward his Jeep.

"Oh, shit!" Ray yanked the steering wheel right, careening

off the highway. He looked back just as the missile struck the patrol car, which disintegrated at 100 miles an hour. The blast from the Sidewinder's strike blew out the Jeep's back window, pelting the interior with flying shards of glass.

Lisa screamed.

"Son of a bitch!" Wrestling the Jeep back onto the highway, Ray looked all around, his chest throbbing so hard he thought it would burst.

"Where'd it go?" Janis shouted, looking out the windows in every direction, his voice filled with panic.

"Goddamn Devin!" Ray yelled.

"That thing belongs to Devin?"

"He keeps it at Edwards."

"What for?"

"The Pentagon wants nukes on the battlefield," Ray said, his eyes still scanning the sky. "Small ones capable of wiping out entire divisions. The Cobra is Devin's experimental delivery platform. Of course—he ordered it with all the options."

"What kind of pilot would use it against us?"

"His brat nephew, Burt. What a brown-noser."

"Bad blood run in family," Lo put in.

Ray steered onto the shoulder to get around a pack of slower cars. A horn blared. He looked up through the windshield, searching for the Cobra—saw nothing but hazy blue sky and smoke from the burning patrol car.

Up ahead, a column of California Highway Patrol troopers approached with lights flashing and sirens wailing. Heat waves, rising from the highway, distorted the procession like some kind of vision in a dream, a bad dream.

"Help's on the way," Ray trumpeted. But his elation was short-lived when the Cobra appeared again, this time circling around behind the line of patrol cars. "What's he doing?"

Another Sidewinder snaked from the chopper and blasted a patrol car off the highway. The other cars skidded and spun around. Gunfire rang out as officers tried to defend themselves against the military menace. A trooper frantically called out on the radio. "Dispatch! We're under attack by a Cobra! Scramble the National Guard right away…" The chopper from hell unleashed another Sidewinder and the squad car exploded in a ball of fire.

Other officers, crouched behind fenders and open doors, continued to fire their handguns at the Cobra, which answered with blazing machine guns. Exploding projectiles ripped the patrol cars to shreds, sending metal and glass flying in all directions. Several officers fell victim to the lethal debris and murderous rounds. Black smoke pumped skyward and drifted west on a lazy breeze.

"Those guys don't stand a chance against that Cobra," Ray said.

"W-why he shooting the cops?" Lo asked.

"Probably doesn't want any witnesses that can ID his chopper."

"We need to get off this highway," Janis said. "How about that way?" He pointed to a road beyond a field.

"Quick, Dad—while the Cobra's busy!"

"Hang on!" Ray careened the Jeep off the highway, through a bumpy field, over an irrigation ditch, and onto a dirt road that curved west under the smoky veil. The Jeep bounced and fishtailed, but Ray managed to keep it on the road. In the distance, he spotted a forest, and hopefully, shelter from the airborne killer. He pushed the accelerator to the floor.

Passing a clump of bushes, the road made a sharp turn to the left. Ray wrestled with the steering but his tires lost traction. Loose gravel pummeled the undercarriage as the Jeep skidded off the road, slid down an embankment into a rocky ravine, and landed in a creek with a bone-jarring bang.

Undaunted, Ray floored the throttle and slammed the four-wheel-drive into gear. The tires spun wildly, slinging mud and rocks as the Jeep bounded up the creek bed, bouncing and jerking. Nobody said a word as he negotiated a couple of tight turns and headed into the forest where he encountered a bridge spanning the creek. After parking between its concrete pylons, he turned to check on his daughter. "It's not much but it'll have to do." She wouldn't even look at him. He heaved a sigh of relief anyway. They were safe—for now.

Janis threw the door open and got out. In the distance, he could hear the battle raging on the highway, machine guns rattling, handguns popping. He climbed an embankment to the roadway above, hoping for a better view. But the trees were too thick.

He looked up the road, spotted a sign that read *Hollister 42*. He slid back down the embankment, ran to the Jeep, and leaned in. "You got a map?"

Ray pulled one off the visor.

Spreading the map on the hood, Janis quickly figured out where they were. Lisa walked up beside him, her eyes scanning the underside of the bridge where chirping birds fluttered about. Ray approached. "What do you think?"

"Obviously, the highway is too wide open," Janis said. "We'll need to stick to these back roads—cut over to 101." He paused. "But there's something I don't understand."

"What?"

"How does Devin keep finding us?"

Ray looked up from the map and twitched his mustache. "It's gotta be Leonard."

"Who the hell is Leonard?"

"He operates Devin's SSS—his Sky Spy Satellite—and he's damn good at it. They can track our every move from orbit."

"How did Devin…?"

"The SSS is nuclear powered. Atomtech got the government contract. It's Devin's favorite toy."

"Is there a way around it?"

"Not without giving its probing eye the slip. We'll need to switch vehicles." He pointed to the map. "Maybe here—in Hollister."

"W-what about the Cobra?" Lisa asked. "How are we going to hide from it all the way to Hollister?" She glanced back and forth between Ray and Janis.

Ray shrugged. "We may have to wait it out here."

"It'll need to refuel sometime," Janis said, listening again for the sounds of battle. He only heard leaves rustling in the breeze and water trickling from the creek. Smoke blotted out the sun.

"Is it gone?" asked Lisa.

"We'll stay here for a while—in case the Cobra comes around. In the meantime, let's check the terrain upstream." Janis took Lisa's hand. "Come on."

Ray folded the map, climbed back into his Jeep, and watched

his daughter and Janis disappear around a bend. "What's with those two?" he asked Lo. "We're about to get blasted into eternity and they go for a lover's stroll?"

Lo looked at him—like a father would his son. "Love and friendship come from heart. Take time to smell the roses, appreciate the ones you love."

"You think...?"

Suddenly, the roaring din of thumping rotor blades and whining turbine engines filled the air. Ray braced himself, hoping he'd hidden the Jeep well enough. The death machine hovered above the bridge, pivoting around as if hunting for a victim. Ray glanced at Lo then looked up the creek bed. Lisa and Janis were nowhere in sight. Panic rippled through him. Where were they? As if his worse nightmare had just materialized, the chopper flew upstream.

Janis held Lisa's hand as they made their way up the creek, looking for a suitable way out of this mess. His stomach knotted the moment he heard the Cobra. Their stroll had left them with no cover, the nearest clump of bushes too far away. He searched the sky. Where was it? It had to be close by. Suddenly, the chopper came around a bend, flying low over the creek. The black and ugly machine looked heavy, cold, and deadly. He pulled Lisa under his arm and watched the awesome power approach. Adrenaline spilled into his veins. He felt suddenly dizzy.

Lisa yelled, "Run!"

"No!" Janis held her. "Wave! Wave at him and smile. He doesn't know us. We're just two lovers out for a walk. Just act like it."

Lisa clutched his arm and mustered a smile. They waved at the chopper like happy children at a parade. But the roaring menace inched closer and closer. Turbulent winds from its rotating blades kicked up a wall of water from the creek, creating an eerie wave of power and fury. The noise was deafening but Janis stood his ground. He waved and smiled in spite of the terror swelling inside him. Again, the Cobra inched forward. Any wrong move and the chopper would unleash its arsenal of death.

As the Cobra came closer, he could see the pilot, a young man wearing sunglasses and a headset, staring down at them. Lisa smiled brightly and waved harder. A few heart-stopping moments later, the pilot smiled and waved back. Turbine engines throttled up and the Cobra rose out of the ravine. Janis felt a wave of relief. He looked at Lisa and hugged her.

A screech suddenly ripped through the sky. He looked up just in time to see the Cobra explode into an expanding ball of red and yellow fire. The concussion from the blast knocked them into the creek. Like a flaming waterfall, burning jet fuel rained down and chopper wreckage crashed into the ravine. A big chuck of debris tumbled down an embankment, spewing black smoke and throwing off broken pieces, rolling toward them at breakneck speed. Janis leaped up and yanked Lisa to her feet.

"Run!"

The wreckage slammed into the creek, just missing them. It hissed and spewed steam like some kind of demon.

Dripping wet, Janis pulled Lisa toward the bridge. He had to dodge clumps of smoldering debris and pools of burning fuel. The air reeked of fire and oil. At a bend in the ravine, he stopped and looked back. Only then did he realize he was shaking.

His eyes followed the smoke churning skyward. "What happened?" he yelled. As if answering, the sky boomed with the thundering wail of four National Guard F-15 Strike Eagles screaming above the treetops. The formation of fighters zoomed overhead, pitched upward, and disappeared in the sun's glare, their roaring engines resonating away.

Ray and Lo ran around the bend. They stopped abruptly, their wide eyes scanning the carnage in the ravine. Black smoke pumped from wreckage strewn along the creek bed. Nothing resembled the Cobra. Burning fuel flowed into the creek and fire danced on the water. Mangled and flaming debris popped and groaned in its own kind of agony.

"Right on!" Ray cheered. "Did you see those fighters blow that bastard away? Damn—that was awesome!"

Lisa turned slowly toward her father, glaring. Janis saw the hate in her eyes again. But he knew what she was feeling—for he too had felt sorry for the young pilot that waved them off with a smile and spared their lives. So quickly he was dead and gone.

"Let's get back to the Jeep," Janis said, turning Lisa away from another conflict with her father. Ray and Lo followed silently behind.

When Janis dropped the tailgate, broken glass scattered everywhere. He sat and looked at Lisa—then at her father. Though the Cobra was no longer a threat, he wished he could say the same for them. They were their own worst enemies. What a waste. But right now, getting to Simi Valley alive was more pressing than their feud. "Let's head to Hollister," Janis said. "We'll need another vehicle to slip the SSS. I've got a bad feeling Devin has more dirty tricks up his sleeve."

Chapter Thirty-Seven

LEONARD

"Damn it!" Devin went berserk when the Sidewinder struck the patrol car. He threw his cigar on the floor and jumped up from his chair. A simple surprise attack on the Jeep had turned ugly—now the authorities were involved. "Shit!" The press was going to have a field day with this. He had no time for that kind of publicity. "Get Burt on the radio, NOW!"

"Racer 10—come in," Leonard said.

A column of patrol cars suddenly appeared on the SSS monitor. "Christ! This thing is going from bad to worse. Give me that." Devin snatched the headset off Leonard's head.

"Racer 10—over," came the reply.

Devin adjusted the mouthpiece. "Squad cars approaching from the south. Eliminate them first, then go after the Jeep."

"Affirmative."

The chopper maneuvered around the troopers. Two patrol cars were destroyed—then another. But the carnage produced so much smoke that the view on the monitor became useless.

"Where are they?" Devin yelled at Leonard.

The SSS didn't move.

"Maybe they've stopped," Leonard said, as the Cobra continued its deadly assault on the California Highway Patrol.

"Racer 10. Abort. Find that Jeep."

A few moments passed before the pilot reported, "I don't see it around here. I'll sweep the area. Over."

The Cobra began circling under the drifting smoke, at times becoming completely obscured. As Devin and Leonard watched the monitor, the other technicians went back to their duties, not wanting to get in the middle of their boss' new problem.

Devin leaned on the console. "Move the SSS to the west."

The monitor's view changed as Leonard worked the joystick, but no Jeep came into sight.

"Racer 10—follow that dirt road," Devin ordered. The pilot didn't reply as the chopper flew over a winding road that came to a bridge just inside a forest.

"Got something there?"

The radio squelched. "I don't know. Wait—I see someone." The chopper flew up the ravine. "Two people—by the creek. They're waving at me."

"I can barely make them out," Leonard said.

"Witnesses!" Devin growled. "Terminate them!"

A few moments passed. The airborne assassin didn't fire.

"What are you waiting for?"

"Negative," came the pilot's response. "They're harmless." The chopper began to rise out of the ravine.

A warning horn suddenly sounded throughout the control room. Leonard checked his computer. *Radar Lock Detected*, flashed in red across the screen. Too late. An air-to-air missile had been launched from somewhere outside the SSS's view.

Devin watched his Cobra disintegrate in living color. "What?" He threw the headset down and glared at Leonard.

"Not my fault, boss," Leonard said, throwing his hands up.

But Devin must not have heard, or agreed. He grabbed Leonard by the lab coat and slammed him against a super computer, knocking the breath from his lungs. "That was your last stupid mistake, pea brain."

Leonard tried to protest but Devin flung him to the floor like a rag doll. As he struggled to crawl away, a boot slammed into his rib cage. Stabbing pain curled him into a fetal position. With an outstretched hand, he pleaded to his coworkers, but no one made a move in his defense.

Like a rabid dog, Devin attacked him again, punching and kicking until he felt numb. Then Devin grabbed Leonard's throat. Hacking and gagging, he tried to break free of Devin's fierce grip. But a dizzy blackness began to envelop him.

Just then, Devin's goons burst in, dripping wet. "Raven! He's escaped!" yelled Toothless.

Releasing Leonard's throat, Devin jerked his attention to his henchmen. "How the hell did that happen?" Moving toward them with balled fists, he shouted, "Nobody's ever escaped the pit!"

"Miss Rivers done it. We tried to stop 'em..."

"Bring her to me," Devin ordered in a slobbering rage.

But any faint flicker of sanity that he may have possessed disappeared as the goons explained how she and the slippery sleuth got away in his airplane.

"Fools!" Devin turned to the main control console and flipped a switch. A round opening appeared and an active radar screen blinked on. All the bleeping images were labeled with transponder codes—except one. The unidentified bleep had to be Raven's Cessna, close to the outer ring on the screen.

Devin pulled a lever that extended a radar-locking-beam antenna. He punched the plane's coordinates on a keyboard. A moment later, the computer beeped a solid tone.

TARGET LOCKED.

He lifted a cover that concealed a red key. "Raven! You're a dead man!" He turned the key. An anti-aircraft missile streaked into the sky, bleeping on the radar screen with its trajectory homed in on the Cessna. Devin cackled.

Suddenly, a dinging chime echoed through the control room. *Range* flashed in red on the screen. He quickly rechecked the coordinates. What the…? Raven's Cessna had crossed the outer ring and was now out of range.

"Son of a bitch!"

The missile arced back to earth and exploded on the desert floor. Bleeping weakly, the Cessna's fuzzy image faded off the radar screen. Devin slumped in a chair. Raven had to be the luckiest bastard on earth.

Leonard sat up, shaking and pale.

"Get back to work!" Devin growled. "You've got a Jeep to find."

Leonard limped to his monitor and grabbed the joystick. He knew that once this problem with Curtis was resolved, they could all get back to business as usual. But right now, it hurt to breathe. If this were any other job, he would have walked out; he would have sued. But not this job. He'd never find another one like it—anywhere. Besides, this was his home. He had a cushy suite in the employees' quarters, three square meals a day, and better than average pay. His whole life revolved around Atomtech and he wasn't leaving—no matter what. He looked at Devin who was staring at the radar screen as though its rhythmic beeping had hypnotized him. Wincing from a sharp pain, Leonard wondered what was going on inside the madman's mind.

Chapter Thirty-Eight
ROCKSLIDE

On the monitor, Leonard spotted the Jeep Wagoneer speeding toward Hollister.

"There you are." A self-gratified smile formed on his lips as he locked the SSS with a click of his mouse button. As he watched the Jeep racing down the highway, he rubbed the top of his head. A plan came to him. RJ's Rock and Gravel Company, just outside Hollister, had bid on a construction contract coming up for Atomtech—a six million dollar deal. Leonard licked his lips. Maybe Pete could help. Switching to the mainframe computer, he brought up the phone book. After finding the number, he clicked the mouse to dial it.

"RJ's. Pete here," came the answer.

"It's Leonard. I need your help with something important." He explained his plan, emphasizing that cooperation would assure them the big contract they sought.

Pete was all ears.

*   *   *

The gravel road wound through the forest and came to a paved highway. Ray turned left and headed toward Hollister, heavy on the throttle again. The Cobra's demise had been a great relief. Now, the unknown awaiting them up ahead had him worried. He was sure Devin wouldn't stop until they were dead.

Lo smacked his lips. "Let's find burger joint in Hollister. What you guys say?"

"I'm thirsty," Lisa said with a whimper. "A soda would taste *so* good right now." She wiggled in her seat and showed Janis her lips.

He gave her a kiss.

Ray felt an urge to punch him again.

"That'll have to hold you for a while," Janis said.

Lisa put on a spoiled-brat frown. "It's gonna seem a lot longer now that you guys got me thinking about my stomach. Thanks a lot." She winked at Janis.

Ahead, a flagman stood on the centerline. Behind him, rocks and boulders blocked the highway. Ray hit the brakes. "That's all we need—a rockslide."

The flagman waved his red flag. "Just pull behind the dump trailer over there. We'll have this thing cleared up in a few minutes." He pointed to a tractor-trailer rig parked near a pile of rocks. As a huge front-end loader with a bucketful of rocks roared toward the truck, Ray parked the Jeep as he was instructed.

Rumbling, the bucket dropped its load into the dump trailer. Dust swirled. Backing up, the big machine beeped loudly and bounced along on giant knobby tires. Hydraulics whined as the bucket came down and the loader turned toward the rocks for another load.

Looking up the hill, Ray couldn't tell where all those rocks had come from. There was no sign of the rockslide's path, no broken trees, no rubble—just weeded ground and stands of young pine.

Just then, another big rig pulled up behind his Jeep. Brakes set with a shrill rush of air. A lump formed in his stomach, spurred by a feeling of being suddenly boxed in.

Again, the huge loader rolled toward the truck, its bucket of rocks raised high. But instead of maneuvering over the dump trailer, it suddenly changed direction and was now looming over the Jeep. "Everybody duck!"

The bucket came down on the roof like a crusher. Glass exploded. Metal crunched. Lisa screamed. Suddenly, they were trapped, entombed on the seats by the collapsed roof.

"Lo! Y-you okay?" Terror choked Ray's words.

"It's a little cramped in here."

Ray wriggled around and looked out through an inch gap left between the roof and door. Backing up, the huge loader banged its bucket on the ground. The diesel engine roared like an angry monster, and as black smoke spewed from the exhaust stack, the loader lunged at the Jeep.

"Hang on!"

The loader rammed the Jeep, picked it up in the bucket, and raised it high in the air. Lisa screamed again. Another terror engulfed Ray. "Lisa! Hang on!" *God, please don't let anything happen to her.*

Terry Wright

Like an amusement park ride gone bad, the Jeep tilted, teetered, then plummeted, rolling upside down and impacting the bottom of the dump trailer with a gut-wrenching jolt. Fragmented glass pelted him. Something in his neck made a crunching sound. But he was less concerned about himself and more for his daughter. "Lisa! Are you all right? Are you hurt?" She didn't answer. "Lisa!" Oh, damn!

He twisted around and looked back between the bucket seats. Janis had already released his safety belt, and crawling on the ceiling now, was brushing aside broken glass. Lisa was with him. They were making a path toward the tailgate. Suddenly, gasoline vapors reached Ray's nostrils, irritated his eyes. One spark—that was all it would take.

"Let's go!" Ray said to Lo.

"Hold on," Janis said. "Let me get this seatback unlatched." He tugged on the release lever and the seat swung forward. Bracing it with a suitcase, he pushed aside the other luggage and crawled to the tailgate. After pulling the latch, he kicked it open. Wincing, he grabbed his bandaged hand.

"Must hurt," Ray said.

"Like hell."

Suddenly, a diesel engine roared, lurching everything into motion. The Jeep teetered, slid on its roof, scraped across jagged rocks, and slammed into the trailer's steel wall with a bang.

Lisa yelped.

Cringing, Ray braced for an explosion and fire.

Nothing happened.

As the tractor-trailer rig accelerated down the highway, the Jeep vibrated and creaked, sending shivers rippling down Ray's spine. Another wave of fear rushed over him. If the wrecked Jeep shifted one more time, the back of the dump trailer would block their only exit. They'd be doomed. "Go!"

Janis propped the tailgate open with his foot. "One at a time! Hurry!"

"How are we going to get out of this trailer?" Lisa asked, scurrying under the tailgate.

"We'll have to convince the driver to stop," Janis said.

"How?" Ray asked, crawling out after his daughter. "Making up a plan as you go?"

"Any other way?"

"You'd better hurry." Ray grabbed the tailgate and held it up for him. "This thing could blow any minute."

Janis helped Lo get out and then followed him.

It was tricky walking on rocks in a moving truck. Clumsily, Ray followed Janis to the front of the dump trailer, and with clasped hands, gave him a foothold and boosted him up to the rim. Janis peered over the edge, and then Ray lowered him back down. "What did you see?"

"The driver—through the back window. He's alone and no one's following behind us, at least not yet. They're probably busy cleaning up that mess they made on the road back there. We've got to hit this guy fast and hard."

"How?" Lo asked.

Janis rubbed his chin.

"Unhook the air hoses to the trailer," Lisa said. "Without air, the spring-loaded brakes will automatically engage."

"What do you know about it?" Ray asked harshly.

Lo said, "Lisa knows..."

"This rig will come to a screeching halt, Dad. Trust me." She glared at her father.

"How do you...?"

"It's worth a try," Janis said, bracing himself against the rocking trailer. "I'll climb down to the tractor and unhook an air hose." He looked at the Jeep. "But watch out for that thing. It may come flying up here."

"What we do when truck stop?" Lo asked.

"We'll make a run for it," Ray answered.

Janis said, "We wouldn't get far."

Lo put a hand on Janis' shoulder. "Don't look gift horse in mouth."

"Lo's right," Janis said, smiling as if he'd read Lo's mind. "It's a long walk to Simi Valley. We need this truck...so..." He paused, looked around. "When the driver gets out to see why his trailer brakes locked up, let's hit him with some of his own rocks." Janis crouched down, picked up a big one, and handed it to Ray. "Bomb him from up there." He pointed to the trailer's rim.

Ray knew he couldn't hit the broad side of a bus but thought Janis' idea might be their best shot. "Got it!" he said and grabbed a couple more rocks.

Janis turned to Lisa. "Watch out for that Jeep."

She looked back at the wreck, wide-eyed.

Ray helped Janis over the rim. "Here goes nothing."

Lo said to Lisa, "Tiger no like it when you grab him by tail."

Chapter Thirty-Nine
ROSES

Rushing air whistled. Brakes locked with a deafening bang. Ray braced himself as tires screeched and smoke billowed from both sides of the dump trailer. The air suddenly smelled of burnt rubber. As the rig jerked to a halt, the Jeep lunged forward, spun sideways and jammed between the trailer's steel walls. Quickly, Lisa helped Ray and Lo climb up to the rim.

On rusty hinges, the cab door squealed open and the driver jumped out. Ray shuddered at the sight of the trucker's big hairy arms, tattooed with skulls and snakes, and how dangerous he looked in that sleeveless shirt and baggy blue jeans. The top of his head reflected sunshine.

Ray took aim and threw the first rock, which merely hit the trucker's shoulder. He reeled around. But the look of confusion on his face melted into a smile when he spotted Janis standing on the tractor, holding a whistling air hose. Before Ray could throw another rock, the trucker grabbed Janis and threw him to the pavement.

"You dumb shit!" the trucker bellowed and stomped on Janis' right leg like a WWF wrestler.

Janis hollered and rolled on the asphalt.

Ray hesitated to throw another rock for fear he'd hit Janis.

Lo reached down for Lisa's hand and pulled her up to the rim. "Janis need help with little guy down there."

She straddled the edge.

Ray gasped. "Where do you think you're going?"

"Just watch." She jumped to the tractor and onto the ground. The trucker was about to land another blow on Janis.

Putting her hands on her hips, she wooed, "Hey—big boy. Wanna try a piece of this?"

The trucker spun around, a look of surprise on his face. His eyes scoped the little blonde up and down. He grinned. "Don't mind if I do." He started unzipping his pants. Janis jumped on his back but the trucker threw him off like a bothersome child. Walking bull-legged toward Lisa, he said, "Come to Daddy, little girl. I'll..."

She didn't let him finish. A spinning left kick to his throat sent the trucker to his knees, gasping for air like a fish out of water. As he held his injured larynx she said, "You talk too much, fat boy." With a swift kick to his temple, she delivered the knockout blow. He fell over and lay motionless on the pavement.

Ray swallowed hard and stared at Lisa, speechless. His little girl was definitely capable of taking care of herself. Why hadn't he known that?

"Let's get out of here," Lisa said disgustedly, brushing her hands together. She climbed into the cab and grabbed the big steering wheel while Janis reattached the air hose, recharging the brakes with a whoosh. He climbed in after Lo and Ray. Lisa slammed the transmission into gear and dropped the clutch. The truck lunged forward.

Lo smiled. "Look like we found new wheels for trip. Now get burger and fries."

Lisa shifted gears. The turbo diesel whined to her commands.

Ray rubbed his chin. "Lisa—I didn't know you could drive one of these things."

She ignored him.

"And how did you learn to fight like that?"

With an icy glare she said, "Isn't it fun to get to know some-one?"

A wave of guilt rushed over Ray. She was right. He'd spent so much time trying to protect her that he'd never taken the time to get to know her. Lo's comment about smelling roses came to mind. Though he'd never given that old cliché any thought before, he now realized that only a fool would go through life without taking time to enjoy the gifts he'd been given. And right now, he was feeling damn foolish. What else would he learn about her? In awe, he watched his daughter maneuver the big rig down the highway.

Hollister was just ahead.

Chapter Forty

HOLLISTER

The pirated tractor-trailer rig idled in a Burger Haven parking lot. Janis helped Ray pull bags and suitcases from the wrecked Jeep and pass them down to Lo, who stashed them in a storage compartment under the semi's cab. Lisa ran in for burgers and drinks.

Janis broke the rhythm of their assembly-line-like chore. "No telling when they'll show up looking for this truck. We'll have to ditch the trailer and go on in the tractor." He paused. "Too bad about your Jeep, Ray."

"Dr. Curtis will buy me a new one."

"*Mister* Curtis," Janis corrected him.

"Whatever!" Ray said with a huff. "Truth is, if the SSS is still locked on us, Leonard will see this switch anyway. We could still end up dead."

Janis detected frustration in Ray's voice. Had Atomtech's high technology suddenly become a formidable foe? It had certainly turned Ray's pride into fear. Janis could see it in his eyes. "We aren't dead yet."

Ray just shook his head and tossed another suitcase.

Pulling the bloodstained towel off his hand, Janis winced and threw it down with the Jeep. The nasty bandage had become more of a nuisance than anything medically useful. He caught a bag from Ray and tossed it down to Lo.

The afternoon sun ducked behind a drifting cloud and offered a little relief from the heat. Janis wiped his brow with the back of his hand. What he wouldn't give for the cool mountains of Colorado right now. Was this how Dorothy felt when she was ripped away from her home and dropped into a land of beauty and danger? Looking at his feet, he almost expected to see the ruby slippers that would send him back to Boulder. Was Devin the wicked witch of the West? Janis shuddered. *There's no place like home.* He tossed the last suitcase down to Lo.

After Lisa returned with three bags of food, she unhooked the air hoses and electrical cord from the dump trailer and pulled the fifth-wheel release rod. Without bothering to drop the landing gear wheels, she joined the others who were already in the cab. "Let's go!"

She popped the clutch. The truck lurched forward, dropping the trailer to the ground with a shattering bang. Startled birds took flight. The engine hammered as they headed for the junction just up ahead. From a bag on Lo's lap, Janis grabbed a burger. He felt as though he could eat a hundred of them.

A door panel rattled and suspension springs squeaked as Lisa pulled the high-range knob on the gearshift and negotiated the on-ramp. The turbo whined. Slamming another gear, she aimed the semi south on Highway 101.

Chapter Forty-One
KING CITY NIGHTMARE

Janis looked at his watch. Two hours had passed as the semi raced toward Simi Valley. The sun hung low, about to be extinguished behind a thick bank of clouds hugging the ocean's horizon. Lisa scanned radio channels for another rock and roll station. Janis preferred country music but let Lisa have her way. He enjoyed watching her bebop in the seat.

The radio squelched through stations.

"And the Lord said unto Jesus..."

Lisa pushed the seek button.

"The big black brother told the little mother..."

Squelch.

"...on I-5 just south of Volta."

Janis put his hand on Lisa's. "Wait." The cut in his palm began to sting.

"Colonel Fallon, the Air Force Security Police Commander, is investigating the possibility that the pilot, Lieutenant Burt Evans of Edwards Air Force Base, was disgruntled over a promotion he hadn't received. Again, the California Highway Patrol suffered heavy losses in the attack."

Janis balled a fist. "Bullshit. They don't have a clue. Devin did it—you idiots."

"They'll figure it out, cowboy," Lisa said. "Give them some time." She pushed the seek button, again.

"For your love, for your love..."

Janis leaned back on the raggedy green seat, cramped with the four of them crammed together in the cab. The diesel droned under the hood, vibrating the floor and making his feet tingle. He curled his toes inside his shoes. How had he gotten himself into this mess?

The traffic into King City moved along at seventy miles an hour and the semi lumbered along with the flow. Janis caught Lisa trying to cover a sleepy yawn. Was the big truck wearing her down? Any wonder. Should he insist she rest? He decided to let her voice her concerns if she felt the need.

Lo kept his eyes on the highway traffic and the flow on the

145

frontage road where the speed limit was much slower. The truck always overtook vehicles bound in the same direction. Except one. For several miles, a four-door sedan had been keeping pace with the highway traffic, always behind his right shoulder whenever he looked back. Once, the traffic on the side-road forced the sedan to run recklessly on the shoulder in an attempt to keep up. At first, he dismissed it, maybe a drunk driver or some clown in a hurry to get home. But given the events of the day, he finally succumbed to his fears and gave Ray a nudge with his elbow. "Check out that car."

The sedan passed a slower car and almost hit another head-on.

Ray tapped Janis on the shoulder. "I don't like the looks of this guy."

Janis eyed the sedan. "What's it say on the fender?" he asked, squinting. "I can't read it from here...Lisa—slow down to 55."

Releasing the throttle, Lisa hit the Jake Brake and the truck slowed noisily. The sedan didn't react to the change in speed and was quickly within reading range.

"Sheriff," Lo said.

The number 2885 had been painted on the roof. Tinted windows hid the interior, so Lo couldn't tell if anyone inside was looking at them or not. As the sheriff continued on ahead without incident, Lo decided his worries were unfounded. "False alarm."

"Steady as you were, Lisa," Janis said with a sigh.

The turbo whined in acceleration.

A highway sign boasted King City, two miles ahead with gas, food, phone, and lodging at all exits. Janis noticed the tank gauges hanging on a quarter each. "Let's find a truck stop. We'll fuel up and get some dinner."

"I need pit stop, too," Lo said eagerly.

"Of course," Janis replied.

The flow of vehicles began to congest the freeway as day turned to dusk. Traffic slowed to 50, then to 40. Lisa started downshifting and working the Jake Brake.

Janis looked behind them, worried that some fool might plow into their decelerating semi. For an instant, he thought he glimpsed the sheriff's sedan as it changed lanes and disappeared behind a delivery truck. When it didn't show itself again, he figured he'd been mistaken and returned his attention to the traffic in front.

Suddenly, a speeding blue van careened down an on-ramp, veered wildly into traffic and smashed into a pickup truck, sending it slamming into several other cars. They all skidded and crashed into a pile. Flying metal, glass, and blue tire smoke filled the air. A tractor-trailer rig locked its brakes. The trailer jack-knifed across an inside lane, crushing a compact car, which burst into flames and plowed into the growing pile of twisted vehicles. Now, hungry flames fed voraciously on spilling fuel and grew into a brilliant wall of fire. Black smoke swirled skyward. Two Fords spun into the inferno, the fire billowing like a belching monster.

"Oh, shit!" Janis braced himself against the dash. "Lisa!"

She cranked the steering wheel right and nailed the throttle down. Tandem tires squawked in protest but the wailing turbo-powered diesel battered them into submission. With vehicles sliding and spinning everywhere, the semi reigned to Lisa's command, bounced off the highway, plowed through a weed-belt, and careened around the pile of death.

"Holy shit!" Janis yelled as he turned to look at the carnage behind them. Several other vehicles had followed their escape route, headlights bouncing, but a second later, a city bus bashed its way through the flaming pile and rolled end over end across the weed-belt. A huge wall of yellow flames licked skyward, illuminating the California twilight. The highway was completely blocked.

"T-that was meant for us!" Ray shouted, his voice charged with hysteria. "You—you saw the blue van. Where did it go?"

"It rolled over, skidded on side," Lo said.

"A-a kamikaze van?"

"I don't think on purpose—just ended up that way. Devin may be crazy and his henchmen run close second. But they're not that crazy. Odds of us get in pileup too great against."

"What do you think he was doing?"

"Devin wanted to stop us with wreck, block road. Attack come from behind."

Janis looked back at the distant fire's glow. Only three pairs of headlights dotted the highway behind them. Nothing seemed unusual. "Let's just get some fuel and get the hell out of here."

She turned off the highway at an exit advertising free showers at Don's Truck Plaza. One car followed them but pulled into a

24-hour convenience store across the street. Lisa stopped in front of a diesel fuel pump where a young man wearing dirty coveralls and grease on his face greeted them.

"Fill both tanks," she said.

Everyone headed for the rest rooms.

At a counter inside where customers paid for fuel, Janis looked out the big front window and noticed the suspicious car was still parked across the street, headlights on and facing the truck plaza.

Ray walked up to Janis. "Is he waiting for us?"

Janis wondered about that as he noticed Lisa and Lo walking across the brightly lit parking lot toward the semi. But before he could answer, the ominous car suddenly accelerated across the road. Dust swirled in the air as it careened into the truck plaza and headed straight for the semi. Janis' guts clenched when he recognized the 2885 car marked *Sheriff.*

"Oh, shit!" He ran outside as the sedan screeched to a stop beside the semi. Lisa and Lo stood in the middle of the lot, their eyes wide with fear. Janis ran to Lisa and tucked her under his arm. Lo and Ray stood next to them. What were they going to do? The sheriff had blocked their way to the truck. If only...

Suddenly, three more sheriffs' cars squealed around a corner, surrounding them. Car doors flew open and a dozen guns came out. How many years would they get for grand theft auto?

Ray, Lisa, and Lo huddled around Janis as he stared through swirling dust at the tinted windows of the sheriff's sedan. The driver's door clicked and slowly opened. Janis swallowed. One shiny black boot appeared, then another. The sheriff stepped out, a big man, with a big belly, dressed in a sharply pressed blue uniform and sporting a brown Smokey-The-Bear hat. He puffed on a fat cigar as he approached his captives.

"Well, well. What do we have here?" His gruff voice chilled the air. Pacing, he eyed his prisoners through military-style sunglasses.

"Should we just shoot 'em here?" he asked his comrades. No one answered. The sheriff, puffing on his rank cigar, circled around his huddled captives, the heels of his boots clicking on the concrete.

A crowd gathered, whispering.

The big sheriff walked up to Ray, face to face, and blew smoke in his eyes.

Without flinching, Ray just glared at him.

"You some kind of spies?" the Sheriff asked loudly. "We don't like spies around here."

Ray said nothing, his eyes locked on the lawman.

Janis gritted his teeth. What's with the spy crap? Maybe the sheriff knew all about them—and Devin. And why wasn't he concerned about the hijacked truck? Maybe he was just being an asshole cop. One way to find out. Janis cleared his throat. "Do spies drive semis around here?"

The sheriff jerked his attention to Janis. "I ask the questions around here!" he barked, pulling his service revolver from its holster. He poked the barrel against Janis' temple and snarled into his face. "You got that?"

Janis stiffened. He could feel the heat of the sheriff's cigar and smell tobacco on his breath. But Janis wasn't backing down. Lisa gripped his arm as if to restrain him from further conflict. But all his contempt was focused on the menacing lawman's face.

"Go ahead—shoot me! That's what Devin wants—some dumb cop to do his dirty work."

The sheriff twinged at the mention of Devin's name.

"Shoot me, damn it!"

Pressing the muzzle against Janis' head, the sheriff cast a quick glance toward his comrades and the crowd. "Damn!" he grumbled.

Janis stared at him. There must have been too many witnesses to the murder he was about to commit.

The sheriff looked down at Lisa.

She cast up her eyes to the officer. "Please don't."

He looked again at Janis, shoved him away, and dropped the revolver to his side. "I don't know what it is you people are up to, but I aim to find out." He turned to his deputies. "Cuff 'em," he ordered and walked toward his car.

The California evening air echoed with the clicking of cocking firearms. "Hands behind your head!" the sergeant shouted in a voice filled with anger. "Now!"

Janis looked at Ray. He sneered and raised his hands. Janis turned to Lo who shrugged and put his hands behind his head.

Lisa's hands were over her face, trembling. In defeat, Janis assumed the position.

"On your knees!"

They dropped to their knees and submitted to handcuffs dealt out by several officers. Janis watched a deputy climb into the semi. The brakes released with a whoosh of air and the truck headed out of the plaza, speeding toward town.

"Shit!" Janis said under his breath.

The sheriff got into his sedan and closed the door, again hidden by tinted windows.

Roughly, a deputy pulled Janis to his feet and directed him to a waiting squad car. His wrists ached from the handcuffs. He saw Lisa and Lo being put into one car, and Ray, in another.

"Watch your head," the officer said as he forced Janis to duck into the back seat.

The door slammed and he fidgeted, trying to get comfortable sitting with his hands cuffed behind him, if that were possible. Two deputies got in front, shut their doors, and began talking quietly. A thick wire screen stretched across the car, caging him in the back seat like some kind of animal. The driver accelerated out of the truck plaza in the same direction the semi had gone. Looking out the back window, he saw the other patrol cars following behind.

"Where are you taking us?" he asked, interrupting his captors' conversation.

"The station."

"Are we under arrest?"

"We're just following orders. Sheriff Doogan will answer your questions later."

"Sheriff Doogan?"

"Shut up and enjoy the scenery."

Janis looked around the speeding patrol car. City lights whizzed by and a dark sky showed just a hint of where the sun had disappeared behind a cloudy horizon. Again, he looked back at the procession of squad cars and shivered. He thought Lisa must be terrified—as well as Ray and Lo, too. But there was nothing they could do to save themselves now. He felt a bleak hopelessness envelop him as the caravan of cars turned into a garage marked "County Sheriffs Only."

The line of patrol cars stopped in front of a set of double steel doors. Several deputies emerged, rushed to the squad cars, and plucked out their new prisoners. Janis clenched his jaw as a deputy yanked him from the car. Quickly, he noticed an oil-stained concrete floor, gray cinderblock walls, florescent ceiling lights, and video cameras mounted high in the corners. The place smelled like gasoline. As the garage door rattled down, he heard Ray yelling, "Keep your filthy hands off the girl!"

Seems Lisa had attracted the deputies' attention. They acted like they'd never seen a woman before. Three grinning lawmen volunteered to restrain her. Respectful of the law, Lisa didn't resist, but grimaced when a big fat deputy with mustard on his mouth said, "I get to frisk her."

"Don't touch her!" Ray struggled to break free of a deputy. Another rushed up. "Got a real fighter there, huh?"

The fat man approached Lisa with groping hands. When his blubberous body shielded her from view, Lisa cried out. "Daddy!"

Ray kicked the deputy in the shin and yelled, "You bastards. Leave her alone!"

The deputy hit Ray with a nightstick, right upside the head. Ray staggered. "Goddamn it!"

Janis watched in horror as the crazed deputies went about their gruesome work. Glancing up at a video camera, he wondered if the damn thing even worked. Or maybe the deputies didn't care if this atrocity was being recorded or not.

Lisa's screams echoed down the corridor and landed on helpless ears. The hoggish man finally backed away. Her blouse was hanging open, her black bra crooked. Janis wanted to kill the fat bastard, but couldn't get away from the deputies restraining him.

"Knock it off or you'll get a bashing like your buddy," one of them said.

The leader of the mob stepped out of his car. Janis spit. "Sheriff Doogan! Can't you control your men?"

The fat deputy flashed a sick smile at Janis and licked his tongue across his lips in defiance, smearing the mustard. Janis tried to lunge at him but the deputies held him back.

Sheriff Doogan stepped up to the belligerent fat man, grabbed his flabby throat with one hand, and slammed him into a wall. "Enough fore-play, you pig." Doogan kneed him in the groin and dropped him to the ground.

151

Holding his crotch, the fat man writhed on the floor, wailing in agony.

As if satisfied, Doogan turned to his deputies. "The rest of you idiots better pack up your hormones and get these prisoners into lock-up—RIGHT NOW!"

Janis felt relieved.

The sheriff turned to a tall, stocky deputy with a scar on his face. "Lawson! You're the Sergeant in Command around here. Start acting like one."

Lawson sneered at his boss and mumbled something under his breath. He herded the captives, single file, through the double steel doors and into lockup.

Before the doors swung closed, Janis looked back at the sheriff who was now leaning against the front fender of his sedan, a short stub of cigar smoldering between his teeth. The big sheriff held their future in his hands. They were at his mercy. A burning fear seared through Janis' veins as the doors slammed shut with a bang.

At a cell door, deputies removed their handcuffs and shoved them inside. Someone tossed Ray an ice pack for the lump on his head. The heavily barred door squeaked as it swung, shutting with a clang that echoed ominously down the corridor.

Sergeant Lawson twisted the key. "End of the line for you guys."

Janis shuddered and sat on a steel bench bolted to the wall. Lisa cuddled up next to him. He wondered who was to blame for this predicament they were in. Was it Ray? He'd followed his lust for fame into this jail cell. Janis looked at Lisa. Her hate for her father had gotten her into this mess. And what about Lo? Revenge was his demise. Then Janis looked inward. Money. Curtis had bought him with a million-dollar deal. None of them could hide from the truth. Their own human frailties had put them in harm's way. Now, cast into this dingy cell, they awaited their punishment for persisting in the quest for self-gratification, the most dangerous quest of all.

Chapter Forty-Two
THE INTERROGATION

Jingling keys attracted Janis' attention to the cell door. "Mackey," a deputy called out, "Doogan wants to see you." He led Janis, handcuffed again, down the hallway. Sergeant Lawson got up from his desk and followed them without saying a word.

Fighting off a nervous quiver in his stomach, Janis wondered what Doogan wanted. Was there anything Janis could say that would set them free?

A shove from behind sent him stumbling into an office where the sheriff sat at his desk, a cigar clenched in his teeth. His hat hung from an antler rack on the wall above his head. The room was dimly lit except for a lamp shining above a metal folding chair set in the middle of the floor. The deputy pushed Janis into the chair.

Leaning against the doorframe, Lawson folded his arms over his chest, grinning.

Janis sat facing the man who had imprisoned him. The sheriff's cold eyes made him shiver. The bright light made him sweat. His glasses started sliding down his nose.

Doogan pointed a hairy-knuckled finger at Lawson. "Get back to your station."

Lawson said nothing, just left the room and closed the door.

The deputy switched on a recorder.

Doogan seemed puzzled, looked Janis up and down and leaned forward. "Devin tells me you guys are enemy spies. What do you have to say about that?"

Janis glared at the officer. "Are we under arrest?"

The sheriff didn't answer.

"What are the charges against us?"

Again, Sheriff Doogan remained silent.

"I want to make a phone call—right now," Janis demanded.

"Dr. Mackey," the deputy said. "I suggest you cooperate with this investigation. We can hold you for seventy-two hours. Make it easy, make it hard, it's your choice."

Janis looked at the deputy and then the recorder. Satisfied it was running, he looked at Sheriff Doogan. "Devin is a liar. He's been trying to kill us since we met in San Francisco two days ago."

"Why?"

"He doesn't want us working for Dr. Curtis."

Sheriff Doogan squinted, closed one eye.

Janis wondered how he could explain their problem any better. He had to find a way to make him understand. But how...

Doogan blew cigar smoke. "You're a math professor, right?"

"So?"

"And Crawford is an atomic physicist?"

"The best."

"How do I know you're not using that against our country?"

"It's Devin and Curtis you need to worry about."

Eyebrows raised, Doogan mouthed his stogie.

Janis leaned forward, wishing he wasn't handcuffed. "Ray and I made a deal with Curtis to do an experiment involving nuclear time and space—the 13th Power to be exact." He elaborated as if the sheriff would comprehend the science involved. "Devin doesn't want us to do the experiment, for whatever reason. We are not spies."

With the cigar clamped between his fingers, the sheriff motioned toward the recorder. The deputy turned it off. Frowning, Doogan said, "Is the 13th Power worth dying for?"

Hot adrenaline lit fires in Janis' bloodstream. Dying? "You're going to murder us?"

"That's right."

The deputy grinned. "How we gonna kill 'em, boss?"

"Later!" the sheriff snapped. "Again, Dr. Mackey—is the 13th Power worth dying for?"

Janis' fear turned to anger. "No!" he shouted. "But those people in your jail cell are. I gave my word to Ray and I would die to keep it. I would die for my friend, Lo Chin, too. But most of all, I would not only die for Lisa, I would *kill* for Lisa."

The sheriff's eyebrows lifted. "Oh? Do you think they'd do the same for you?"

"I think the question here is whether *you* would die for Devin."

Looking at his deputy, Doogan snarled. "Get him out of here before I put a bullet in him myself."

The deputy pulled Janis to his feet and pushed him toward the door.

"Devin will have you burning in hell!" Janis yelled as he was shoved into the hallway. "In hell, I tell you."

*   *   *

Sergeant Lawson quickstepped down the hall. He was sure they didn't know he'd been listening through the door. The conversation went as he had hoped. He ducked into the next office. The deputy and Janis passed by without seeing him. He rushed back to Doogan's office. The door was closed. As he reached for the doorknob, he heard Doogan's voice booming.

"Killing them won't solve anything, Devin!"

Lawson stopped to listen.

"I don't care about the money. Murder was never an option."

A moment of silence.

"You're out of your mind!"

Doogan slammed down the phone and kicked over the folding chair.

Lawson didn't like the way that conversation sounded. Retreating down the hall, he slipped back into the office and dialed Devin in Nevada.

*   *   *

The deputy keyed the handcuffs and pushed Janis back into the cell. His insides burning with anger, Janis noticed a tray of food on the table—mashed potatoes, roast beef, and something that looked like baby food. A small carton of milk sat next to it. Empty trays told him the others had eaten.

"Our last supper?" he said and sat down. He felt defeated, out of hope.

Ray looked at him, concerned. "What was that all about?"

"Nothing," Janis said for lack of a better answer. "How's the lump on your skull?"

Ray lifted the ice pack and rubbed the side of his head. "Still there."

"The bastards will get theirs some day." Janis looked at Lisa. She was looking at her father—but not with her usual hateful glare. Did he see a hint of pity in her eyes? Was she feeling sorry for him? Or was she impressed with his futile attempt to protect her from the crazed lawmen? Was her hate beginning to fade?

He looked at Lo who was sitting on a cot with his legs crossed and staring straight forward.

"Lo. You okay?"

Lo didn't respond. Janis shrugged and turned his attention to the meal in front of him. It tasted horrible. When he finished, he cuddled into Lisa, closed his eyes, and drifted into an uneasy sleep.

Lisa stroked his hair and whispered in his ear. "Good night, cowboy." She knew he didn't hear her but it made her feel better, just the same.

Chapter Forty-Three

THE ASSASSIN

Janis awoke to a dreadful clanking—a nightstick striking the bars. Through sleep-laden eyes he saw Lo and Ray standing by the cell door, which hung wide open. A second deputy stood behind them, his hand on his revolver. The sight triggered foggy memories of Doogan, this jail, and murders yet committed. Though he couldn't recall what he'd been dreaming, he knew it had to have been better than the nightmare into which he just awoke.

Lisa moaned. "Huh?"

"What time is it?"

"3:30," Ray said without checking his watch. "Looks like Doogan has decided what to do with us."

Janis and Lisa got in line.

The lead deputy said, "Let's go."

"What? No handcuffs?"

"Shut up!" the trailing deputy said.

The line of the doomed shuffled out of the cell. Halfway down the hall, Janis caught a glimpse of Sergeant Lawson lurking around a corner. What was he doing? The procession turned down an intersecting hallway and passed through double steel doors into the parking garage where Sheriff Doogan stood by his squad car, engine running, headlights on.

"Looks like we're going for a ride," Janis said as sarcastically as he could.

"Shut up!" barked the deputy behind him.

The column of prisoners approached the sheriff and stopped. The lead deputy spoke with him, but too softly for Janis to hear their words. As he strained to listen, he heard a sound behind him, a kind of scraping that drew his eyes toward the double doors, which were now teetering on their hinges. He spotted Lawson slipping behind a concrete pillar. Why was he sneaking around?

Doogan stepped aside. The deputy opened a rear door of the squad car. He motioned to Lo and Lisa. "You two—get in."

With wide eyes, they did as they were told.

Looking into the car, Janis noticed it had no wire partition between the seats. And why weren't they being handcuffed? What was Doogan doing? Did he really think he was going to get away with this?

The deputy shut the back door and opened the front passenger door. He motioned to Ray.

Ray got in and the deputy shut the door. What? That left only Janis and the driver's seat.

With a quick wave of his hand, the sheriff signaled the deputies to leave. They disappeared through the double doors. Doogan walked up to Janis. "Your belongings are in the trunk." With a firm grip, he shook Janis' hand, and then pointed to his squad car. "She's all yours."

Wide-eyed, Janis said, "Why?"

"Good luck. You've got a long way to go." A smile lit Doogan's face, a smile that surprised Janis, warm and sincere. He slid in behind the wheel and shut the door. *We're free.* He couldn't believe it.

Doogan backed away from the car. "Drive safely... "

The blast of a firearm echoed through the garage. Janis whipped around. Out the rear window, he saw Lawson standing by a pillar, his gun held out, straight-armed. He yelled, "Double-cross Devin and die!"

Two more shots rang out.

Lisa screamed and ducked down on the seat, clutching Lo. Janis looked at Sheriff Doogan, who lurched backwards from two rounds tearing into his chest. Blood spewed from his shirt, staining it red in an instant. The big man grimaced and grabbed for his gun.

"You think you're so tough!" Lawson yelled. "Take this!" He fired again.

The slug tore mercilessly into Doogan's shooting arm, ripping away any chance he may have had to defend himself. Hunched over and holding his shattered arm, he glared at his killer. "Now Devin has your soul." Another round ripped into Doogan's throat, blood gushing to the concrete floor. His eyes rolled back and he collapsed.

A bullet shot into the car. Janis' stomach knotted. *He's gonna kill us all!* "SHIT!" Panic raced through his mind as he grabbed the gearshift and slammed the transmission into drive. He stomped the accelerator to the floor. Tires squealed. Several more shots rang out. Bullets pummeled the car. Janis ducked. Engine roaring, he steered toward the exit and, as if propelled by a force greater than the 13th Power, crashed the speeding car into the garage door. Aluminum panels exploded. Lisa screamed. The car careened out of the garage and into the early morning darkness.

Chapter Forty-Four
THE RESCUERS

Simi Valley lay in a sleepy darkness. Saturday night—the town had all but closed down. Only light traffic trickled through city streets, most of the residents having settled in for the night. At a local park, two teams slugged out a baseball game under bright lights. Roaring turboprop engines suddenly overpowered a group of cheering fans. At Solartech Field, Red stood in the glow of floodlights as the C-130 Hercules warmed up for takeoff. His small paramilitary army of professional soldiers boarded the big transport. A Jeep slid to a stop at the cargo ramp. Red saluted Alex.

"Get her aboard." The loadmaster waved him in.

As the Jeep rolled into the aircraft's belly, Red sprinted up after it. Buckled into webbed seating, his men secured their weapons in sling-holsters. He knew it had been a long day for his men, forming assault squads and mapping out individual phases of a difficult mission. Alex had supplied high-tech equipment that would enable them to sneak-up on Devin. The morale of his men was high. They talked and joked freely while awaiting takeoff.

Red made his way to the flight deck as the loadmaster pushed the ramp control lever up. Hydraulics whined and the ramp closed with a bang, sealing the soldiers inside a crimson-lit cargo hold.

"Ready when you are," Red informed the Captain with a sharp salute.

Seeing the green light glowing on his console, Captain Baine taxied his huge transport to the runway threshold.

"Flaps 30," announced the copilot, sliding the control lever. "Go for takeoff."

Captain Baine pushed the brake pedals down and shoved the throttle handles forward. Four huge turboprop engines revved to a thunderous roar, shaking the aircraft violently. At maximum power, he released the brakes. His aircraft began its deafening rumble down the runway. The airspeed indicator came alive.

Suddenly, a blinding light appeared directly in front of him, a hundred feet off the ground and heading straight for them.

Squinting, he yelled, "Abort!" and yanked the throttle handles back, shutting down the massive engines. But they were slow to respond. He jammed on the brakes as the blinding light came closer and closer—lower and lower. Tires squawked and smoke billowed from the brake casings.

"Brace yourselves!" He careened the transport off the right side of the runway. The soft, grassy beltway helped slow the aircraft and, quickly, he regained complete control. Looking out his left window, he saw a blue and white Cessna settle on the runway, its landing lights bright. "Idiot," he sneered. "You trying to get us all killed?" He bounced the transport back onto the runway and swung it around to taxi back to the threshold.

But the Cessna made a U-turn and headed straight for them. "Now what?"

"Is this guy totally nuts?" the copilot said.

Again, the Captain applied the brakes, stopping the big transport in the middle of the runway.

The Cessna taxied up to the C-130, nose-to-nose, its propeller clunking to a stop and a man jumping out. He signaled them to kill their engines with a slicing motion of his hand across his throat.

"Shut 'em down," said Captain Baine.

The turboprop engines whined to a stop and the California night fell silent. Satisfied, the Captain turned to find Red. But he was already out of his seat and scrambling for the jump door. He swung it open and leaped to the runway, his Glock .40 drawn. Captain Baine watched him run around the left wingtip and approach the troublesome pilot.

Steve Raven gulped as a gun-wielding soldier ran toward him. Quickly, he pulled back the flap of his flight jacket, revealing his holstered .45. "Put the shooter away. We're both on the same side."

"What the hell do you think you're doing?" the old soldier yelled, still brandishing his weapon. Another soldier ran up from under the right wing. Steve recognized Alex Gibson from their encounter in the mailroom. Several other armed men followed behind him.

Steve started feeling out-numbered but he held his ground. "I had to stop you bone-heads somehow. I heard your pilot's transmission to flight service, filing a flight plan to Desert Rock. I made the connection with Devin. In case you didn't know, he protects his airspace with ground-to-air missiles. You'll be scrap metal within twenty-five miles." He looked at Alex. "Do you recognize me without my fake beard?"

"In the mailroom," Alex said with a huff. "You have a lot of nerve coming back here."

Steve spit on the runway. "I didn't come back to play patty cake with you guys. I want Devin dead. If you're out to get him, I want in on it." He offered the old soldier a handshake. "Steve Raven, private eye, at your service."

Red holstered his Glock. "James Colburn." They shook hands. "But you can call me Red," he said with the proud tone of a patriot. "And you're the guy who beat Alex's security. You know, he's still a little touchy about your escapade, so let's not rub it in. If..."

A movement on the Cessna caught Red's eye, stopping him in mid sentence. Steve looked toward his airplane. First one shapely leg, then another, appeared under the passenger door. Red's eyes narrowed and he cocked his head as Miss Rivers peered around the door. "Is it safe to come out now?"

Red's eyes lit up. "Please—come join us."

Steve cleared his throat. "This is Susan Rivers. She saved my life."

Susan ducked under the wing and joined the group of men.

"It was nothing, really," she said. "Steve is the hero here." She strolled to his side and took his hand.

One of Red's soldiers had been examining the Cessna. "This aircraft has seen some action," he announced. "Looks like ground fire."

"That's right," Steve said. "Atomtech is under a full security alert."

Chapter Forty-Five
THE RAID

Alex swallowed a lump in his throat. If Steve Raven was right, their plan for a landing on the desert floor ten miles from Atomtech's compound would be a death sentence. The missile threat called for a change in plans. In order to neutralize that threat, the missile guidance and radar systems would have to be jammed within twenty-five miles of Atomtech. He turned to Red, motioned him to the side, and voiced his concerns.

Red touched his cheek. "How are we going to jam his air-space?"

"We'll need the Aircraft Advanced Sensor Eliminator aboard the C-130. With the AASE, Devin's radar won't be able to detect our approach nor will he be able to zero in on the aircraft if we're spotted visually. It's another one of Solartech's new hi-tech toys, on the cutting edge of stealth technology."

"Like the PASE units that our advance team, Jackal One, will wear for the tower assaults, only bigger?"

"You got it. The Personnel Advance Sensor Eliminator is just a smaller version of the AASE." He looked at his watch. "One call and about two hours. That's all we need to get it onboard."

"Do it!" Red spun around and marched to Steve. "You saved our lives with that stunt you just pulled. The mission is on a two-hour hold."

Alex activated his wrist radio. "Station two—get the bus back here."

"Affirmative."

Red saluted Captain Baine and gave him new instructions, concluding with, "and don't file a flight plan next time."

"Clear the runway," Alex ordered.

Steve jumped in the Cessna, started the engine, and taxied to the parking area.

Whining hydraulics echoed as the cargo ramp dropped to the runway. A soldier backed the Jeep out. Alex, Red, and Susan climbed in. They sped after the Cessna to pick up Steve. In cadence, the soldiers marched down the ramp and paraded toward a gate where the bus would arrive. With a whine, the cargo ramp closed again. A tug drove up to the nose wheel, hooked a tether rod, and groaning defiantly, pulled the transport toward the tarmac.

As the Jeep approached Steve's parked Cessna, Alex turned to Red. "I don't know if our people will last two more hours. With Devin having marked them for death, time is crucial."

"They're on their own until we can intervene." He looked at his watch. "We'll still make our predawn strike time. It's the best we can do."

Alex felt as though Red was just trying to ease his concerns. He might have succeeded if he could've hidden the worry in his eyes. Alex was sure that Curtis' new mathematician was crucial to the success of the 13th Power project. He had to be protected—at all costs. *The Ark's* orders.

Steve jumped into the Jeep's back seat with Susan. Speeding through the airfield gate toward C-Wing, Alex radioed the tech lab and ordered the AASE prepped and transported to the C-130. "Meet you on the flight line at 2300 hours sharp."

"Roger."

Arriving at C-Wing, the men climbed out. Alex offered Susan a hand.

She accepted with a smile. "Which way to the ladies room?"

"Just inside to the left." Alex pointed.

Steve watched her walk away, and then said to Alex, "What are you soldier boys up to?"

Alex glanced at Red, looking for a hint of how to handle Steve's question.

Red just shrugged.

Steve persisted. "You got some kind of raid going on here?"

Alex didn't answer.

"I'm right, aren't I? You're going after Devin—aren't you?"

"Tell him," Red said. "Or he'll hound us to death."

Alex hesitated, thinking. "We're going to Atomtech."

"To get Devin?"

"That's right."

"Good," Steve said. "I'm going with you. Any luck, I'll be the one to pull the trigger on the bastard." He slapped his holstered .45.

Alex saw the hate in Steve's eyes. He wasn't going to take this news lightly. "You can't go."

"Like hell!"

"Let *us* get him for you," Red said. "It's safer that way—for all of us."

"No way. I'm going."

"What about the lady?" Red pointed in the direction Susan had gone. "Stay here with her. Let us do the dirty work."

"But..."

"I insist."

"Then I want to see his bloody carcass—dead at my feet."

"No problem," Red said.

Alex patted Steve's shoulder. "Then it's settled." But Alex knew Red had lied to appease Steve. They had made no plans to retrieve *any* bodies.

Red turned his attention to the busload of troops approaching C-Wing. The brakes squeaked and the door swung open. He clunked up the steps. "At ease men. We have two hours to kill. The phones are still off-limits. Cafeteria's open but no smoking. We'll meet back here at 2200 hours. Any questions?"

"What's the delay about?" a young mercenary asked.

"Just an equipment change aboard the aircraft. Our plans are still the same. Remember, this is not a drill. Devin's security force will put up one hell of a fight." He smiled. "Just the way we like it—right men?"

"Yes, Sir!" came a unison response from his troops.

He saluted his men. How many of them wouldn't see tomorrow's sunrise? Should he tell them they were being sacrificed for *The Ark?* No. He thought it best they die without knowing.

Chapter Forty-Six

2300 HOURS

Red joined Steve and Alex in the cafeteria. They had already found the coffee. A few minutes later, Susan came in, her hair freshly brushed. Steve offered her a chair. "Coffee?" he asked.

"With cream and sugar."

As Steve headed toward the coffee maker, she asked Alex, "What's next?"

"You'll be staying here tonight."

"With Steve?"

"If you like." Alex activated his wrist radio. "Housekeeping."

The speaker squawked. "Yes, sir?"

"We have a special guest for this evening. Pick her up at C-Wing in thirty minutes."

"An executive suite?"

"The best one you've got."

"Anything else, sir?"

"Take good care of her. First class all the way."

* * *

At 2300 hours, floodlights illuminated the C-130 as the AASE arrived in the arms of a forklift. A staff car pulled up, its doors flying open. Six technicians in white lab coats jumped out and surrounded the forklift with its beeping cargo. Alex watched the loadmaster wave them aboard.

The ensemble made its way up the ramp and into the cargo bay. Gently, the forklift set the AASE down and backed away. Technicians began hooking up electrical cables to the big box, the looms of wire stretching across the fuselage, into the power converter, and up to the cockpit.

At the flight engineer's seat, a supervisor secured a control terminal to an instrument panel with a Velcro strip. He typed a secret code on the keyboard. A red light started flashing and "Stand By" pulsed on the display screen.

"All set," he reported to Alex and left with his men.

"That's it. Let's go!" Alex ordered.

The pilots strapped themselves in. A few minutes later, as the bus drove through the airfield gate, massive turboprop engines roared back to life. Black smoke drifted in the glowing floodlights. The troops buckled in and slung their weapons while payload specialists secured the Jeep with tie-down straps.

The ramp closed with a bang. Crimson lighting illuminated the cargo bay and cast an eerie glow over the soldiers inside. Noticing they were in a more somber mood than earlier, Alex knew reality was setting in. They would soon be putting their lives on the line for someone else's sake. No one spoke. Droning engines set an ominous tone for the scene.

Red gave Alex a thumbs-up. He climbed into the cockpit and tapped Captain Baine on the shoulder. "Let her rip." Buckling into the engineer's seat, he watched the pilots go to work. A few moments later the roaring engines blew the massive aircraft down the runway and blasted it into a moonless California night sky.

* * *

From the window of their executive suite, Steve stood behind Susan, his hands on her hips, and watched the massive transport roar down the runway and rise into an ink-black sky. Sound waves shuddered the glass but subsided quickly as flashing navigation lights dimmed in the distance. When the plane was out of sight, he slid his hands round Susan and hugged her. In a few hours, his friends would be in grave danger. By dawn, the madman would be dead, his reign of terror over.

A tear ran down Susan's cheek. Steve wouldn't have noticed except for her sniffle. "What is it, babe?"

Susan relished the warmth she found in Steve's embrace. But she was thinking of a happier time at Atomtech—before Ray Crawford left on his relentless pursuit of the 13th Power—when her job had given her a great sense of pride. Sure, Devin had been a strict boss and a shrewd businessman. But he had always been good to her. Most of the time, he'd even been fun to be around. For a while, back then, she thought she might have been in love with him. Sometimes she had found it hard to keep her feelings professional. She remembered his laughter, before it became a sinister sort of cackle.

Now, that same man must die. His life meant someone else's death. His death meant someone else's life. And her life had changed so suddenly. Nothing was the same anymore. She turned to Steve, unafraid to let him see the stream of tears.

"Everything is happening so quickly." She buried her face in his chest. "Hold me until morning," she said. "Hold me until it's over."

Chapter Forty-Seven
THE DECEPTION

As the sheriff's car sped away from King City, Lisa whimpered in Lo's arms. Ray turned around, put his hand on her shoulder in an attempt to comfort her. She'd seen more blood and death in the last two days than most people see in a lifetime. In her eyes, he saw the pain she felt for the victims of this deadly fiasco.

She wiped away a tear. "W-when is all this dying going to end?"

Ray didn't know how to answer that. He only wished she could've been spared this grief. Was it his fault? Had his blind ambition, his obsession with the 13th Power, put his daughter in danger? Not entirely. If only she didn't hate him so much, she'd be home—safe. Nevertheless, his stomach churned with guilt. He'd really made a mess of her life—and his, for that matter. But he had no choice—back then—when Kate had forced him to do things he didn't want, things that he had come to regret.

He braced himself on the armrest as the car roared down Highway 101, the speedometer quivering at 120 miles an hour. The gas gauge indicated someone had filled the tank. "Guess the sheriff wasn't a bad guy after all."

Janis clutched the steering wheel with both hands. Ray was right about Doogan. Though fully capable of carrying out Devin's wishes, he must have drawn the line when it came to murder. Janis admired his courage. By standing up to Devin, the sheriff had paid the ultimate price. Was he even aware of Sergeant Lawson's allegiance to the madman?

Changing lanes to get around a slower car, Janis glanced at Ray. "Doogan told me he was going to kill us."

Ray's eyes went wide.

"But for some reason he changed his mind. During the interrogation, I asked him if he would die for Devin. He must've decided the answer was *no*. How ironic—he died for us instead." A shiver ran up his neck, his eyes again on the highway, its centerline racing along in the headlights like a yellow-striped snake.

Ray sat silent for a moment, as if digesting the sour truth.

"We'd all be dead right now."

"That's right," Janis said and pushed his glasses up.

Again, Ray turned to his daughter in the back seat and reached for her hand. Janis watched her reaction in the rearview mirror. Without moving her cheek from Lo's shoulder she took her father's hand.

It was time to smell the roses.

*   *   *

In the parking garage under the police station, two deputies ran through the double steel doors with their revolvers drawn. They stopped and stared at the lifeless body of their leader, lying in a pool of blood. Lawson holstered his revolver, walked up to his victim and stooped to check for a pulse. Nothing. "Damn it!" He looked at his comrades.

"What happened?" one deputy asked as he dropped to his knees. The other deputy stood next to him, holding his pistol at his side, his eyes wide and mouth hanging open. Several more deputies ran to the scene of the sheriff's demise, reacting the same way. Lawson saw the terror in their eyes.

"What the hell happened?"

"Mackey jumped me," Lawson began. "He took my gun and shot Sheriff Doogan before I could wrestle it away from him. Then he tried to kill me. Hell—look at the skid marks. He tried to run me over. He's a cop killer."

"That doesn't make any sense," a deputy called out from the crowd of lawmen. He was the lead deputy who'd brought the prisoners out to the car. "Sheriff Doogan was releasing them. He was giving them his car. Why would Mackey kill him?"

Lawson paused, thinking. "Mackey grabbed my gun before the sheriff could explain. He thought Doogan was going to kill them."

"That's right," another deputy put in. He had operated the recorder during the interrogation. "I was there when Mackey asked Doogan if he was going to murder them. Doogan said 'that's right'. I thought he was just trying to scare the professor. I played along."

The crowd of officers began talking among themselves as if trying to assess the information they were getting. Then the deputy added, "Mackey also said he would kill for Lisa."

"Let's get 'em!" one officer yelled.

Lawson joined in. "Cop killers. Shoot 'em on sight." The mob of officers raced for their squad cars and peeled out of the garage. Like a horde of avengers, with sirens wailing and overheads flashing, they swarmed toward the highway. Sergeant Lawson transmitted his emergency to the world.

"Attention all cars—attention all precincts. This is an All Points Bulletin. Be on the lookout for a King City sheriff's sedan southbound on 101, headed for Simi Valley. Four suspects, three men and one woman. Use extreme caution. Wanted for the murder of Sheriff Doogan in King City. Repeat. Use extreme caution. Suspects are armed and dangerous."

With that, he ended his transmission. He knew he'd just issued their death sentences. Every trooper, sheriff, policeman, and cop in California would be out to avenge the murder of a fellow officer. Mackey and his friends would surely die—they'd never make Simi Valley. More important to Lawson, the truth would be murdered along with them. He swerved around a patrol car, took over the lead, and grabbed his cell phone to call Devin.

A sleepy voice answered. "Atomtech, Devin."

"Doogan is dead, sir. The scientists you wanted escaped. We are pursuing them down 101. Can you help us out here?"

"Can't you do anything right?"

"They're driving a sheriff's car with 2885 painted on the roof—you know how they do that for the police choppers?"

"I'll get Leonard on it right away. How long before sunrise?"

"Another hour and a half," he replied. "Sky's clear. Nice morning to die."

"Enjoying your job, are you?" Devin injected with a tone of approval. "Don't let me down Lawson or *you'll* be the one dying this morning."

"You just have Leonard call me when he's locked on the squad car. I'll take care of the rest." He rudely hung up. Though he was paid well for his loyalty, he wasn't paid near enough to put up with Devin's idle threats. But Lawson's stomach tightened as Doogan's last words suddenly echoed back to him. *Now Devin has your soul.*

Leading his posse down Highway 101, Lawson strengthened his resolve to terminate the scientists.

Chapter Forty-Eight
THE ROADBLOCK

From a plush apartment adjacent to his third-floor office at Atomtech, Devin phoned the employee quarters. The phone rang several times before anyone awoke to answer it.

"Get Leonard up here right now!"

He threw on a pair of brown slacks, a T-shirt, and his boots, then made his way down to the main control room. Grumbling to one of the graveyard-shift technicians for a cup of coffee, he walked up to the SSS monitor, which revealed a vast span of dark ocean. The SSS wasn't locked on anything so it wandered with the rotation of the earth. Devin grabbed the joystick and yanked it to the right. An unfamiliar scene of city streets and buildings came into view. *Rochester, NY* scrolled across the bottom of the screen.

"Shit!" He cranked the joystick a little to the left. A tractor appeared on the monitor, kicking up dust, plowing a field. *Russell, Kansas.*

"This is ridiculous! Where the hell is Leonard?" He backed away from the frustrating machine. At times like this, he appreciated an experienced man at the controls. It could take all day to find King City, California.

A technician handed him a mug of steaming coffee. With it cupped in his hands, he sat down and tried to think, a hundred questions rolling through his mind. The news of Sheriff Doogan's death was unnerving enough on its own, without the added complication of Curtis' hired scientists on the loose again. How the hell had they gotten away? Sipping coffee, he watched the farmer plow his field.

With a bang, Leonard burst through the doors, still buttoning his lab coat. "What is it now?" Pointing to the coffee maker, he motioned a technician to get him a cup.

"Fix this piece of crap machine of yours," Devin said and flipped a finger at the monitor.

"What is Kansas doing here?" With the mouse, Leonard clicked the *Undo* command. That brought up New York instead of California. He grabbed a chair. "Move it!" he said scooting Devin out of the way. "This thing is a mess!"

As Leonard cross-file coordinates and type commands on the keyboard, Devin scowled. "This is taking too long."

Still typing, Leonard grumbled. "What the hell is going on now?"

"Crawford and his band of traitors got away from King City..."

"I'm sick of this shit!" Leonard cut in. "Every time you get into trouble with this deal, you come screaming for me to bail you out. When are you going to drop it and let us all get back to our real jobs?"

"When Curtis and his scientists are out of business."

Leonard said nothing, worked the keys and mouse until his hi-tech spy machine finally zeroed in on King City, California. "What am I looking for?"

"A car with 2885 on the roof. It should be southbound on 101. When you find it, call Lawson on his cell phone."

Leonard worked the joystick, searching for his target. But there wasn't enough light. Sunrise was still an hour away. He had to strain his eyes to make out images on the screen.

Devin stood. "I need a cigar. Call me when you find them."

Leonard didn't look up until he heard the door close. Coffee cup in hand now, he stared into the screen, working the joystick, following 101 south. Suddenly, flashing emergency lights came into view—a dozen police cars barreling down the highway. Moving the SSS ahead of them, he came upon a lone sedan with 2885 painted on its roof. "Ah ha!" With a click of his mouse, he snared his prey, then picked up the phone and dialed Lawson. "I found 'em—halfway between Bradley and San Miguel. They're really moving—one hundred twenty miles an hour."

"Let me know if they make any turns," Lawson ordered. "Hell—we must be thirty miles behind them."

Lawson picked up his mike and pressed the button. "State Patrol, this is King City Sergeant Lawson. Come in."

The radio squelched. "State Patrol dispatch. Go ahead."

"We need a roadblock as soon as possible on southbound 101—say somewhere around Paso Robles. The cop killers are approaching San Miguel. Can you help us out?"

"Stand-by." A few minutes passed before the dispatcher returned. "Okay, Sergeant. We'll roadblock at Atascadero. San

Miguel has an officer in pursuit right now. We're on it."

"King City out." He put the cell phone to his ear. "Leonard. You see that? San Miguel is in hot pursuit."

"Don't get all excited," Leonard said. "2885 just ran the San Miguel cruiser into a tree. It was awesome. They're almost to Paso Robles. You guys had better hurry up."

Chapter Forty-Nine

DESERT JACKALS

Through the dark Nevada night sky, the C-130 transport roared toward Atomtech's crucial twenty-five-mile mark. Captain Baine notified Alex of their position. "Time for you to work this contraption of yours."

Alex picked up the activation terminal, his heart beating faster. "Okay. Here goes." He pressed the *PROGRAM* button and typed in coordinates from the navigation computer. *READY* pulsed on the display. He turned the *ACTIVATE* knob. The device beeped three times and the red light went out. *CLOAKING* glowed in green across the display.

"This baby had better work."

The pilots glanced at each other, uneasily.

"Start your descent to the landing zone." Alex switched on the intercom. "Red! We're going in."

Captain Baine eased back on the power. The engine drone subsided and the transport began to sink in the air.

Alex looked out the front windows—saw nothing but blackness. "I hope you know what you're doing," he said with a nervous twitch.

The Captain smiled. "Relax. Desert landing at night is tricky but I've done it more times than I care to remember. This stretch of salt flats outside Desert Rock is a piece of cake compared to the sandy dunes of Iraq." He dimmed the cockpit lights. "Flaps?"

"Check," the copilot said. "Landing lights, check." He scanned the instruments. "Set her down, Captain."

The transport had descended to one hundred feet above the ground when the automatic night-landing system activated, firing flares from the aircraft. Alex squinted as they illuminated the desert floor, brightly.

"Okay, ease her down..." the pilot said, coaxing his big bird back to earth. Massive tires rumbled on the desert floor as the giant aircraft flared out of the night sky. Clouded by dust, the burning flares glowed eerily in the wake of the landing plane. Reverse thrusters roared and slowed the aircraft to braking speed. A few moments later, the C-130 stopped, its mighty engines whining down. Hissing and spitting flares quickly burned out, returning the desert to darkness.

Whining, the cargo ramp came down. From the cargo hold's crimson glow, a Jeep backed out. Soldiers assembled into squads. In the dim light, Alex looked them over.

Lion One was his command team with Red. They would drive the Jeep, loaded with munitions and the radio isolator that would keep their transmissions hidden from detection.

Jackal One carried the PASE equipment. Each of the men had clipped cloaking devices on their belts, which rendered motion detectors and infrared sensors worthless. Undetectable, they would assault the guard towers first.

Jackal Two had the technical equipment required to circumvent perimeter security.

Jackal Three would destroy the main circuitry complex with C4 explosives and sever Devin's link to the outside world.

Jackal Four was prepared to storm the main building and eliminate Devin himself. With assault rifles, hand grenades, and bayonets, these soldiers would do battle with Devin's security force and end his reign of terror. The Desert Jackals executed an about-face and began a ten-mile hike to their assigned positions.

Red, his face now blackened for combat, climbed into the Jeep. "See you at sunup," he said to the pilots. Alex hit the accelerator. The Jeep sped off toward Atomtech under a moonless, starlit sky.

Chapter Fifty

THE TOWER GUARD

Harry Thales swallowed the last of his chicken sandwich and helped it down with a throat-burning gulp of soda. After a relieving belch, he glanced over the video monitors lining the wall in front of him. These monitors were linked to surveillance cameras and motion detectors positioned on electrified fences enclosing the Atomtech compound.

Below his tower, the main circuitry complex held the master terminals for all the wiring, computer links, and electronics used by technicians in the control center. All antenna and satellite dishes mounted on the roof were funneled through the main circuitry complex, fed into backup computers, and branched out to various departments within the compound. These connections tapped into a main computer database, which the control room had access to at all times. Harry felt proud to be the protector of such a great technological wonder.

After crumpling the paper bag that his wife had packed his dinner in, he tossed it into a wastebasket, thinking how long it had been since he'd eaten a home-cooked meal with his family and wondering how long it would be before he'd have dinner with them again. Any employee of Devin's not willing to work the long hours would become an ex-employee and Harry wasn't about to give up a steady job. After all, he had a wife and three kids to worry about.

He stood from his chair and stretched, relieving the stiffness in his muscles. After a few knuckle-pops and cracks, he decided some fresh air would do him good and walked to the window. As he opened it, a cool breeze swept across his face. God, that felt good. He closed his eyes and took in the scent of desert sage. Satisfied, he looked out toward the other guard towers. Automatic spotlight turrets swept the perimeter with ever-moving cones of light. Should the motion detectors sense anything, the computer would sound an alarm and all the lights would automatically zero-in on the movement.

Harry gasped. Something must not be working right. He had spotted a dark figure climbing up the adjacent guard tower. An alarm had not sounded. How could that be? Shaking, he grabbed his binoculars and focused on the ascending figure, a helmeted soldier with a rifle slung across his back and a knife clenched between his teeth. He was almost...almost up to the guard's cabin.

Fred! I gotta warn Fred!

He tossed the binoculars on the table and reached for a walkie-talkie on his belt strap. A stinging pain rifled through his brain. Sudden blackness engulfed him.

Chapter Fifty-One
ASSAULT WITH MALICE

Alex spit. "Why didn't you shoot him when I told you to?"

Red, lying prone on the ground, lowered his rifle and turned onto one shoulder, glaring. "If I *had* fired, that guard might have dropped his binoculars from the window. The motion detectors would've sounded an alarm and brought every damn security guard in the compound down on us. All our asses would have been nailed. So I waited until the binoculars were out of the picture."

"You were taking too big a risk. What if you had m...?"

Red shot him a stern look. The last man who had said *missed* to Red took the butt of his rifle in the teeth. Red never missed. Alex relented. "Nice shot."

"Damn right." Red looked down the fence line at his closest soldier. All his men were in position. Jackal One had taken out the other guard towers, as planned.

"Phase two. Open the bridge," Red ordered into his wrist radio.

Jackal Two went to work on the perimeter fence, bypassing ten thousand volts and the alarm system. Then they cut out a large section of isolated chain-link.

A few minutes later: "Jackal Two to Lion One—the bridge is open," came the report.

"Phase three. Cross the river," Red commanded.

Jackal One and Jackal Two teamed up, man for man, so they could enter the motion detection zone under the cloak of a PASE. In pairs, they slipped through the breached perimeter fence and ran across an open area toward the main circuitry complex. Alex held his breath for an alarm that never sounded. He exhaled when they reached the building.

Jackal One entered and eliminated the only graveyard-shift worker in the control room. With a slash across his throat from behind, the execution was silently carried out.

Jackal Two went to work disabling the motion sensor system. Bypassing this system without alerting the main control room required some sophisticated electronics and several well-placed jumper wires.

A few minutes later, the next transmission came. "Jackal Two to Lion One. The river is crossed."

"Jackal Three. Phase four. Plant 'em," Red ordered.

The explosive experts quickly crossed the compound without sounding an alarm. They carried satchels of C4, wiring, and detonators into the doomed main circuitry complex. The lethal C4 was deployed, wired, and armed.

A few more minutes passed before the next transmission. "Jackal Three to Lion One. We're hot."

"Jackal Four, Phase five. Huntin'—Fishin'!"

Soldiers funneled through the hole in the fence and stormed the main building. Red turned to Alex. "Let's go get him." As they followed their men into battle, Red went to his wrist radio again. "Jackal Three. Blow it!"

A second later the Nevada desert rocked from a mighty blast that tore the main circuitry complex from its foundation and shattered every window in the compound. A fireball billowed into the night sky. Walls fell. The roof collapsed. Debris flew in every direction and rained down around the compound.

Jackal Four infiltrated the main building. Gunfire marked their first encounter with Devin's security forces.

Red stopped running a moment—to take it all in. The explosion and gunfire made his blood boil with excitement, the rush of adrenaline like a drug-induced high.

Alex called out. "Come on!"

Red sprinted toward the action. Jackal One joined forces with Jackal Four. The fighting escalated.

*   *   *

As Leonard watched the 2885 car speeding toward Paso Robles, he wondered about the roadblock at Atascadero. Moving the joystick, the SSS tracked ahead of the sheriff's car. The monitor soon revealed a dozen patrol cars parked across 101, lights flashing.

"All right," he said into the phone. "They're dead meat." As Lawson's laugh echoed in his ear, Leonard worked the joystick, returning to the place where he had last seen the 2885 car. A surge of panic rippled through him. Something was wrong. 2885 wasn't there. It must have turned off 101. But where? Frantically, he worked the joystick, sweat now trickling down his neck. They have to be around there somewhere...

Suddenly, the SSS monitor went black followed by a deafening blast that rocked the building. Leonard hit the floor as ceiling plaster rained down and dust choked the air. He put the phone to his ear. "Lawson!"

The line was dead.

"Oh, shit!"

*   *   *

When Devin left Leonard in front of the SSS monitor, he went upstairs for a fresh cigar. He found his faithful goons hanging out in the darkened foyer that once was Susan Rivers' office. Toothless lay awake. Little Man, his shadow of a partner, slept snoring on the couch.

"Mornin', boss," Toothless said.

"What are you doing up here?" Devin turned on the light in his office and plucked a plump cigar from its case on the desk. The light beamed sharply off the foyer floor.

Toothless put a hand over his eyes. "Figured sackin' out here was no harm, seein' as how you don't got no use for this office right now."

"No thanks to you," Devin snapped. "Raven got away with more than just his life yesterday—the bastard!"

"Raven will get his!" Toothless roared. "Our time will come!"

Devin stood in the doorway mouthing the end of his stogie, lighter in hand. "Yeah, yeah, yeah," he said with a deliberate bite of sarcasm. "You and whose army? Raven has more dumb luck than the two of you have brains."

"Luck don't last forever, boss. Raven is going to screw up and I'm gonna be there to cash in—with blood." He clenched his fist in the air.

Devin, liking the hate in Toothless' voice, flicked the lighter into flame and lit his cigar. The smoke was like nectar to his nostrils. He really didn't have much respect for his goons but they were loyal as little puppy dogs. He liked having followers around him. Leaders always made waves.

Little Man stirred on the couch. "What are you bellyaching about now?" he mumbled.

Toothless fluffed him off with a swipe of his hand. "Ah, nothin'!" He propped his feet on the coffee table, settled back in the chair and closed his eyes.

The light in Devin's office went out.

With a horrendous boom, the darkness erupted in a flash of yellow light. A concussion busted windows into lethal shards of flying glass. The walls shook. Like a clap of thunder, the explosion rolled across the desert. The night glowed with fire.

Toothless found himself lying on the floor, shaking. In the eerie yellow glow that painted the walls, he spotted Little Man sprawled on the floor, his forehead bleeding.

"Little Man!" Toothless pushed away a broken end table and pulled a shredded curtain off his partner.

"What hit me?"

"Hell if I know!" Toothless crawled toward the wall where the window had been. He peered over the jagged edge.

"We got big problems here!" Panic laced his words. He turned back to the disheveled room. "There's a whole frickin' army out there...and...they're comin' this way." Gunfire echoed through the building. "We gotta get out of here!"

Devin crawled from his office, pushing debris out of his way with his arms, the glowing cigar still clamped in his teeth. He looked angry as hell. "Security will deal with them. Meantime, get your weapons." He got to his feet, grabbed hold of the couch, and started muscling it toward the stairwell. "Make a barricade. We'll blast anyone who comes up."

Toothless started to help him but paused. "Boss, I hate to tell you but this furniture ain't gonna stop no military ammunition ... "

The building shuddered from the blast of a grenade.

"...Or explosives. We have to get out!" He grabbed his machine gun, locked in a clip, and headed toward the stairs. "Come on!"

*   *   *

"What was that?" Leonard shouted.

The control room lights flickered. With a sound like popping corn, sparks spewed from computers and the room went dark. A second later, emergency lighting blinked on, its piercing glow revealing a haze of acrid electrical smoke swirling in the air.

Coughing, a technician yelled, "Let's get the hell out of here!"

Leonard scrambled to his feet but froze in terror at the sounds he heard next. "Wait! Listen!" Gunfire?

Again, he heard the reports of automatic weapons coming closer and closer.

"Everybody get down!" The room fell silent. Every man found a spot under a table or counter—somewhere to hide. Horrified, Leonard listened to the battle raging outside the doors. The rattling of machine guns, banging and popping of rifles and pistols, yelling and screaming voices. The din would get louder and closer, then quieter, as if moving away, only to return louder than ever before.

Suddenly, the doors burst open. A grenade thudded across the floor.

Leonard covered his head.

Like being hit by a truck, the explosion slammed him into the wall under the SSS console, knocking him senseless. He couldn't breathe. His eardrums ached and a burning pain raced through his body. Rancid sulfur laced the air. Choking, his throat burned. Blood streamed down his face. The sound of gunfire became muffled and distant like the pounding of his heart in his head.

Suddenly, men appeared above him, their faces clouded by smoke, blurry. They wore helmets and carried rifles. Either something was wrong with his eyes or he had been dropped into the middle of a war. He tried to scream but only gurgled. He tried to breathe but only gagged.

Footsteps clunked. He felt movement. Was he being dragged across the floor? *What's happening to me? What are they doing? Stop! Let me go!*

Someone lifted him up by his belt. Burning air rushed into his lungs. His stomach ejected a wave of nausea. After coughing up vomit and blood, he groaned. *Is this what it feels like to die? No! I don't want to die! What have you bastards done to me?*

Soldiers were leaning over him now, yelling at him. "Where is

Devin?"

Leonard strained to focus but only saw the blurry faces of two soldiers, identical twins.

"Where is Devin?"

He could barely hear the words. The soldiers shook him repeatedly.

"Where is Devin?"

"Upstairs," was all he could manage to say, not recognizing the sound of his own voice as his consciousness started slipping away in a dizzying swirl.

Alex stood, the balding technician at his feet now jerking with spasms, an eyeball half out of its socket.

Red approached, Glock in hand, and looked down at the man hacking on the floor. "Poor bastard doesn't even know his leg is gone." Red raised his gun, pulled the trigger, and put an end to Leonard's suffering with a fatal blast that echoed down the battle-scarred corridor.

Alex stepped back. "Devin's upstairs."

Chapter Fifty-Two

THE BATTLE OF THE STAIRWELL

Locking a clip into his machine gun, Little Man followed Toothless down the stairwell. Devin stopped short of following them. He leaned on the couch, trembling from a sudden wave of shock. Why was this happening? Had Curtis struck back? How did he come up with a goddamned army?

As if all hell had broken loose, a fierce gun battle erupted from the stairwell. Cursing voices mixed with rapid gunfire. Someone screamed. Devin shook with fear. Backing away from the stairwell, he retreated to his office and closed the door. There was no way out. Crouching behind his desk in the fire-lit darkness, he thought about the end of his life. "The 13th Power isn't worth all this," he mumbled in disbelief and took a drag off his cigar as if it would be his last. "That bastard Curtis!" Rage now boiled in his stomach.

He leaped to his feet and paced the floor, kicking broken glass and debris out of his way. As gunfire became more intense in the stairwell, he walked to the window and looked out across the desert, which flickered in the glow of the burning circuitry complex. The eastern horizon was ablaze with the start of a new day. A chill went through his bones. "Damn it! It's not going to end like this!"

The door flew open.

He whipped around, muscles taut.

Toothless bolted in. "Little Man's holding them off."

"Jesus! You scared the shit out of me!"

"We gotta jump, boss. It's the only way." He ran to the window with desperation in his eyes. He didn't seem to care that a three-story fall to concrete could be fatal.

Devin grabbed his arm. "Wait!" he said, suddenly remembering how Raven had left his office earlier. "The pit! Didn't you say it was full of water? Is the rope still there?"

Toothless looked at him blankly. He didn't answer. Just stared. Devin shook him. "Think, man!"

His face contorted into an ugly smile. "Yes! The pit!"

"I'll be a son of a bitch!" Feeling like a condemned man getting a last minute reprieve, he ran to his desk, stabbed his cigar into the ashtray, and pressed the hidden button. The trapdoor released with a clank in the dark. "Over here!" He led Toothless to the opening.

The fearless goon stood there for a moment, looking into the black abyss. "It'll be like a ride at the water park," he said and sat down on the edge. "Geronimo!" He pushed off and was gone. The trapdoor began to close but Devin caught it with his foot. After taking a deep breath, he followed his faithful goon down into the pit of horror. The trapdoor snapped shut as darkness swallowed him.

*   *   *

Little Man had taken several rounds in the battle of the stairwell. He lay on the floor of the second landing, back propped against a wall, shooting short bursts down the steps, his last clip loaded and half gone. Blood covered his sleeve and hand, his fingers now sticky on the rifle grip and trigger. As soldiers pressed their relentless attack and bullets ricocheted around him, he thought of Devin and Toothless. What would become of them? He had to hold his position, hold off the attack, give them time to get away. But it was getting harder to move, more painful by the minute. Either his machine-gun was getting heavier or he was getting weaker. The pool of blood around him was getting bigger. Feeling light headed, he could smell baked bread from his mother's kitchen now, and he could hear music, music that floated in the air, violins, flutes, and harps. Everything seemed so peaceful. He squeezed off the last rounds in his clip. Somehow nothing mattered anymore.

*   *   *

Alex stood next to Red as the soldiers battled for the stairwell. It seemed brutally defended. The smell of gunpowder permeated the air.

"He's up there," Red said, his voice as cold as an executioner's. "I can feel it."

The battle raged for several minutes until finally, there was no more gunfire coming down the steps. Soldiers rushed the stairwell, firing as they went. But a lone defender, lying on the second landing in a pool of blood, was already dead. They stepped over his body and systematically swept the upstairs offices and attached suite. Finding no more resistance, they gave the all-clear signal.

"Let's go!" Red yelled.

As they scrambled up the smoky, battle-scarred stairwell, Alex got a creepy feeling that Red was wrong about Devin being up here. Something about this siege didn't seem right. It was too easy.

Reaching the foyer, a team leader, sweating and breathing hard, reported to Red. "Nobody in the elevator shaft, Sir." Another soldier ran up. "Nobody on the other end, either."

"Nobody hell! Find the son of a bitch!"

The soldiers ran back to their search as Alex walked into an office he presumed to be Devin's. He looked around the flickering darkness. On the desk, he spotted a crushed cigar still smoldering in an ashtray. He picked it up. "Red—check this out. It's still hot."

"Devin was here, damn it!" Red shouted. His face had the look of a man who'd been cheated at poker.

Alex looked out the window and saw a glowing horizon. "We can't stay any longer. One more sweep and we're out of here." Walking out of Devin's office, he noticed the nameplate on the receptionist's desk. *Susan Rivers.* He picked it up. "Souvenir for the lady. She'll know how close we came to Devin."

As he put it in his pocket, he saw anger rising in Red's coal black eyes. A sudden chill rippled down Alex's back. He'd seen that look before—in that Vietnamese rice paddy.

"The rat has a hole to hide in," Red snorted in a voice rasping with rage. "But he has to come out sometime. I'll make him wish he never had!"

With a warrior-like cry, Red snatched the bayonet from its sheath on his belt and ran downstairs to the bullet-riddled body on the second landing.

Puzzled and concerned, Alex ran after him.

Red grabbed the corpse by the hair.

"What are you doing?" But even Alex's worse nightmares had not prepared him for what he saw next. A sudden wave of nausea gripped his guts as Red slashed the bayonet through the dead man's neck with the force of a butcher. The torso fell away with a thud, its severed head now dangling in Reds grasp, blood dripping.

Alex's stomach cramped with a dry heave.

Holding the gruesome decapitation out in front of him, Red ran upstairs and into Devin's office.

Alex scrambled after him. "Are you crazy?"

"Just watch this," Red said, his voice reeking with insanity. He set the head on the desk, raised his bayonet, and slammed it through the skull like a toothpick through an olive. The steel blade embedded in the desktop with a thunk. Blood and brain matter spurted out and oozed.

"Take that, you bastard," Red yelled and stepped back, now folding his arms across his chest and cocking his head slightly, like an artist admiring his work. In the shadowy glow of the burning circuitry complex, the message he left for Devin looked like it could have come directly from hell.

Alex, shaking, raised his wrist radio. "A-all teams assemble and disperse," he ordered. Grabbing Red's arm, he pulled him toward the door. "Let's go soldier. You've had enough fun for one day." Red's snarl turned into a smile. Not a happy smile—a satisfied smile that didn't reach his eyes.

Without finding the man they sought, the soldiers regrouped at the transport. Sunup was in ten minutes, the fiery horizon announcing its coming as black smoke billowed into the Nevada sky.

Alex looked back toward the war-torn compound and tried to justify what they had done. The killing was necessary. To prevent death, he had to cause death. Devin had taken many lives and he could have taken many more. This morning, they'd avenged those he had murdered and saved countless others. But where was the madman now? Would he leave the 13th Power project alone, or would he come back with a vengeance? Alex had a bad feeling this wasn't over yet.

Chapter Fifty-Three

A GUN IN THE GLOVE BOX

With sweat beading on his brow, Janis drove the sheriff's car down highway 101. He felt the hum of the powerful Chevy in the palms of his hands as the speedometer hit 130. Determined to put the most distance between themselves and King City in the least amount of time, he pressed his meager driving skills to the limit. Through every curve and straightaway he was thankful the traffic was light in the twilight hours of this California Sunday morning.

"They're coming after us, aren't they," said Ray.

Janis thought that was a possibility. "Try the radio."

Ray fiddled with the knobs. The radio only squelched. "Nothing," he said. "Maybe that's good news."

"I doubt it," Janis replied, passing two trucks laden with cargo. "We saw Lawson kill Doogan. You can bet he's made up some bullshit story to cover it up."

"What kind of story?"

Janis contemplated the answer.

Lo said, "Crooked cop will blame us. Tell comrades we did it. Get help to kill us that way. Witnesses are no good alive."

Ray turned to the back seat. "Now that's a chilling thought," he said. "Can't you think of something else that would put us in a *bigger* jam?"

"No."

"Well if you're right, every cop in the country will hunt us down like mad dogs."

"You think?"

Janis felt a cold shiver seep through his veins. "He's right, Ray. That's what I'd do. Try changing frequencies. Maybe we can get something."

Lisa leaned over the seatback. "Look in the glove box," she said. "Maybe there's a directory of some kind."

Ray hit the latch. In the glow of the glove box lamp, the blue steel of a service revolver glistened. The smell of fresh cleaning oil rose in the air. He stared at it, his silence attracting Janis' attention.

"What is it?"

Reaching in, Ray took hold of the gun, slowly removing it as if it were a vial of nitroglycerin.

"It's a gun," Janis said. He saw silver bullets shining in the cylinder. "Loaded too, so don't shoot anybody."

"Very funny. Watch the road or we won't need one of these to get killed."

Janis concentrated on the highway again. Had Doogan put that gun in the glove box deliberately? He didn't seem the type of man who'd forget it was in there. What if.—?

"Let me see it," Lisa said.

Ray gave her the gun. "Careful." Returning to the glove box, he pulled out a lot of loose papers, half filled-out forms, a map, and some receipts from various places. After discarding the stuff on the floor, he kept digging and found a couple of pens, a comb, some toothpicks, and a handful of ketchup packs.

"Why do they always give you too many of these?"

Janis shrugged and, on a hunch, reached up and pulled the sun-visor down. Taped to it, neatly typed on a piece of paper, was a list of frequencies, the California Highway Patrol's on top. "Here we go. Try this one."

Ray twisted the dial. The radio remained quiet.

"Leave it there," Janis said. He looked at the rear-view mirror and caught a glimpse of Lisa examining the gun. She seemed entranced by the power of life and death in her hands.

Chapter Fifty-Four
THE SAN MIGUEL MANEUVER

"San Miguel is up ahead," Ray said.

Janis saw a police car pull onto the highway in front of them. He blew around it without even trying to slow down. Shifting his eyes to the rearview mirror, he saw the overheads come on and the cruiser speed up behind him. "Damn it!"

"J-Janis?" Ray said. "Why would one cop chase another cop?"

"Shit!"

"He must know who we are."

"Guess we're back to Lo's theory," Janis said. "I can..."

The radio began to crackle. Ray fine-tuned it.

"...Cop killers...approaching San Miguel...Can you help us out?...Stand-by..."

Janis looked at Ray. He was white as a ghost. As Lisa and Lo leaned forward, Janis glanced at the rearview mirror. The cruiser was on his bumper now. Visions of spending the rest of his life in jail raced through his mind, or worse, if Lo was right.

"... Lawson ... roadblock at Atascadero. San Miguel ... in pursuit ...We're on it ..."

Ray slapped the dashboard. "Shit! Lawson knows where we are. It has to be Leonard. He's locked the SSS on us again."

The San Miguel cruiser pulled up beside Janis, shining a spotlight that nearly blinded him.

"What are we going to do now?" Ray shrieked. "They're waiting for us with a roadblock."

"Get rid of tail. Take different road," Lo said, as if it were an easy solution.

"We can't outrun this guy," Janis said. "Hell—all he has to do is hang with us 'til we hit the roadblock. If we change routes, he'll radio the others. We're..."

Captain Ben crashed back into Janis' mind. How did that go—emergency brake, yank the steering wheel? That's it! He looked at Ray and gritted his teeth. "You know the saying, the best defense is a good offense?"

"So?"

"So, hang on!"

Janis stomped on the emergency brake pedal and cranked the steering wheel hard to the right, spinning the car around. He clutched the wheel so tight his knuckles burned. Centrifugal force plastered him against the driver's door. Darkness swirled past his windshield until the taillights of the cruiser came around into view. Now! He pulled the brake release and floored the gas. Wrestling the steering wheel back and forth, the car fishtailed up behind the cruiser and rammed its rear bumper with a violent jolt. Janis clenched his jaw as the cruiser skidded sideways in front of him. Smoke swirled from its tires, forming a blue cloud that glowed in the headlights. He could see the officer struggling with his steering wheel. But it was no use. Out of control, the stricken cruiser veered off the highway and slammed into a tree.

"Wow!" Ray said. "Where did you learn that?"

"From a cab driver. Look! Up ahead! Highway 55! That's our way out!"

"Until Leonard gets 'em headed in the right direction again," Ray said with the sarcasm of a condemned man. "Remind me to kill that little shit next time I see him."

"Want to use this gun?" Lisa asked, holding the weapon in the palm of her hand.

Ray seemed content with her suggestion.

But the thought made Janis shiver. Killing only led to more killing. Would it ever end? He turned off Highway 101 onto 55, a southbound side-road out of Paso Robles. They were going to need a miracle.

Chapter Fifty-Five
THE POSSE

Lawson and his band of enraged lawmen raced toward the roadblock at Atascadero. He drove with the cell phone pressed to his ear. When he heard Leonard say "dead meat," he laughed, his confidence soaring. He looked in the rearview mirror at his pack of misinformed followers and grinned.

Suddenly, a muffled sound came over the cell phone, a short commotion, and then silence.

"What the...?"

He pulled the phone from his ear and examined the display. The *in-use* light was out.

"Damn cell phones!"

He re-dialed Leonard. It rang and rang with no answer.

"Shit!" He tossed the phone on the seat. We got 'em anyway. He leaned forward on the steering wheel. *They're dead meat.* Remember?

Just past San Miguel, Lawson and his speeding posse of patrol cars came upon the flashing lights of emergency vehicles along the highway. A fire truck and ambulance blocked his view of a crash on the shoulder. In spite of flares and warning lights, he didn't slow down. As his formation blew past the accident scene, Lawson caught a glimpse of a San Miguel officer standing by an ambulance with a white bandage around his head.

"What's the matter, dumb ass? Can't drive?"

When Paso Robles was in his rearview mirror, he passed two loaded semis like they were standing still. His radio squawked.

"Sergeant Lawson—change to tack-two. Officer Snyder at the roadblock wants a word with you."

"10-4." Lawson twisted the tack switch. "Lawson here. You got 'em? Are they dead? Over."

The radio squelched. "What are you King City boys up to? Over." The voice sounded gruff and irritated.

Lawson swallowed hard. "What's the problem? The stolen sheriff's car should've reached your position by now. Over."

"What makes you so sure they were headed this way? Over."

"Never mind that," Lawson replied, his mouth turning dry as

sandpaper. Where had they gone? He pushed the mike button. "San Miguel was in pursuit. They have to be somewhere between the crash and your roadblock." He paused a moment. What if they'd figured out how to use the radio? Damn it! "They might have ducked around you. Hold your position. We're six minutes out. Over."

"There must be a dozen side roads between Paso Robles and here. They could be anywhere by now." The radio went silent for a moment. "I'm calling for the helicopter. Out."

Lawson reached for the cell phone and re-dialed Leonard. He got nothing. "Damn technology ain't worth a shit!" he muttered to himself. An idea came to him. Repositioning the switch to tack-one, he radioed again. "Mackey—I know you can hear me. We *will* find you. You can't kill a cop and get away with it." He hoped that would get a response. But the radio remained silent.

*　*　*

Ray reached for the mike.

Janis grabbed his arm. "No! Let him sweat. Lawson must've lost us. That means Leonard has lost us, too. Sudden invisibility—just what we needed."

"A miracle," said Ray.

Looking at the sky, Janis saw a new day dawn in blazing yellow. He glanced at Ray, then to the back seat. Lisa smiled at him. The revolver was still in her lap.

Chapter Fifty-Six

OFFICER SNYDER

Lawson skidded his patrol car up to the roadblock at Atascadero, his band of faithful followers right behind him. Putrid tire smoke permeated the air and lingered in the breezeless morning. Early rays of sunshine cast long shadows across the highway. Before getting out of his car, Lawson re-dialed Leonard. Again, nothing.

"Damn!" He tossed the phone down and climbed out of the car. With overheads flashing behind him, he walked toward the troopers huddled around their command car. Officer Snyder stepped forward, an open pouch of chewing tobacco in his hand. His belly hung over his belt and heavy jowls swung from his cheeks. Double chins made him look like he had no neck. Lawson ignored the cold look in his eyes. "When's the helicopter going to be here?" Looking skyward, he turned a full circle.

Officer Snyder pinched a plug of tobacco and tucked it under his lower lip. "Five minutes—maybe ten," he said gruffly.

Lawson felt the trooper's icy stare and didn't like it.

Snyder stashed the pouch in his pocket, tucked his thumbs under his belt, and puffed out his chest. "You know—Doogan and I go back a long way," he said with a huff of pride. "As Military Police, we served in the same infantry division in 'Nam. Pulled two tours, back to back." He spit a slug of spittle on the pavement.

Lawson scowled.

"After that, we attended the California Highway Patrol Academy. Graduated top of our class."

"Congratulations," Lawson said, in no mood for a history lesson. But Snyder seemed intent on continuing his story. His eye contact was unnerving. What was the point?

"Then we spent several years together patrolling these California highways before he became Sheriff."

"So?"

"His murder hit me pretty hard."

"I'll bet."

Snyder spit again. "What happened in King City that got my best friend killed?"

As Lawson trolled out his well-rehearsed account of the events that led up to Doogan's death, Officer Snyder hung his head. An experienced cop, gunned down by a lowly math professor from Colorado. What an insult to Doogan's career. Anger boiled inside Snyder. He glared at Sergeant Lawson. "You must be the biggest pantywaist cop in California," he said. "How could you have let a pencil-pushing professor take your gun away from you? How tough can a mathematician be for Christ's sake?" He pointed his finger, shaking it in Lawson's face. "As far as I'm concerned, you're responsible. Your gun killed him."

Lawson took a step forward. "Damn you ..."

The air-slapping sound of helicopter blades interrupted. Snyder turned his attention to the landing aircraft. Noisily, the Bell D-47 chopper settled on the roadway in a whirl of dust, several yards away. The pilot motioned through the doorway of the glass bubble, a signal for Snyder to come forward. He and two other troopers ran under the rotating blades, ducking the blast of air.

"We need a search pattern around Paso Robles," Snyder shouted to the pilot.

"I can stretch the fuel two hours, tops."

Snyder turned to Lawson. "I'll finish with you later," he yelled over the clattering helicopter and climbed aboard. The other troopers ran back to their command car. With a rush of swirling wind, the helicopter ascended into the sky, vibrating, hammering. When it cleared the treetops, Snyder signaled his troopers to open the highway. A few moments later, all the patrol cars were lined up on the shoulder. Snyder gave them a thumbs-up sign and pointed the pilot toward Paso Robles. Something stunk about Lawson's story. Snyder needed to find the mathematician. Just how tough could he be?

Lawson walked back to his squad car, got in, and slammed the door shut. He noticed his deputies gathered together—one of them bounded over to the car and signaled him to roll down the window.

"What is it?"

"M-me and the boys think we should get back to the station," he said. "It'll be way past shift change by the time we get there and Lieutenant Nelson will need to be filled in on this. You know—paperwork."

"Just go!" Lawson said with a huff. "I'll stay here and see to it those bastards pay for what they did." He rolled his window up in the deputy's face and slammed the transmission into drive. In a swirl of tire smoke, he spun the squad car in a circle and headed toward Paso Robles.

Anger at Snyder festered inside him as he drove in the direction the helicopter had flown. *Pantywaist?* "I'll show you!" he yelled. That smart-ass Snyder had just pissed off the wrong man.

In the distance, east of Paso Robles, he spotted the circling helicopter. He set his radio on tack-two and cranked up the volume. When they found the 2885 car and radioed its position, he'd be closer than the others, faster to respond. It was now apparent—he'd have to do the killing himself. His future depended on the witnesses being dead. Again, he tried the cell phone but there was still no connection with Leonard and his high-flying spy machine.

Chapter Fifty-Seven

TIME TO DIE

Janis backed off the throttle. Highway 55 was a two-lane road that wound its way through the hilly California countryside. No place for a mistake. Tires squealing through a right hand curve, Janis gripped the wheel like a race car driver, both hands sweating. Roadside trees, posts, and signs whizzed by at a dizzying pace. The world seemed to be spinning by. At any moment, their perilous flight could be terminated, probably with deadly force. The safety of Simi Valley seemed far away.

He glanced at Ray. "We have to call Solartech Labs," he said and quickly returned his attention to a left-hand curve. "Curtis needs to know we're in trouble out here."

"Use this." Lisa offered Ray her cell phone.

"No thanks. It's not a secure line. Besides, my Vidphone will reach Curtis no matter where he is."

"Vidphone, cell phone, pay phone, I don't give a damn what phone," Janis said. "We need help."

"Pull into that gas station up ahead," Ray said, pointing down the road.

Janis drove into the dirt lot of an old countryside fuel stop. Two antique gas pumps fronted a log cabin store. A big black Lab lying on the porch lifted a brow to the visitors, growled instinctively, and returned to his nap. Janis hit the trunk release button. Ray pulled out his suitcase. With Vidphone in hand and juggling cords, he headed across the parking lot to a phone booth by the fence. Janis followed him, pulling change from his pocket. Ray activated the box and set the payphone receiver into its cradle. Janis dropped in a quarter and the box began to emit special tones.

Curtis answered, his voice excited. "Ray! Where the hell are you?"

"We're in a big mess, sir. Every cop in the world is after us. They think we killed the sheriff of King City."

"We didn't do it," Janis injected into the phone.

"We're about twenty miles south of Paso Robles on Highway 55," Ray said. "Devin seems to have lost us for the moment."

"You won't need to worry about Devin anymore," Curtis

said. "But those cops are a big problem. Keep moving south on 55. I'll find Alex and send help right away. Get moving."

"Yes, sir."

"We didn't do it," Janis added again.

The connection terminated. Ray unplugged the Vidphone and turned back toward the car.

"What kind of help can he send?" Janis asked.

"A helicopter would be nice."

As if words could turn to sound, a helicopter appeared, hovering over the fuel store. Janis stopped and stared. Was it friend or foe? The helicopter rotated sideways, revealing a California Highway Patrol emblem.

Janis thought his heart had stopped. "Lawson!" But the aircraft just floated there—it didn't approach—it didn't land. What was he waiting for?

* * *

Sergeant Lawson followed the State Patrol helicopter as it circled search patterns around Paso Robles. Trees and hills hindered his view from time to time but he was able to guess its position, never losing sight of it for long. The helicopter worked its way south of Paso Robles. He tailed it down highway 55.

Suddenly, tack-two came alive with Snyder's voice. "Ok boys. We've got 'em here on five-five about twenty miles out. Roll 'em!"

Lawson sneered. They were just around the bend. He switched off his radio and floored the accelerator. They were dead meat.

* * *

Over the racket of the engine and whipping rotor blades, Officer Snyder heard his name called on the radio. Keeping his eyes on the men standing in the parking lot looking up, he grabbed his mike.

"Snyder, here."

"Switch to tack-three, sir."

The emergency frequency? He twisted the dial. "What is it?"

"This is Lieutenant Nelson. You there, Snyder?"

"I'm kind-a busy right now, Lieutenant. What can I do for you?"

The radio squawked. "I'm at the King City Sheriff's department. Doogan is dead all right. But Dr. Mackey didn't do it. Video surveillance cameras in the garage told an entirely different story. Lawson did it. So tell your boys to leave those people alone. And find Lawson. He's wanted for first degree murder."

"The son of a bitch."

"That's *dumb* son of a bitch, sir. He forgot about the security system. Killers always forget something."

"Roger that. Out."

Officer Snyder switched the radio back to tack-two. He had to call off his men. Those people had to be scared to death. "Put her down," he said to the pilot, and as he was about to call his troopers on the radio, a squad car suddenly careened into the gas station's parking lot below him. It was a King City car. Snyder grinned. *I just found the dumb son of a bitch.*

*   *   *

Screeching tires jerked Lisa's attention out the back window, sending the revolver tumbling to the floor. She saw a sheriff's car slide to a dirt-flinging stop. Wide-eyed, she looked for her father who was standing with Janis between her and the phone booth, their eyes on the King City car, their faces flushed with surprise. She looked back as Lawson got out. He had a gun in his hand. Without warning, he shot her father. She stifled a scream as the round ripped into his right shoulder, spinning him around and dropping him to his knees.

Oh God, No!

The Vidphone smashed on the ground. Janis dove for cover behind the car. Hovering overhead, the helicopter's downdraft swirled dust around her wounded father and his attacker. Ray had been hurt. He looked so helpless. This couldn't be happening.

"Drop your weapon, Lawson!" Officer Snyder ordered over the helicopter's loudspeaker. "You're under arrest."

Lawson looked up. Through the cockpit door, he saw Snyder pull a service revolver out of its holster.

"Damn you!" Lawson yelled and stepped back to his car. He grabbed a flare gun from the seat pouch, turned quickly, and fired a projectile at the hovering helicopter. It twisted a trail of smoke into the glass bubble's doorway and ignited. A ball of bright white light glowed inside the chopper. The engine sputtered. The helicopter pitched and yawed in the air, then nose-dived into the fuel pumps.

An explosion rocked the country store. A bright yellow fireball churned skyward, fueled by severed pipes that fed gas to the pumps. Flying aircraft debris pummeled the 2885 car. Black smoke billowed into the California morning sky.

Lawson turned his back to the inferno and walked up to Ray. With hell's fury burning behind him, he put the gun to Ray's forehead. "Time to die."

Chapter Fifty-Eight

THE GATES OF HELL

Paralyzed with fear, Ray begged his muscles to move. They refused. He looked up at the crazed lawman standing there, his eyes narrow slits of anger, his teeth bared. The cold steel of the gun barrel on Ray's forehead sent a chill through his body. Heat from the roaring inferno hit his face like a devil's wind. With his shoulder burning from the bullet, he realized there was no way out—nowhere to run. Numbed by fear and resigned to his fate, he closed his eyes. So this was how his life would end—a bullet to the brain. The hammer clicked. He flinched. *Time to die* echoed through his mind.

The report of a handgun rocked his body. But there was no black void of eternity spiraling around him. The fire still roared; his shoulder still burned. Huh? It took only a split second for him to realize that the blast had not come from the murderous cop's gun. He popped his eyes open in time to see Lawson buckle over.

Ray looked quickly toward Doogan's car where Lisa was standing with a gun clasped in her hands, elbows locked, face aglow from the billowing inferno, and her hair wisping in the hot wind.

Again, the gun spit fire as she squeezed off another round. The bullet jarred Lawson's body as it tore into his chest. His handgun clunked on the ground and he dropped to his knees, his arms hanging limply at his side. With a wide-eyed look of disbelief on his face, blood spurted from his mouth and gushed down his chin.

Another blast from Lisa's gun knocked him to the dirt.

Janis bolted around the car, grabbed Lisa's arm and pushed it down, pointing the gun to the ground. Again, she squeezed the trigger. The round struck the dirt, and as if she were locked in a nightmare of her own, she fired again and again until the revolver resounded only hollow clicks from empty chambers.

"Lisa. It's over."

She dropped the gun and moaned. Her knees buckled but Janis didn't let her fall. She clung to him, trembling. "I had no choice."

"I know."

Ray started shaking. Still on his knees, he couldn't believe his eyes. His daughter had saved him. Holding his wounded shoulder, he looked up a wall of fire towering into the sky. Had he crossed through the gates of hell? He was sure of it. The heat was like a blast furnace. Why did he feel so cold and numb? He looked back and forth between Lisa and the inferno, unable to move, his mind locked in horror.

The King City cop lay sprawled beside him, blood pooling underneath the lifeless body of Devin's secret henchman. Were there any more around here? Was the whole damn country infested with them?

Dazed, he suddenly realized Lo had come to his aide, checking his wound. "Hang on, Ray. It's not too bad," he said unreassuringly. "Must hurt like hell." He pulled on Ray's other arm. "Let's go. More cops coming to kill us."

But Ray couldn't move. He just stared at Lo's face.

Lo looked at Lisa, still clutching Janis and weeping. "This not good, you guys. Run now—cry later." He slapped Ray's face.

The sudden sting on his cheek yanked him back to reality. Shaking his head to clear the fog, he staggered to his feet and slowly but deliberately walked to Lisa. Though his shoulder burned, they hugged each other anyway.

Chapter Fifty-Nine

THE CHASE

Crossing in front of the car to get behind the wheel, Janis spotted a chunk of black helicopter wreckage stuck in the grill. Dripping green liquid made a small puddle under the radiator. Though he knew nothing about car mechanics, he was sure of one thing—that drip didn't look good.

Sirens wailed in the distance.

"Let's go!" Ray yelled.

Janis jumped in and spun around the inferno, squealing onto southbound 55 just as a horde of State troopers rounded the curve. He floored the accelerator and looked in the rearview mirror. It seemed like a million flashing lights were behind him.

Gripping the wheel, he raced down the winding road, pushing Doogan's car to its limit. Life or death hung on every curve. But it became obvious very quickly that he wasn't going to shake his relentless pursuers. Dogging him blindly and oblivious to the truth, they had but one thing on their minds—revenge. He could only hope to stay out of their grasp long enough for Curtis to intervene. Could the Money Man be a Miracle Man, too?

Winding its way down from the hills, Highway 55 finally broke out on the Carrizo Plain where it became straight and flat— like a drag strip. Humming under the hood, the powerful V-8 engine pulled the car ahead of the police. Janis counted nine cars in his mirror. God only knew how many more lay in wait up ahead. Another roadblock would be a disaster. The chatter coming over the radio sounded like a foreign language of code numbers and meaningless jabber, giving him no hint of what the troopers were planning.

Lo studied a map he'd found on the floor. "No side roads for sixty miles. No way out."

Janis glanced at Ray and Lisa in the back seat. She was wrapping her father's shoulder with a piece of his shirt. Her cheeks glistened from streaks of tears. She looked like...

Suddenly, the car surged. The engine bucked and jerked. "Oh, oh!" He scanned the instruments. The temperature gauge was pegged in the red zone. Again, the engine bucked. But this time a vibration shook his teeth. Though he had the gas pedal pressed to the floor, the engine was losing power, smoking as if it were on fire. The car began to slow. He glanced at the rearview mirror. The patrol cars were getting closer. His stomach sank. "We're in trouble."

Everybody looked out the back window.

From a misty California sky, an aircraft flying low and slow banked left and flew over the posse of State troopers.

"Look at that," Lisa said, pointing.

In the rearview mirror, Janis saw a C-130 Hercules rocking in the air, its cargo ramp hanging down and wing-flaps deployed as it dropped lower and lower, heading straight toward them.

Ray's eyes got big around. "What's he doing?"

Janis backed off the throttle. "Landing!"

The massive transport roared over the roof. Turbulence buffeted the car violently. Flaring out of the sky, the plane settled on the highway in front of them, the cargo ramp dragging on the pavement and throwing up sparks like a curtain of glittering rain. An oncoming car swerved into the ditch.

"That's our ride out of here," Janis said. Heart pounding, he floored the gas pedal again, aiming for the ramp. The car, bucking and lurching, veered through the shower of sparks and hit the cargo ramp with a bone-jarring bang. Janis slammed on the brakes. The car screeched to a stop inside the plane. Steam spewed from under the hood. The overheated engine squealed and seized. Janis clung to the steering wheel, a cold sweat on his forehead. He thought his chest would burst.

Chapter Sixty
A TOAST TO THE DEAD

As the sun rose above the Texas horizon, a shiny white and gold Learjet cruised toward Simi Valley at thirty-five thousand feet. The sleek aircraft cut effortlessly through a frozen sky, leaving a white ice-crystal contrail behind it. Whining engines hummed softly inside a cozy cabin where Curtis sipped a Bloody Mary that Jonathan had prepared in the aft bar. They'd spent the weekend partying in Dallas. Though Sleazy Susie had kept Curtis entertained, his mind wasn't entirely on the frivolities. Devin's relentless assault on the 13th Power project had made Dallas an uneasy respite. During the night, Curtis had tried to reach Alex on his Vidphone but there was no answer. Something big was going down and he wanted to get back to Solartech Labs as soon as possible.

Curtis eyed the concoction in Jonathan's glass. An umbrella protruded over the brim, shading what appeared to be a fruit salad floating in a pink slush. "What kind of drink is that?"

Jonathan plunged a straw into the swill. "A cross between a Daiquiri and a Kamikaze. Looks pretty. Tastes sweet." He took a swig. "But it's lethal."

Shaking his head, Curtis returned his attention to his own drink. Jonathan wasn't much of a drinking man, but the morning booster seemed appropriate, if not necessary. Though Curtis had a tendency to make spur-of-the-moment plans, Jonathan never complained. He was paid well for his tolerance.

Bright sunlight glared in through the windows. Curtis looked out beyond the wing. A thick bank of clouds hung over the mountains. Lake Powell snaked across the landscape ahead. He pulled the shade down, sat back in his seat, and sipped his drink again.

Jonathan handed him the morning paper. "Early edition of the Dallas News," he said. "It's the Captain's."

"Be sure to thank him for me."

As the paper unfolded in Curtis' hands, the headlines quickened his pulse. *Nevada Desert Atomic Plant Explodes.* That could mean only one thing, Devin was out of business. The 13th Power was close at hand.

Curtis turned the front page toward Jonathan. He read, "Fearing radiation leaks, officials rush to the remote area. No communications have been received from the site."

Raising his drink to Jonathan, Curtis said, "A toast to Devin's demise." They drank to the good news.

Curtis downed the rest of his Bloody Mary and picked up his golden staff, caressing its smooth surface and eagle-head handle, taking care not to exert too much pressure on its emerald eyes. Nothing could stop him now, unless…his scientists…where were they? Curtis lifted the shade and looked out his speeding aircraft. Were they safe, somewhere out there? The 13th Power project depended on them. His new wealth—his new power. Ray and Janis had to be safe. Leaning back in his seat, he closed his eyes and let his mind savor the possibilities.

Two hours later, the sleek corporate jet turned on final approach to Solartech Field. "Buckle up," the copilot said over the intercom.

Curtis tugged on his seat belt and turned his attention out the window. The descending jet's shadow raced along the valley floor, rippling over burnt orange grasslands strewn with boulder fields and scrub oak, which soon gave way to city streets, rows of houses and lines of traffic. Sifting through a chain-link fence, the shadow danced over an array of approach-light towers and slid across the runway threshold, finally converging with the jet, its tires squawking and reverse thrusters roaring as it slowed to taxi speed.

"Smooth," Jonathan said.

The executive car, a long black Lincoln with Solartech flags flapping from its fenders, raced toward the tarmac as the jet swung around and stopped. A chime echoed through the cabin. An auxiliary power unit hummed to life. The copilot opened the door and steps dropped down. A gold carpet unrolled automatically.

Curtis donned his black hat and coat and grabbed his golden staff.

Jonathan gave him a two-fingered salute. "Catch up with you later, sir. I'll clean up around here first."

"As you wish." Curtis turned to the copilot. "Great flight."

"Enjoy your day, sir."

Curtis deplaned and headed for the executive car where an attendant greeted him. "Good morning, Dr. Curtis."

"Security Central—right away."

Chapter Sixty-One
THE ULTIMATE SACRIFICE

Down in the pit of horror under Atomtech, Devin swam in darkness, shivering from the cold water. Anger kept his adrenaline pumping as he battled panic. Gulping air, he heard Toothless treading water nearby.

"Over here, boss. I've got the rope."

Devin dogpaddled toward the voice in the dark. He felt his strength dwindling. His water-soaked clothes and boots kept trying to pull him under. Had his age become a handicap? Would he drown in this stinking pit? Spitting water he yelled, "Over where?" He swam into a slimy wall. "Shit! Talk to me you bonehead!"

"To your left, boss. Keep coming. You can make it."

Reaching out toward the voice, a strong hand grabbed his arm.

"Take the rope," Toothless said, guiding Devin's hand. "Follow me."

Toothless climbed the rope to the upper deck and pulled himself out of the pit. Dripping and shivering, he lay on the concrete floor, gasping air. "Come on!" he yelled.

Devin clung to the rope, his hands weak from the cold and burning from the strain. "Pull me up," he shouted. "I don't have enough strength to climb the rope."

"Who do you think I am, Mister Universe? I can't pull your fat ass up here."

"Fat ass?" Devin spit. "Who are you calling a fat ass?" If he didn't need his goon so badly, he'd have killed him for that. "Turn the water on."

Toothless sloshed over to the water valves sticking out of the wall. "Which one is it?"

"Hell if I know. Just pick one, damn it!"

"Okay, boss. Eenie, meenie, minie, moe." He turned the valve.

Devin let out a scream as a sudden whirlpool nearly dragged him off the rope. "Wrong one, you idiot!"

"Oops." Toothless shut the valve quickly and opened the other one. The pit filled with water. He reached out a hand and helped Devin climb out. Together, they sat on the cold wet floor, shivering and dripping. Devin stared up the stairwell, listening for any portentous sounds. Nothing.

An hour passed. Devin trembled the whole while, thinking pneumonia was setting in and fearful of what he would find up those stairs. Should they risk leaving the sanctuary of this hole? Were the soldiers gone? Could the silence be a trap? He ordered Toothless to go upstairs and see if it was safe to get out of this sewer.

While Toothless clunked up the stairs, Devin wondered how much damage Curtis had done. In a mental rage, he damned Curtis' quest for the 13th Power, damned Ray Crawford's blind devotion to the impostor, and damned his daughter, too.

"Boss—you better get up here."

Shivering, Devin walked the wracked halls of Atomtech. He felt numb, stunned with disbelief. The place looked like a war zone, his company in shambles. Scattered throughout the debris lay the bodies of his workers and security men. Painful moans of the wounded echoed eerily down desecrated corridors. Gunpowder and sulfur hung heavy in the air. Lingering dust and smoke burned his throat.

In the main control room, he came to realize the magnitude of his loss. The nerve center of all his technological wonders lay in ruins around his mangled technicians. Atomtech could no longer function. It would take years to repair the damage to his empire. He could never replace the professionals he had lost. Seeing Leonard lying in a pool of coagulating blood left him racked with nausea. Disbelief collided with reality. Curtis had to be stopped. Somehow.

A scream from the stairwell sent a chill down his spine. Toothless! What would make the big goon scream like that?

Devin ran up the bullet-scarred stairwell. What he saw on the second landing made him reel in horror. The headless corpse of Little Man lay in a pool of blood. And the stench was something awful.

Toothless pounded his fist on the wall. "Why?" he yelled. "Why did I let him stay here alone?"

"Come on!" Devin said, his guts churning. "Keep going. Upstairs."

"What kind of animal would do this?"

"The worst kind!" Devin replied. "The *human* animal." He stepped over Little Man's torso and climbed the remaining stairs to the third floor foyer. Early morning sunbeams shined through blown-out windows.

"Somebody's going to pay for this, boss!" Toothless pledged as he shuffled through the room, dust swirling from his footsteps.

As he approached his office, Devin saw the bulging eyeballs of Little Man's severed head staring out from the shadows. Blood streaked his face like tears. A bayonet held him upright on the desk. Devin's stomach cramped. "The bastards!"

Toothless ran to the doorway. "Little Man!" The big goon buckled over, fell to his hands and knees and vomited on the floor.

Devin turned his head away, his stomach heaving from the smell of bile in the air. Fighting a reflex to expel his guts, he swallowed hard and looked back into his office.

Like a wraith in flesh, the hideous image of Little Man's decapitation reflected the haunting truth about this real-life nightmare. Was there no limit to what men would do to each other? Devin slammed his fist into the wall. Why had he been condemned for trying to end Curtis' quest for the 13th Power? If only Colonel Fallon had believed him. Devin felt like a lone soldier in a war the world knew nothing about. Curtis was winning; the world was losing. Something had to be done to turn the tide. Maybe *now* Fallon would help him defeat Curtis.

"Get up!" He yanked on Toothless' arm.

The burly goon rose, snorted in his sleeve, and spit on the floor. "Where we goin', boss?"

Devin walked into his office, ignoring the gruesome head skewered to his desk. "Indian Springs to find Colonel Fallon. Any objections?"

Toothless didn't answer.

"Make yourself useful and find us a van."

Scooping up a handful of cigars, he watched Toothless disappear down the stairs. Alone now, Devin turned his attention to the severed head on his desk. Lower lip trembling, he felt the sorrow of losing his faithful aide. But he couldn't find the words to thank Little Man for saving his life, for making the ultimate sacrifice.

Chapter Sixty-Two
JAWS OF TIGER

Steam swirled around the overheated sheriff's car, giving Janis an eerie sense of entombment. He couldn't see beyond the crimson mist. A droning vibration shook the car violently as the massive aircraft climbed under full power. Clinging to the steering wheel, he felt as if he'd jumped on a fast elevator. His stomach turned queasy. Though it seemed like forever, the shaking finally subsided and his vertigo relented as the plane leveled off. He quickly turned his attention to the back seat.

"Wow!" Ray grimaced in pain as he held his daughter. "Nice driving!"

"How about that," Janis said, reaching back to touch Lisa's shoulder. "We're safe now..." Hesitating, he scanned the tinted windows. "I think." He looked at Lo. "You all right?"

Lo didn't answer. He just stared straight forward in his usual trance.

Janis turned to Ray. "That was... "

A thumping sound came from the driver's door window. "Time to deal with these guys," he said, noticing the steam had begun to dissipate.

He rolled down his window. "I'll have the burger and fries combo, please."

"Welcome aboard," a soldier said.

"Alex! Where the hell did you come from?" Ray said, his voice beaming with surprise.

Alex stooped, looked in, steadying himself on the doorframe as the aircraft rocked. "Ray! How the hell are yah?"

"I'm shot, damn it! Get me a doctor."

"You don't look like you're dying." He looked at Lisa. "Is this your nurse?"

"Cut the bull. I'm serious."

Alex said to Red, "Get the medic."

A moment later, a young doctor dressed in combat fatigues, climbed into the back seat and attended to Ray's wound.

"How's it look?" Janis asked, noticing blood on the medic's pants.

"I've seen worse."

Janis asked Alex, "How'd you find us?"

"Curtis said you'd be on 55 with a pack of police on your tail. So we took a detour to see if we could help. You were easy to find. The Captain decided to drop the transport down in front of you, figuring you'd take the ramp rather than deal with those cops. What did you do—kill somebody?"

"Something like that." Janis looked at Lisa who was holding Ray's hand as the medic dressed his shoulder, her eyes still shiny with tears, her lower lip trembling. Killing Lawson must have been tormenting her. But now, she seemed concerned about her father's condition and attentive to the medic's work.

The intercom crackled. "Ten minutes to touchdown."

As payload specialists attached anchor straps to the axle, Alex opened the driver's door. "Everybody out." The aircraft banked right. He braced himself on the door. "Find a seat and buckle in," he said as the plane rolled back to level flight.

Janis climbed out of the car. "I'm Dr. Mackey," he said to Alex.

"You had us worried for a while, Professor."

"It was one close call after another. I just don't understand why Devin was so hell-bent on stopping us."

"Beats me. But it cost him plenty." A wry smile formed on Alex's lips but a turbulent bump of air jarred the aircraft and quickly changed his expression to a frown. "I hate when it does that."

After applying adhesive tape to a gauze bandage, the medic got out of the car and reported to Alex. "That'll hold him for now. Get the doc to pull the slug when we're on the ground."

"Let's go!" Alex ordered. He held his hand out to assist Lisa but she refused it.

"Help my dad."

Alex helped Ray to a web seat and strapped him in. Lisa sat next to him.

Janis and Lo found seats among the troops and buckled in. Lo mumbled something in Chinese.

"What's the mumbo-jumbo, Lo?"

"We go now into jaws of tiger," he translated. "Bad feeling about this..." he pointed to his stomach, "... here."

Janis shrugged. But when he looked around and noticed sweaty soldiers and smelled the lingering odor of gunpowder, he wondered if Lo was right. Sooty M-16 barrels slung here and there made Janis suspect these troops had been in some kind of skirmish, probably for Curtis and probably against Devin. Had the gladiators done battle?

He glanced around the cargo bay, trying not to be obvious as he took note of the men's faces. Some were stern and unfeeling. Others were blank and distant. None were happy. All were tired. Looking toward the cockpit, he suddenly realized Lo was right. Two soldiers lay wounded and bandaged on evac gurneys. Damn! Was Curtis just as dangerous as Devin? Was he equally capable of causing death and destruction? Could Janis trust him, or Alex, or any of these soldiers? He felt as though he couldn't see the snake pit for all the snakes.

The engines quieted and the aircraft pitched down for landing. Janis looked at Lo. *We go now into jaws of tiger.*

Chapter Sixty-Three

THE HYPOTHESIS

The long black executive car, flags flapping from the fenders, cruised through the airfield gate. Several black staff cars followed behind it. The procession headed for the tarmac where a staging area had been decorated with banners. Curtis sat in the back seat and scanned the sky for any sign of the approaching transport. He had been elated when Alex radioed news of the successful rescue of his scientists. That, and Devin's defeat, brought him joy. "Today has been a great day," he said to himself, still looking skyward. His golden staff lay across his lap.

As the plush luxury car came to a graceful halt, the trailing staff cars fanned out on both sides. Like a choreographed precision driving team, they all stopped in formation. Staff car doors swung open and top supervisors and department heads of Solartech Labs, dressed in dark suits, got out and padded toward the executive car. Jonathan opened the door for Curtis, who emerged into sunshine and donned his black hat, tipping it to his supervisors. Again, he turned his attention to the sky. Nothing.

He tapped his staff on the concrete. "Let's go."

His men joined him as he made his way to a covered bandstand fronted by rows of folding chairs. As they walked, they talked and laughed among themselves. He was pleased to see everyone's excitement over the 13th Power project's new mathematician, the man who would make it all work. Not smiling, he scampered up the steps to the shaded podium as the others found seats to their liking.

"Gentlemen," he spoke into the microphone. "Today is a proud day for Solartech Labs and for all of you, the men who made this possible. In a few minutes, Dr. Janis Mackey will be joining us. As you know, his help is vital to the 13th Power project.

"This isn't new territory for him. Twenty-five years ago, he and Ray Crawford developed the hypothesis that you have been working with. Simply put, our reality is the world we live in. It's made up of atoms and surrounded by the universe. The magnitude of each of these things is dependent upon perspective."

He paused looking over his assembly, sweltering in the sunshine.

"The hypothesis proposes that since the earth is a ball so big that everywhere on its surface appears to be the top, then the same goes for the atom or the universe. As the perspective changes, the physics and math change, too. If we look at the earth from a different perspective—say from space, we can clearly see that there is a bottom, and sides, as well as a top—its dimensions are quite perceptible.

"So the hypothesis proposes there is a place inside the nucleus of an atom where the space around it is as vast as the universe, a perspective I believe to be attainable. Does that mean smaller equals larger? The hypothesis says it does. Can negative equal positive? The hypothesis says it could. Do the rules of physics and math apply in this place beyond our reality? The hypothesis says probably not. So where is this place? The hypothesis says the 13th Power."

The assembly stirred and talked together softly. Waiting for them to return their attention to the bandstand, he felt as if he had a whole school of suckers on his hook. If these brainards knew what he was really after, they'd all want a cut. No way. Milk them with their own science. Make them think big. Keep them on the hook.

"Think of the possibilities of the 13th Power. Without the rules of physics to shackle our technology, we can harness the speed of light, alter gravity, and tap the energy that generates the atomic force. E equals M C squared will be obsolete, gentlemen. The new rules will be more powerful than we ever imagined."

He raised his fist and pulled it down forcefully. "YES! THEN *WE* WILL HAVE THE POWER!"

His audience stood and cheered. He smiled, raised his golden staff, and turned his back to the podium. The clamor behind him grew louder and louder, suddenly turning into a roar that stifled the applause.

Curtis whirled around and saw it in the misty sky, the huge form of a flaring C-130 transport. Massive belly-tires smoked on the concrete and, as the nose wheel gently settled to the runway, reverse thrusters roared the aircraft to braking speed. Vibrations pounded the onlookers. Some of them turned their backs to the onslaught and covered their ears. But Curtis stood upright and took it all in. The power was like a high. He loved the feel of it.

Chapter Sixty-Four
THE NEW ARRIVALS

From the perimeter fence twenty yards away, Steve stood with Susan, watching the spectacle played out on the bandstand. They hadn't been invited to this event but when he saw the activity from the window of their suite, he decided they should take a walk.

As he listened to Curtis' speech, he recalled what Devin had told him about the impostor. Judging from Curtis' obsession with power, Steve figured Devin must have been right. Melvin Anderson was, indeed, a dangerous man. And as he listened to what sounded like another madman, Devin's warning didn't go entirely unheeded. *I need to be careful with this guy,* he reminded himself. Curtis wouldn't want his real identity revealed because his followers wouldn't be so loyal if they knew they were working for a fraud. It had to be worth a fortune.

Steve spotted the C-130 transport approaching from the west, dark and eerie and seemingly gliding down an invisible string. The wing flaps were fully deployed, giving it the appearance of a giant aberration that somehow defied gravity. He pointed to the aircraft, turning Susan's attention away from the podium. A cold shiver ran down his spine when the quiet day suddenly turned into a clamoring roar of turboprop engines and screeching tires from the landing aircraft. Susan gripped his arm.

Questions raced through his mind, questions about the raid and the men that went to stop the madman. The thought of Devin's death excited him even more. He couldn't wait to hear how it happened. His hate for Devin was unmoved by the madman's incredible insight of the impostor.

Susan watched the aircraft come to rest on the tarmac. She had mixed feelings about Devin and didn't want to hear how he'd been killed. A flight-line crew unrolled a gold carpet from the bandstand to the cargo ramp. Curtis came down from the podium and stood at the carpet's edge as if he'd practiced this ceremony before.

Soldiers marched down the ramp to the cadence of their leader. When they cleared the aircraft, Red barked, "Column right, huh! Company halt!" They stood in formation and Curtis saluted them with the golden staff. Red saluted back.

Two men made their way down the cargo ramp, followed by a woman and an Oriental man. One of the men had a bandaged shoulder, his arm in a sling. Susan thought they looked important. Then she saw Alex walking behind them, long-faced. Why? Had something gone wrong? They all stopped at the gold carpet and faced Curtis.

"Those are the guys Devin was trying to kill," Steve told her.

"The girl, too?"

"I guess."

"Who are they?"

"I don't know. I wonder how they ended up on the plane." Steve took Susan's hand. "Come on. Let's find out."

At a full run, they headed for the gate.

Chapter Sixty-Five
NESTING

Janis looked at Curtis standing pompously at the other end of the gold carpet and wondered what he'd gotten himself into. He started to complain to Ray. "This is... "

"Just humor the guy, Janis, for Christ's sake. He got us here alive, didn't he? So smile."

Janis gritted his teeth—pretended to smile. The rich man seemed more interested in his stupid ceremony than the well being of his new arrivals. "Let's get this thing over with." He started walking without an invitation. Ray and the others followed him as the assembly stood and applauded.

Curtis greeted them with his hand extended. He seemed especially delighted to meet Ray's daughter. Smiling at her, his gold tooth glistened in the sunlight. "Welcome to Solartech Labs." He took her hand and turned it palm down. Janis saw her tremble as Curtis kissed the back of her hand the way a prince would kiss a princess.

Janis sneered. A prince of *darkness*. He wanted to belt Curtis for being overly suave with his girl. But he had to chuckle when Lisa pulled her hand away and wiped it on her shorts.

Seemingly unconcerned, Curtis turned his attention to Lo. "I hear you do computer consulting, Mr. Chin." He shook Lo's hand. "I hope you are planning to stay on with us. We could certainly use your help."

Lo bowed. "I have to see what help you need. Right now, we're tired. I would thank you very much to help us with that." Lo smiled but kept eye contact with Curtis.

"Very well," Curtis said and turned to Ray. "Looks like I need a damage report on you. Does it hurt?"

"Like hell, sir."

"I bet it does. We'll get that taken care of shortly." Curtis looked at Janis who had Lisa safely tucked under his arm. "And how are you, Professor? Glad to see you could make it."

As Curtis reached to shake his hand, Janis was quick to protect it. "I've been nursing this cut since Devin blew up Lo's house. Needs stitches."

"We'll have to fix that, too," Curtis said. "From the looks of you all, I'd say you had a rough trip."

"That would be an understatement," said Janis.

Curtis turned to his security chief. "How...?"

"I need to brief you about last night—in private, sir."

"Shall we get together on that—say—later this afternoon?"

Alex nodded.

"Good. Now I'd like to introduce my staff to Dr. Mackey."

Janis glowered. "Look, *Mister* Curtis. This is a bad time for a party. So save it. We need medical attention, food, and rest. Just point us in the right direction."

Curtis tapped his golden staff on the tarmac. "Alex will take care of all the details, gentlemen..." He hesitated. "...And Lisa, of course. All in good time..." Curtis paused, his eyes now fixed on a couple sprinting toward them. "Alex, who do we have here?"

"That's Steve and Susan," Alex said, waving to them. "It's a long story. Let's just say they're your guests."

Curtis didn't look impressed. He turned to the bandstand. "Ray—Dr. Mackey. Follow me." They went up the steps to the podium. Lisa held Janis' arm and Lo followed them.

The assembly stood and applauded the newest members of their team. Curtis raised the staff. But his attention was not on his audience. He was watching Alex greet the couple, Steve and Susan. Shaking hands, they stood together talking. Steve suddenly clenched his fists. Curtis' interest spiked. Were they arguing about something?

The clamor from the small crowd began to subside. Curtis pumped his staff in the air, prodding them to continue cheering, buying him a little more time to observe Alex and his guests.

Susan clasped her hands in front of her mouth and dropped her head. Was she praying? Or crying? Steve shoved Alex. They scuffled for a moment, then embraced as if consoling each other. Alex took something from his pocket. It looked like a nameplate. He handed it to Susan. She, too, joined the embrace.

Curtis frowned. What was that all about? He made a mental note to ask Alex later. In fact, he had a lot of questions for his top security man. Alex had better have plenty of answers.

Janis noticed the soldiers marching up the cargo ramp with

their leader. A tug had hooked onto the nose wheel of the massive aircraft. Then he saw the broken-down sheriff's car hanging from the sling of a tow truck, which rumbled away. "Hey—our stuff's in there!" he yelled.

"Later!" Curtis shouted harshly. He tapped the golden staff on the microphone. A clunking sound reverberated through the speakers and the assembly came to order.

"Gentlemen," he began. "I present to you Dr. Janis Mackey from the University of Colorado."

Janis acknowledged the crowd with a slight wave of his hand.

As the applause began again, Curtis raised his hand to silence it. "Tomorrow we'll meet in Tech-Com Control at 0900 hours. In the meantime, our cafeteria personnel have prepared a big barbecue party for this afternoon. I suggest we celebrate today for there will be no time to play once we get this project on track." He raised his staff once again and the assembly responded with cheers.

Janis nudged Curtis aside and blew into the mike. "I want you to know we are happy to be here." He paused and looked over the group. "Hell—we're happy to be alive."

The assembly laughed lightly.

"We're looking forward to working with you people. After tomorrow's meeting, we want a complete tour of Solartech Labs. But today we want to get cleaned up, rested, and fed. Any objections?"

"No" and "no, sir" could be heard among the heightened applause. Janis hugged Lisa. Ray pushed his way to the microphone.

"This is going to be the big one, boys," Ray trumpeted to his fellow workers. "My lifelong dream will become reality and the 13th Power will soon be ours." He raised a fist and the crowd cheered wildly.

Janis tapped Ray on the shoulder. "Shut up and let's go." Janis led the way down from the bandstand. Everyone gathered at the bottom of the steps where they could mingle with the new arrivals. Janis kept Lisa tucked snugly under his arm as they made their way through the crowd, shaking hands and patting shoulders as they went. Short greetings and quick introductions could not be avoided. The group conversed and moved slowly toward waiting staff cars.

Straining, the tug pushed the C-130 transport back onto the runway threshold. As Red stood in the jump-door, he saluted Alex and Steve. They saluted back and Susan waved goodbye.

Four massive engines cranked, spewed smoke, and roared to life. Red swiveled the door shut. The prestigious crowd stopped to watch the giant aircraft poised for flight. A few moments later, the thundering aircraft rocketed down the runway and clambered into the midday sky.

Janis and Lisa watched their rescuers disappear in the distance. Ray and Lo joined them. As Janis made eye contact with Ray, he wondered if they had chosen the right direction in this. Many people had paid a high price for them to get here, many with their lives. Was the 13th Power worth all that?

Lisa's eyes welled with tears. "Is the dying going to end now?"

"Yes," Janis said and rubbed her shoulder, hoping he was right about that. But Lo was shaking his head *no* in answer to Lisa's question. Janis felt a chill. Lo was never wrong. Were they really safe in the cradle of Simi Valley, or actually nesting in a pit of vipers?

Chapter Sixty-Six

COLONEL FALLON

Colonel Fallon paced the floor in the control center at Nellis Air Force Base. His shiny black boots clunked on polished hardwood as he listened to radio transmissions coming over the ComLink. He wore jungle fatigues, which hung loosely on his stocky frame. Beads of sweat trickled down from balding temples. Removing thin wire-framed glasses, he wiped his brow with a handkerchief. His day had started with a disaster.

The ComLink crackled with static as his helicopter squadron neared the Atomtech compound. From this third floor control room in the Central Communications Building, Fallon was in constant contact with the mission specialists. He stopped pacing at the plate glass window overlooking the flight line. They should've been there by now.

The radio on the ComLink squawked. "We've got smoke—ten miles out. Towering black column."

"Roger that—Green Leader," the controller answered. "Send in the remote Geigers."

"Sensors away."

Remote radioactivity sensors were rocketed into Atomtech's compound ahead of the advancing squadron. A few minutes later: "We're not getting any signals. It's clean down there."

Colonel Fallon felt instantly relieved.

"ComLink—Red Leader, please," the speaker blared with the urgent voice of a pilot.

Fallon cocked his head to listen.

"Go ahead, Red Leader," the controller answered.

"I've spotted a blue van speeding across the desert like hell's on fire. Request clearance to intercept."

The controller looked at the Colonel.

"No."

"Negative, Red Leader. Stay with the mission."

"Put out an APB on the van," said Fallon.

"Yes, Sir."

An airman breathlessly arrived holding a phone, the mouthpiece covered by the palm of his hand.

"It's the media again. What should I tell them?"

"No comment." But he knew he couldn't hold them off forever. He was still trying to ascertain the severity of the disaster. Until he had more answers than they had questions, he would keep the press in the dark.

As his staff collected statistics from the troops at the scene, he began to realize the staggering cost in human life. He dispatched another Med-Evac chopper to handle the flow of wounded. A triage team at the site was reporting injuries consistent with a battlefield scenario. Those reports made him think he was dealing with a terrorist strike rather than an accidental explosion. But he couldn't understand why terrorists would be interested in the heavily guarded remote facility. What did they want?

And the fate of his friend, Walter Devin, was also on his mind. Although he thought of him as a cheat at cards, he still favored his friendship and was concerned. He could only hope Devin wasn't among the dead.

An airman handed him a decoded secret communiqué. "Get a load of this, Sir."

"Now what?" The Colonel read the note aloud. "A decapitated corpse was found in a stairwell. The head had been bayoneted to a desktop."

He looked up, a surge of horror running down his spine. "What are we dealing with here?"

The airman shrugged. "Something bizarre, that's for sure," he said, turning back to his terminal at the com-station. Another airman signaled the Colonel's attention.

"Sir—report coming in. Munitions has discovered C4 residue…" He paused to listen into his headset, his eyes on the ceiling. "…M-16 shell casings are everywhere and…hand grenade blast zones with shrapnel scoring." He looked at the Colonel with a frown. "They say it looks like it was a military operation, Sir. They're interviewing survivors right now." He jotted down some more notes.

The Colonel walked back to the window and looked out past the flight line—out into the vast span of desert to the north. What evil had lurked beyond the horizon last night? Who would have done such a thing?

Suddenly, the window glass rattled as a formation of F-16 fighters flew over the runway, pitched upward, and banked gracefully to the west. Its thunderous splendor only sidetracked his attention for a moment. He returned to pacing the floor.

A few hours passed before the final assessments were compiled. The good news—no radiation leaked from the compound. The rest—all bad news. Thirty-seven dead, ninety-four injured, some seriously. Most of the injuries, lethal or otherwise, were multiple gunshot wounds or shrapnel trauma. One building was a total loss, along with the sophisticated equipment that it housed. Most of the other buildings were blast damaged. Someone familiar with security circumvention had cut the perimeter fence. It had been a professional operation. Colonel Fallon, standing at the window again, decided he had enough information to prepare a press release.

He watched the last Med-Evac chopper land on the flight line below. Medical personnel transferred wounded Atomtech workers to waiting ambulances that raced off toward the base hospital, lights flashing and sirens wailing. A makeshift morgue had been set up in Atomtech's gymnasium. The dead would be evacuated later, after autopsies and identifications were completed. He rubbed his temples. This was going to be a long day.

* * *

Sending a plume of dust into the air, a blue van rumbled down a road that cut its way across the desert. Though the midday heat had dried Devin's clothes, his boots and socks still sopped from the pit. But now he missed the coolness of a wet shirt.

For the past thirty miles, he had said nothing to Toothless. The terror of the raid ravaged his mind. Anger boiled inside. He was now more determined than ever to end Curtis' quest for the 13th Power—he was too dangerous to possess it. Devin decided he'd concentrate on putting Atomtech back together after the impostor was put out of business. For that, Colonel Bruce Fallon was his only hope. Devin wiped away a bead of sweat trickling down his cheek. Maybe the Colonel would believe him now—after what had happened at Atomtech.

Devin stared out the window of his speeding van. Cactus and sage streaked by. As a dust devil swirled in the distance, dancing across the sandy flats, Devin thought about Colonel Fallon. A trusted friend, he was one of the few people with whom Devin socialized. Poker was their bond. On occasion, they'd head up to Reno for a few high-stake hands.

A smile cracked his lips as he remembered one of those all-nighters. He had beaten the beleaguered Colonel with the draw of an ace. Fallon lost it—accused him of cheating. What a fistfight. They ended up on the sidewalk out front with bloody noses and a warning from the casino—*never come back again.* As the memory replayed in his mind, a high-flying hawk, riding the thermals, lifted his hopes. The Colonel would surely help him stop Curtis now. Satisfied, Devin lit up a rank cigar.

"Smoke that damn thing outside," Toothless complained, batting at the smoke.

"Don't like it—don't breathe." Devin blew a puff in his face. "Just keep driving. Twenty miles to the highway—then go left. Got that?"

"Whatever you say, boss."

*   *   *

Toothless braked at the main gate to Indian Springs Air Force Base. The guard, a burly Security Policeman dressed in jungle fatigues, stood in front of a drawbar, signaling the dusty blue van to halt. Another guard with SP on his helmet approached the driver's window cautiously, as if expecting trouble. "What's your business here?"

Toothless just stared at him.

"We've come to see Colonel Fallon," Devin said.

"Let's see some IDs."

Toothless pulled a wet wallet out of his back pocket and fished out a soggy driver's license. "Flash flood."

Devin shrugged his shoulders. "I left home without it."

"Get out of the vehicle!" the SP ordered, backing away from the door.

Toothless heard the click of an M-16, a round from the clip sliding into the chamber. A guard, standing by the shack, brandished the weapon as if he intended to use it. Toothless snickered. Soldier Boy with the big gun didn't scare him. Shaking his head, he reached for the Luger tucked under his belt.

Devin held his arm. "We'll play their silly game."

As they got out of the van, several more SPs ran toward them with weapons drawn.

"Hands on your heads! Now!"

At gunpoint, they were led to the front of the van.

"Hit the ground—right here. Belly down!"

Toothless, trying to keep his chin off the hot pavement, glared at Devin. He should've let him shoot the bastards. Roughly, SPs slapped on handcuffs and frisked them. The Luger was quickly discovered.

"This has to be them," the guard said.

A siren wailed in the distance. Toothless craned his neck, looking down the street. Flashing lights on a security Jeep sped toward them. He spit. Did all Devin's friends treat him this good?

"Keep 'em covered," the guard ordered as he turned to meet the approaching officer.

As Lieutenant Briggs approached the main gate, he saw a group of guards surrounding two prisoners on the pavement. Some of his men were searching through a blue van. The squawk on the radio was barely audible over the wailing siren. "We have them in custody," came the report.

Briggs was relieved. All bases in southern Nevada were on a full-scale security alert in response to the disaster at Atomtech. An APB had been posted for a blue van seen speeding from the area. Now the suspected terrorists were at his front door. He stopped at the drawbar and shut off the siren. Leaving the overheads flashing, he jumped out and ran to the waiting SPs. "What's their story?"

"One has no ID," the guard said as they walked toward the prisoners. "Says his name is Walter Devin. The ugly one was armed with this." He showed him the Luger.

"And the van?"

"Nothing, Sir."

Briggs stepped up to the subdued men. They looked uncomfortable with their hands cuffed behind them. "Get 'em off the ground."

Several SPs grabbed the prisoners by their arms and lifted them to their feet. Devin's cold eyes and stern face caught Briggs' attention immediately. A shiver went up his spine. "What do you people want?"

"I demand to see Colonel Fallon."

"What for?"

"My company was attacked this morning. We barely escaped with our lives."

"You're referring to the explosion at Atomtech?"

"That *explosion* was a military assault on my facility—commandos and all." Devin spit. "Now take me to the Colonel and stop wasting my time."

Briggs stepped back and looked at his prisoners standing there shackled like criminals. They certainly looked like they'd had a bad day. Maybe Devin was telling the truth. Briggs went back to his Jeep and keyed the radio mike. "We're bringing them in 'til we talk to Colonel Fallon. Over."

* * *

As the Colonel sat at his desk writing his report for the media, an airman summoned him to the phone. "Indian Springs, Sir."

"What is it?"

The airman shrugged.

"Fallon, here."

"Sir—Lieutenant Briggs. We've got two men here. They drove up in a blue van. One guy claims to be Walter Devin. Says he's a friend of yours."

"Is he all right?"

"Claims to have been attacked by a military force of some kind. Wouldn't elaborate any further. Insists on seeing you—personally."

"Military?" A confirmation, Fallon thought.

"That's what he says, Sir."

"Put him on a chopper—ship him down here right away. Who's with him?"

"An ugly looking goon, his aide."

"Send them both."

Fallon hung up and turned his attention to the flight line outside his window. He crossed his arms over his chest and watched a Med-Evac helicopter rise from the pad. As it flew into the distance, he decided to hold off the press a while longer, at least until after he'd spoken with Devin. There had to be an accounting for the dead and wounded at Atomtech. A surge of anger gripped him. Vowing to track down the marauders, he swore he'd bring them to justice. The murderous military operation within his jurisdiction would be avenged.

Chapter Sixty-Seven
THE DEAD MAN'S WALTZ

At Indian Springs, Devin's handcuffs were removed and he was ushered into a holding cell with Toothless. Briggs thought they weren't dangerous but elected to be cautious anyway. Devin's complaints about being locked up fell on deaf ears. Toothless didn't complain about anything, except the loss of his Luger. Chow was served on green metal trays. Devin wasn't hungry. Toothless ate enough for three men.

While they waited for the Colonel, they showered and shaved. Afterwards, Devin took a nap. The Lieutenant woke him up. "Let's go," he said, unlocking the cell. "You're going on a chopper ride."

Blackhawk helicopter engines whined and rotors slapped overhead as Devin climbed in, Toothless right behind him. A spotter gave the pilots an all-clear signal. The chopper lifted from the pad with the smoothness of an elevator.

Watching out his window as the flight line fell away, Devin thought about how he would expose the impostor to Fallon and derail Curtis' dangerous quest for the 13th Power. He would pay dearly for what he had done to Atomtech. A satisfied smile came on Devin's face as the desert streaked by below.

The twenty-minute flight was over before he realized. Nellis AFB stretched out below him. As the chopper neared the landing pad, he spotted Colonel Fallon standing at the edge of the platform. "Shit is going to hit the fan," he said as the ride came to a gentle end. The engines whined to a stop. He jumped to the sun-scorched pad and rushed to the Colonel. "Am I glad to see you." They shook hands.

But the Colonel's greeting was more official. "What happened out there at your place, Devin?" he asked as he directed them toward the communications center.

"They came to kill me..."

"And me," Toothless put in, pacing along behind them. "But they killed Little Man."

"Who came to kill you?" the Colonel asked, looking first at Devin, then at Toothless.

"Let's talk about that inside—say over a cold beer and a good cigar." Devin reached in his shirt pocket and plucked out a fat one to tempt his friend.

"Follow me."

They pushed through the double doors of the Central Communications Building. Cool air-conditioning made the desert's heat seem far away. As they rode the elevator, Colonel Fallon said, "I have the body count, Walter. We've been evacuating them all morning. More to come this afternoon."

"Just how many people did I lose?"

"So far—thirty-seven dead, ninety-four wounded, and some of those, seriously."

The elevator door slid open but Devin just stood there, anger and shock rooting him to the floor. Thirty-seven dead? If it weren't for Toothless and Little Man it would have been thirty-eight.

And if not for Susan's rescue of the aggravating private eye, the pit of horror wouldn't have been an escape route, only the death trap he'd intended. It was fate. He believed in fate. Move a single grain of sand on the shore and change the history of the world. He felt suddenly dizzy. This time fate was good to him— bad for thirty-seven of his people, and the ninety-four who were wounded. For their fate, Curtis must pay.

Stepping out of the elevator, Devin lit a cigar with his Zippo. "Get me that beer," he said. "We've got to talk about Curtis' fate. And when the bastard's dead, I'm gonna waltz on his coffin."

Chapter Sixty-Eight
SCIENCE FICTION AND HISTORY

A foaming mug of beer slid along the bar, sloshing to a stop in front of Devin. Another slid toward Toothless who smiled his spacious grin and chugged the mug dry. Belching like a sailor, he slammed the empty mug on the bar. "More." The bartender worked a gurgling tap. Toothless picked up a magazine.

Colonel Fallon lit his cigar. Resolving the tragedy at Atomtech was top priority. Though the officers' lounge wasn't his idea of an official meeting place, given the circumstances, it would have to do. He faked a smile and took a puff. "All right, Walter. You've got your beer and cigar. Now tell me what happened at Atomtech last night."

"I warned you about him, Bruce. But you wouldn't listen." Devin took a swig of beer.

"I'm listening now. Who did it?"

Elbows on the bar, smoke swirled from Devin's cigar. "I told you Curtis was up to something. And I was right. Now my people are dead and Atomtech is in ruins. This could have been avoided."

"Just tell me where he is."

"At Solartech Labs in Simi Valley, searching for the key to our existence. The 13th Power is at his fingertips."

Colonel Fallon took a drag on his cigar. Maybe he should've listened when Devin had warned him about Curtis. But there was nothing he could have done. Curtis hadn't broken any laws or caused any trouble, not that anyone knew about. Fallon couldn't beat down Curtis' door if he wasn't throwing a party. But now things were different. First he had to get the facts. "What's the 13th Power?"

Devin looked up, face pinched with concern. "The end of the world, Bruce."

An awkward silence permeated the officers' lounge as the Colonel pondered Devin's words. The end of the world? He looked at Toothless for a reaction but found him thumbing through a girly magazine, unconcerned. When he looked back at Devin, he saw a familiar look in his eyes—one he'd seen before, in the eyes of a young bombardier over Hanoi in 1972, just before he pushed the bomb release button for the first time. Carlton Nash, a fine lieutenant back then, seemed to be crying out for some way to stop what was about to happen. The dread in Devin's eyes was as real as Carlton's. But Fallon couldn't comprehend the threat of the 13th Power. The end of the world couldn't be real. He sat down on the barstool next to Devin, his friend, the harbinger of doom. "Tell me about it, Walter."

Devin clasped his hands around the beer mug. "This goes back a long way, Bruce."

Toothless turned another page of his magazine.

"Einstein predicted mathematically that matter could be converted into energy. Then Cockcroft and Walton put Einstein's theory to the test by splitting the first atom in a machine they called a particle accelerator. By violently dissecting the atom, they succeeded in locating and measuring its nucleus—ten to the minus power of twelve in centimeters. The 12th Power was theirs.

"But it wasn't until the United States put together the Manhattan Project in New Mexico that the 12th Power showed its muscle. Remember Alamogordo on July 16, 1945? With that first atomic bomb blast, Oppenheimer proved that chain-reaction fission made the 12th Power an awesome power to possess. The world was changed forever. Missiles of death were pointed at everyone, just waiting for one lunatic to push a button. We built our bomb shelters and our missile silos and propelled the civilized world into a Cold War of threats and counter threats. Our only hope for survival was the promise of mutual annihilation. It's a miracle we survived." Devin took a swig of beer. "We won't be so lucky with the 13th Power."

A vein in Fallon's forehead throbbed. "Why not?"

"In theory, there exists a subatomic particle, a boson called the Higgs, the particle that generates the atomic strong force—hidden deep within the atom's nucleus—the ultimate power that gives matter mass. Take away the Higgs and Einstein's relativity goes out the window. E won't equal M C squared anymore. No, sir. The rules of physics that govern our universe could be altered forever."

Fallon still wasn't any closer to solving the Atomtech tragedy. "Get to the point, Walter. What's all this science mumbo jumbo have to do with what happened last night?"

Devin took a breath. "Enter Ray Crawford. He wants to add his name to that elite list of famous scientists by achieving the 13th Power. Curtis recruited him to conduct the experiments. But the sons of bitches don't have the professional restraint or moral convictions to safeguard the atomic cosmos. They would plunder the atom's nucleus to meet their own selfish agendas and damn the rest of the world. On top of that, Curtis is an outsider, uneducated in the field. But he's assembled the equipment and scientists that will do it for him. If he gets his hands on the Higgs, he'll exploit the 13th Power at the expense of the entire world. Believe me, he doesn't give a damn about anybody but himself. Don't underestimate him like I did." Devin chugged the mug and summoned the bartender for another.

Colonel Fallon waited. "Tell me, Walter. What threat of worldwide destruction could the 13th Power produce that is worse than the 12th Power anyway? A bigger bomb?"

"Disintegration. By stripping an atom of the Higgs, it comes apart, violently, sending tiny particles outward at the speed of light. They collide with other atoms releasing still more Higgs and more atoms come apart. Poof. They're gone. Elements and molecules disappear. No big bang. Just silent oblivion."

Devin trembled and took another drag on his cigar.

"Worse yet, the 13th Power experiments are dangerous. Disintegration is the side effect of siphoning off the Higgs. If they screw up, our reality could be altered forever. They could open a void into the universe, a giant swirling funnel of anti-matter, consuming the atoms of everything around it and sucking the world out of existence. Talk about a science project gone bad! The Russians tried it—they failed miserably. Pretty scary stuff when you consider the amateurs that are about to attempt it now."

Fallon examined his cigar. "Just what do they expect to get by doing this?"

"My guess would be the Higgs boson, at any cost. Once they have it, there's no way of knowing *what* they will end up with. But you can bet it won't be what they expected."

"But what could they do with it if they got it?"

Devin stared into his beer. "Who knows? Maybe they could develop some kind of doomsday weapon orbiting in space like Star Wars, or Buck Rogers' ray guns or something. The government's been trying to do that for years now. Since Reagan anyway."

"That's not possible, Walter. It's pure science fiction."

"Tell that to Jules Verne, Colonel. His science fiction is now history. Don't discount the power of science to turn fiction into reality. It happens all the time."

Chapter Sixty-Nine
ENLIGHTENMENT

The Colonel stood and paced. Devin watched him for a moment, and then went back to his beer. He thought he'd let Fallon stew over the possibilities of the 13th Power for a while.

Several minutes passed in silence. Except for the sound of Toothless flipping through pages of his magazine and the Colonel's footsteps, nothing else stirred in the officers' lounge. Anymore, Devin didn't care what Curtis wanted with the 13th Power. Now he was only concerned with settling the score—to destroy Curtis' precious project and snuff out his life. Smiling at the thought, Devin took another swallow of beer.

Fallon walked up, frowning. "Are you sure Curtis could do this, Walter?"

"Absolutely."

"Then we have to stop him." He hesitated. "But how?"

Devin rotated the cigar in his fingertips, ashes dropping on the bar. "Military force, Bruce—just like he did to me last night."

Fallon sat on a barstool. "Why did he attack *you*?"

Devin gulped. He knew he was in trouble now. People had been killed, property destroyed, all on his orders. But he had to do something to stop Curtis. The truth would surely make it look like Curtis had acted in self-defense. But the 13th Power experiments had to be stopped, and to that end any means was justified. Now Devin had to think of a way to enlighten the Colonel without looking like some kind of homicidal maniac. First rule of survival, always blame someone else. Devin put the mug on the bar. "I was trying to derail his 13th Power project."

The Colonel looked concerned. "What did you do, Walter?"

"At first, when I found out Curtis was recruiting Janis Mackey from Colorado, I sent some men to delay his cab so he would miss his flight and a meeting with Curtis in San Francisco. My men ended up dead.

"So I sent some other guys to persuade Ray Crawford that he could get hurt dealing with Curtis. Shook Ray up a bit is all.

"Then I sent three of my toughest bruisers to detain Janis for questioning. They got the shit beat out of 'em. So I told them to disable Janis' limo. The boneheads decided that blowing it up was a good way to do that. When they followed Janis to a mansion, I told them to send him a message. They sent him a bomb instead. I tell you—can't get good help these days."

Fallon didn't look sympathetic.

Undeterred, Devin continued with his tale. "I hired a private eye who discovered Curtis was after the 13th Power. From then on, I tracked his scientists by satellite, trying to neutralize them as they made their way to Simi Valley. I thought that eliminating his hired minds would derail his project."

"Don't play word games with me, Walter. *Neutralize* and *eliminate* sound like *kill* and *murder* to me. Say it isn't so."

"I was desperate, Bruce."

The Colonel glared. "Desperate enough to use your Cobra? Lieutenant Evans didn't go loony—did he? He was acting on your orders—wasn't he?"

"Burt went on a rampage. He never did like cops." Devin gulped a swallow of beer. That was his story and he was sticking to it. The Colonel would play hell trying to prove otherwise.

"Your story stinks, Walter."

"Look! Curtis had to be stopped. I failed. Somehow, he caught on and executed a military strike against Atomtech. I never thought he was capable of anything like that. I tell you, Bruce. He's a dangerous man. And his real name isn't Frank Curtis either. Try Melvin Anderson. Check him out. You'll find he's supposed to be dead."

The Colonel stared, his eyes still disbelieving. "How did *you* get wind of all this?"

"I met Curtis during an official visit at Solartech Labs, right after he took over the place. I recognized him as Melvin Anderson from a carbon-dating seminar I attended in Zurich some twenty years ago. We sat across from each other at the conference table. Yeah, Melvin Anderson, a con man if ever I saw one. His alias made me suspicious so I hired a private eye to keep tabs on him. Melvin may have been well-respected back in those days, mostly because of his father, but history showed him for the snake that he really is."

Fallon thought about that for a moment. Back home on the farm in Idaho, when a snake escaped into a hole, they'd flush it out with fire and cut its head off with a shovel. Devin had opened a viper pit. Fallon could see it was going to take a lot of fire and a big shovel to deal with Curtis and his 13th Power project. Now was the time to start thinking about how to put an end to it. He crushed his cigar in an ashtray.

"Finish your beers, boys," he said as he got up and headed toward the door. "I'll send someone to show you to your quarters. Get some rest. You're going to need it." He walked out of the officers' lounge, his footsteps fading down the hallway.

Devin looked at Toothless. "Like I said, shit is gonna fly."

Toothless tossed his magazine on the bar and grinned his ugly grin.

Chapter Seventy

STONEWALLED

Fallon slammed the office door and walked past his desk to the window. As he looked out at rows of Apache helicopters parked on the tarmac, he mulled over what Devin had told him. How could Curtis have come up with enough firepower to launch a military attack against Atomtech? A civilian with military capability didn't seem possible. And the armament that was used—C4 explosives, M-16s, and hand grenades, made it all the more impossible. How many men had it taken? How had they gotten in and out? By land? By air? He picked up the telephone.

"Sergeant—get me the tower." The phone rang almost immediately.

"Tower. Airman Brown."

"Colonel Fallon, SP," he said. "I need the radar recordings for last night's air traffic. Who do I need to talk to?"

"I'll connect you with Las Vegas Center, Sir."

"Very well." The phone clicked and rang again.

A woman's voice answered. "Las Vegas Center—how may I help you?"

"This is Colonel Fallon calling from Nellis Air Force Base. I'm investigating the Atomtech tragedy."

"Horrible."

"I need last night's radar recordings for southern Nevada."

"They're tied up by the FAA right now," she said.

"Isn't that unusual?"

"Who are we to question them?"

"Why is the FAA interested?"

"Probably has something to do with a radar echo that disappeared from our screens about twenty-five miles southwest of Desert Rock this morning. Our controllers thought the aircraft had been destroyed in midair or something, but before they could initiate a search of the area, the echo returned—going the other direction. Just disappeared and reappeared—like magic."

"How long was the aircraft lost on radar?" The line was suddenly muffled, as though she had put her hand over the mouthpiece.

A moment later she replied, "I can't answer that, Sir. You'll have to take your inquiries to the FAA. Sorry." The phone line clicked dead.

"The FAA, hell!" He slammed the receiver down. That tape was important. It could help him determine the origin and destination of that aircraft. Maybe it wasn't significant, but then again, it might be a breakthrough. Needing to know for sure, he grabbed the telephone again.

"Get me the FAA Regional Office."

"Right away, Sir."

A recording came over the line. "Thank you for calling the FAA Nevada office. The regional director wishes to convey to the traveling public that we are doing everything possible to insure the safety of air traffic in this country."

"Yeah, yeah."

"All of our agents are currently busy with other calls. Please stay on the line and we will answer your call as soon as possible."

"Shit!" He pushed the speakerphone button. The music playing on hold annoyed him. He paced the floor waiting for it to end. Excited about the discovery of a mysterious aircraft in the vicinity, he was impatient to get some answers. Too many people were awaiting his report. The music stopped and another recording came on.

"Thank you for holding. Someone will be with you shortly."

Colonel Fallon sighed in disgust and sat at his desk. On a pad, he began writing notes in an effort to piece together a time line of events related to the Atomtech disaster. His outline had a lot of blanks to be filled in.

"Agent Lester—may I help you?" came from the speakerphone.

"This is Colonel Fallon at Nellis. I'm investigating the Atomtech tragedy last night and I need a copy of the radar recordings from Las Vegas Center. Have one available for my courier."

"Sorry, Sir. A malfunctioning player accidentally destroyed the tape you're referring to. Burned to a crisp." The agent cleared his throat. "Is there anything else I can help you with?"

Without replying, Fallon hung up in disbelief. The FAA was no help at all. He flexed his jaw. A crucial piece of evidence destroyed? Or so they claimed.

Thinking of another possibility, he picked up the phone again. "Get me General Brigham at the Pentagon."

"I'll ring you when I get connected, Sir."

"Very well." He went back to his outline of events and wrote *Curtis* and *Solartech Labs* on top of the page. He drew an arrow between them. Below them he wrote *Melvin Anderson*. He drew an arrow to *Curtis*. The phone rang.

"General—how are you?"

"Late for my tee off, Bruce."

"I'll make this brief. I'm investigating the Atomtech tragedy..."

"Horrible accident," the General injected. "It's all over the news. What's going on out there, Colonel?"

"That's what I'm trying to find out but my investigation has been stonewalled at every turn. I think the military is involved. Can you help me with that?"

The General coughed. "What are you suggesting, a United States military operation against its own citizens? Not out of this office, I tell you."

"Certainly not, General. But how about the Corbett satellite? Could we get some reconnaissance information from it, radio transmissions, audio, video, anything?"

"The CIA commissioned it yesterday for something in Central America. You know how much trouble they're getting into down there."

"Then will you check with some of your CIA contacts—see what you can learn?"

"The CIA can *rot* as far as I'm concerned."

Colonel Fallon understood. General Brigham and the CIA had a falling out two years ago. He recalled the flack over it. In fact, the President had threatened to bust Brigham down to Corporal if he persisted with his accusations of a conspiracy between the White House and the CIA. A special committee, appointed by the Justice Department, convinced Congress the General was just pissed off because the President had taken Star Wars away from him. He was nearly imprisoned for misappropriation of funds. In the end, Brigham held no fondness for the President, either.

"Sorry, Sir. I wasn't thinking. Enjoy your golf game." The

Colonel hung up with yet another dead end. Frustrated, he looked again at his outline, focusing on *Melvin Anderson.* Devin had been adamant about Curtis being his alias—an impostor. Fallon double underlined Melvin's name. What could the FBI dig up on this guy? He reached for the phone again.

Chapter Seventy-One

SOLARTECH LABS

Curtis watched the C-130 transport disappear over Simi Valley. He decided to concentrate his attention on the arrival of his scientists. They had made a grand entrance.

Scanning the crowd for Alex, Curtis noticed the newcomers huddled together, the bond between them obvious. He could only wonder what they had been through. But there would be time to get that story later. Ray and Janis needed medical attention and they all needed food and rest. He would give them that much before pressing them for details.

For now, the California sun shined much too intensely to be standing around in a full-length black coat. The air-conditioned executive car beckoned him. He handed his hat to Jonathan and ducked inside. The door closed and the cool air surrounded them.

"That went well, sir," Jonathan said.

"Very well, indeed. Let's go!"

Jonathan motioned to the driver. The executive car weaved its way through the lingering crowd toward the airfield gate.

* * *

Alex commandeered the nearest staff car and invited Susan and Steve to ride along. Sitting in the front seat, Steve's gaze went to Curtis' car. "There he goes."

Susan squeezed his arm. "Don't do anything stupid. Please."

He didn't answer.

Alex asked, "Do what?"

"Nothing," Steve said. "Don't you think you better get your boys some medical attention?"

Alex, seeing Ray standing on the tarmac holding his arm, spoke into the wrist radio. "Station two, get the Doc ready. He's got customers."

The tiny speaker squawked. "Roger."

Alex drove around the crowd to where Ray stood with Janis, Lisa and Lo. "We gotta get you to the clinic, Ray. Hop in."

Lisa opened the door and slid in after Ray. Janis and Lo

squeezed in next to them.

Steve turned to the back seat. "I'm Steve Raven and this is Susan Rivers." He looked at the bandage on Ray's arm. "How did you catch that bullet, Ray?"

Ray looked at him for a moment, a deep frown across his brow. "How did you know my name?"

"I know a whole lot more than you think."

Susan patted his shoulder. "He's a private eye."

Steve smiled slyly. "I saw you at the Balli Club when I was disguised as a janitor. Remember?"

"Ah—yeah," Ray said. "Disguised?"

"The beard makes me invisible. Devin hired me to find out what you brainards were up to. We've since had a falling out."

Janis shot him an angry glare. Alex wasn't sure if Janis was going to hit Steve or not. Driving on, Alex listened while watching Janis in the rearview mirror.

"Now don't get the wrong idea, here," Steve said. "I had nothing to do with your problems."

Janis didn't look relieved.

Alex could feel the tension in the air. "He's on our side now. That's what counts."

Steve bobbed his head in agreement. "Who shot you?"

Ray recounted his brush with death as Janis stared at the private eye. By the look on Janis' face, Alex thought he wasn't convinced about Steve's loyalty. Nor was Lisa. But he wasn't sure if she felt uneasy about Steve or the story Ray was telling him.

Susan seemed especially interested in Ray's story. Her mouth hung open when he got to the part about Lawson's death. She looked at Lisa. "You shot the bastard?"

Lisa looked at the floor. She didn't seem proud of herself, but sullen, like she wished there had been another way to deal with the crooked cop.

Finishing his short rendition, Ray grimaced in pain.

Steve said, "Damn! You're lucky to be alive." He looked at Alex. "Devin isn't going to let this thing go—you know that."

Alex ground his teeth, frustrated. He accelerated the staff car toward the airfield gate.

Solartech Field Road was paved and neatly striped, lined with swaying palm trees and well-groomed grass waysides. A sign directed traffic to go left for the main gate and Simi Valley, or right for the compound security checkpoint. Alex went right.

The staff car slowed at a stone archway, where video cameras recorded their arrival. A heavily armed security officer saluted as the car went by. Alex activated his wrist radio. "Station two, ETA three minutes."

"They're waiting," came the reply.

Ray's heightened pulse rate made his shoulder ache. He just wanted to get this over with. Doctors, needles, and blood were nowhere on his list of favorite things. His stomach churned just thinking about it. He watched out the window to get his mind off what was to come. Lisa held his hand. Though he found some comfort in that, he wished she wasn't attracted to Janis. The thought of those two together rekindled an anger he'd been harnessing. Pain stung his shoulder again—this time with intensity.

The staff car stopped in front of C-Wing. Steve and Susan got out.

"The cafeteria's inside," Alex said. "Catch up with you later. Save some food for us."

Janis moved to the front seat and closed the door. "I'm starving."

"Doc needs to look at that hand first." Alex drove away from C-Wing. At a stop sign, he turned right and headed up a ramp to an elevated viaduct between two stainless-steel buildings, five stories high. Tinted plate glass windows on both sides reflected images off each other, giving the illusion of driving through a kaleidoscope. Ray watched Janis' expression—his face beaming like a kid admiring a Christmas tree.

"Incredible!" Janis said.

The staff car passed under glass enclosed pedestrian walkways, catwalks that bridged the gap between the two buildings high above. Up ahead, a huge steel arch spanned the viaduct, its facing inscribed with the words, *Welcome to Solartech Labs. Gateway to the Atomic Universe.*

"Oh, my God," Lisa said. "Will you look at that?"

Lo looked impressed in spite of his reservations about tigers and teeth.

"I told you, Janis," Ray said. "This place isn't like anything you've ever seen."

Alex cleared his throat. "This is the main complex, the heart of Solartech Labs. All the technical work is done within these walls. You'll get the grand tour tomorrow."

The staff car sped under the archway and into a vehicle reception lobby. Centered in the lobby, an array of huge glass doors marked the entrance to this hi-tech facility. Chrome and black escalators moved up and down just inside the atrium where video cameras swept back and forth in ever-silent vigil. Ramps to an indoor parking garage extended up both sides of the lobby. A horn reverberated from somewhere.

Alex hung a left. Squealing tires echoed through the steel-girdered lobby as the staff car swung onto a ramp that spiraled upward. Around and around he drove higher and higher until the car broke out onto the rooftop parking area. Ray squinted from the sudden burst of sunshine.

To the right, a helicopter pad extended out from the roof, its windsock swaying lazily in the breeze. To the left, a fountain, which erupted every hour from a pool five stories below, gushed water as high as the roof. Ray was pleased with the amazed expression on Janis' face.

The staff car stopped in front of an elevator lobby. Double doors swung open. Several personnel in white gowns wheeled a gurney out. Ray's stomach rolled over. They were coming for him.

Chapter Seventy-Two
THE RULES OF PHYSICS

The executive car screeched to a stop under a carport in front of the presidential quarters. A little gray lizard darted across polished granite steps and scurried up a white marble pillar. From the safety of its lofty perch, it peered at an attendant rushing out the revolving door to greet the CEO of Solartech Labs. A pop from the car door made the lizard cock his head sideways to get a better look. When Curtis emerged and donned his black hat, the light-footed little creature ran for cover under a shaded eve.

Curtis tapped the golden staff on the driveway. He had to maintain his facade even if he was at home. Jonathan followed him into the lobby, the staff ticking on the tile floor as they made their way to the Penthouse elevator. Curtis punched a code on a keypad mounted to the wall. The door opened with a ding and he stepped inside.

Jonathan didn't follow him. "See you at the barbecue party." He headed toward the elevators on the other side of the lobby.

The door closed, encasing Curtis in a chamber of mirrored walls draped in gold velvet. Soft lights around the ceiling made the golden draperies glimmer. Mirrors projected the light, giving the illusion of sparkling glitter floating in the air. The elevator ascended smoothly.

Removing his hat, he wiped sweat from his brow with his coat sleeve. He was tired but too excited to care. As he leaned against the back wall, he caught a glimpse of his face in the mirror. Wrinkles on his forehead and cheeks reflected the wear and tear of time. Sagging skin under his eyes made him look older than he felt. But he grinned anyway. This was the face of the master.

When the elevator reached the Penthouse, the door opened into a spacious parlor. A large crystal chandelier hung from the ceiling. Golden light beams scintillated around the room. After hanging his hat and coat on a rack by the elevator door, he walked briskly into the front room.

He headed straight for the bar, poured himself a glass of brandy, kicked off his boots, and settled into an easy chair by the fireplace. He laid the golden staff across his lap and stroked its smooth, shinny surface, cautious of the eagle head's emerald eyes. After he propped his feet up on the hassock, he took a moment to savor the sweet vapor of his drink. Peach—his favorite. He loosened his tie, took one sip—then another, and began to relax. Enjoying the moment, his mind wandered as he settled lower into the chair. Another sip or two later, he felt himself slipping into slumber.

Suddenly, a crash of thunder rumbled through the room and jolted him from his seat. His golden staff fell to the floor. He threw up his arms, shielding himself from a blast of wind that whipped in through a shattered window. The broken sash flailed violently as the tempest blew in a torrent of rain.

Shards of glass littered the carpet and cut his feet as he struggled, step by step, to reach the window. Something was drawing him to look out. Whatever it was, terrified him. When he peered out the window, he saw a world that made his stomach twist in horror.

Lightning bolts cracked the dark sky and lit up the valley's boulder fields. The ground rolled like an ocean in a gale. Thunder banged again. Wind blew. Rain pelted his face as he looked up at spinning clouds glowing red, then orange, then yellow, and then back to red. Rotating like a giant pinwheel, the storm spun off funnel clouds that twisted down and snaked across the ground. Flashing blue streaks of lightning spit fingers earthward and made sinkholes appear. They gobbled up trees and rocks, filled with water, and froze over.

"What in God's name?"

An icy hail began to pelt him, bouncing across the room, and melting into sparkling fireballs. He spun away from the window, ducked and covered his head with his hands.

Again, the sound of thunder rolled into the room. He watched in horror as jagged fingers of static electricity arched over the sill and wormed their way toward him, randomly forking to the ceiling and the walls. They crackled, sizzled, and hissed as they moved blindly about the ravaged room.

Heart pounding, he screamed and turned to run from the stormy window and its lethal tongue. He ran hard but he wasn't moving—he wasn't getting away.

"OH, SHIT! RUN, DAMN IT! RUN!"

But he couldn't. He felt a heavy weight on his back. It was more than he could carry. His feet were sluggish and hard to move. The room was going by in slow motion as the deadly electric limb arced closer and closer. There was no escape. With adrenaline rushing through his veins, he turned back into the tempest to face the approaching nemesis. But the arching death had disappeared, leaving behind the ionized smell of battery acid hanging in the air.

Suddenly, the window raced toward him. Through the jagged opening he looked down at the lab complex from where the storm was spawned. "BASTARDS!" he yelled above the gale. "YOU STARTED WITHOUT ME!"

Without warning, the wind and rain stopped. The storm held its bitter breath with the stillness of a funeral parlor.

"What...?"

A shove came from behind. He tumbled out the window into thick, sulfur-laced air. The dizzying sensation of falling engulfed him as he looked up to the window. Jonathan was waving goodbye. The horror of death swirled in his mind. So this was how it ended. He struck the ground, numbed by the impact.

His body jerked. Breaking glass ripped at his consciousness. He grabbed the golden staff and leaped from the chair. With his heart hammering in his chest, he looked around the room. Except for the brandy glass lying shattered on the fireplace hearth, nothing was broken. Everything was in place, including the ominous window. Gasping, he tried to shake the cloudy nightmare from his mind. But the terror lingered.

Hot shower water tingled his body, which still trembled in the wake of his terrifying dream. Had he seen a premonition? Though he knew that fooling around with the atomic structure was tricky, he wondered if his imagination was being fed by unfounded fears. Could mutated atoms spread like a cancer, changing natural events into bizarre phenomenon with catastrophic consequences? Would the rules of physics be nullified?

Steam fogged the shower stall glass, blurring his reflection. The hot water dissolved the tension in his back. With steamy mist swirling around him, he thought about other scientists who'd been splitting atoms for decades, attempting to study the building blocks of matter. They'd slammed nuclei together in supercolliders without changing the basic nature of things. So what if he was going to do the same thing—only at higher speeds—the speed of light to be precise. Nuclei would just be broken into much smaller pieces of short-lived particles. That's all. How could the results be any more dangerous?

Or was it more dangerous because he was going to contain the atomic strong force, to capture the Higgs boson, to possess the 13th Power? Unlike other scientists, he wasn't going to let the prize get away.

He put his head under the shower spray. Containing and controlling the atomic force could be dangerous. It was risky. His father's words came back: *Risk nothing, gain nothing. Risk nothing, gain nothing.*

He twisted the shower knobs and stepped out. Grabbing a towel, he thought about Ray and Janis. They weren't so smart. Interested only in the science of the 13th Power, they were completely unaware of the power they would unleash. But the only man that could have stopped them knew. Devin! And he was dead.

Chapter Seventy-Three
THE BARBECUE PARTY

Holding Susan's hand, Steve strolled onto the patio behind the cafeteria at C-Wing. Smoke, rising from the barbecue pit, scented the air with the aroma of hickory and tangy sauce. His stomach churned with anticipation.

Several cooks wearing white aprons and towering chef's hats attended the grill, flipping steaks and burgers. Other servers worked behind a long table of sides and fixings. Curtis had spared no expense for this occasion. The finest meats, produce, and junk food were abundant—enough to feed an army.

A light breeze rustled the canopy above the bar, shifting Steve's attention to Solartech Lab's employees and supervisors gathered around, drinks in hand, sipping and talking among themselves. Boisterous laughter occasionally rose above the hubbub. Hawaiian music drifted across the patio, giving the festivities a Polynesian flair.

Susan tugged on his shirt. "Over there." She pointed to the food tables.

"All right—I'm coming." He scanned the crowd looking for Curtis, even as she pulled him toward the buffet. Not seeing Curtis around the bar, he quickly surveyed the courtyard. Most of the patio tables scattered about the lawn were vacant, their gold umbrellas flapping lazily in the breeze. Swaying palm trees adorned the walkway leading to a swimming pool. Again, he didn't see Curtis.

As he followed Susan's persistent lead toward the food, he glanced down at the .45 holstered under his short-sleeved shirt. It wasn't concealed very well. But he believed it was better to have a gun and not need one, than to need a gun and not have one. And this was no place to be caught without one.

Before they got to the table, Susan stopped abruptly and pulled him close, her eyes filled with concern. "Do you have to go through with this?"

"Don't worry."

"If I don't—who will?"

He pursed his lips and stared at her. Back in their suite, while dressing for the party, she had expressed concern for his safety. Not being used to dealing with someone else's feelings, he felt annoyed by her persistence. Hell—he'd been dealing with bad guys all his life. Now all of a sudden she thought he needed worrying about. "I can take care of myself."

Her beautiful eyebrows arched. "Like you did in Devin's pit? You'll end up dead."

So...okay...she was right about the pit. He'd still be wallowing in the slop if she hadn't saved his neck. "But that was different."

"Dead is dead, Steve. There is *no* difference." Looking as if she had made her point, she started walking toward the table again.

Steve followed her, thinking maybe he should be extra careful.

She looked over the selections at the food table and handed him a plate. "Don't make this your last meal."

Feeling mothered, he scooped up some potato salad and coleslaw and grabbed a handful of hot wings as he walked down the buffet line behind her. She looked great. Her dress, a flowing silk gown brought up by housekeeping, accented her fluid motion. Smiling to the server, she requested a chicken breast. He set an especially plump one on her plate. She was good with people, not shy to talk frankly and with an air of confidence. He liked that. Her sweetness seemed contagious to those around her.

He looked over the menu on the chalkboard. The skewered shrimp kabob with green peppers and artichoke hearts looked good. "I'll have the shrimp thing." He pointed to the chalkboard.

The server looked at the board. "Sorry—we're all out of that, sir. You'll have to pick something else."

"What?" He was sure he read it right. Looking again, there it was in white on black. His cheeks burned. The solution seemed obvious. "Why is it still on the chalkboard? You run out of something, you erase it. Don't make me out to look like an idiot." His angry voice boomed above the crowd. He pulled back his shirt panel, revealing the .45.

A spoon clanged on the floor. The server stepped back, trembling. The din of conversation went silent, everyone's attention now on Steve.

Susan tugged on his shirt. "Never mind, dear. Have a steak kabob instead," she said, forcing a smile. Steve's tough-guy attitude and hair-trigger temper was probably the only reason he'd survived in his line of work. Could his anger go so far as blind rage? She didn't think so. She'd seen his softer side. But now he had the attention of these partygoers, a dangerous thing if someone were to take him seriously. She needed to defuse him before he got himself killed. "Just don't shoot the poor guy 'til *after* dinner."

Steve covered up his gun and growled at the server. "Erase it before you piss off somebody who's not as nice as I am."

"Right away, sir." The server went to the chalkboard and rubbed off the shrimp selection with the palm of his hand. Another server took his place and held up a juicy skewer of steak adorned with plump mushrooms and green pepper slices. "This one satisfactory, sir?"

"Fine." Steve shot a menacing glance at the bar crowd. They quickly went back to minding their own business.

Sitting alone at a patio table, dressed in a Hawaiian shirt and green Bermuda shorts, Judas slid sunglasses down his nose and watched the fracas in the serving line, just the kind of thing he was policing for, troublemakers within the organization. Because he was the kind of weasel who would rat on his own mother, he liked spying on the employees of Solartech Labs. His reputation had instilled fear in them. Fear meant control. Control meant power. And Curtis gave him a free rein. He took another sip of his iced tea, and crossing his hairy legs, kept an eye on the irritating stranger.

With heaping plates and napkins in hand, Steve led Susan to the courtyard and selected a shady table. He sat facing the patio, as he would never have his back to a crowd or the center of a room. It wasn't safe that way—especially after the show he'd just put on. Now, everyone knew he had a mean streak. They'd step aside for him. They wouldn't dare interfere with his plans.

He forked a chunk of steak off the skewer, keeping one eye on the patio. The rich impostor could appear at any time.

Payday.

Chapter Seventy-Four
SOLARTECH MEDICAL

Janis, with Lisa at his side, stood in front of the rooftop entrance to Solartech Medical and waved goodbye to the staff car as it spun around and drove away. Alex and Lo were headed for the maintenance garage to get their luggage out of the car. They were going to take everything over to Tamarack Hall, the employee's quarters, a place with a soft bed, a place Janis longed to be, fast asleep. But not yet. He followed Ray into the clinic, the medical team leading the way.

Inside the atrium, large ferns grew to the ceiling on both sides of the elevators. A huge chrome-framed photo of a Rega air-ambulance helicopter hung over a waterfall that flowed down tiers of moss-rock and trickled into a shimmering pool. Coins, glittering reminders of wishes once made, reflected from the shallow bottom. Lisa knelt at the pool's edge and ran her fingers through the water. Janis wondered what she was thinking. Was she silently wishing for something? What could it be? The elevator doors slid open. He reached for her hand and they went in after Ray.

On the ride to the infirmary, an antiseptic smell permeated the elevator. Ray hugged Lisa, and with a nervous smile, looked at the nearest attendant who must have noticed his apprehension. "We'll have you fixed up in no time," he said assuredly.

"I'm hungry enough to eat the damn bullet," Ray said.

"You'll be eating ribs at the barbecue party before you know it."

The door opened into a brightly-lit corridor.

"We'll be waiting," Lisa said as the medical team led Ray down the hall.

Another doctor approached Janis. "I'm Dr. Lucero. Let me take a look at that hand, Professor."

"Oh—this little cut?" He showed the doctor.

"This little cut needs cleaning and stitches."

Janis knew he was going to hate this.

"Follow me."

They walked down the hall and turned into a small room.

"Sit right here." Dr. Lucero pointed to a folding chair next to a table. "And set your hand like this." He situated it precisely—palm up, fingers straight. "Now hold it right there." He turned to a drawer under the counter and started rummaging through it.

A nervous shudder went through Janis' stomach. The room shined bright white and smelled of alcohol, not his idea of a fun place.

"Let's see. I need this—and some of this. Oh yeah, and this for sure." Lucero held up a big plastic hypodermic.

Janis grimaced.

From a brown glass jar on the counter, the doctor drew a liquid into the syringe. "Peroxide and water solution—to clean the wound." He laughed, probably at Janis' wide eyes.

"Very funny," Janis said with a sigh of relief.

"You'll think *funny* until I start scrubbing that little cut. It'll feel like the Grand Canyon is on fire in the palm of your hand, Professor."

With that, the doctor sat down at the table and began to wash the dried-up wound. Janis winced. But he was tough. He didn't want Lisa to think he was a big baby.

The wound came open and began to bleed as the doctor rubbed away the scab. He squirted the solution from the syringe into the gaping cut and rubbed some more.

Janis meshed his teeth. Excruciating pain knifed up his arm. He almost didn't care *what* Lisa thought. Almost.

Satisfied the wound was clean, the doctor grabbed a small vial and another syringe—a smaller one with a skinny needle on it.

Novocain began to numb the pain. Janis never thought he would be so happy to get a shot. He only wished it were a shot of Scotch. Double.

"Let that go to work for a few minutes," Lucero said, placing a clean gauze pad on the open wound. He popped the needle from the syringe, tossed it into the disposal chute, and patted Janis' shoulder. "I'll be right back." He walked out the door, closing it gently behind him.

Lisa strutted toward Janis, smiling. "Way to go, cowboy." She kneaded his shoulders.

Her fingers felt as soothing as the medication numbing his hand. "Lisa...?"

"Just, relax," she said, massaging him gently.

"You need to keep your guard up around here," he said, turning to face her. "I know this all looks like paradise...but I have my doubts."

She stopped massaging him and looked into his eyes. "It's beautiful here."

"It's an illusion."

"You think?" She turned his head back around and resumed the massage.

"On the plane, did you notice the soldiers?"

"Smelly bunch, huh."

"They looked like they'd been in a war. Did you see the wounded men?"

"No."

"Lo said we were going into the jaws of the tiger coming here. Those men were in a fight on behalf of Curtis, I'm sure, probably with Devin." He turned around to face her again. She resisted and he persisted. "I'm telling you—Curtis isn't any better than Devin. Our safety is an illusion. Promise me you'll be careful."

"Of what?"

"I didn't like the way Curtis looked at you."

"He's just an old man—eccentric but old."

"He's dangerous."

"I think you worry too much."

"Maybe."

"Then I'll be careful." She said it like an annoyed child and pushed his head around more forcefully than before. "Are you going to relax now?"

Janis slumped in the chair, letting Lisa's fingers work on his shoulders. He closed his eyes. He'd never met anyone like her before. The women he'd encountered in his life had always been the snooty professional types. They were extremely educated and so driven to be better than their male counterparts that they regarded men as competition, not companions. There was no tenderness in their manner—no care-giving. Janis never had any success with women like that. Lisa was young enough—she hadn't developed any of those unattractive traits.

He opened his eyes and looked at her over the top of his glasses, her smile, her hair hanging down. Was Lisa the woman he'd been looking for all of his life? Would Mother approve of her—if she could? What would she find wrong with Lisa? Her age for one—and she was Ray's daughter for another. Did any of that really matter? Or was the allure of California, the sunshine and Lisa, warping Janis' sense of reason? His head had been in a whirl since he arrived. First the 13th Power, then a million dollars and the love of his life. Had he somehow been plucked from the real world and deposited into a dream? Was any of this real?

The cut in his hand was real. He lifted the bloody gauze and looked at the wound. "It looks worse now than when we came in here." He turned it up for Lisa's inspection.

"Yuk," she said. "Leave it alone and close your eyes. Lisa will kiss it and make it better—later."

Janis closed his eyes. It had to be a dream.

Chapter Seventy-Five

DOCTOR DOOM

"Can we see Ray now?" Lisa asked Dr. Lucero after he secured the bandage to Janis' hand.

Lucero examined his work, seemed satisfied and said, "Keep this dry for two days. I want you back here on Tuesday."

Janis tested the bandage, wiggled his fingers. "Nine stitches?"

"We'll take 'em out soon."

"I want to see my dad now, Doc." Lisa smiled as she hugged Janis' neck. She showed Lucero her warm childish charm. Knowing how to get her way, she batted her eyelashes.

"I'll see if he's ready for visitors." Lucero slipped out the door.

She needed to talk to her father. If she wasn't going to hate him anymore, she needed to know why. She needed to know he really cared for her. She needed to know why he'd sent her away so long ago.

*   *   *

Dr. Lucero walked down the hallway to the surgical area. When he pushed through the double doors, he spotted the *Occupied* light flashing over the door to operating room B. Taking note, he scrubbed up, donned a gray surgical robe and mask, and placed a cap on his head. Satisfied, he headed for the OR.

The bright light over the operating table silhouetted the team and their head surgeon who held up a pair of forceps. "There it is." A dull clang echoed through the room as he released the slug from Ray's shoulder into a metal tray. "A few stitches and you'll be good as new."

"Thanks, Doc."

Lucero introduced himself.

"Mind if I don't shake your hand?" Ray said.

"Lisa wants to know how you're doing. She can be very persistent."

"Tell me about it."

"Looks as though Dr. Randolph has things well in hand."

Lucero picked up the metal tray and examined the bloody bullet, flattened like the head of a mushroom. "What bone did it hit?"

"The scapula," Randolph said. "Another inch, it would have passed clear through. We'd be eating barbecue by now."

"Dumb luck, huh." He set the tray on the instrument table. "What should I tell Lisa?"

"I want to see her when they're done with me." Ray paused, thinking. "Then I'd like to get some sleep. I'm beat."

"We'll put you on twenty-four hours bed rest."

"By then you'll be begging to get out of here," Dr. Randolph said.

"Don't bet on it." He closed his eyes.

Lucero patted Randolph on the shoulder. "See you at the barbecue party." He walked out.

Dr. Randolph sutured the wound and stepped back from the table. "Wrap him up, boys." He peeled off his rubber gloves. "Put him in post-op. He can rest there."

Ray opened his eyes. "Thanks again, Doc."

"My pleasure, Ray. After all, you're the celebrity around here and we, merely your humble servants—at least to hear Curtis explain it—that is."

"Do I detect a tone of sarcasm in your voice?" Ray asked, not sure why he was getting that impression.

"All we ever hear about anymore is this 13th Power project and how prioritized it is." The doctor pulled his surgical mask off. "Most of us dummies around here don't have a clue what the big deal is about. Personally, I think it's gotten way out of hand." He walked to the door.

"Wait," Ray said and turned on his side. "This experiment will be the greatest advancement in nuclear research since the Manhattan Project. Just because you people don't understand it doesn't mean you're dummies. It'll take all of us to do this. It's a team project in which everyone here has an important part. We're going to make history, Doctor."

"History?" Randolph huffed. "Just what do you expect to find at the end of this experiment, Ray?"

"Fame," he answered and rolled onto his back again, smiling. "The Nobel Prize, at last."

"Maybe for you, but what about Curtis? You can bet he isn't in this for the glory. No way. That man runs on two things—power and money. He has more money than he knows what to do with. That leaves only power. Something tells me the 13th Power will give him more of that than he'll know how to handle." Dr. Randolph opened the door. "This 'history in the making' is big trouble for us all—if you ask me."

"Well, I didn't," Ray mumbled and turned his head away. He heard the door close and set his jaw. How dare the doctor question Curtis' intentions. Curtis was a man of science. Ray had brushed off Janis' skepticism because he didn't want to hear it. He didn't want to hear what Dr. Randolph had to say either. Just because they were doctors didn't mean they were so smart. They lacked the vision that drove true scientists toward new discoveries.

The room light went out. Ray closed his eyes and stewed over their shortsightedness.

Chapter Seventy-Six
LIKE A FATHER'S LOVE

Lisa followed Dr. Lucero down the corridor toward the operating rooms. The hallways seemed to go on forever. Her head felt suddenly light. She didn't want to confront her father—but she had to. It was overdue. During the harrowing trip to Simi Valley, she'd had no time to reassess her feelings for him. But now, after saving his life, was there hope for them after all?

Though the hate lingered, she wanted to be free of it. Could she forgive him for alienating her—for the years she suffered from the loneliness he'd cast her into? A little girl, alone in a big world. Big jets full of strange people. Big schools full of strange kids. Why? Why had he done that to her? It was cruel. How could she ever lose the hate? It had been so much a part of her.

Dr. Lucero stopped in front of operating room B. "He's resting in there. Don't be long."

Lisa pushed the door open and walked into a dimly lit room. The smell of disinfectant was strong. She saw her father lying on a gurney, covered with a white sheet that draped to the floor. He looked helpless, nothing like the man she hated. As she walked up to him, he opened his eyes. The unexpected motion startled her. "I thought you were sleeping."

"Glad you could come." His voice was firm, like a father's.

She leaned against the gurney and took his hand. "Does it hurt?"

"No." But he nodded yes, contradicting his words. "Thanks to you, I'm still alive."

"I wish ..."

"I know—I wish you didn't hate me so much either."

"I wasn't thinking that."

"I was."

"What did you expect?"

"Certainly not this." He scooted over on the gurney. "Sit." He patted the pad. "Come on."

She sat next to him, looking down into his eyes. They were strong eyes, like a father's. She'd really missed having a father—all those years wasted. "Why?"

"What?"

"How *could* you?" She squeezed his hand, almost wanting to hurt him. But he didn't complain. "How could you send me away like that?"

"I had to."

"It was your damn job—wasn't it? I was in the way so you got rid of me like you did my mother." Hot tears stung her eyes. She tried to restrain them but they flowed as if they had a will of their own. "Why?"

Ray lifted his head off the pillow. "You were too young to understand."

She let go of his hand and stood. "That's a lame excuse."

"It's the truth."

"The truth is I hate you for what you did to me and Mother." Her back to him now, she wiped tears from her cheek. "But when I thought you were going to die today, I suddenly realized I had to stop hating you long enough to help you. If I hadn't helped you, I'd never had a chance to do anything *but* hate you, forever."

"Hating me was a small price to pay," Ray said. "You think I didn't want you? I ached for you. All those years, from the time you were six, I had to live without you to keep you safe."

"Safe?" She sniffled and turned toward him, her heartbeat rising. "From what?"

He reached out his hand. "Never ask a question you really don't want the answer to."

She looked at his hand then turned her head away. "I want the answer... "

"Please, Lisa. You don't want to hear it and I don't want to tell it."

"Why not?"

"Your image of your mother will be destroyed. What you thought you had all those years will be gone. And then you'll hate me for that, too."

"What's my mother got to do with this? You cast her out just like you did me."

"I did not." He took a deep breath. "Kate left *us*."

Slowly, Lisa turned her head toward her father, her chest tightening. "That's not true. You threw her out. Nanny Jean told me so."

"Nanny didn't know the truth. I never told her that your mother came back strung out on cocaine again. Her umpteenth bender had left her dead broke."

"She was a junkie?" Lisa put her hand on her heart.

"Worse yet—she came back to get you."

"I don't understand."

"I told you you wouldn't."

"Then help me." She sat by his side on the gurney again and took his hand. "I don't even remember my mother. She has no face, no smile, no form. Why is that?"

Her father's eyes drooped.

"Why, Dad?"

He looked like a man about to confess to murder. "I knew it wouldn't last—Kate and I. We met on the strip in Las Vegas. She was a working girl."

Lisa felt a surge in her bloodstream. "A hooker?"

"A working girl. I fell in love with her. She was so sweet—so much fun. And beautiful. But when I found out it was cocaine that made her happy, I decided to rescue her from herself. I convinced her to swear off drugs, prostitution, her seedy way of life on the street with the pimps and dealers. I tried to help her."

Lisa put her hands over her ears. "Daddy—I don't want to hear anymore!" She thought she'd rather die.

But he continued anyway. "We married. She said she was clean—drug free. But she'd lied and hid it very well. I found out the day you were born. Your heart was racing. Your blood pressure was off the scale. The doctors thought you were going to die 'til the blood tests came back. You were high on cocaine. Your withdrawal was agonizing."

"Oh God! No!"

"She addicted her baby. My baby. You."

"No!"

Like a man obsessed with freeing his soul, he went on with the seamy story. "But she tried. For two years she fought the battle—we fought the battle of her addiction. But the sober Kate was a basket case. I often thought something was tormenting her—something she wouldn't talk about. She'd run off in the middle of the night, leaving me to lie awake and listen to every car that drove by. Was this one hers? No. Maybe the next one. All night long, worried to death.

"When she finally came home, she was a mess—throwing up drunk, crying, saying she was sorry, promising to never do it again, promising to get professional help. I'd forgive her and she'd do it again anyway—pulling tricks for dope and not giving a rat's ass about us, the ones who loved her, the ones she was supposed to love. Finally, she gave up. She left and didn't come back until you were five."

"When she came back for me?"

"That's when I divorced her. Enough was enough. The custody battle was bitterly fought, Lisa. Her higher-ups in the drug world went to bat for her. I spent a fortune. But she lost. You were safe from growing up like her."

Lisa sniffled. "So why did you send me away?"

"Kate was a sore loser. In the middle of the night, she took you away. By God, I was never so afraid in my life. I got up and you were gone."

"Gone?" She felt like she would faint, not wanting to know any more.

"For eight agonizing months I was on the verge of insanity, not knowing where you were, where she'd taken you. I hired a private investigator who specialized in the underground world of missing and exploited children. He tracked Kate to a little trailer town in the desert outside North Las Vegas, plying her trade while you wallowed in filth, underfed and abused."

"Abused? How?"

"Remember what I told you about questions you don't really want answers to?"

"No, Daddy! No!" An unknown terror engulfed her. She fell on her father's chest and clutched his bed sheet. Tears flowed again. He stroked her hair, soothing strokes, like a father's.

"When I finally got you back, I swore she'd never find you again, even if it meant I'd have to live without you. With the pain of a thousand daggers in my heart, I sent you away."

"Why didn't you tell me about her?"

"Like I said, you were too young to understand. Besides, I didn't want to risk jarring any memories you had of her. The things you've forgotten are best forgotten. Besides, every child deserves a loving mother, even if it's only an illusion."

"And all this time I thought I had a father that didn't care about me. An illusion?"

"The price I had to pay to keep you safe."

She looked into his eyes. "The price *we* had to pay."

"I'll be damned if I'll lose you again."

"Is that why you disapprove of Janis?"

His chest rose. "Not entirely. But don't you see? You deserve a man in your life with whom you can plan and build a future of your own—not a man living in a future he'd planned for himself decades ago."

"But I love him." She ached for him to understand.

"I know you think you do."

"You love me?"

"More than anything."

Lisa blinked. "Anything? Like more than the whole world?"

"More than the whole world."

She hoped he'd never have to prove that.

Chapter Seventy-Seven
TROUBLE

Susan finished the last bite of her potato salad and glanced up to the patio when a flurry of activity caught her attention. She quickly looked at Steve who was already concentrating on the commotion.

Dignitaries emerged from the cafeteria with an entourage of security personnel. A smile crossed Steve's lips as he reached for a napkin and wiped away barbecue sauce. She knew he was headed for trouble—that look was unmistakable. He had the searing glare of an eagle as he scanned the scene, taking mental notes and calculating his next move. She put her hand on his arm but he didn't take his attention off the patio.

Curtis emerged a moment later, dressed in his long black coat and wide-brimmed hat. The golden Pharaoh's staff thudded on the patio deck.

"Soon," he said with a crafty smile.

Judas, noticing the stranger's sudden interest in Curtis' arrival, repositioned his sunglasses, uncrossed his legs, and sat upright. Not knowing the man's intentions, he wanted to be ready for anything. His hand closed over the cold steel of his Glock .45, just in case. But the stranger didn't make a move. He just sat there, seemingly satisfied to do nothing else. Judas knew better. He knew the stranger had more than a casual interest in his boss. Glancing at the woman seated with him, Judas took note of the worried expression on her face. He'd been trained to read those expressions when he was with the Secret Service. That and common sense told him to be wary of these two.

Curtis stood on the patio, noting how many people had gathered for the festivities. Pleased by the large crowd, he smiled at Jonathan.

A young waitress wearing a short black skirt approached the new arrivals. "Drinks, anyone?"

"I'll have a Margarita," Curtis said. "On the rocks with salt."

"Right away, sir." She turned to Jonathan. "And for you?"

"A red beer will be fine."

Curtis led the way to the head table. He enjoyed being treated like royalty and his table especially pleased him. As if for a king's feast, the places were set with gold tableware and delicate china. A red satin tablecloth fluttered in the breeze. In the center, an ice sculpture of an atom with a key inserted into it, slowly dripped into a champagne bowl. He couldn't resist touching it. The chill reassured him it was real ice.

Tipping his hat to the waiters standing ready, he claimed his seat at the end of the table. Jonathan sat to his right. His Margarita and Jonathan's beer were delivered with a smile. All around him, the atmosphere was light and jovial and he soon became engrossed in petty conversation.

Steve tossed his napkin on his plate. Now was as good a time as any. He stood and walked toward the head table.

Payday.

Susan ran up behind him, tugging on his arm. "No, Steve. Not now."

"I just want to introduce myself," he said with a huff. "Don't get all... "

A nauseating dizziness suddenly engulfed him. His knees buckled. The sound of Susan screaming was the last thing he heard before a black silence cloaked his consciousness. He never felt himself hit the ground.

Chapter Seventy-Eight

THE RAT CELLAR

Judas, holding the butt of his Glock in one hand and Susan, struggling and screaming in the other, stood over the man he had knocked unconscious. Susan fought to slip from the hold he had on her arm but he wouldn't let go. She kicked him in the leg.

He squeezed her arm tighter. "Cool it lady or I'll send you to never-never land with your boyfriend."

"Go ahead, tough guy!"

The party fell silent. Two other plain-clothed security men ran up. Judas shoved her at them and knelt down, frisked Steve, found the .45 and held it up for everyone to see. "I got the bastard!" he yelled. "He made a move for Curtis and I got him."

Curtis stood, staff in hand, and padded toward Judas with Jonathan following behind him.

"Are you people nuts?" Susan yelled. "He didn't do anything."

"Get her out of here," Curtis ordered.

They dragged her away, screaming. She couldn't fight them off. They wouldn't listen to her. They were all crazy!

"What's with this guy?" Curtis poked at Steve with his golden staff.

Judas handed Curtis the .45. "He was acting suspicious."

"You think?" Bending down, Curtis grabbed the man's hair and turned his face up. "I've seen this guy earlier, at the ceremony." He dropped Steve's head to the turf and stepped away.

"Alex knows him," Jonathan said.

"Yeah—and I thought that screaming broad looked familiar." Curtis pointed his golden staff at Steve. "Toss this fool in the rat cellar. And his girlfriend, too."

Judas smiled.

Curtis walked back to the head table. "And get Alex up here. Right now!" He opened his coat and tucked the doomed man's .45 under his belt. "Now—where were we?" he said to the men gathered around.

While Curtis made light of the matter, Judas signaled for help from his security personnel. He knew his boss wasn't going to let this incident overshadow the celebration at hand. The 13th Power project was not going to be upstaged by a stranger with a gun.

Security struggled with Steve's limp body as they dragged him out of C-Wing and tossed him into the back of an all-terrain vehicle. Judas pushed the rear hatch shut, which slammed with the bang of a dumpster lid. He climbed into the driver's seat. Two of his men jumped on the running boards and grabbed the suicide rails.

The diesel engine clattered to life. Black smoke puffed out the vertical exhaust stack. A security car, with overheads flashing, passed the ATV and Judas accelerated after it. He could see the woman in the back seat flanked by two men. It looked like they were still struggling with her. He grabbed the communications headset from the dash and positioned it over his ears. Adjusting the mouthpiece close to his lips, he pressed the mike switch mounted on the steering wheel. "Salvo—just knock her out."

"No fun that way," came the response.

"Morons." He switched the channel to *Supervisor.* "Alex?"

"Now what?" Alex's voice sounded tinny through his wrist radio.

"Curtis wants to see you right away. Trouble's brewing big time."

"What happened?" The radio squelched.

"We're taking your buddy to the rat cellar. Got his girlfriend, too."

The radio went silent for a moment. "Not Steve and Susan! Don't do it! I'll meet you there in fifteen minutes."

"No you won't. Go see Curtis right now. He insists. Besides, we can take care of these two just fine." He held the mike switch just long enough to broadcast a moment of cynical laughter.

"Touch them and you'll have me to deal with, Judas! Fifteen minutes! Got that?"

"You don't scare me, Alex. I could have you swimmin' in concrete by morning." He released the mike button. Just who did Alex think he was dealing with anyway?

Judas careened the six-wheeled ATV onto a dirt road running east toward the valley flats. As the diesel growled under the hood, he choked in the tail of dust kicked up by the security car in front of him. He spit. Enough of this shit.

He glanced at both big rearview mirrors attached to each side of the ATV. The men clinging to the suicide rails were hanging on, their hair and clothes lashing in the wind.

Slamming the throttle to the floor, he swerved off the road, crashed over a drainage ditch and down an embankment, and after plowing through a clump of bushes, raced past the security car. "Yahoo!" Judas yelled as he veered back onto the road in front of them. "Now you morons can eat my dust." Again, he checked the rearview mirrors. His riders were gone.

He pressed onward, unconcerned.

Two miles down the dusty road, the turnoff to Morrison Ridge wound past several abandoned gold mines and ended in a town that had been left to rot in the sun. The ATV slid to a stop in front of a dilapidated hotel. Judas pulled the fuel valve closed. The diesel engine rattled to silence. He jumped off the ATV and smiled at the thought of what awaited Steve and Susan inside.

The security car slid to a stop alongside the ATV and the doors flew open. Susan was still struggling with her captors as they pulled her out of the car. From the look on her face, he could tell she was concerned for her safety—and rightly so. He opened the rear hatch of the ATV.

"Salvo. Get 'em inside."

*   *   *

"Damn it!" Alex switched off the wrist radio, hit the brakes, swung the car into a spin, downshifted and accelerated in the opposite direction. Tire smoke clouded the air.

Lo coughed and tightened his seat belt. "What's a rat cellar?"

"Under an old hotel at Morrison Ridge there's a large cellar, once used by the local vineyards to store and age their wines. Now in ruins, the only inhabitants are vicious Kangaroo rats.

"Kangaroo rats aren't vicious."

Alex aimed the car toward the valley flats. "These are. A hundred fifty years ago their ancestors roamed the valley floor and were drawn to the cool cellar. Wine kegs were easy pickings and the drunken orgies that followed spanned thousands of rat generations. Their young were genetically altered forever. Deranged.

271

They became vicious and insane, hunting in packs, feeding on carrion and even taking a cow now and then."

Lo made a sour face.

"During the morning and evening hours they hunt in the valley. But when the day heats up, they travel back to the cellar where they nap and breed some more—a living sea of undulating fur. Scared me half to death when I first saw the little bastards. Their lethal nest is no place for man or beast."

"So Curtis found a use for the rats?"

"When he took over Solartech Labs, he discovered the rat's peculiar behavior. The rat cellar became the last stop for people Curtis wanted to get rid of. Rats left no remains."

No remains echoed in Lo's head. "Steve! Susan! Go faster!" A bad feeling churned in his stomach. Jaws of tiger. Jaws of rats. Insanity. He felt helpless to do anything but hang on for the ride.

The staff car careened onto a dirt road.

* * *

Salvo and his men pulled Steve out of the ATV and carried him into the old hotel. They dragged Susan along, kicking and screaming. But before Judas went in behind them, he looked to the west and spotted a plume of dust rising from the dirt road in the distance. *You're too late, you dumb bastard.*

"Toss 'em in right now," he ordered his men.

Chapter Seventy-Nine
CHITTER

Susan recoiled in horror. The opening to the cellar looked like a black hole into hell. The stairs must've rotted away decades ago, leaving no escape from within. Steve hit the floor with a thud.

"You bastards!" Susan screamed.

She fought to free herself from the men who dragged her to the edge of the abyss. A moment later she felt herself falling but clung to Salvo's arm. He tumbled into the darkness with her. They hit the bottom together.

Stunned, she fought off a surge of terror that rippled through her. From the cold, damp darkness, a musty fecal smell assailed her nostrils. The heavy air made her nauseous. Bile burned the back of her throat.

But Salvo's antics distracted her from her sudden misery. He was running in circles, stomping his feet and screaming to his comrades above. "Get me out of here, Judas! Get me out of here!"

The terror in his voice frightened her more than the darkness and stench. She felt around for Steve. The floor crumbled in her fingers—felt like a thick layer of Rice Crispies. Could this be what smelled so horrible?

In spite of all the noise Salvo was making, she could hear gasping in the darkness. Guided by the sound, she groped her way toward Steve. Suddenly, a stinging pain shot up her leg. She yelped and heard a thud in the darkness. Salvo! The idiot had tripped over her ankle and fallen on the floor. He scared the shit out of her. Screaming, he struggled to his feet, again pleading for help from above. She thought he was going insane. Why?

"Steve." She shook him.

He coughed.

"Steve?" She thought he was slowly becoming aware of her. She shook him again. "Steve."

He grabbed her arm and pulled her close, sucking in large breaths of air. "What ... happened?"

"Steve. Are you...?"

A flickering light suddenly pierced the darkness. She turned and saw Salvo's face lit up by the flame of his lighter. His wide-open eyes revealed unimaginable terror. He glared into the darkness beyond the dancing light.

Steve hacked. "W-what's out there?"

"Nothing." Salvo laughed out loud. "Not a damn thing." He looked up to the opening in the ceiling. "Judas! There ain't no stinking rats down here."

"Rats?" Susan put her hand on her mouth. "What rats?"

A light scratching sound echoed through the cellar now. Susan's stomach tightened. The scratching sound came again.

"T-those rats," Steve said, pointing to a commotion in the corner, eerily lit by the flickering lighter.

From the crevices in the walls, one, then two small rats wiggled through and fell to the floor. A few more followed them and several more after that. She froze with fear as an eerie chitter began to echo within the cellar. More and more rats poured in through the cracks, like a living waterfall cascading into a growing pool of rats. Susan thought her heart had quit. *My God.*

"Judas! Get me out of here!" Salvo yelled again.

Judas just stood at the opening above the doomed and laughed. "Sorry, Salvo. Looks like you're gonna have a really bad day."

Susan watched in horror as the horde of rats spilled toward her. She tried to pull herself to her feet, but Steve held her down. "Stay still," he whispered softly. "Don't do anything to piss them off." He reached into his shirt. "Shit! My gun's gone."

"Curtis took it after Judas clobbered you." She cocked her head toward the man silhouetted in the light above. "What do you think you're going to do, shoot every rat in here? Better have a lot of bullets."

"Just one rat—up there." He pointed at Judas.

Salvo yelled up to his comrades but no one made a move to help him. He trembled with fear as a wave of rats flooded the cellar floor. Using their large back feet, they hopped around each other like little kangaroos. Bushy hair on the tip of their tails made them look cute but their numbers made them look horrendous, an army of distorted shadows now dancing on the walls to the rhythm of lighter flame.

Salvo cracked. He made a running leap for the opening.

"No, don't!" Susan yelled.

He missed and landed in the mass of teeming rats. Holding the lighter at arm's length, he ran in circles, stomping rats, kicking rats, and screaming. The chitter became deafening as the pack hunters attacked him, jaws snapping, teeth gnashing. His screams changed from fearful to painful, eerily mingling with the chitter and echoing within the cellar walls.

With Steve clinging to her arm and her eyes wide with horror, Susan watched the gnawing horde force Salvo to his knees. He fell backwards into the sea of crazed rats. Only his rigid arm stuck up from the writhing mob, still holding the flaming lighter. His muffled screams turned to gagging as the rodents infested him. A moment later, the lighter went out and darkness hid the hideous feast.

Susan buried her face into Steve's chest and sobbed. He held her tight. Not knowing how long before the rats would turn their attention to them, she tried to calm the terror welling up inside. More so now than in Devin's pit of horror, she feared for Steve's life—and hers. Dear God, how had she gotten herself involved in this deadly fiasco? Now she would pay the price for Steve's get-rich-quick plan. It wasn't supposed to turn out this way.

Chapter Eighty

NO REMAINS

The staff car fishtailed down the dirt road as Alex raced toward the old mining town. He clutched the steering wheel so tight his knuckles turned white. He was furious. The existence of the rat cellar had never bothered him before—as long as it didn't interfere with his mission for *The Ark,* he didn't care. But Judas had just changed all that. "Damn you, Judas!"

"Who's Judas?" Lo asked.

"A snake in the grass—that's who. I should've known it would come to this. We've had bad blood between us ever since Curtis hired him. He was supposed to provide security against threats from within Solartech Labs' community. But he turned it into a sneaky underhanded crusade against anyone he didn't like personally."

"Make no friends that way."

"He doesn't care. The brown-noser reports directly to Curtis. Every time I complained about him—Curtis exemplified him. A 'valuable asset to Solartech Labs,' he told me. The menace was untouchable. But this time he's gone too ... "

As the staff car rounded a curve, Alex saw two men walking in the middle of the road. He slammed on the brakes and swerved to miss them. The car skidded out of control, careened off the road, and ended up sideways in a drainage ditch, suspended by the bumpers. The engine roared. The rear wheels spun uselessly.

"Shit! Where the hell did they come from?" Dust lingered thickly around the staff car. Alex couldn't see the men he'd almost run over. He threw open the door as they ran up to the car. What were his security men doing in the middle of the road? Why did they look like they'd already been run over?

"That was close," said one of the haggard men. "You all right?"

"What are you doing wandering around out here?"

"Judas—the crazy bastard—bounced us off the ATV."

Alex groaned then rushed to the front of the car. "Let's get this thing out of the ditch." He signaled Lo to get behind the wheel.

Together, they pushed and pulled and dug in the choking dust to free the car. A few minutes later, it lurched back onto the dirt road.

"Hurry!" Lo yelled. "We wasted too much time already."

They climbed in and Lo hit the gas. "You point the way," he told Alex.

A few minutes later, Lo slid the car to a stop in front of an old hotel and cut off the engine. An eerie chitter echoed from within the rotting walls. He turned to Alex. "What's that?"

Alex looked like he'd just seen a ghost. "We're too late." He turned to his men in the back seat. "Stay here." Raising his Glock .40, he pulled the breach back. A round chambered with a click. "Judas is mine." He kicked open the door and climbed out.

Lo watched him walk up creaky steps to a porch and disappear inside the hotel. Without turning his attention from the doorway, Lo said, "I can't sit here doing nothing." He got out of the car and tailed Alex.

Floorboards creaked beneath Lo's feet. Sunshine beamed in through cracks in the wall timbers and ceiling boards, splitting the darkness with razor-thin lines of light. Chittering filled the air, echoing, getting louder as he tiptoed deeper into the building. He felt a twinge of panic. Where was that sound coming from? Were the rats feeding?

No Remains.

The image in his mind of rats eating people made him want to vomit. He thought about running outside and all the way back to San Francisco. But he had to go on. He had to help, if he could. Following footprints on the dusty floor, he stalked through a doorway, then right, down a long dark hallway. The chittering got louder.

No Remains.

*　　*　　*

Alex ran toward the room above the rat cellar, his neck hairs tingling from the chittering of the rats. At the door, he put his back against the frame, held his Glock in both hands, pointing at the ceiling. Carefully, he peered into the room. He saw Judas standing at the opening above the rat cellar looking down, probably admiring his handiwork. The smile on his face sent a burst of rage through Alex. The thought of Susan covered by those gnawing rats turned his rage into vengeance. He stepped into the room, aimed the Glock at Judas's head, and tightened his finger on the trigger. "Judas!"

A sudden flash of black boot leather sent a burning pain rifling up his right arm. What the...? The Glock flew from his grasp, slid across the floor, and flipped over the edge of the rat cellar. Down it went. Gone. His arm stinging, he realized too late his anger had made him careless. The maniac he stalked was not unguarded.

Before he could react, another kick slammed into his left kidney, arching his back and sending him to the floor. Pain blasted through his guts. Wind rushed from his lungs. He tried to gulp air. Another kick rocked the side of his head, numbing his senses. He rolled on his back. The blurred images of two men circled above him. He tightened his muscles against the pain. Get up! Fight back!

He rolled to his right. An adrenaline rush fueled his defense and, with a scissors kick, he snared one of his assailant's legs and sent him to the floor with a thud.

In a dusty brawl, he grappled with the two men. He recognized Harold Petty. Pitiful Petty they called him—a longhaired-hippie-brown-noser of the first degree. He smelled of old sweat. The other puke looked like Jeff Tillman. Someone said he had sold his sister to the Mexicans. Judas had shit for friends.

Alex peered under a smelly armpit to see what Judas was doing. The smile on the bastard's face made him angry as hell. He connected an elbow to the jaw of one of his attackers. Must have been Tillman. He squealed like a stuck pig.

Out the corner of his eye, a motion at the door caught his attention. Lo? Alex tried to yell, to tell Lo to get back, but took a left hook in the nose. His head buzzed with stars. This was no place for Lo. He could get hurt. Alex shifted his leg from under the pile of bad guys and kicked the door shut in Lo's face. Maybe he got the hint. Alex grabbed a handful of long hair. An elbow caught him in the eye. He shook off the blur in his mind and fought harder.

Chapter Eighty-One

HOTEL HELL

Lo ran back outside to recruit the help of the security men waiting in the staff car. Shit! They were gone. He looked down the road, saw a plume of dust speeding away.

"Not good."

He thought about running back into the hotel. A little karate lesson would do the bad guys some good. But that could be a problem. Three against one was no big deal, but all those guns bothered him. Bullets always won. With the chitter echoing in his brain, he spun a full circle, looking for a better idea.

The ATV caught his eye, a six-wheel drive steel-reinforced off-road-monster truck. It reminded him of his training in the National Guard. He climbed aboard and fired up the engine.

"Like ride bike—no forget."

He slammed the transmission into low range and powered toward the old hotel. Six knobby tires ripped at the porch steps, tearing away boards and cracking joists. The front tires crashed through rotting porch planks, but the trailing wheels drove the ATV forward. Diesel engine roaring, the ATV plowed through the front door, ripping the doorframe from the wall.

Driving through the lobby at full throttle, Lo turned on the flood lamps and hit the back wall head-on. Wood planks and wallboards exploded, flying in all directions. The ceiling buckled and sagged. Dust choked the air. The old hotel shuddered and the chittering suddenly stopped.

*　*　*

Steve heard the gun hit the floor of the rat cellar. He reached out, groping, patting the ground until he found it in the darkness, swearing it had fallen from heaven. The cold steel gave him a new hope. He could hear a fistfight knuckling above him, cursing and swearing.

Suddenly, the building shook, as if from an earthquake. The rats went eerily silent.

Susan flinched. "What was that?"

In the darkness, Steve sensed a change in the rat's behavior. As the building rumbled above, the horde began moving in waves, first to the left, then to the right, as if panicking. Now they were coming toward him, a thousand little footsteps scampering in the dark, getting closer and closer. He clutched Susan in his arms. At least he could *try* to protect her. Terror gripped his mind. To be eaten alive—what a horrible way to die. He held his breath, tightened every muscle in his body. And then they were on him.

Like a furry carpet being dragged over him, he felt the lightness of their lethal touch. He thought he would go insane. As the wave of rats bounded over him, he suddenly realized there was no pain—no attack. The rats were scrambling to escape something that had frightened them. In a few seconds that seemed like eternity, they were gone, the last of them scratching their way back into the cracks from which they had come.

He glanced up to the cellar opening. It sounded like the place was falling apart up there—a diesel engine roaring, lumber cracking, voices yelling and then the familiar sound of gunfire.

"What the hell is going on?" He got up and pulled Susan to her feet.

"Whatever it is ..."

An explosive shower of splinters and debris rained down into the cellar. Steve pulled Susan away from the opening, hunkered her in his arms, and closed his eyes. Behind him, there came a horrendous crashing sound. Then silence. Susan trembled in his arms.

When he opened his eyes, the cellar was ablaze with light. He squinted and turned around, completely dumbfounded at what he saw. An ATV had crashed nose-first into the cellar. Lo was hanging onto the steering wheel. Floodlights illuminated a smile on his face. "Need a lift?" he asked.

Susan shrieked and clung to Steve's arm. He followed her eyes. Not far from the ATV, now visible through the dusty haze, lay Salvo, or what was left of him—a yellowish ribcage protruding from half-eaten flesh, pink intestines spilled on the floor, shiny strands of tendons glistening, and one eyeball still intact, staring out from a faceless skull.

Steve's stomach clutched. The rats would be back to finish their meal. He had no intention of being around for that. "Let's get out of here," Steve said. As he lifted Susan up to the ATV's suicide rails, a thought came to him. "Wait!"

"Who's up there?" he asked Lo, checking the clip in the Glock from heaven.

"Alex and one man he called Judas. The other two guys I ran over—squish. Sorry—they not look first where they were going."

"One bad guy left, huh." He looked at Susan. "I'll go get the bastard. You stay here."

"But he'll kill you."

"He tried that already." Steve climbed up the ATV to the room above and spotted Alex and Judas fighting on the floor, Judas on top, fists swinging, apparently beating the crap out of Alex. Steve rushed up behind Judas and put the Glock's muzzle against the back of his head.

"Enough!" Steve yelled.

Judas took another swing at Alex.

"You don't listen too good." Steve jabbed the muzzle again.

"All right, damn it. All right!" Judas let go of Alex and raised his hands.

"Get up!" Steve forced Judas to his feet and pushed him against the wall, pressing his face into the wallboards. Steve ached to pull the trigger, to kill the bastard for what he'd done to Susan, to him. But one glance at her face and her pleading eyes convinced him that she didn't want to watch Judas die. Without a second thought, Steve raised the Glock and slammed the butt down hard on the back of Judas's head. He hit the floor like a wet towel. "See how you like it, prick!"

Alex, still sitting on the floor and panting, looked at Steve. "Thanks."

Steve gave him a hand, pulled him to his feet.

Looking at Lo, "The ATV was brilliant," Alex said. "Those piles over there," he pointed to the crushed remains of Petty and Tillman, "were about to tear me apart when all the noise distracted them." He turned to Steve. "You should've seen it. Before they could open the door to see what was going on—wham-o! The door and the ATV flattened the bastards. Judas started shooting at Lo just as I tackled him."

"Bullets were flying everywhere," Lo put in.

Alex brushed the dust off his pants and went over to Judas, lying motionless on the floor. "Help me with this piece of shit."

They dragged him to the opening above the rat cellar, his limp body leaving a trail in the dust.

"Turnabout is fair play." Steve kicked Judas over the edge. "If he's lucky, he'll wake up *before* the rats come back."

"Sleep tight, you cockroach," Alex yelled down.

Steve handed the Glock to Alex. "Thanks for the loaner."

As they stood above the rat cellar, Susan peered down into her would-be tomb. In the floodlights' dimming glow, Judas lay sprawled on the fecal floor not far from Salvo's haunting remains. "Nighty-night," she said and walked away.

Lo picked up the gun that Judas had dropped when Alex tackled him. He handed it to Steve who ejected the clip and took inventory of the rounds. "Well, it's not my .45, but it's better than nothing." He slammed the clip back into the grip. "Let's get out of here."

They made their way through the wrecked hotel and into the sunlit afternoon. The security car overheads were still flashing. Alex shut them off. "What now?"

Susan leaned against the fender. "Let's leave this place, Steve. These people are crazy."

"First we pay Curtis a visit."

"No!" Susan shouted. "Curtis was the one who told Judas to throw us in there." She pointed to the hotel. "Don't piss him off any more."

Steve huffed. "He's a wimp. But there's something he needs to know. Right Alex?"

"What?"

"Have you told him that Devin is still alive?"

"No."

"Good," Steve said. "I want to be there to see the look on his face." He kicked at the dirt. "Better yet, I have some bad news for him, too."

Alex frowned. "Such as?"

"It'll rattle Curtis' cage."

Glaring into Steve's eyes, Alex saw a man that had been pushed to the limit. But Alex's first priority was to protect Curtis from *any* kind of interference, including cage rattling. It was his job, his mission for *The Ark*. "What are you going to tell him?"

"And spoil the surprise? No way. I'm not giving up my ace in the hole. You'll find out *after* I talk to Curtis. So let's get going."

Alex grabbed Steve's arm. "Don't be confused about where my loyalty lies, Steve. Mess with Curtis and I'll put you down."

Steve pulled his arm away. "You'll find your loyalty is misplaced, pal. So don't get cocky with me. You don't know all the facts." He turned and walked around the car, paused and glowered at Alex over the roof. "Are we going or not?"

Alex just stared at Steve. What was he thinking? What did he know? One thing was certain—Steve wasn't the kind of man who could be bullied into doing anything. Alex made a flash decision. "Have it your way, Steve. Get in."

Chapter Eighty-Two

FEAR

The barbecue party was in full swing as Janis led Lisa out onto the patio, hand in hand. He quickly drew the attention of those mingling around Curtis and his table of dignitaries. Janis held Lisa a little closer as a group of well-wishers and avid conversationalists flocked toward them. He held his bandaged hand up to thwart off the onslaught. "Give us a break, you guys," he said above the loud music. "Don't interrupt your party on our account. Just carry on as you were. The 13th Power can wait until tomorrow." To his surprise, they returned to their frivolities.

Curtis tipped his hat to Lisa, then returned his attention to his guests.

"Impressive, darling," Lisa said with a smile.

"Curtis must've given me a lot of clout with his people."

"I wonder how long *that* will last."

"Let's eat."

Janis carried a pitcher of iced tea and two cups, while Lisa juggled several heaping plates and followed him to a table in the courtyard. Seated, he scanned the area for any sign of Lo.

As Lisa arranged the table, Janis took a moment to admire her again. His mind replayed the events of the past three days since they'd met. Seemed more like three years, for all they'd been through together. Her hair darted about in the breeze. She was beautiful. But was she the one for him? It all seemed so impossible: Ray's daughter, young, spoiled, moody, and completely wrong for him. Mother would say so too—if she could. Maybe.

She caught him staring. "Penny for your thoughts, cowboy."

Janis blinked. "Just looking, California Girl."

"Then just look at this." She slid a plate of barbecued chicken at him.

He picked up a plump thigh. The jailhouse food from King City had long since worn off.

Lisa sighed and discarded a wing bone.

"What is it?" Janis asked, concerned.

"I was just thinking about my father. He really loves me, you know."

"I'm sure."

"But he's not ready to let me go. He's overprotective. That won't change overnight."

Janis forked some potato salad. "He must realize you're a grown woman now."

"To him I'll always be six years old. That's how he remembers me—when he sent me away."

"That'll have to change before you two will ever get along."

"Wouldn't that be a miracle?" She looked around. "I wonder where Lo is."

"No telling."

A gentle breeze rustled the palm trees lining the courtyard. Shade from the patio crept motionlessly across the lawn as California's sun settled westward.

"The pool looks good. Want to go for a dip?"

He showed her his bandaged hand. His fingers were free enough for typing—but swimming? He really shouldn't.

"Maybe a hot bath then." She plucked another thigh from the pile on the plate.

Janis sipped his iced tea as he watched the patio party progress. The music had escalated to a loud kind of rock and roll he didn't like. Shrill guitars and pounding drums overpowered the words, but the beat seemed enticing to Curtis' guests. They humped and gyrated like overactive lovers with their clothes on. Many of the women looked like they'd been hired-out from Los Angeles, not looking like professionals from *this* community. But the men, groping and flirting, were enjoying their company.

Lisa rubbed his shoulder. "I really like the music but I'm too tired to get into it. The meal made me sleepy."

"How can anyone sleep with all this noise?"

"Let's go anyway." She tugged on his arm.

Janis didn't get up. Even though their staff car was waiting out front, he took a moment to watch the revelers, basking in their pseudo-glory over a hypothetical intrusion of the atomic cosmos. They couldn't have been more joyous at a wedding reception. As he watched, he occasionally glanced at Curtis, who wasn't any better behaved than the rest of his band of lunatics. Janis huffed. They were all crazy.

He tossed his napkin down. "I'm ready."

Down the concrete steps from C-Wing, he spotted their staff car, its driver leaning against a front fender leisurely smoking a cigarette. When he saw them approaching, he tossed the butt and opened the car door. But before they got in, the sound of squealing tires filled the air.

"Now what?"

A security car screeched to a stop. The doors flew open. Steve and Alex jumped out, arguing about something. "I'll tell him about Devin first," Alex was saying. "So keep your pie hole shut 'til I say it's okay—got that?" Without so much as a nod of recognition, they stomped up the steps to C-Wing. "But I'm talking to him in private," Steve returned. "Don't screw me up on this, damn it!" They disappeared inside.

Janis thought everyone had gone crazy.

Lisa rushed up to Lo as he got out of the car and flung her arms around him. He was dusty and sweaty. "Where have you been?"

"Long story. I'm going to eat now."

"What happened?" Janis asked.

Walking backwards toward C-Wing, Lo said, "Tiger really pissed-off." He turned and tromped up the steps, mumbling something in Chinese.

Lisa spotted Susan sitting in the back seat with dirt on her dress, her face smudged, and chin down. "I wonder what happened to her."

"Find out," Janis said, holding his bandaged hand. The Novocain was wearing off. "I'll wait in the car."

Sliding in next to Susan, Lisa asked, "What's all this?" pointing at her dirty dress.

Susan threw her arms around Lisa's neck. "Oh God, it was horrible."

Lisa patted Susan's back. "What was horrible?"

"J-Judas…and…the rats. They were everywhere."

"What rats?"

"Now they're…they're both going to get themselves killed. These people…they're animals, I tell you. We have to get out of here."

"You're not making any sense."

Susan sat back and stared into Lisa's eyes. "Steve and Alex are going in there to confront Curtis. They're both angry as hell. Somebody's going to get killed, I tell you." Her eyes welled with tears. Her chin quivered. She looked terrified. Was she afraid for herself, for Steve and Alex, or for all of them?

"They're big boys," Lisa said. "They can take care of themselves."

When the look in Susan's eyes didn't soften, Lisa recalled Janis' warning while they were waiting at Solartech Medical. He must've been right—their safety *was* an illusion. An ominous feeling began rising in her stomach. Susan's fear was real. Lisa couldn't find any words to comfort her. But from the looks of her, a hot bath and clean clothes would be a good start.

"Let's get you back to your room."

Chapter Eighty-Three
THE GAME

Susan clutched a fistful of dirty dress as the staff car headed toward the executive suites. Why did men have to be so bullheaded? Whenever they got a hair-brained notion, they'd run off half-cocked. And Steve took the prize. Didn't he know there were people's lives at stake here? Didn't he care? Why was the money so damned important? Or was it the winning? Was it a game to him? *The tough-guy wins, nice guys finish last.* It was all macho bullshit. Now all she had to do was figure out why she cared so damn much for him. If he got himself killed, she'd never speak to him again. That'd teach him. She felt the urge to cry—but didn't.

The car stopped in front of the executive suites. Susan followed Lisa through the front doors. Janis and Lo trailed behind. Upstairs in Tamarack Hall, Sheila, the housekeeping supervisor, used her cardkey to open the door to Susan's room.

A wave of relief rushed over her. The room felt cool—and safe. She plopped on the bed, exhausted. Sheila closed the curtains and left. Janis walked in and handed Lisa a cardkey. "Your room is 319."

Taking the card, she sat next to Susan. "Steve will be all right. You'll see."

Susan didn't find Lisa's words reassuring. "You don't realize what Curtis is capable of," Susan said, sitting up. "I do. I was there. I saw it. They're killers and they don't care who lives or dies. Christ, Lisa. Steve's going to get killed."

"What does he want with Curtis that's worth risking his life for?"

"Money—what else? Devin ripped him off so he came here to collect from Curtis. I tried to stop him...before...at the barbecue."

"How does Steve figure Curtis is going to give him any money?"

"He wouldn't tell me." Susan trembled. Not knowing was the hardest part.

Janis walked to the window, parted the curtains, and looked out, his glasses riding low on his nose. "It's apparent there's bad blood between Steve and Curtis. I suggest we let them settle it."

He looked at Susan. "One thing's for sure—you're lucky to be alive."

She dropped her chin to her chest.

"Let's round up our luggage and get some rest," Janis said. "My hand aches." He looked at the bandage, scowled, and walked out.

Lisa stood. "Steve will be back soon. Get cleaned up for him." She patted Susan's knee and walked toward the door.

Susan said goodbye, restraining tears. When the door closed, she fell back on the bed and stared at the ceiling. This trip to Simi Valley had turned into a nightmare. Steve's obsession with Curtis was unnerving, as though he had no fear of him—or anyone else for that matter.

Still, she smiled at his reckless bravery. An unwanted tear trickled down her cheek. At first, she'd hoped he would abandon his scheme and take her away from this awful place. But now, as she thought about the situation she and her new friends were in, she realized they were all in grave danger here.

The horror of the rat cellar came back. She closed her eyes. The room spun. She tried to ward off the dizziness, but it was too strong. In submission, she rolled over and cried for Steve—wanting only that he make it back to her—alive. Game or no game.

Chapter Eighty-Four

THE CONFRONTATION

The patio door swung open. Alex went outside first, Steve following close behind. Dancers took up most of the floor so he had to weave a path through them to get to the tables on the other side. No one paid the intrusion any mind.

Alex spotted Curtis sitting at the head table, talking with a lab-tech supervisor. Alex interrupted his conversation.

Looking annoyed, Curtis growled. "I told Judas to summon you more than two hours ago. What took you so…?" He hesitated, his wide eyes suddenly locked on Steve, his breath caught in his throat. Eyes shifting between Steve and Alex, he looked as if he didn't know what to expect.

"We need to talk," Alex said. "Now."

"I'm busy."

"This is important."

"It can wait," Curtis said sternly.

"Don't bet on it."

Curtis looked toward his guests. "Excuse me, gentlemen. It appears I have some urgent business to attend to." He got up from his chair. "This way, if you will."

Steve followed Curtis and Alex through the cafeteria and down a hallway, his pulse racing with anticipation.

Payday.

The golden staff's tapping and their footsteps echoed down the corridor. Music from the patio faded. Stopping at a conference room door, Curtis pushed it open. "This should do nicely." He turned on the ceiling lights and set his staff on a long table.

Steve looked around the lavishly appointed room. "Very impressive…"

Curtis turned suddenly, grabbed him by the shirt and slammed him against a wall. The wind rushed from his lungs. "Just who the hell do you think you are?" Curtis snarled in his face.

Steve gulped air, searching for a good answer. He didn't want to overreact and escalate the situation. But before he could say anything, Curtis threw him to the floor and pressed a knee into his chest. He could hardly breathe under Curtis' weight. Steve saw

Alex standing spread-legged, arms folded across his chest. He was obviously serious about his loyalty to Curtis. Diplomacy was no longer an option.

Curtis sneered. "I should kill you ... huh!" Suddenly, his face twisted in pain.

"Get up or I'll blow your balls off, you bastard!" Steve rasped. Judas's .45 had come in handy. "I'll kill you." Steve jabbed the gun into Curtis' groin. Curtis slowly released his grip on Steve's shirt, rose cautiously, hands raised.

Alex drew his gun. "Drop it, Steve!"

"*You* drop it, Alex." Steve got off the floor, still aiming at Curtis. "I'll kill him."

Alex pulled back the breach of his gun. "Have you forgotten where my loyalty lies?"

Steve forced a smile. Why did Alex have to make this so damn hard? "Tell him about Devin, Alex. Go ahead—tell him. See how far your loyalty gets you."

Alex looked at Curtis, who glared back.

"What about Devin?" Curtis bellowed and put his hands on his hips. His black coat fell open as he stared at his security officer.

"Well..." Alex looked back and forth between Steve and Curtis. "We had a problem at Atomtech."

Steve turned his attention to Alex.

"We couldn't find Devin anywhere. He disappeared."

When Steve glanced back to catch Curtis' reaction to the bad news, he found himself looking down the barrel of his own .45. He flinched instinctively but held his gun on Curtis, whose eyes were throwing daggers at Alex.

"Are you telling me Devin is alive?" he yelled.

"You better believe it, bozo." Steve put in. "And he's really pissed off at you guys. How do you like them apples, asshole?"

"Who the hell is this guy?" Curtis barked and pointed the .45 at Alex. "What is he doing here, damn it?" He looked as if he ached to pull the trigger on both of them.

Alex took a step backwards. "Now, everybody calm down." Sweat suddenly appeared on his forehead. He held his gun on Steve and his eyes on Curtis.

"Shoot him, Alex," Curtis ordered. "Or I'll put a bullet in you first."

"Go ahead, Alex," Steve said. "I'll put three rounds into your boss before I hit the floor."

"Don't bet on it," said Curtis, aiming at Steve now.

"Try me!" Steve shouted. "I'm waiting. Go ahead—shoot him. I'll blow you away before he hits the floor. Either way—you die."

"This is ridiculous," Alex said. "Nobody is shooting anybody." He paused a moment, and then tossed his weapon down.

"Nice move," Steve said and turned to Curtis. "Now you. Throw the gun down or shoot. I'm ready either way."

"I should shoot both of you," Curtis said, showing teeth.

"Go for it!"

Curtis raised the gun to Steve's head.

His heartbeat went up a notch.

"He just wants to talk," Alex said.

"I don't want to listen." Curtis pulled the trigger. The gun resounded a harmless click. He tried two more times.

Steve lunged forward and grabbed the gun from Curtis' hand. "You're a bastard." He pushed Curtis backwards.

"It was empty?" Curtis yelled.

"Secret safety," Steve said. "I made it myself." He slid a slider on the barrel back. "Never know when some dumb-ass might take my gun away. Hell—he might even be stupid enough to try to shoot me with it." He pointed the gun down and pulled the trigger. The report was deafening. Point made.

Curtis stood dazed, his mouth hanging open, cheeks mottled with rage. "You knew all along—I couldn't have shot anyone. Who the hell are you, anyway?"

"Your worst nightmare."

Steve grinned and faced Alex. "It's my turn to talk to him."

Shaking his head, Alex didn't move.

"I need to be alone with him."

"I'm not going anywhere," said Alex.

"We made a deal."

"Screw the deal!"

Steve pointed the .45 at Alex. "Get out!"

Curtis glowered. "Go ahead, Alex. But I'm not through with you on the Devin matter."

"Yes, you are," Alex said and left the room, slamming the

door.

"Never mind him," Steve said, reaching into his pocket. He pulled out a folded piece of paper and handed it to Curtis. "Read it."

Curtis unfolded the paper. A look of confusion crossed his face. "What's this?"

"My bank account number. Feel free to transfer a million dollars into it. In fact, I insist."

"Oh, do you?" Curtis sneered. "Suppose I tell you to go to hell?"

"Suppose I blow the lid off your charade?"

"Who are you?"

"Name's Steve Raven, private eye." He crossed his arms. "In fact, your good friend Walter Devin hired me to keep tabs on your little shenanigans around here."

Curtis didn't look impressed.

"Problem is, the bastard stiffed me for my fee. But I learned something from him, something much more valuable."

"Like what?"

"Something you would want kept quiet."

"Sounds like blackmail," Curtis growled. "Are you loony?"

Steve looked Curtis in the eyes. "Loony enough to mess up your little science project here—put an end to it real quick like." He turned his back on Curtis, took two steps.

"I'll have you killed."

"Singapore will get a letter."

Curtis took a step back. "What did you say?"

Steve turned around. "Transfer the million dollars or kiss your phony ass goodbye, Melvin Anderson."

Chapter Eighty-Five

THE TAMARACK HALL BRAWL

Janis went to the lobby where he found their luggage neatly sorted. After picking up his bags, he headed down the hall and spotted Lisa gently closing her door. Good—she was going to get some rest.

He looked at the cardkey in his hand. Room 317. That should be right over here. No. Over here? Something wasn't right. He swore his room was the same door Lisa had just closed.

Sheila brushed by him, smiling slyly. What was that all about? He slid the cardkey into the slot. It clicked and he went inside.

Hearing water running, he walked toward the bedroom where he tripped over a sandal. Huh? A pair of denim shorts lay on the floor—and a white blouse not far away. Lisa? What was she doing?

He threw his bags on the bed next to a black lace bra and silk panties. Shaking his head, he pulled the knob on the bathroom door. Inside, the lights were dim and steam clouded his view. But he found her lying in the tub, up to her neck in bubbles, smiling at him.

"Hello, cowboy," she said breathily and raised a handful of bubbles. "Come on in." She puckered her lips and blew the bubbles at him.

His heart skipped with surprise—not by how beautiful she looked—but by how apprehensive he felt. She was Ray's daughter for Christ's sake. Janis' accelerated heart rate made his hand throb. "I better get some ice."

"Don't be long, cowboy. The water's fine." She leaned forward and shut off the faucets. The bubbles barely covered anything.

Janis ran to the ice machine, hardly able to keep up with his feet. They wouldn't slow down. What did they think he was going to do with Lisa? He couldn't believe he was even considering it. No way in hell.

Why not?

Ray would never stand for his daughter being intimately involved. Not with him—maybe not with any man, especially an older man. That would be asking for trouble and God knew they'd had enough of that already.

Ice bucket in hand, Janis made his way back down the hall, driven onward by the thought of Lisa's bubbly body.

The elevator doors slid open. Steve and Alex bolted out, pushing each other. "Just like that?" Alex shouted. Steve shoved him. "You can't stop me!" Janis dropped the ice bucket, trying to get out of the way. He felt invisible.

Alex grabbed Steve's arm. "Watch me!"

Steve showed him a fist. "I'll knock you into next week!"

"Just try it!" They went face to face in the middle of the hall, neither looking like he'd back down to the other.

"Tomorrow morning, I'm out of here!" Steve growled. "Susan, too!"

"Like hell!" Alex yelled. "What kind of deal did you make with Curtis? I saw him leave. He was fuming. What did you tell him?" He shook Steve. "I have to know!"

"None of your damn business! How many times do I have to tell you?" Steve pushed him. In the shoving match that followed, they fell against the wall and Alex clamped Steve in a headlock. Cursing, they tumbled to the floor.

Janis stepped in. "Knock it off."

Susan ran out of her room. "Steve! Oh, thank God! Steve!" She jumped onto the pile. "Let him go!" she shrieked, pounding on Alex's back.

Janis took a step back to assess the new complication, watching the three of them grapple with each other on the floor.

Lo was standing beside him now. "What? You don't want to play with them?"

"You first," Janis replied.

Lo chuckled and, assured no harm was being done, walked back into the library, mumbling something in Chinese. He'd been doing a lot of that lately.

Stepping in again, Janis shouted, "That's enough!" He grabbed Susan around the waist and lifted her off the pile, kicking and screaming. He tossed her to the carpet and again tried to separate the men. "Alex—let him go! What's the matter with you guys?"

"He's got something on Curtis," Alex said. "The shit told me

I didn't know all the facts."

Steve punched Alex in the stomach. Susan ran back to the pile. "Stay out of this," Steve warned her.

Standing with her hands on her hips, her eyes tense and angry, she seemed unaware of the tear in her nightgown, which revealed more than she would have wanted them to see.

Alex looked up at Janis as he wrestled with the private eye. "He said he would tell me what he told Curtis—if I let them talk in private."

Steve elbowed Alex in the ribs.

"He lied. I kept *my* end of the deal, but he reneged." Alex balled a fist and hit Steve in the jaw.

"Get this—you piece of shit!" Steve yelled. "I can't tell you. I promised Curtis I'd keep my mouth shut—so back off." Steve belted him in a kidney. "You're his hot-shot security chief. Go ask him yourself. I'm out of here tomorrow ..."

"Tomorrow?" Susan said. "Steve—are you serious?"

"As a heart attack—if this shit-ass ever lets go of me." He slugged Alex again.

"Stop it!" Janis yelled and yanked on Alex's arm. Steve broke loose, kicked Alex in the shin, and sat up against the wall, gasping.

Alex yanked his arm from Janis' grasp and sat next to Steve. The private eye was a hard head. A shit. Alex had a hunch that Steve knew something about Curtis, maybe even his real name. But who could have told him and how much did he know? Was the mission at risk? If he detained Steve for questioning, it could blow Alex's cover—blow the whole operation. *The Ark* would have his ass. It wasn't worth the risk. Besides, Steve had said he was leaving tomorrow—maybe that would be the end of it. Alex got up, straightened his shirt collar, and walked to the elevator. "I hope you haven't done anything stupid this time, Steve." He turned and left Tamarack Hall.

As the elevator door slid shut, Susan ran to Steve and hugged him, her eyes filled with tears. "You made it back."

"What else?" He held her warm body, which trembled in his arms. He was beginning to like how she cared about him. The rip in her nightgown was rather sexy, too.

Janis picked up the spilled ice bucket and walked away, grumbling.

"We're leaving tomorrow," Steve said.

She whispered in his ear. "We can't go."

Steve saw a flash in his brain. "Like hell we can't."

"Don't you see? These people are in trouble, too. We have to help them. We can't just leave. Look around. There's something horribly wrong here. Don't you see?"

Steve looked at the ceiling. "So what if I do?"

"Then help them."

He stood and pulled Susan to her feet. "I know what I'm doing."

Chapter Eighty-Six

LOVE IS BLUE

In Janis' room, music was coming from the bathroom. He removed the luggage and underwear from the bed and pulled down the sheets, an apprehension in his chest as heavy as a parked truck. What was he going to do about Lisa? Why was she doing this to him? To get at her father, to piss him off some more? Janis didn't want any trouble from Ray; they had to work together. He undressed to his boxer shorts. At the bathroom door, he stopped and sighed. It wasn't going to happen. Not today. Not ever.

Maybe.

Slowly, Janis swung the door open and walked into the steamy bathroom. "Love is Blue" played from the radio, the instrumental version—the sexy one. It made him feel all mushy inside.

A floral fragrance drifted in the bubble bath mist. Lisa was lying in the tub, her head on a water pillow, fast asleep. Bubbles floated all around her. She looked beautiful, even with her hair wet.

Reaching into the water, he gently lifted her from the tub. The bubbles cascaded off her body like a foamy waterfall. As he wrapped her in a fluffy bath towel, she sleepily put her arms around his neck and moaned. His heart raced. He carried her to the bed, his mind swimming in emotions and desires. *Could* he make love to Lisa? Yes. Certainly she'd be willing. But *should* he make love to Lisa? No. She was Ray's daughter, goddamn it.

He laid her on the bed and covered her with a sheet. Standing there, he watched her sleep for a few moments. He knew she was too young for him. They had nothing in common. But more so, she was a California girl with a lifestyle far different from his quiet existence in the university community of Colorado. She would soon become bored with him, wander off, and break his heart. Love wouldn't be enough to keep them together. In this complicated world, it took more than love—much more.

Sadly, he returned to the bathroom and showered. The water felt wonderful, made him sleepy. As he dried off, he felt relieved—he'd made up his mind about Lisa. At the window, he looked out over Simi Valley and up at a star-lit sky. Somewhere in the universe, the woman he was meant to love still waited undiscovered, as elusive as the 13th Power.

After donning a new pair of boxer shorts, he slid under the sheet next to Lisa. She rolled over. The towel fell away. In the darkness she cuddled into him, the warmth of her body like torture. But he was sure he'd made the right decision.

"Good night, my cowboy," she murmured.

They slept in each other's arms.

Chapter Eighty-Seven
FLIGHT FROM SOLARTECH

Steve rolled over and picked up the phone that was ringing in his dream. The damn racket was real. He shook off sleep. "Yeah?"

"Steve Raven?" The voice on the phone sounded harsh and cold.

"What?"

"You've got your money. I suggest you get the hell out of here before Curtis changes his mind about letting you live."

"Who is this?"

The phone went dead.

Steve rubbed his eyes. Was that good news or bad? Didn't sound good. Dazed, he held the buzzing receiver and glanced across the bed. Susan was lying on her stomach—her bare back uncovered. He hung up the phone, not taking his eyes off her. Unbroken by tan lines, her sun-kissed skin looked smooth and inviting. He scooted next to her and wrapped her in his arms. She stirred sleepily. He wondered if last night's passion fires were still burning embers waiting to be rekindled.

Susan opened her eyes, pleased to see his face. His warm, strong arms around her felt like heaven. He smelled of Stetson. Clean. Sexy. Last night drifted in her mind like a hazy dream. He'd survived the confrontation with Curtis. Relieved, she left no doubt about her feelings for him. Never before had she been attracted to a man so strongly. Last night she wanted all of him. She took all of him. It was heaven.

And this morning, as she kissed him, she hoped that nothing would ever change the way she felt right now. The warmth, the love, the strength—last night he gave it all to her. She moaned and held him tighter. He responded to her touch. She kissed him from his lips to his ear and hugged him. She couldn't get close enough. As the bed sheet shifted and fell to the floor, the damn phone rang again.

Steve picked it up. "What do you want?"

"Mr. Raven?"

"It's your quarter."

Susan rolled over on top of him, the teasing smile of a naughty girl on her lips. With her long black hair hanging down in his face, he tried to divide his attention between her foreplay and what the man on the phone was saying.

"Mr. Olson, here."

Steve blinked. "First National?"

"You requested we notify you when a transfer into your account had been completed. I am happy to report it came through this morning. Looks like you finally got a decent paycheck."

"How many zeros?"

"Six."

"I'll be damned."

"May I make a suggestion?" the banker said. "I think this might be a good time to settle up on those bad checks you have in collections. We'd certainly like to have them off our backs. And let's get your airplane out of hock, too."

"Handle it, Mr. Olson." He tossed the phone down, smiling. He was a goddamn millionaire. Rolling over, he put Susan on her back.

"Six big ones, baby. Let's get out of this dump." He kissed her and jumped up from the bed. As he pulled his trousers on, he looked at her lying there, uncovered. Wow. But she wasn't getting up. "Come on. We're leaving. Get your clothes on." He gave her a wink. "Or are we flying naked this morning?"

She smiled and stretched out her arms, beckoning him to come to her.

"Hurry."

She sat up, frowning. "We're not going, Steve."

Steve ignored her, zipped his pants, and reached for his holster.

"I wasn't kidding last night. We can't go."

He put his shirt on over his .45 and tucked in the tails without buttoning it. What was she talking about? She was going to mess up everything.

He dropped to his knees in front of her and stared into her eyes. For several moments, he didn't say anything, searching for the words she'd understand. This was important; it meant life or death. He couldn't risk her life any longer. The rat cellar was a close call—too close. How many more of those would she survive? The first phone call lingered in his mind—the threat.

"I need to get you out of here," he said. "Trust me to do the right thing."

"Blind trust is a lot to ask of someone."

"You have to," he said.

"Then you have to take them with us."

"Ray won't go. You heard his speech."

"Janis and Lisa will. And Lo."

"The plane can't carry everyone."

"Take a staff car," she said.

"They'll just run us down. We'll get caught."

Steve saw tears shining in her eyes. But she *had* to understand, she *had* to trust him. This was the only way. "We have to go now." He got up and held his hand out to her. Slowly, she grasped his fingers and he pulled her up. For a few moments, he held her. Then she dressed quietly and they slipped out of Tamarack Hall.

Steve hailed the first staff car he saw. "Airfield," he said. The driver seemed happy to have somewhere to go.

As they raced toward the main gate, the ominous phone call lingered in Steve's mind. He knew these people didn't make idle threats. His eyes keen for trouble, he tensed as the car approached the security checkpoint. The driver stopped and talked with a guard.

Looking into the back seat, the guard asked, "What's your business at the airfield?"

Steve was about to snarl that it was none of his damn business when Susan jumped in.

"Officer," she said with a wink, "my friend here," she hung on Steve's shoulder, "is taking me up in his air-o-plane. He promised to get me higher than anyone else ever had. I suspect, though, it'll be the other way around." She slowly pulled her dress above her knees, adding to the effect.

The security guard touched his helmet. "I'll bet you're right about that, pretty lady. Have a nice flight." The draw bar went up and he waved the car through.

Steve couldn't believe it. Susan was truly amazing.

On the tarmac, the Cessna had been parked next to Curtis'

gold and white Learjet, its turbine intakes covered with gleaming gold caps to keep the birds out. His little blue and white airplane looked so unimpressive next to the sleek jet, but he didn't care. Flying was flying. Little planes and big jets all flew by the same rules—pitch was airspeed, power was altitude and any landing he walked away from was a *good* landing.

He unlocked the door of his plane.

Susan buckled in.

The engine cranked and fired with a puff of smoke, the propeller's drone filling the California morning air. Steve taxied to the runway threshold where he performed his run-up and pre-flight checklist. Satisfied, he set the *Com-One* radio to 121.3 and dropped the flaps ten degrees. He looked at Susan. "Ready to get high, baby?"

She smiled and gave him the thumbs-up sign.

He pushed the throttle all the way in. The knob vibrated in his hand as the engine revved to full power. He released the brakes. The cool morning air was perfect for flying. The airplane quickly accelerated to sixty knots and he pulled back on the yoke. Holding the nose high, the Cessna rose from the runway. Easing the nose over to gain airspeed, he slowly retracted the flaps. As he turned south, climbing, he picked up the radio mike. "So-Cal Approach— Cessna niner-four-niner, twenty-four miles north. Request radar vector to Orange County."

"Cessna niner-four-niner—squawk three-three-two-seven ident," came the reply over the ceiling speaker. Steve reached down and turned the transponder dials.

"Three-three-two-seven coming at you." He pressed the *Ident* button. A little yellow light glowed on the console. A few minutes passed as the controller talked with another pilot.

"Niner-four-niner—radar contact, two-one miles northwest. Turn to heading one-two-zero and maintain one-five-hundred. Clear to Orange County. Maintain VFR."

"Niner-four-niner on one-two-zero at one-five-hundred. Thank you." Steve put the mike back into its holder on the panel.

"What was all that?" Susan asked above the engine drone.

"He told me to fly a compass heading of 120 degrees at 1500 feet above sea level." He pointed to the instruments. "And here," he pointed to the transponder, "I'm squawking this number, which identifies our bleep on their radar screens. Now they know who we are up here."

"So we won't run into anyone else?"

"True to a point. But he said to maintain VFR, or visual flight rules, which means I am ultimately responsible for the safe separation of aircraft, visually."

"Why didn't you do all this on the flight from Nevada to Simi Valley?"

"We didn't need to." He looked around. "But now we're entering the most congested airspace in Southern California. Up here, we all have to work together to make it safe for everyone. It's amazing though, the number of people working down there to make this flight possible." Steve spotted a 737, off to his right, dropping through his altitude. A United emblem adorned the tail.

"Niner-four-niner," the speaker blared. "Traffic, three o'clock, descending to LAX through one-five-hundred."

Steve grabbed the mike. "I have the traffic—niner-four-niner." He put the mike in his lap. "See how they can help? But not always. We have to keep our eyes open all the time."

Susan looked out the window at the city below. Los Angeles skyscrapers reflected off the underside of the wing. It was a beautiful morning to leave Solartech Labs. But thinking of those they had left behind, tainted her excitement over this flight to Orange County. She had no idea what Steve was up to. That worried her even more.

"Why are we going to Orange County?"

He pulled a piece of paper out of his pocket and handed it to her. "If we should get separated for any reason, this is where you'll be safe. Tom and I go way back." He checked his airspace with a visual sweep and picked up the mike again. "So-Cal Approach—niner-four-niner still with you."

"Niner-four-niner—stay on course," the controller answered. "In four miles expect heading zero-niner-zero and one-thousand. John Wayne tower is on frequency one-one-niner-point-niner."

"Call my turn."

"Roger."

Steve set the tower's frequency on the *Com-Two* radio. "When we're on the ground, we'll rent a car and I'll take you to

Tom's. You'll stay there 'til I get back."

"From where?"

"Just some unfinished business I need to attend to."

She didn't like him leaving her in the dark and was about to voice a protest when the speaker crackled. "Niner-four-niner—turn to heading zero-niner-zero and begin your descent to Orange County. Contact tower. Frequency change approved. Have a good day."

"Thank you," Steve replied. He switched to *Com-Two*. "John Wayne tower—niner-four-niner with you." The engine drone subsided as Steve pulled back on the power and the airplane began to sink toward the airport in front of them.

"Niner-four-niner—welcome to Orange County. Winds light and variable. Make right traffic. Clear to land—one-niner right."

"Roger," Steve radioed. "One-niner right—clear to land."

Susan tightened her seat belt. When would this really be over?

Chapter Eighty-Eight
SOLARTECH SECURITY

The morning sun beamed down from a misty California sky. Janis, having left Lisa sleeping, followed Lo out of Tamarack Hall to a staff car idling under the carport. An attendant opened the door. "Good morning, gentlemen."

Janis got in. "Smile," he said to Lo. "It's a beautiful day."

"So you say. I'm not so sure this day is any better than last the three." He looked at his watch. "They called meeting for 9:00 AM. We're already late."

"Relax. Half of them are probably wrecked with hangovers. They won't mind the delay."

"Maybe not the workers—but Curtis is a different story." Lo touched his nose. "Something stinky about rich man, Janis. Nothing on the Internet about him. I look for hours. It's a mystery to me."

"Nothing?"

Shaking his head, Lo looked out the window as they raced toward the lab. "Tiger jaws clamp tight," he said and mumbled something else in Chinese.

"Will you quit that?" Janis was in no mood for Lo's Oriental soothsaying. Besides, the Internet didn't have information about everyone—did it? He fidgeted in his seat. All he knew for sure was the sooner he got this project started, the sooner he'd be finished and on his way home. He leaned forward and tapped the driver's shoulder. "Step on it."

They barreled up the ramp between the towering stainless steel buildings and under the steel archway to the vehicle lobby. The driver stopped in front of the glass-encased entrance. They got out and the staff car drove away.

Lo held open the atrium door. "Enter tiger's lair."

Janis smirked. They rode the escalator to the lobby. His shoes ticked on the marble floor, which was inlaid with a gold atomic symbol that spanned the foyer. Walking toward the reception counter, he looked up at the ceiling some five stories high, supported by six gold pillars. At least they looked like real gold.

Under the "Security" sign at the end of the counter, a bank

of video screens lined the wall. Monitoring various areas within the building, they were under the watchful eye of a security officer dressed in a white shirt and red tie. A smile lit his face as they approached. "Dr. Mackey," he said with a handshake then turned to Lo. "Mr. Chin. Nice to meet you."

Lo bowed.

From behind the counter, a woman with silver hair brought them two folded white lab coats. Squinting behind her spectacles, she helped Janis into his coat, wrestled with a stubborn button, and inspected the fit.

Janis thought it felt stiff from too much starch.

"Very nice." The woman turned to Lo and helped him with his coat. "Such a handsome man."

Lo gave her a funny look.

Smiling, she shuffled away.

The security officer opened a folder, shuffled through some papers, and removed two ID tags. "You'll need these." He clipped an ID tag to each of their coat pockets. Lo inspected his. He didn't seem impressed. There was no picture—just a black-on-white barcode under a Solartech Labs insignia, a gold shield and a blue atom pierced by a yellow lightning bolt. Janis noticed the security officer didn't have an ID tag clipped to his pocket.

"Where's yours?"

With a proud smile, he pulled up his left sleeve and displayed a twenty-four-pin microchip that had been surgically implanted in his arm, complete with a flashing red LED. The black-on-white barcode was sealed in clear plastic. "Never leave home without it," he said. "The halls and labs are randomly laser scanned. Our main computers track the whereabouts of everyone in this building." He pulled his sleeve down. "This one is electronically encoded. Yours have to be in plain view so don't be sticking them in your pocket or under a lab coat. We don't like false alarms. Got that?"

As Lo patted his tag, Janis quickly rechecked the position of his.

"We're ready," the officer said. "They're waiting for you in Tech-Com Control."

Chapter Eighty-Nine
TECH-COM CONTROL

Janis followed the guard down a long hallway and into the depths of Solartech Labs.

"Mr. Chin," the guard said to Lo as they walked. "Weren't you on the ISIS programming team a couple of years back?"

Lo nodded.

"I read somewhere that you debugged the transcription program single-handed. Pretty impressive feat considering the number of brainards that had tried it."

"Thank you. But please, all in a day's work." He looked at Janis. "Magazine make big deal over nothing."

"Maybe to you," Janis said.

At an intersection in the corridor they entered a glass-enclosed catwalk that connected the two buildings. Janis looked down to the ramp. A car went by. He looked up at the steel archway with its ominous message towering above.

At the end of the catwalk, they entered a room skirted by electronic control panels and dozens of monitors. Several video screens hung from the ceiling. Technicians, wearing white lab coats, sat on swivel chairs in front of their stations. A row of windows overlooked a room where six rows of super computers hummed in servitude to the technicians.

Crossing the control room, Janis went to another window in the wall. About eighteen inches high and six feet long, it was made of glass a foot thick with rounded corners. A light beyond the ominous window blinked on and off in one-second intervals. When the light came on, he saw a steel-ribbed chamber with tunnel-like walls laced with piping. When the light went off, he saw a red glow coming from somewhere beyond his view. What kind of contraption was this? It looked like something from a horror movie.

Lo stood next to him, staring into the strange window. "Eye of tiger," he said hauntingly.

His words sent a chill down Janis' spine. As his mind tried to calculate the meaning of all this technology, a voice from above broke the silence.

"Dr. Mackey."

Curtis stood on a landing above the control room, an office window and door behind him. He made his way down the steel stairs, tapping the golden staff with each step. The metallic twang reverberated around the room. Several other personnel emerged from the office and followed him down. "Glad you could join us this morning. We've been waiting for this moment for a long time."

On the control-room floor, the technicians fanned out around Curtis. Dressed in his black hat and long black coat, he looked out of place among the men in their white lab coats, ID tags dangling from their pockets. But Curtis didn't have an ID tag. Janis got goose bumps, recalling the security officer's implant, and warily shook Curtis' hand.

The others went to their stations.

"Before I show you around, I'd like to introduce my staff," Curtis said and walked up to the first man sitting at the console. "This is Roger Deadford."

Roger smiled, his black hair slicked back with a greasy shine. He looked about thirty. Clean-shaven.

"Our electrical engineer," Curtis said. "Power plant and distribution. Keeps us plugged in, so to speak."

Janis scanned all the meters and dials on the console then smiled at Roger.

Curtis patted Roger on the back and walked to the next station.

"Good morning, sir," the longhaired young man at the monitor said.

"Good morning, Stan." Curtis put a hand on his shoulder. "Stan Burton. Mechanical engineer, Harvard grad, and a genius at keeping the nuts and bolts tight around here. Nothing he can't build."

"With a little help from my team, sir."

"Ah, yes. Your team. Of course." He moved to the next station.

Janis lagged behind to acknowledge Stan, who looked more like a hippy than an engineer.

Lo stayed one step behind Janis.

The man at the next station was much older than Stan, mid sixties Janis figured, thin gray hair and wrinkled cheeks. Curtis shook the man's hand. "Robert. How are you this morning?"

"Tired, sir."

"Sorry to hear that." He turned to Janis. "Best damn synchrotron operator in the business. Goes way back, 1952, wasn't it? Worked with Glasser on the Brookhaven Cosmotron. He's busted a lot of atoms in his time. Right, Robert?"

"A smashing career, sir."

Curtis laughed lightly and moved on.

"And this, gentlemen, is Dr. Tracy McClarence. She joins us all the way from Cavendish Labs at Cambridge, Great Britain."

Janis' mouth fell open. The redhead looked much too beautiful to be a scientist. What was it about her, those sparkling green eyes or the little freckles on her nose? Or maybe her thin pink lips and perfect teeth. She sat at a keyboard, returning his smile. He almost didn't hear Curtis explain that she was a laser physicist, tops in her field. As Curtis moved on to the next station, Janis followed him but continued smiling at Tracy as he walked backwards, his heart in a flutter. Every line. Every curve. She was gorgeous.

"This is Ray's station," Curtis explained as he placed his hands on the back of an empty chair. "From here, he controls the hydrogen atoms. He'll be joining us later."

"How's he doing?" Janis asked.

"Rested well last night, or so Doc tells me." Curtis moved to the next man seated at the console. The monitor at this station grabbed Janis' attention because it was the most beautiful thing in the place, except Tracy. A computer-generated funnel rotated like a tornado, color coded in green, yellow, and red. Mesmerized, Janis watched in awe as it whirled and twisted.

Lo leaned forward. "Gravity generator?"

"That's right!" Curtis said. "We call it the MIGGS. Johnson here is our expert."

Johnson smiled. His straight brown hair hung down past his shoulders and he wore black-rimmed glasses. He looked like he'd eaten too many Twinkies. "The MIGGS is our Mass Imitation Gravity Generating Simulator," Johnson explained as he pointed to the strange window in the far wall, the one with the thick glass. "She's capable of simulating a 3M star mass rotating at the speed of light." He turned back to the monitor. "This is a rerun of the last test…let's see…14 July last month. Got her up to full speed.

We can identify the event horizon on the monitor, right here, in red. Escape velocity 186,000 miles per second. Nothing will get past her."

"An artificial black hole?" Lo asked with a mix of curiosity and disbelief etched on his face.

"Mathematically, yes," Johnson explained. "The Supers work the numbers." He pointed to the super computer window.

"What's it for?" asked Lo.

"Containment," Curtis said.

"What has to be contained?" Janis asked.

"Later!" Curtis barked.

Janis flinched, puzzled at the harsh reaction to a simple question. Why?

"This way." Curtis motioned them on to the next station. It had two swivel chairs, twin monitors, and dual keyboards. "And this Janis, is where you will work your mathematical magic. We've modified this station to accommodate both of you." He wagged his finger between Janis and Lo.

As Janis inspected his terminal, his eyes caught the motion of an old man entering the control room. He wore a white lab coat with the familiar ID tag dangling from a pocket. The old guy looked like the mad scientist in a Frankenstein movie. Maybe it was because of his scraggly gray hair and bushy eyebrows.

Curtis pointed to the old man. "Ah, yes, gentlemen. Last, but not least. I'd like you to meet our Tech-Com Director of Operations, Mr. Ted Benning."

Slightly hunched over, Ted limped up to Janis, shook his hand and smiled through half decayed teeth. "We velcome you."

"It doesn't get any better than this," Curtis proclaimed as he walked to the windows overlooking the Supers. He raised his arms and held the golden staff above his head. The black coat spread open, making him seem larger than life against the glare of the glass. "Together, we'll make the calculations to the 13th Power." His words echoed through the control room.

Janis looked at Tracy, checking her reaction to Curtis' theatrics. She just shook her head and went back to her keyboard, typing. Janis pushed his glasses up. He wanted to get close to her, to get to know her, but feared she might be the snooty professional type, the type of woman he'd never had any luck with before. The competition. Would she be any different? He planned to find out later, when Curtis finished showing off.

Lo sat down at his workstation and began typing. The monitor blinked on. Numbers and symbols began scrolling down the screen.

"Leave him to play with his new toy," Curtis said to Janis. "Follow me. There's more to see."

With Curtis at his side, Janis walked out of Tech-Com Control through a set of swinging doors that opened to a long hallway. Windows lined the wall overlooking the Supers below. Several technicians passed by. They seemed preoccupied with their duties and managed only cordial nods in passing.

Curtis motioned a turn down a hallway to the left. At the end, a set of huge steel doors blocked their way. Curtis gained admittance by placing his hand on a scanner. A light beam traversed his palm and a buzzer sounded. Door locks clicked open. "Let's go," he said, letting Janis enter first. It seemed as though they'd entered another world.

"The heartbeat of Tech-Com Control," Curtis yelled over the loud drone of machinery. A technician driving an electric cart whizzed by—another passed from the other direction, towing a trailer full of workers wearing gray jumpsuits and white hard hats. The place buzzed with activity.

Janis looked up to a brightly lit ceiling some three stories above him, skirted by steel catwalks and supported by I-beam pillars. Pipes, electrical cords, and air ducts snaked throughout the massive room chaotically. Huge steel-encased machines towered up the walls. Welders spewed molten slag down to the floor while several men held a beam in place. A man standing on a ladder must've been their supervisor.

Hauling a large wooden crate, a forklift whined by and the driver waved. Several men dressed in white lab coats and holding clipboards were standing around a cylindrical tank, concerned about vapor escaping from a valve on top. Another electric cart went by with a diesel generator in tow. The whole place smelled like wet cement.

"What's all this?" Janis yelled to Curtis over the drone.

"This is where it all begins—the race to the speed of light." Tucking the staff under his arm, Curtis directed Janis' attention to a group of men wearing thick gloves and stacking silver cylinders that were covered with frost. "Liquid hydrogen for the 13th Power experiment," Curtis explained at the top of his voice. "They go in the ionizer, that rust colored machine with round doors. It reverses the polarity of atoms, strips off electrons, and injects them into the synchrotron, over there."

He pointed to a twenty-foot high steel ribbed tube that seemed to end at a concrete wall. "It's sixteen miles in length and can accelerate nuclei to about a quarter light speed." Curtis turned. "See that glass tube? A linear accelerator, four miles long. It goes into the MIGGS."

Janis noticed doors painted with hazard stripes mounted in the walls next to the glass and steel tubes. "Where do those doors go?" he hollered over all the noise.

"Service access tunnels," Curtis shouted. "Almost fifty miles of them honeycombing under Simi Valley, with dozens of access doors like that—some from inside this building and others from outside locations throughout the valley. Makes it easy for us to service the synchrotron and laser resonator."

Janis looked around. "So where *is* the laser?"

"At the other end of the glass tube four miles away. Activated by the Supers, it shoots a beam into the linear accelerator. In a millisecond, it will boost nuclei to the speed of light."

"A particle beam," Janis said loudly, smiling.

"If it works right," Curtis said and looked at the ceiling, pointing to a chrome-plated pipeline. "Up there," he yelled, "electrons stripped from the atoms are directed into the MIGGS and electro-magnetically aligned into a target. When impacted by the particle beam, we should get fission and containment." Curtis smiled. His gold tooth glistened. "Wham-o!" He slammed a fist into his hand. "That's where you come in."

"How's that?"

"Get with Ray. He'll tell you what he needs." Curtis looked around, his hands outstretched. "All this is for naught if you guys fail to make the calculations to the 13th Power. We've got the equipment but we don't have the formulas to make it work. Don't let me down on this, Janis."

They walked out through the steel doors, the silence a welcome relief. But it didn't make Janis feel entirely comfortable. He now realized the huge investment Curtis had in the 13th Power project. Was he chasing a fantasy? Could Janis help him catch it? He guessed it didn't matter. Succeed or fail, Janis was getting paid to try. One question lingered.

"What about containment?" he asked as they walked toward Tech-Com Control. "What needs to be contained?"

Curtis stopped in the middle of the hall. "The MIGGS is no bubble chamber, Janis. We're not going to smash atoms into tiny particles, take pictures, and name the debris. No, sir. We're going to contain the particles, re-accelerate, and re-collide them, over and over again until we find the 13th Power." Curtis began walking. "It's a good plan but we can't get the math right."

Janis decided to be blunt. "So what's in it for you? I mean— Ray wants to be famous. That's no mystery. But what about you— an archeologist turned atomic scientist? Doesn't compute with me, *Mister* Curtis."

"Never mind what's in it for me, Dr. Mackey." He shook his golden staff. "Just do your job and we will get along just fine."

Janis stiffened. Curtis and his damn attitude problem. He certainly didn't have all his cards on the table. Why? Could he be holding jokers—or an ace up his sleeve? Whatever the case, this wasn't the time to force his hand or call his bluff. After all, Janis didn't want to blow his million-dollar deal. As they walked through the doors into Tech-Com Control, he decided to play along, for now. Besides, this project had become very interesting. He was looking at the redhead.

The doors closed behind Curtis as he walked into Tech-Com Control. He went up the metal stairs to his office above the control room, wondering if Janis was being stubborn or careful. Would he perform to the caliber required for the project? He'd better.

Inside, Jonathan sat waiting for him, his face long.

Curtis laid his staff on the desk. "Why the look?"

"I transferred the money, as you requested."

Curtis didn't answer. He poured a cup of coffee.

"The P. I. has been notified. He'll be leaving soon."

"Good riddance."

"Are you sure you don't want me to get Judas on him? The bastard deserves to die."

Curtis stirred sugar into his coffee. His mind raced back to the Jungles of Borneo. Memories of Fred Jenkins sent a cold chill down his spine. Not the killing—the punishment. A Sumatra prison and death by hanging or beheading, if he was lucky. Should the Malaysian authorities ever find out he was still alive, they'd stop at nothing to get him back. His life wouldn't be worth a nickel.

Was Steve Raven bluffing about the letter to Singapore? Curtis couldn't afford to take the chance. It had been a long time since Borneo and he had a lot invested in this project, too much to let a greedy P. I. ruin. Killing him seemed like a good idea. But they'd tried that, and failed. Steve had guts and luck, the kind of man who was hard to kill. He had to be dealt with wisely.

"Steve Raven is like a bad dream," Curtis said. "He keeps coming back. Just let him go." He took a sip of coffee. "You know—he acts tough. But right now his tail is tucked between his legs and he's running like the chicken-shit that he really is."

Jonathan walked to the window overlooking Tech-Com Control. "I don't think so, boss. You should've killed him when you had the chance. The bad dream may come back to haunt you."

Curtis stood beside Jonathan, thinking he'd better be wrong about that. Below, on the control room floor, a commotion caught his eye. Lo seemed excited, waving at Janis who ran to Lo's terminal and leaned over his shoulder. Lo pointed to something on the monitor. What had they found?

"What is it, Lo?" Janis asked.

"Run file checks here—get feel for system."

"It's all Greek to me."

"But look." Lo scrolled down a list of files. "All these reside in upper memory. Most are program files in directories like this." He clicked on one for demonstration. An error flag appeared. *No Application Associated.* "See. Okay to do that." He clicked on several more with the same result.

"So?"

"Now look here. Mixed up with files I found these." He pointed to one. "File extension *w-m*. I've not seen anything like that before."

"Is that bad?"

"Look what happens." He clicked on a *w-m* file and got

Access Denied. He clicked on several more with the same result. "See?"

"What does that mean?"

"System bugged. And I bet..." he worked the keyboard. The monitor flashed to a program manager called the Worm. All the information for the program appeared.

Janis said, "What does it do?"

"Spies on data and reports to a host computer—off site somewhere. Very complicated."

"Who's bugging the system?" he asked as Lo clicked through several windows.

"No telling. Worm has read-only files. Changes locked out. Can't break into program."

"Then delete the damn thing and be done with it."

Lo closed the program manager for the Worm and went back to the list of files. He typed the command to delete them. *Access Denied* flashed on the screen. He looked at Janis, shaking his head. "No can do."

"What?" Janis swallowed hard. "Curtis better know about this." He turned, found Ted at the MIGGS console with Johnson. It looked like they were busy with something. Tracy was with them. Janis walked over to the huddle.

"Hi," Tracy said with a smile.

Janis said, "Hello," and quickly turned his attention to Ted. He didn't want to seem overly anxious to talk to her. Tapping the old man on the shoulder, "Ted—get Curtis down here."

"Vait one minute." He didn't turn his attention away from the MIGGS monitor.

Janis looked at Tracy. She shrugged. He tapped the old man's shoulder again. "Now!"

Ted handed Janis the phone. "Dial *G-O-L-D*, 4-6-5-3."

"Thanks." The phone rang. Gold? How pompous.

"Curtis." His voice sounded harsh, as if the interruption annoyed him.

"Better get down here right away," Janis said. "The Supers are bugged."

The phone clicked. A moment later, the sound of Curtis' voice filled the control room as he stormed down the stairs. "What are you talking about?" He ran to Lo's station. "Bugged? Bugged how?"

"Memory resident program," Lo said. "The Worm."

"A virus?"

"A bug. A spy." Lo pointed to the monitor. "Every time something happens in computer, the Worm analyzes it and sends data out on Modem2, secondary device running in upper memory. Main modem not used so computer not report to terminal. Very sneaky."

"Can you get rid of it?"

Lo thought a moment. "Aside from pull plug—no."

Curtis picked up the phone, dialed quickly and groaned. "Get Alex up here. Now!" As he put the phone down, Ray stormed into the control room, arm in a sling and eyes on fire.

"Ray—how are you?" Janis said. He was still smiling when Ray pushed him against the console. "What the…?"

"You think I don't know, you bastard!"

"What?" Janis put up his guard.

"She wasn't in her room all night!" Ray grabbed Janis by the lab coat. Curtis and two technicians jumped in to restrain Ray. During the scuffle, he kept yelling, "That's my daughter, you bastard! My daughter! How could you?"

Janis, seething, pulled free as the others held Ray back. After straightening his ruffled lab coat, Janis clutched his throbbing hand. Ray was making this job impossible. How could anybody work with him like this? He was going to ruin everything. "What's with you?" Janis glared at the maniac.

"I called your room this morning. Lisa answered, you son of a bitch!"

"She was sleeping."

"In your bed!"

"Nothing happened!"

"That's what you say."

Janis felt like beating some sense into Ray though it probably wouldn't do any good. Lisa was right—her father was overprotective. An understatement. "Did you ask her? You said she answered the phone. Did you ask *her*, damn it?"

"No." Ray looked down to the floor.

"Why not?"

"I hung up and assumed the worst." He readjusted the sling

on his arm. "Maybe I was wrong. I'm-I'm sorry."

"Sorry? You're obsessed. Accuse me of having my way with your daughter—is there nothing you won't do?"

"Nothing."

"That's what you've given her. Nothing. No love. No happiness. No freedom. Nothing."

"That's not true. I've sacrificed a lot for her. And I'd sacrifice a lot more. My life—even the whole world if I had to."

"Stop talking like an idiot."

The room fell silent.

Ray's shoulders slouched. "All right—I said I was sorry. I lost my head. But you know how I feel about her. Why do you have to push it?"

"I pushed nothing. She fell asleep in my tub so I put her to bed and left her there this morning. She's not six years old any more, Ray. Let her make her own choices. She's really quite capable... "

Alex stormed into the control room, followed by two of his security men. "What's going on in here?"

"It's the computers," Curtis said. "They're bugged. What do you think?"

Alex looked at Lo's monitor, still flashing *Access Denied.* "What can I to do about it?"

"I want a full investigation," Curtis bellowed. "Find out who put the bug in here, who it's reporting to, and how to kill it. I suggest you start with Devin. Get on it right away." Curtis climbed the stairs to his office, cursing.

Rubbing his throbbing shoulder, Ray thought there was no end to Devin's interference. "How could anyone plant a bug in here?" he asked Alex.

"Stranger things have happened."

"What about the private eye? Could he have penetrated security this deep?"

Alex furrowed his brow. "I wouldn't put it past him."

"Well—go get him—find out."

"He left this morning."

Looking at the door, Ray said, "So we'll never know."

Alex shrugged and walked out.

Ray blinked. Steve couldn't have had anything to do with the message flashing on Lo's monitor. The P. I. may have been cunning and resourceful, but he wasn't knowledgeable enough to access the Supers. Why had Alex been satisfied with that explanation so quickly?

Turning to Janis, who looked disgusted with him, Ray said, "Lisa will always be my little girl. I can't help it. Kate forced me to do things you'd never understand—you've never been a father. "

Janis sat down, stared at the monitor. Was he even listening? Ray went on anyway. "I've been overprotective—I know it. Lisa's never had a mother, Janis. She has no recollection of Kate. We talked about that yesterday. She understands why I sent her away. She'll forgive me—I'm all she's got."

"But not all she'll ever have."

Janis, still boiling with anger, looked at Tracy. She was shaking her head as if unimpressed with the madness around her. Great first impression. Maybe she wouldn't be any different than the other women he'd known, but he wished Ray hadn't made him look like a womanizer. Tracy, wearing a green skirt and white blouse, walked back to her station, her red hair swaying. She was perfect. Perfectly professional, perfectly wrong for him.

Janis swiveled his chair toward Ray who had leaned against the console and was now futzing with his sling. "Are you done with your temper tantrum?"

"I told you I was sorry."

"What's on the agenda for today?"

"A test fire," he said.

"What?"

"A full-systems run. Go over the math first, check the formulas. Lo can reprogram the Supers. How long will it take you?"

"Maybe six hours."

"Let's go with that." He turned to Ted at the main control console. "Start the clock."

Ted pushed a button on his panel. Above the window overlooking the Supers, a black digital clock with red numbers started running backwards, one second at a time. A program schedule appeared on all the monitors. "Let's keep the countdown on schedule," Ray said. "Six hours."

"What if we're not ready?" asked Janis.

"Wouldn't be the first time. We'll just abort and restart, later."

"You've done this before?"

"Not the whole program."

"What if the formulas are still wrong?"

"Then we'll have to fix them and try again."

Janis adjusted his glasses. "So what makes this experiment any different than the hundreds of atom-smashing projects going on around the world every day?"

"First of all," Ray said. "We're using a carbon dioxide laser to boost accelerated nuclei to the speed of light. At least that's the plan. This high-speed collision will produce the smallest subatomic particles ever.

"Secondly, we're going to contain the fission in a gravity chamber. No one else has ever done that. A multiple-collision strategy increases our odds of success, but it's dangerous. Without the MIGGS, the atomic reaction would level the place. Nothing like Hiroshima, of course. But we're still at ground zero."

"Curtis said you couldn't get the math right. What's the problem?"

"We have some formulas the Supers keep spitting out as errors. When we couldn't reformulate them properly, I thought of you. I'm hoping you can correct the formulas so the programming accepts them. Then the Supers will be able to make the measurements to the 13th Power instead of bleeping out a bunch of errors."

Lo cut in. "When we calculate and measure the 13th Power, how do we see what we find there?"

"The monitors will display a computer-enhanced nucleus. It will appear to be expanding and you'll get the illusion of traveling into its core."

"How?" Janis asked.

"Colliding at high speeds, things happen pretty fast, so we're using a triangulation of electron microscopes to transmit a 3-D image of the event to the Supers. As the nuclei come apart, the MIGGS will contain the particles and the CEI, the Computer Enhanced Imaging program, will record it in slow motion. When we play it back, it should be quite a show."

Janis rubbed his chin. "But Curtis said we were going to contain the particles and smash them over and over again. That's what the MIGGS is for."

Ray touched his mustache. "I wonder why he would say that. It's not true. We need the MIGGS to contain the particles so the electron microscopes and the CEI can analyze them. Without it, the debris would be hurled into oblivion. Why would he lie?"

"I think he has an ulterior motive for the MIGGS—maybe even for the 13th Power project."

"Like what?"

"You're the atomic physicist. What else could be contained?"

Ray wrinkled his brow, thinking. Then his eyes widened and he snapped his fingers. "That's it!" Excitement lit up his face. "The Higgs! He's after the Higgs boson."

"The Higgs bos-what?" Janis asked.

"The Higgs boson, the particle that generates the atomic strong force. It gives matter mass." Ray ran to the MIGGS window and tapped on the thick glass. "He's going to contain it in there. Curtis is going to make history."

"History?" Tracy asked.

"That's right. If the Higgs boson is at the 13th Power, it makes sense to contain it. He'll have proof that it exists."

"More than that," Tracy added, "he'll have the power."

"What power?" Janis asked.

"The power to change everything," she said and turned back to her monitor.

Janis looked at Ray. "Change everything? Ray? What does she mean by that?"

Ray didn't answer. He was staring into the MIGGS window as if mesmerized by the blinking light.

"Come on. What do you say to that?"

Ray turned around. "I say we get cracking on those formulas."

"What about the Worm?" Lo asked.

"We can't let *that* stop us."

Tracy smiled.

Chapter Ninety

THE INVESTIGATION

At FBI headquarters, an elevator opened. Agent Lou Marston stepped out with another passenger who was folding a copy of the *Washington Post*. The disaster in Nevada had taken the headlines. Lou walked to his reception desk where Miss Jennings greeted him with a smile.

"Good morning, Lou."

"For a Monday, I guess." He set his sunglasses on top of his pepper-gray hair. "Anything for me?"

"Your wife called this morning—told me to tell you, and I quote, 'Don't even try it.' What do you suppose that's all about?"

"S-she must have heard from my lawyer," Lou said, loosening his tie.

"And this." She handed him a memo. "Answering service faxed it over this morning."

He read the note. "Hmm. Atomtech." Handing it back he said, "Get this Colonel Fallon on the line. I'll be in my office."

"Right away."

He closed the door, removed his suit coat, and tossed it over a chair. Straightening his vest, he walked to his desk and picked up a silver-framed picture of a beautiful woman hugging a young girl. They were dressed in their Sunday best. His eyes watered.

"Sorry, Sandy," he said to the photo. "Somebody has to end this madness." He hoped his lawyer hadn't been too hard on her.

He replaced the picture, walked to the window, and opened the blinds. The Capitol building stood majestically before him, a sight that inspired him every morning. But he felt sad today. He was missing her already. The phone rang.

"I have Colonel Fallon on line one," Miss Jennings announced.

He picked up the phone and walked back to the window. "How can I help you, Colonel?"

"The Atomtech tragedy, Lou. I'm sure you've heard about it."

"I read you're heading up the investigation." He paced in front of the window. "How's it going?"

"The FAA and the Pentagon have been jerking me around. I'm hoping you'll check out a lead I have."

"Depends."

"Some dead guy—went by the name of Melvin Anderson. I have sources telling me he's alive and well, going by the name of Frank Curtis, an archeologist turned atomic researcher. Can you help me with that?"

"This kind of thing is out of my jurisdiction—more down your alley, don't you think?"

"Thirty-seven Americans are dead, Lou."

"It was an accident."

"Hardly. I have reason to believe they were murdered by government soldiers."

Lou swallowed. "Outrageous."

"Get your nose out of the reg book and help me nail the bastards."

"You got any proof?" Lou went to his desk, pushed aside some paperwork, grabbed a pad and pen.

"First of all, the dead and wounded sustained battlefield injuries. Military!" the Colonel said with a sting. "Second, the place was littered with M-16 shell casings and hand grenade shrapnel. Military! And third, C4 explosives leveled one of the buildings. Military! Better yet, survivors said they saw heavily armed soldiers, equipped for war. Military! And get this—Air Traffic Control recorded an aircraft in the area that mysteriously disappeared at altitude, then reappeared some time later going the other direction."

"How much later?" Lou asked, jotting notes on his pad.

"They won't say. Claim the tape was accidentally destroyed."

"You suspect a cover up?"

"Something big."

"What's that name again? Marvin Anderson?"

"Melvin. Melvin Anderson."

"How does he fit in?"

"He may have ordered the assault against Atomtech in a defensive move to protect his project at Solartech Labs in Simi Valley."

"What project?" Lou asked after he finished writing.

"The 13th Power project."

He wrote it down, not having a clue what it meant. "Defensive, you say. Had Atomtech been on the offensive?"

"That's the way I understand it. Regardless, I need to know about Anderson. If he's a bad guy, like my information suggests, we need to stop his project and lock him up."

"What about this project?"

"I've been told it's a dangerous experiment in sub-nuclear technology, atomic force stuff."

"Dangerous?"

"Something about disintegrating the world."

"Pretty scary."

"That's how I see it, and so did Atomtech's people. They tried to stop Anderson from conducting the experiments. The guy may have struck back."

"A civilian with military capability?"

The line went silent for a moment. "I'm surprised you have the same concern. Check out Anderson. We may find out how he did it."

"I'll do that. And I'll send a task force to Nellis. Give 'em all the facts."

Lou ended the call, jotted down some instructions, and grabbed his coat on the way out the door.

"Miss Jennings," he said, handing her his notes. "Type this up with a case number and fax it to the field office in Las Vegas. I want them at Nellis within the hour and in this office by six PM, report in hand. I'll be downstairs."

Before she could reply, he stepped into the elevator and the doors closed.

The basement housed master files, stored on magnetic tape and managed by a mainframe computer. Here, fingerprint and identification records were safeguarded for use in FBI investigations worldwide. With modem connections to the databases of Interpol, Tokyo, Sidney, Singapore, and Scotland Yard, the system was the most complete record of the population ever compiled. Lou Marston hoped it knew something about Melvin Anderson.

The elevator stopped and a buzzer sounded as the door opened. Lou flashed his badge to the clerk in a steel cage. The door clicked and unlocked.

Inside, he sat at a computer terminal. Though the room was

brightly lit, the air smelled stale. He was alone.

"Let's see." He typed. A search form appeared on the monitor. He filled in the blanks. Name- Melvin Anderson. Occupation- archeologist. *Enter.*

A few moments later the monitor flashed: *MATCH - Singapore System*, then, "Standby for Download" scrolled across the screen.

"Bingo!"

Within moments an empty picture frame appeared with blank information boxes under it. The computer bleeped. *Record Deleted* flashed in red on the monitor.

"What...? How...?"

He pressed *reload* and got the same result. Lou bit his lower lip. Somebody had tampered with this file. But who? He left the basement, disappointed and concerned.

Back in his office, he sat at his desk, this problem rolling around in his brain. A pile of paperwork sat unattended, his caseload already burdensome enough without this addition. But the record deletion seemed more important. Ominous. There had to be another way to find out about Melvin Anderson, the ex-archeologist turned nuclear scientist.

He stood and paced in front of the window. The Capitol building glistened in the sunlight. He wondered if archeologists had a union or an organization where members of the profession could congregate or contact one another. Sitting at his computer, he searched online. There it was—The World Society of Archeologists. They even had a toll-free number. He picked up the phone.

Dr. Benjamin Church, whom the secretary had said was a leading archeologist in the United States, answered the call.

"Dr. Church—sorry to bother you this morning. It's urgent. I'm Agent Lou Marston from the FBI and I'm wondering if you could tell me about a colleague of yours, a Melvin Anderson. Does that name ring a bell?"

Silence.

"Dr. Church?"

"I'm sorry," he finally said. "You caught me by surprise, you did. It's been a long time since that name's been mentioned around here."

"What can you tell me about him?" Lou held his pen in hand.

"He was a bad apple, I tell you. Heard he died in Indonesia some years back. What do you need to know?"

"You say he was a bad apple?"

"In the ninety-seven years of this organization, he's the only archeologist we publicly banned from digging. Blacklisted him."

"Why?"

"The man was a good digger, all right. Trouble was, he was a better thief. Robbed the host countries blind—more than a half billion from Malaysia alone." He grunted. "Spawned a lot of hostility and killing. Did some killing of his own, too. Funny thing about greed—there's no satisfying it. Never enough. Feeds on a man's soul." The doctor paused, blew his nose. "Devil's got it now, I'm sure. So why the questions?"

"Oh, just heard his name from a friend. Can you tell me how he died?"

"Helicopter crash in Borneo. Rumor has it, he shot his own pilot and ended up as crocodile bait. A fitting end to the scoundrel, just the same."

A fitting end to the scoundrel. Lou could hear the doctor's words long after the conversation ended. Had Anderson's life and death really been erased? He pushed the intercom button.

"Miss Jennings?"

"Sir?"

"Help me with something. I searched for a file downstairs. The computer downloaded an empty form. It had been deleted. How's that possible?"

"Somebody must've deleted the data file but not the index file."

"Who would do something like that?"

"Someone unfamiliar with our system and its safeguards."

"Safeguards?"

"Index files not only keep track of data files, they also record every user. Lets us keep track of who's interested in who, how many hits a file gets."

"Hits?"

"Inquiries."

"Can you get me that information?"

"Sure," she said. "What's the file name?"

"Melvin Anderson, archeologist. Came up on the Singapore system."

"Right away, Lou."

Curbing his impatience, he picked up the picture of his wife and child again. God, what was he doing? He'd spent his whole life solving problems—sometimes big problems. But this one, his marriage, was bigger than he could manage. Married at 40, it was simple at first. But before long it became the most complicated project of his life. Between *his* job, *her* alcohol, and the constant bickering over both, after nine years he believed only divorce could bring them peace.

He looked into the hazel eyes of his little girl—his baby. Trisha would bear the brunt of the pain. If only there was a way to spare her from it. A tear stung his eye. He set the picture back down—carefully.

Miss Jennings knocked and opened the door. "Here it is."

She handed him the printout. It showed the record of his inquiry this morning. The only other entry was two years ago, logged on by *The Ark*, the CIA operative with White House authority. Lou couldn't breathe. He couldn't believe it. The White House? Colonel Fallon was right. The civilian did have military capability, as only the CIA would be so bold to orchestrate.

Still staring at the paper in his hand, Lou got a sick feeling in his stomach. The government had killed its own citizens for Melvin Anderson. Why would they do such a thing? Who the hell was this guy? Certainly, Anderson was dangerous, the 13th Power project was dangerous, and *The Ark* was backing them both. Why? He again paced in front of the window. The Capitol building didn't look so majestic anymore.

Chapter Ninety-One
TEST FIRE

In Tech-Com Control, the digital clock counted down the seconds from ten minutes to laser firing. *9:59, 9:58, 9:57.* The MIGGS hummed to life, sounding distant at first, then getting louder with each passing moment. Janis pushed up his glasses and looked into the thick window. The blinking green light went out— a red glow now flooding the interior.

Ted worked a lever on his terminal, opening a panel in the ceiling of the MIGGS. The high-pitched whine of electrically driven gears echoed through the control room as a shiny titanium cylinder, bullet-shaped and blunt-nosed, slowly descended. A single folding arm with little hydraulic muscles suspended the cylinder in the MIGGS.

"Sighting beam," Ted said.

Tracy typed on her keyboard. A thin red beam of light appeared in the MIGGS.

Looking at Ray's monitor, Janis saw a gun-sight, which Ray maneuvered with a joystick at his terminal. Moving it left and right and up and down, he aligned the titanium cylinder with the sighting beam of the laser. *Laser Locked* displayed on the monitor, flashing in red. Janis thought that didn't look too hard.

Satisfied, Ray clicked off his sighting screen and brought up the scheduler from the Supers. He adjusted his arm in the sling and looked at Lo's monitor, hoping Janis' new formulas would make the programming statements work. Only one way to find out—put them to the test. A bead of sweat trickled down his cheek. *Ready* scrolled across the screen. He clicked on the *Load* button. A status window on the monitors opened as the Supers charged the Ionizer with liquid hydrogen. The clock above the window read *7:15.*

Load Time remaining: three minutes, scrolled across the monitors. Ray glanced up to the office window above Tech-Com Control. He saw Curtis looking down at them. Jonathan handed him a tall glass. Ray looked at Ted. The old man's face shined with sweat. He looked like a nervous father in a delivery room. Ray hoped the Russian wouldn't crack under the strain.

Load Time remaining: two minutes. Ray looked at Robert. He seemed calm, waiting for the Supers to verify ionization and request access to the synchrotron. Ray turned to Johnson. His eyes were on the monitor where a faint wisp of a vortex was beginning to form, the gravity generator building its artificial black hole, humming louder and louder. Ray looked at Tracy. She scrolled through formulas on her monitor, which displayed the laser firing sequence.

Load Time remaining: one minute. Ray glanced at Roger who was adjusting the main power dial, increasing the supply as the machinery demanded more. Meters were steadily rising. Stan was on the phone with one of his team members at the Ionizer, verifying a tight seal on the injection tubes. He typed something as he held the phone to his ear with his shoulder.

Ionizer ready. As a fail-safe, the load program stopped automatically and a new window opened indicating: *Ionizer Command Sequence Start / Abort.* The countdown clock read 4:15. The scheduling program showed *3:38.*

ERROR.

"Damn!" Ray shouted. "Hold the scheduler, Lo." Something wasn't programmed right. Wiping sweat from his forehead, Ray waited for the countdown to catch up, a thirty-seven second hold. His shoulder ached. The temperature of the liquid hydrogen was rising. In thirty-one seconds it would be a useless gas. With precious seconds ticking off the clock, Ray glanced at Lo, whose monitor began flashing errors.

Lo looked at Ray, concerned. "What do we do now?"

"Abort!" Ted shouted.

Curtis tapped the golden staff on his office window. "Proceed!"

Ray entered the *Start* command seven seconds too soon.

The Ionizer buzzed. Inside the hyper-cold machine, the hydrogen atoms were now stripped of their electrons and vacuum sealed in their respective injection tubes.

Across Lo's monitor, the Supers started flagging errors faster than before. He went to work, frantically clicking the *Ignore* buttons as fast as they came up.

Ray's mouth went dry. The program was falling apart. "Stay with it, Lo...Johnson! MIGGS ready?"

"I need those seven seconds, Ray."

Ray turned to Ted. "Can we run seven seconds over in the synchrotron?"

Ted shook like his nerves were on overload. "Seven seconds—seven minutes—vhat's the difference? It's all wrong. We must abort."

"No!" Curtis yelled from the office landing. "Proceed."

Robert's monitor bleeped: *Request Synchrotron Now / Abort.*

"Do it!" Curtis bellowed.

Without another second passing, Robert clicked *Now.*

The Ionizer injected hydrogen nuclei into the synchrotron and electrons into the MIGGS, which trapped them in an electromagnetic field, its magnets rumbling like an oncoming freight train. Tech-Com Control began to tremble.

The Supers engaged the RMS, Refractive Measuring System, and the electron microscopes, which would triangulate the event and digitize it back to the Supers. At least that was working, Ray thought and looked at Johnson's monitor where a vortex swirled wildly, greens and yellows, but no red event-horizon formed. The dial was at full power. He needed more time.

As the synchrotron accelerated the nuclei toward their doom, Ray's monitor switched to the targeting window. The Supers made the electron target look like a disk of quivering little ball bearings suspended inside the titanium cylinder's nozzle. Janis' monitor switched to the CEI, the Computer Enhanced Imaging program that would record the collision and the 13th Power. Janis was cross-checking the formulas scrolling down his screen.

Ray turned to Robert at the synchrotron controls. "Give me seven seconds."

"I can't. We hit 14 trillion electron volts at two seconds before laser firing. Seven more seconds will put us over 16 TEV. The electromagnets won't hold the nuclei on target. We'll be shooting blanks in seven seconds."

"Then give me two seconds."

"You got it." Robert brought up the configuration window and added two seconds.

Satisfied, Ray turned to the MIGGS terminal. "Johnson?"

"No good, Ray. I'm at full power."

Janis looked up from the CEI program. "Roger? Can you

give us more power?"

"A hundred-sixteen percent is all Tech-Com can handle without blowing the breakers. It's a long shot. Everything will get a voltage spike so be prepared for some weird responses."

Ted yelled across the room. "No! Too dangerous!"

"Do it!" Curtis shouted.

Ray pointed to Roger. He twisted the big voltage dial. The ceiling lights brightened. The electromagnets roared like a diesel locomotive, shaking the consoles, the monitors, and the windows above the Supers. But a red band finally appeared on Johnson's screen.

"That's it!" he announced loudly.

Ray rushed to the MIGGS window. A swirling black mist began to grow inside the gravity chamber, expanding, swallowing up the titanium cylinder and snuffing out the red glow from the synchrotron, dowsing the MIGGS in total darkness. The roaring hurt his ears. What aberration were they about to unleash?

The clock ticked down to *ZERO* and the laser fired with amplified intensity. As thick as a flashlight beam and as bright as the sun, the laser, saturated with accelerated nuclei, buzzed into the MIGGS and collided with the target. The Supers began to calculate the 13th Power.

But too many error flags kept popping up on the screens all over Tech-Com Control. The measurement status table began to falter. Janis and the rest of the team rushed to the MIGGS window and crowded around Ray.

Inside the gravity chamber, the thick black mist rotated like a shadowy storm where no light penetrated. The walls vibrated and the floor shook from its fury. A few seconds passed in darkness. Then flashes of light began flickering in the black mist, like lightning in a distant storm cloud on a moonless night.

Johnson ran back to his MIGGS monitor. "She can't hold it," he yelled over the roar.

Ted screamed in terror. "You, I told. You, I told. Vhat more I can do?"

Ray spun around to look at Janis' monitor. The measurement status bar had shut down.

Power = 12.90 flashed on the screen.

Sparks flew from a bank of Supers. Ray ducked. "Damn!"

Tech-Com Control shook. The MIGGS roared. Ray slowly turned his eyes back to the ominous window, his heart now pounding from a fear he'd never known. Light waves were arching across the chamber now, swirling and twisting like the angry snakes of Medusa's hair, lashing out at the walls of the MIGGS, leaping up from the black mist and plunging back down into it like captured beasts fighting to be free of the failing gravity field. As the MIGGS weakened, light waves pulsed and surged brighter and brighter becoming painfully hard to watch, like the glow of a welding torch. Blinding. Ray squinted against its fury, thankful for the protection of the thick glass window.

Suddenly, the pulsating light expanded like a balloon and burst into billions of tiny specs that now sparkled in the darkness like glitter. For what seemed only a second, Ray thought he saw the universe expanding endlessly beyond the vibrating window. Millions of star clusters, swirling galaxies, and pulsing supernovas streaked by. He blinked in disbelief. How the hell was that possible? The universe?

With a crack like thunder, it all went black. The MIGGS stopped vibrating and the roaring subsided to a hum. Tech-Com Control stopped shaking. Inside the MIGGS, the black mist broke into smaller vortexes and twisted down floor grates as the gravity equalized. The green light started blinking again—one second on, one second off. He couldn't believe his eyes. The titanium cylinder was gone, part of its suspension arm left dangling from the ceiling. A loud buzzer sounded, echoing through Tech-Com Control. He looked at the countdown clock. It was stopped at zero and still flashing red. The air tasted like tin.

"Gone!" Johnson said. "The Higgs consumed the gravity that would have contained it." He sat in his chair and looked blankly at his monitor. *Fault* scrolled across the screen. He turned the power dial off and looked at Ray with wide eyes. "What was that?"

"Soul of tiger," Lo said. "It almost got loose."

Chapter Ninety-Two

THE EDGE OF REALITY

Janis turned away from the MIGGS window and its blinking green light. What had he seen? Where did the titanium cylinder go? Why was Ted yelling like a crazy man? He looked at the Russian leaning on his console, shaking, his face flushed. Why? What did he know?

Turning to confront Ted, Janis noticed Tracy at her keyboard, typing feverishly. Eyes intense, she didn't look happy. Her red bangs dripped sweat. Formulas and calculations scrolled down her screen. Janis didn't recognize any of them. He did recognize all the error flags, though. She stopped typing, put her elbows on the console, and cradled her chin in the palms of her hands, still staring at her monitor. Obviously, she had a problem that she wasn't sharing with anyone else. Not looking away, she went right back to typing. Janis returned his attention to Ted. He was gone.

"Damn!"

Frustrated, Janis rushed back to his station where Lo and Ray were working with the Supers. *Programming Replay. Please Wait* flashed on Lo's monitor. A drop-window read: *CEI Engaged.* Janis sat down, checked the bandage on his hand, and glanced up to the office window. Curtis was nowhere in sight.

Ray rubbed his shoulder and looked at Janis. "Next time we'll get it right."

"You think it's that easy?"

"The Supers report every error to *MOM,* a monitoring program that will give us a detailed printout of every point in the experiment that failed, every formula that miscalculated. All we need to do is make the corrections on the list and we'll be ready for a rerun."

Lo nudged Ray. "Coming up." The monitor displayed the Solartech Labs insignia over a screen titled *Replay Ready.*

"Let's see it," Ray said.

Lo clicked the *GO* button.

A computer-enhanced image of the electron target and the titanium cylinder appeared on the monitor. Running backwards in the upper left corner, a digital clock spun off seconds in hundredths. Electron microscopes zoomed in on their quivering target, which was suspended inside the titanium cylinder's nozzle. A white tracking scale, looking like a vertical ruler, came up on the right side of the screen, divided into thirteen increments depicting each calculation to the 13th Power.

The clock hit *ZERO*.

A flash of light arced across the screen as the laser fired. Janis winced, startled by the sudden brightness of the particle beam. The glare subsided quickly and revealed a nucleus of an atom, a shiny gray sphere smooth as polished agate, expanding on the monitor, getting bigger and bigger as it approached the electron target. They collided at incredible speed and the CEI recreated the splitting of the nucleus in a sort of slow-motion virtual tour.

In the upper right corner, the formula, "Power = 1.0" appeared as the nucleus shattered. The Supers made the calculations and the CEI made it all look like some kind of journey into the tiniest place in nature. The tracking scale turned red on the bottom and began to rise like a thermometer as the measurements were mapped.

Janis watched, amazed.

The *Power* numbers changed: 1.10 to 3.25 to 5.38. As the red scale edged upward toward the 13th Power, the illusion of speed increased with each calculation.

"Look!" Ray said, pointing at the expanding image. "A meson of quarks. There should be six of them—the up, down, and strange and their antiquarks."

"Antiquarks?" Janis said.

"Antimatter. They have the same mass as their partners but an opposite charge. When the two meet, they disintegrate."

"Amazing," Janis said as the colors changed inside the nucleus. Reds and blues, reds and greens, reds and yellows—abstract art was never so brilliant.

The *Power* numbers climbed higher: 7.69 changed to 9.70, the particles breaking into smaller and smaller pieces. The CEI went faster and faster. Someone behind him said "Wow." The *Power* number hit 11.80 and the monitor went suddenly black.

Janis leaned forward.

A tiny spot of light appeared in the center of the screen. It seemed far in the distance and pulsated, growing larger and larger as it neared.

The *Power* number climbed to 12.50.

Light beams emanated from the expanding glow, bending and twisting like the tentacles of some kind of luminous squid and giving off rippling rays like an Aurora Borealis.

Ray gasped. "It's the Higgs—the Higgs boson."

"My God—will you look at that thing," Janis said, staring, mesmerized by its beauty.

Streaking toward them at breathtaking speed, the Higgs suddenly broke apart and disappeared, returning the monitor to black again. The *Power* numbers hit 12.90 and stopped rising.

Then the blackness on the screen slowly opened up like the iris of an eye.

Janis felt a chill. He couldn't take his eyes from the monitor now, as if it had cast a spell on him. Icy sweat trickled down between his shoulder blades. He couldn't believe what he saw. Beyond the opening, the CEI revealed a galaxy rotating in the star-studded blackness of space, its middle bulging, glowing fat with white and yellow clusters of supernovas, and its stellar plain swirling tails of sparkling stars in its wake. Billions of stars speckled the darkness around it.

"What the…?"

ERROR flagged diagonally across the screen and the CEI switched to a giant Nebula with three pulsars glowing around it. A comet trailing an icy tail streaked through a swirling mass of colorful gasses.

ERROR.

The opening slowly closed and the monitor went black. *End Rerun* scrolled across the screen. The control room seemed suddenly silent as a morgue. Janis sat stunned, breathless, his mind trying to sort out rampant confusion. He didn't know what to think; the mathematics didn't make sense. How could the universe reside inside the nucleus? He turned to Ray. "We shouldn't be messing with this."

Ray didn't even look at him. He seemed to be in a daze, his eyes on the monitor, staring.

"I told you the 13th Power wasn't real," Janis said. "Light travels in a straight line. It doesn't bend and twist like that." He wiped sweat from his forehead. "It would only do that in a place where the rules of physics don't apply. The Higgs was trying to get out. When it disappeared, it took the titanium cylinder with it. Could've taken us, too. Maybe even the whole world."

"Thank God the MIGGS held up long enough," Johnson said, patting his monitor.

Lo rubbed his eyes. "13th Power like tiger—very dangerous."

Ray looked at Janis, trembling. "You guys don't get it, do you? We've just discovered the key to the universe, a doorway, a portal to the galaxy. This is bigger than anything we could have ever imagined."

"This is disaster, Ray," Janis said sternly.

"Jesus Christ, Janis! The titanium cylinder isn't gone—it's somewhere across the Milky Way, 100,000 light years from here."

"You don't know that."

"All I have to do is prove it."

"It was disintegrated, Ray."

"Hell—I'll be more famous than Einstein."

"You'll be dead—along with the rest of us."

"Just think of it, Janis—space flight without liftoff, interstellar transition in seconds."

"Are you even listening to me?"

"We might even find other planets, other life, other civilizations." Rays eyes went big around. "The age-old question will finally be answered— *We are not alone.*"

"We can't risk disintegrating whole world to prove it, Ray. It's too dangerous."

"But… "

"Lisa could die, Ray."

Silence.

Ray's face went sullen. "My God—you're right. I wouldn't risk her life… But… but couldn't we…?"

Janis snapped his fingers. "Sorry, Ray. We can't."

"But what about my place in history? Is it gone—poof—like the titanium cylinder?"

"Write a book. You can still take credit for discovering the Higgs."

"I wanted the 13th Power."

Janis switched off his monitor. "We're lucky you didn't get it."

Frustration on her face, Tracy got up from her station and stomped across the control room. "We missed the 13th Power and the Higgs boson wasn't contained. We need to try again."

"No!" Janis said. "We could have been sucked out of existence. If we'd reached the 13th Power, you can bet we wouldn't be here right now. There's no way the MIGGS could have saved us."

"That's ridiculous," she said. "You have no proof of that?"

"Show her the rerun, Lo."

Tracy watched the rerun, her pulse pounding in her temples. But she couldn't let them see her fear. She had to convince them to try one more time. The power setting for the laser resonator was too high. The data she got didn't make any sense. She needed another firing at the correct power setting. If not, her particle beam technology would be lost, Directive Number 119 would be dead, and *The Ark* would blame her for failing the President.

End Rerun.

She hugged herself. Quick, Trace. She always called herself Trace when she felt frustrated or lost, when things seemed hopeless. Think of something; keep this project alive. "The CEI made a mistake," she said to the team. "It was flagging errors like crazy. You saw them. The test fire was a failure from the start." She started pacing. "The countdown was wrong, the scheduler was programmed wrong, the hydrogen was too hot, the synchrotron was pumping 15 TEV. Hell—everything was running at sixteen percent overpowered. Even the laser was too intense." She turned to Roger at the power station. "Didn't you say to be ready for some weird responses?"

"Yes—but not that weird."

"See? We have to try again. Take the fail-safes out of the scheduler and let the Supers run the countdown. It'll work, I tell you."

Janis and Ray looked at each other and shook their heads.

"Don't you see?" Janis said. "The fail-safes are what saved us. Our mistakes created the errors that faltered the test fire... "

"Okay—no mistakes next time."

"A perfect firing *is* a mistake. The final errors were inevitable because the computers were multiplying by minus 1/10th. They were expecting a smaller number at the 13th Power. They came up with the universe, a bigger number. It's mathematically impossible so the computers flagged the errors."

"How do you figure the answer was positive?"

"You saw it—the black void. The galaxy. The 13th Power positive, 100,000 light years. The CEI was racing through the space inside the nucleus toward the 13th Power negative. We saw the Higgs boson at the threshold and got a glimpse of what lies beyond the doorway. Open it and the universe rushes in."

"Like turn sock inside out," Lo said.

"Right. It's too dangerous."

"Now you're starting to sound like Boris..." she stumbled. "I—I mean Ted. The old man is paranoid."

Janis' eyes narrowed. "I think the old man knows what we're up against here. He knows, doesn't he?"

Tracy turned away from the conversation and sat at her terminal. She felt Janis' stare. But now she understood why the Russians had abandoned their experiments. They *were* scared to death. Boris was right. *The Ark* should've stopped Curtis. Now her sense of duty and her moral convictions began to tug at her conscience. She needed one more laser firing, but one more might be one too many. They were working too close to the 13th Power, too close to disaster.

"I have to find Curtis," Janis said. "His precious 13th Power project is finished."

"I'm going with you," Ray said.

She didn't envy them for their task as they walked out of Tech-Com Control. Flicking a lock of hair from her cheek, she began typing again. *The Ark* was counting on her. There had to be another way to solve her problem.

Chapter Ninety-Three

NEVER SAY NEVER

After a silent walk to the lobby with Ray right behind him, Janis approached a guard at the security station. The wall behind him glowed with monitors displaying activities in the halls and labs throughout the building. He was watching them closely.

"Where's Curtis?"

The guard looked up. "C-Wing, I think."

"You think? I thought all these fancy computers kept track of everyone around here."

"Only inside this building." He pointed to the escalators. "I saw him go that way, with Jonathan. They usually go to the cafeteria this time of day. Don't need no stinking computers to figure that out."

Janis turned to Ray. "I'm hungry—how about you?"

"Famished." They headed for the escalators. On the ride down to the atrium, Ray put his hand on Janis' shoulder. "What about the money?"

Janis thought about that. The money. Curtis would probably back out of the deal. He had every right to. "It's not important anymore." In the parking garage, he hailed a staff car.

Tires squealing, the car accelerated toward C-Wing. After passing under the towering archway, Ray looked back and read aloud the words inscribed on its steel facing. "Welcome to Solartech Labs. Gateway to the Atomic Universe. Sounds like they knew all along."

"If so—they're crazier than we thought."

The line of employees in the cafeteria was long and moving slowly when Janis and Ray walked in. The air, filled with conversations, smelled of roast beef and apple pie. Looking around for Curtis, Janis spotted Jonathan at a table across the room, alone. After working through the maze of people, Janis sat down without an invitation. Ray grabbed the chair next to him.

Jonathan looked back and forth at them disdainfully then put his fork down. "What can I do for you guys?"

"Where is he?" asked Ray.

Janis snatched the dinner roll from Jonathan's plate, took a big bite, and tossed the remains into the potatoes and gravy. "Like *he* said." Janis swallowed a gulp of Jonathan's milk.

"Better leave him be," Jonathan said flatly. "He's not in a good mood."

"Neither are we," Ray replied, his voice gruff, serious.

Jonathan groaned. "In his office, down at the end of the corridor." He pointed. "Now leave me eat my dinner in peace."

Ray stood without another word. He fixed his sling and Janis followed him, their footsteps echoing down the hallway. At the far end, Ray stopped in front of an office with double oak doors. He didn't bother knocking—just pushed his way in.

Phone to his ear, Curtis looked up from his desk. Janis was surprised at how ordinary he looked without his usual costume, which lay in a heap on the credenza. Slamming down the phone, Curtis yelled, "What's the meaning of this?" He stood and put his hands on his hips. "Get the hell out of here!"

"Funny thing," Ray said. "That's exactly what we intend to do." He leaned on the desk and glared into Curtis' face. "But first, there's the matter of Janis' money."

"What are you getting at?"

"We're done," Janis put in. "The experiment is finished." He said the words calmly because he meant them.

Curtis frowned. "Finished? What the hell are you talking about? The test fire today was a huge success! We're almost there!"

"Not so," Ray said. "We could've ended up in oblivion along with your titanium cylinder."

Curtis glowered.

"Do you know what you're messing with here?" Janis asked.

Curtis didn't answer.

"Then let me tell you. The end of the world."

Curtis shook his fist. "Just like that?" His cheeks turned red, his eyes bulging. "You come in here blowing smoke up my ass because you think you saw something! Truth is, you big-shot brainards don't know what you saw. You turn chicken-shit and run to Mommy because you're afraid of the dark. You're pathetic!"

"This project is dangerous, " Janis said. "Pathetic is not recognizing it for what it is."

Curtis sneered. "I'll tell you about pathetic, Dr. Smart-Ass." He hit the desk with his fist. "I bought you Janis, with money, a million bucks worth. And you, Ray, I bought with the promise of fame. How feeble. I exploited your weaknesses to get what I wanted. You didn't even know it. You think you're so smart—I think you *define* pathetic!"

Ray looked as if he would explode. Red blood vessels in his neck started growing and his eyes narrowed. "All this time I believed your intentions were strictly scientific. Now, I wonder what those intentions really were." His mustache quivered. "You don't care about the 13th Power, do you? I figure you're after the Higgs boson."

"The Higgs will be mine!" Curtis shouted with a curl on his upper lip that made Janis break out in a cold sweat.

"Why?" Ray asked.

"Riches beyond my wildest imagination," Curtis said. "Janis will get his measly million while I control the financial markets of the world."

"How do you figure?"

"With the Higgs I'll be able to rearrange the periodic table. My first project will be to change lead into gold—lots of it." Curtis gleamed as if in ecstasy just talking about it.

"Now look who's blowing smoke," Janis said.

Rays eyes went wide. "No, Janis." His voice was almost a whisper. "Reconstructive fusion has been hypothesized for years. It's as far-fetched as cold fusion but equally intriguing."

"I'll be damned," Janis said. "I knew the 13th Power was a smoke screen. He made us think we were working on one thing when, in reality, he had another agenda all together."

"Genius," said Ray.

Curtis looked impressed with that word.

"Genius or not—you're finished, *Mister* Curtis. You'll get nothing more from us pathetics." Janis headed for the door. "Come on Ray—let's get the hell out of here."

"Not so fast, boys!" Curtis came around from behind his desk, staff in hand. "You have another firing tomorrow at noon. Not another test fire, mind you, but the real thing this time. I..."

"You haven't been listening, *Mister* Curtis," Janis cut in. "You're finished."

"You're wrong!" Curtis snapped. "Tomorrow at noon!" He paced the floor, tapping the staff with each step. "Stan Burton and his team are installing a new titanium cylinder as we speak. Ray—you'll reprogram the Supers to run the scheduler without the fail-safes. Janis—the formulas worked until the Higgs appeared, one-tenth of a second before the void opened. All you need to do now is reformulate the programming to contain it. But you must shut the experiment down before the 13th Power is attained."

"That's impossible," Ray said. "The programming expands fission into usable time—you know—slow motion. In real time—hell—we'd have to snatch the Higgs in less than a millisecond."

"It'll never happen," Janis said.

"Never say never, Doctor. Try—I insist." Curtis stopped pacing in front of a door by the bookcases. "I have confidence in you. Besides, it's your opportunity to save the world."

"Why are you being so bullheaded about this?" Janis asked. "You know the dangers."

Curtis smiled wide. "Risk nothing, gain nothing." His gold tooth glistened.

Janis turned to Ray. "He's insane. Come on—we're leaving. What makes him think he can make us fire that thing again anyway?"

"Wait!" Curtis said forcefully. "I was afraid you lightweights would turn tail and run. So you might say I took out a little insurance. Before you go, I'd like to show you why you *will* do it." He opened the door behind him. "I think you'll be highly motivated."

From out of the darkness beyond the door, Lisa stumbled into the room, shoved from behind, nearly naked and bound in chains, struggling to stay on her feet. Her mouth was gagged, her hair tousled, her wide eyes ringed in white.

Horrified, Ray's face went blank with disbelief.

Janis felt his heart turn over in his chest. He stepped backwards, staring, first at Lisa and then at the man standing behind her, his face and hands bloody, his clothes ripped and shredded. He looked as though he'd been nearly eaten alive.

"I'd like you to meet Judas," Curtis said and laughed. "He's had a really bad day."

In one hand, Judas held the end of a leash, which was attached to a dog collar around Lisa's neck. In the other hand, he held a small gray box with a big red button and a black antenna. Quick to demonstrate its purpose, Judas pushed the red button.

Lisa let out a throaty scream and fell to the floor, writhing in pain as blue electrostatic sparks lashed out from the chains and pierced her body. The smell of singed hair filled the room.

"Don't anybody get any dumb ideas about being a hero," Judas warned. "I'll zap her if I even think you're gonna get brave."

Ignoring Judas, Ray clenched his fists and lunged at him. "You bastard!"

Judas pushed the button again.

Lisa screamed in helpless agony.

"Back off!" Judas yelled.

With teeth bared, Ray stepped back. "You'll die for this!"

"I doubt it." Judas pushed the button again.

The terror in Lisa's screams tore at Janis' sanity. Filled with anger and frozen with fear, he felt helpless to do anything to rescue her. Any move would only cause her more anguish.

"Okay! Okay! No more!" Ray pleaded.

Curtis raised the golden staff. "We've made our point, Judas. Leave us."

Judas snarled and yanked on the leash, pulling Lisa to her feet. They disappeared through the doorway, the rattling of chains quickly fading away.

Curtis closed the door and walked back to his desk. He looked at Janis and Ray is if he'd just won a bet—obviously pleased by their horrified expressions. Sitting down, he laid the staff across his lap and, still looking at his pathetic scientists, smiled.

"I suggest you boys get to work. It's going to be a long night."

Chapter Ninety-Four

THE TASK FORCE

Agent Lou Marston stood on the tarmac at Andrews Air Force Base, his black FBI squad car idling behind him and his gaze on landing lights approaching the runway. Tires squawked as the Hawker jet touched down. After the nose gear settled to the concrete, reverse thrusters roared. He looked at his watch: 8:30. They were late.

Day had turned to dusk, but for Lou, it wasn't nearly over. He had spent the afternoon compiling his report on Melvin Anderson and *The Ark*, while his task force met with Devin and Colonel Fallon at Nellis. They had gathered information about Curtis, his 13th Power project, and the Atomtech disaster. Lou was anxious to put all their information together into one report. Then he'd have enough evidence to get Grand Jury indictments against operatives from the CIA to the White House. The bastards weren't going to get away with it. A hot rush pumped through his veins. His confrontation with CIA Chief Lawrence Higgins was fast approaching.

He watched the Hawker negotiate the taxiway toward him, the shrill whine of its engines getting louder as the glaring lights came closer. As it pulled up, floodlights illuminated the FBI seal on its tail. A soaring Bald Eagle spanned the fuselage. When the door opened, steps descended and the engine whine subsided. Turbine-fans rotated slowly as Lou climbed the stairs and stepped into the plane where the air was tainted with cigarette smoke. His men were shuffling papers and compiling reports on a laptop computer—testimony they'd taken from Colonel Fallon and Walter Devin.

Lou removed a disk from his pocket, the evidence he'd gathered against *The Ark* and Melvin Anderson, and handed it to Agent DeSoto, a young man with thick glasses. "Add this to your report."

"No problem." DeSoto inserted the disk. The laptop copied and merged the files. "Almost finished." He copied the new file back onto the disk, a complete record of the 13th Power case, enough evidence to send some hi-powered operatives to the death chamber, a disk that would avenge the deaths of thirty-seven Americans. It only lacked one thing—*The Ark's* name.

Lou looked over the other task force agents, suddenly seeing a familiar face. "Riggs! What are *you* doing here?"

"Transferred from the LA office," Agent Riggs said, smiling. His muscular frame made up for his short stature. He finished reorganizing an overhead compartment then rubbed his stubbly chin. "Just in time for some excitement. Incredible story."

"Just wait 'til you hear it, Lou," added Agent Bell, a young black man with pearly teeth.

"I can't imagine." Lou looked into the cockpit. "Captain Connors—good to see you."

The pilot glanced up from his checklist. "Lou." He motioned to his copilot. "My first officer, Maggie Collins." They exchanged smiles.

"You're on for tomorrow," Lou said. "0900. Better get some rest."

Nodding, the pilots returned to their post-flight chores.

"What's up for tomorrow?" Riggs asked, approaching with an outstretched hand.

"Listen up, men," Lou announced as he took Riggs' handshake. "It appears this 13th Power project has the backing of the CIA and is connected to the Atomtech disaster. I have evidence *The Ark* is involved."

"No way!" Agent Bell said.

"It's all in my report," Lou assured his men. "Tomorrow we're going to shut down Solartech Labs. Judge Freeman is waiting for us in his chambers. He's agreed to take our testimony and issue a Federal warrant for Melvin Anderson."

Agent DeSoto ejected the disk. "Then let's get to it." He closed the laptop and handed the disk to Agent Bell. "Lock it up."

"It's a copy for the Colonel," Bell explained. "We promised him."

"That's fine," Lou said. "He's really pissed about what happened at Atomtech."

"He wants the culprits caught," Riggs put in.

"There's enough evidence on that disk to indict and prosecute *The Ark*, whoever the hell he is," Lou said. "I hope to find out tonight."

"Only the President knows who *The Ark* is," Agent Bell said as he put the disc into a small air-safe, closed its thick door, and spun the dial. "How are we going to ID him?"

"Before we see the judge, we're going to pay a visit to CIA Chief Higgins. He's at the Marriott, attending a campaign fundraiser. I think he knows something about *The Ark* and Dr. Curtis... or Anderson... or whatever his name is."

"Why should Higgins know?" Bell asked, wiping dust off the FBI seal on the air-safe's door.

"He's the chief—top dog, unless *The Ark* is activated. Then he becomes #2. He'll know."

Agent Bell secured a panel covering the air-safe. Colonel Fallon's copy of the report was safely stowed for tomorrow's flight.

"We're ready," Riggs said.

Lou turned to the pilots. "Nine sharp." He ducked out the door and down the steps, his task force following behind him.

Chapter Ninety-Five

BANQUET AT THE MARRIOTT

At the entrance to the banquet room, Lou and his men flashed their FBI badges to the maitre d' as they walked in. This formal affair had attracted the rich and famous of Washington. The room was filled with the din of their conversations.

Lou led the way between rows of tables draped in white linen and set with polished silver, crystal, and china. His men marched behind him like characters from "Men In Black." The aroma of prime rib and lemon-meringue drifted in the air. Lou's stomach fluttered. The tuna fish sandwich he'd had for dinner seemed so mundane. But he ate a lot of tuna fish sandwiches.

Red, white, and blue banners hung from rafters above a podium at the front of the room. In a corner, a twelve-piece band played softly and several couples were casually dancing.

Near the center of the room, Lou spotted Chief Higgins, sitting with his wife, daughter, and two Congressmen. They all looked so formal in their fancy eveningwear. Lou wondered if Higgins used some kind of wax to make his bald head shine like that.

Task force in tow, Lou marched toward the table. Higgins looked up, put his fork down, and wiped his mouth with a napkin. His wife, in mid sentence, stopped talking, her gaze now on the approaching FBI agents.

"We need to talk, Lawrence," Lou said with an official tone.

"Agent Marston," the CIA chief said, his voice festive, without concern. "You remember my wife, Beverly." She smiled. He indicated an unoccupied chair. "Have a seat."

"No, thanks," Lou said, looking over the party. "Excuse us. We have to go to the men's room."

"Come to think of it," Higgins said. "I'll be right back, dear." He left his guests and led the way through the maze of tables and dignitaries.

In the men's room, a man backed away from a urinal, zipping his trousers. As he walked to a sink, the door burst open and FBI agents rushed in. They fanned out, checking under the stall doors for unwanted company.

"Out!" agent Riggs ordered the man at the sink.

He held up the palms of his hands. "But, I... "

"Wash 'em later." Riggs grabbed the man's collar and threw him out. As the task force agents stood guard, the top Feds stepped up to adjacent urinals.

"What's on your mind, Lou?" Chief Higgins asked and unzipped his pants.

"Tell me about Melvin Anderson and the 13th Power experiments at Solartech Labs," Lou said, urinating.

"You've been playing super cop, have you?" Higgins spit into the urinal. "Take my advice and walk away from this one, Lou. It's way over your head."

"Atomtech was destroyed, Americans were murdered, and the smell of it drifts all the way up to the White House. I suggest you either prepare to explain it to a Federal Grand Jury or come clean right now."

"You're nuts."

"The President assigned *The Ark* to someone. Who is he?"

"Have you been drinking? There's no boogieman."

"I'm willing to cut you a deal—minimum prison time."

"A word of advice, Lou. You're messing with the wrong people. I seriously suggest you boys go back to bank robbers and leave this one alone."

Lou backed away from the urinal, zipped his pants, and leaned into the CIA chief's ear. "Listen real good, you bastard. Judge Freeman is issuing the warrant tonight. Our jet is ready at Andrews. Tomorrow we're goin' in. Solartech Labs is goin' down and Melvin Anderson will be in chains. With a murder rap hanging over his head, he *will* talk and I guarantee you'll be put to sleep right along with your buddy, *The Ark*. Are you clear on that?"

"You're wrong!" The CIA chief zipped his pants with a jerk. "You don't know what you're dealing with here, damn it! Anderson can tell you nothing. It's a covert operation. We're untouchable."

"We'll see about that."

"Don't be stupid, Lou." He pointed his finger at the task force agents posted around the men's room. "Walk away from this. All of you."

"We're goin' in, tomorrow," Lou said with finality. He

turned to his men and signaled an exit.

"Don't do it," Lawrence shouted.

Lou stopped at the door, slowly turned around and jabbed a stiff finger at Higgins. "Don't do it? You should've said that to the Atomtech assault—*before* thirty-seven Americans were executed."

"Let it go," Higgins said.

"Not on your life." Lou led his men out.

"Don't say I didn't warn you!"

Chapter Ninety-Six
A FEDERAL WARRANT

Early morning sunlight beamed through the office window and woke Agent Marston. He opened his eyes and didn't move. Where was he? His arms were folded on his desktop, his head resting on his forearms. He blinked. His mouth tasted like glue. The picture of his wife and daughter caught his eye, propped on top of the Federal Marshall's warrant for the search and seizure of Solartech Labs. Lou wanted to talk to her; he ached to see her. But he had to wait until the 13th Power case was closed. Again, his personal needs were put on hold for the sake of his job and, as usual, his job dragged him into the late hours of the night. They hadn't gotten out of Judge Freeman's chambers until after midnight.

Licking his lips with a cottony tongue, he looked at the clock. 7:05. His task force agents were downstairs in temporary quarters for transients. He had chosen to be alone in his office—his life. Stretching, he got up and walked out. Miss Jennings was sitting at her desk, as usual.

"Get Colonel Fallon on the line."

She reached for the phone.

Lou went into the locker room, showered, and shaved. After jamming yesterday's clothes into the bottom of his locker, he put on a fresh shirt and slacks. After years of never knowing from one day to the next whether he'd make it home or not, he was already accustomed to being separated from his wife. He spent most of his time without her anyway. Suddenly that bothered him. He hadn't been a very good husband.

Over his vest he slung his holster and locked in the .38. What a way to travel to California. He made a final check in the mirror and turned to leave.

Elevator doors slid open as he walked into the lobby.

"They're trying to find the Colonel, Lou," Miss Jennings reported as his task force agents stepped out of the elevator.

"Thanks." He turned to his men. "In here." They followed him into his office.

The picture on the desk attracted agent Riggs' attention. "Sandy—how is she?" he asked as he picked up the picture. "And look at Trisha. What is she, seven now?"

Lou smiled. "Eight, and just a living doll."

The other agents looked over Riggs' shoulder. "How long have you and Marston known each other?" agent DeSoto asked.

"We met in Vietnam some thirty years ago," agent Riggs said with a proud smile and put the picture down. "I was Best Man at their wedding."

Memories of that day came crashing back. Lou stood at the window, grappling with the anguish of his decision to divorce her. Somehow, deep down, he knew her drinking was his fault. If he'd only spent more time with her—more time with his family—maybe she wouldn't have turned to the bottle to fill the loneliness he had left her with. Guilt tore at his soul. He really wanted to make his marriage work again. She deserved better than what he'd been giving her, excuses—the FBI *this* and the FBI *that*. Was the reality of this impending divorce forcing him to see his mistakes more clearly? He'd really let her down. Was it too late to change? Could he make it up to her? God, he had to try. After this assignment—he'd call her then. He'd change.

The phone rang. His task force agents gathered around.

"Colonel Fallon?"

"What's the plan, Lou?"

"We're going into Solartech Labs to arrest Melvin Anderson."

"On whose authority?"

"Judge Freeman issued the Federal Warrant."

"I want Anderson first."

Lou thought about that. "You can have him after we're done with him."

"Do you have my copy of the report?"

"It's on a computer disk—in a safe on the plane."

"What did you find out?"

"It's all on the disk—enough to hang the bastard."

"Who?" the Colonel growled.

"I don't have his name yet. But we'll get it out of Anderson."

"Let me know when you've got him."

"I'll call you."

Lou hung up, grabbed the warrant off the desk, and spoke softly to the picture of his wife and daughter. "I'll call you, too, darling—as soon as I get back." He grabbed his coat off the chair and turned to his men. "Let's go get him."

Chapter Ninety-Seven
THE WRONG PEOPLE

Security waved the squad car through the gate at Andrews Air Force Base. Up ahead, Lou saw the FBI Hawker parked on the tarmac, a ladder by its tail, an engine cover open. As the car came to a stop, he spotted Captain Connors and his copilot standing off to the side, watching a man working on the left engine. He wore navy blue coveralls and a matching ball cap. That was all Lou needed. A delay.

"What's the problem?" he asked the Captain.

"Just a final check on an Airworthiness Directive they performed some time back. I don't know—came up rather sudden. He's about finished."

In the dark engine compartment, the man dressed like a mechanic checked each of the devices he'd attached to the fuel lines and the main hydraulic hose. They glowed faintly, as they should. He knew that these magnesium chips, once ignited, would burn from the inside out and were not extinguishable, ever, not even under water. Like a welding arc, they could burn through anything. The size of the chip determined the amount of time it would take to expose intense heat to the fuel and oil. He'd selected small chips for this assignment. Satisfied, he closed the engine cover, climbed down the ladder, and rolled it to the side. "All set," he said, handing the Captain an official-looking FAA form. "Sign right here."

Captain Connors looked over the form. "Paper work is in order." He scribbled his signature, and smiling, handed it back to the mechanic. "There you go."

"Have a nice flight." The man walked away.

Agent Marston called to his task force. "Get aboard."

The pilots began their pre-flight checklists as the task force agents, armed with their Federal Marshall's Warrant, seated themselves and buckled in. The engines whined to life and the stairs retraced. Hooking up to the nose wheel, a tug operator pushed the Hawker onto the taxi ramp.

First Officer Maggie Collins radioed ground control. "Andrews Ground—Hawker November-zero-four-seven-Echo at Delta-niner request taxi to active one-seven. Awaiting clearance to LA Center."

"Hawker four-seven-Echo—taxi to one-seven. Standby for clearance," the ground controller came back. The Hawker's engines revved and the jet began to roll toward the runway.

"Hawker four-seven-Echo—you are cleared to the Kirby VOR. Expect eight thousand in ten. Departure frequency one-one-seven-point-two-five. Squawk five-three-niner-niner. Awaiting read-back."

Maggie repeated her instrument flight instructions and set the dials as Captain Connors prepared his aircraft for takeoff.

"Hawker four-seven-Echo—read-back correct. Clear for takeoff. Have a nice flight."

Within moments, the jet turned onto the runway and the engines revved to full power, jetting the FBI task force into the sky over Washington, DC.

As the aircraft climbed to altitude and turned on course, the FBI agents sat quietly, glancing back and forth at one another. Lou didn't know what to expect when they arrived at Solartech Labs. He could only hope the seizure would be executed peacefully.

Suddenly, the phone rang, startling everyone.

Lou picked it up.

"Just breaking news, Lou," Miss Jennings said. "When the Justice Department opened at nine this morning, they found Judge Freeman in a pool of blood on the floor of his chambers. The place had been ransacked. Isn't he the judge you were with 'til all hours last night?"

Lou's face contorted with fear.

"What?" asked Agent Riggs, detecting panic.

Lou thought his chest would burst. He couldn't find the words to thank Miss Jennings. Had he signed the judge's death warrant by mentioning his name to Higgins? Would they go so far as to assassinate a Federal judge to protect the 13th Power project? His mouth went dry. Was there nothing they wouldn't do? Nothing? OH MY GOD. NO!

"THE MECHANIC!" He jumped from his seat and ran to

the cockpit. "GET THIS PLANE ON THE GROUND NOW!"

"What...?"

"Just do it. Declare an emergency and get us down. I DON'T GIVE A SHIT WHERE!"

"What's wrong?" agent Riggs demanded, his face white with fear.

"Judge Freeman was murdered in his chambers last night and I'll bet that mechanic was no mechanic. GOD DAMN IT!" He buckled into his seat. "THE ARK IS OUT TO KILL US... "

An explosion jolted the jet.

A cockpit alarm rang out. "Fire on number two!" Captain Connors announced. He hit the extinguisher switch. The *FIRE* light didn't go out. "Shit!" He turned to Maggie. "Call a Mayday." The altimeter started winding down.

Keeping his cool, he trimmed the jet for landing, anywhere, maybe that parking lot down there—no, too small, too many buildings, too many cars on the roads. Where? Check airspeed—okay. Flaps. Another alarm sounded. "What the...?" He scanned the instruments. "Flaps? What's wrong with the flaps?"

"They're not extending," Maggie said nervously. "T-try again."

He worked the flaps lever again and again but nothing happened. Another alarm sounded. "Damn! We've lost the hydraulics!"

The Hawker began to roll to the left. Captain Connors turned the yoke to the right. Sluggishly, the jet rolled right. He turned back toward level flight. The controls went limp in his hands. His stomach clutched. Terror gripped him as the nose pitched down and his aircraft continued to roll to the right.

"Backup hydraulics!" he shouted, fighting for control of his aircraft.

Maggie worked the switches. "Nothing, sir." She tried them several times.

As the altimeter needle spun downward and the vertical speed indicator showed 2,000 feet per minute, smoke began to fill the cabin. The crippled Hawker was in gravity's grip of death. Captain Connors yanked and twisted his useless controls. He looked at Maggie who was desperately trying to restore the hydraulics. When he looked back, the horizon was no longer in view out the windshield—only the ground. "God help us all."

Agent Marston, heavy G-forces pressing on his chest, clung to the armrests as the Hawker plunged toward the ground. He gagged on acrid smoke now filling the cabin. Looking at his task force agents, he could see terror on their faces—each man locked in his own helpless mortality.

"THE ARK WON, DAMN IT!" His men didn't respond, now hanging upside down in their seats. The nose dropped into a steep dive. Lou closed his eyes and fought tears, an ache in his chest, and a sudden sadness in his soul. He swallowed hard. "Sorry, Sandy."

*   *   *

A black ribbon of smoke snaked downward behind the Hawker. It impacted the ground with a massive explosion that shook the ground for miles. The billowing red and yellow fireball pumped churning black smoke into the sky over the nation's capitol.

Higgins saw the smoke from the window of his office in CIA headquarters. "I told the dumb bastards they were messing with the wrong people." He closed the blinds and turned his back on what he had done.

Chapter Ninety-Eight
A HORRIBLE ACCIDENT

Superseding coverage of Federal Judge Freeman's murder, wire services picked up the news of the plane crash in Washington. Video of the carnage quickly hit the airways as local television news teams rushed to the scene to cash in on the catastrophe.

FAA phone lines lit up with calls from investigative reporters attempting to get information on the plane and its ill-fated passengers. A television news helicopter beamed back live pictures of the horrible accident. Dozens of fire trucks pumped water on the raging fire that consumed a jet and the shopping mall it had struck. Not far away, in a cluttered parking lot, lay rows of blanket-covered bodies, some still smoldering underneath.

Rescue workers and firemen went about their gruesome duties. A steady stream of ambulances, laden with wounded, negotiated congested streets toward hospitals throughout the city.

*   *   *

Nathan walked into the Oval Office just as the news about Freeman flashed across the television screen. His office had been ransacked and nobody knew what, if anything, was missing. But *The Ark* knew what was missing—the evidence—the link that would ruin him.

A bulletin interrupted the news report. An aircraft had crashed just minutes after takeoff from Andrews Air Force Base. Nathan sat with the President and watched in horror as the ugly turn of events unfolded.

The newscaster adjusted the knot on his tie as he came on. "We've just learned through unconfirmed sources that the downed plane was an FBI Hawker jet destined for the Los Angeles area with four agents and two crew members aboard."

Nathan took a shot of adrenaline. What the hell had Higgins done? This time the son of a bitch had gone too far.

"Excuse me, Sir," he told the President. Nathan had a phone call to make.

*   *   *

From his desk at CIA headquarters, Higgins answered the phone.

"Lawrence—you did this deliberately."

He recognized Nathan's agitated voice right away. "Relax, John. For Christ's sake." He was standing at the window, blinds parted, peering out at the smoky sky. "Look at it as a confirmed kill."

"It's a needle in our arms," Nathan said. "Damn it! Why wasn't it rigged to crash over Colorado like we planned? Now this mess is in our back yard."

"That pea-brain Marston threatened Grand Jury indictments against us. I wanted to watch his plans go up in smoke. Couldn't have done that in Colorado, now could I?" He let the blind go and walked back to his desk. "Saved both our asses, John."

"You better have a tight lid on this thing, Lawrence. No slip-ups."

"We're the CIA, goddamnit. Besides, Alex says the 13th Power project is on schedule. They're going for broke this afternoon."

"Will the particle beam work?"

"Tracy's had some problems."

"But we're close?"

"She's expressed doubts about the safety of the project. But she's a trooper. She'll hang in there. With any luck we'll be heroes tomorrow."

"I just wish there'd been another way."

"There's always been another way, John. It's called diplomacy. Your White House agenda put peace in the hands of technology. Not a good substitute for a nuclear arms treaty and a handshake. But who am I to tell you guys?"

"The President wants it this way."

"As long as he does, *The Ark* will always be a necessity."

"The same goes for the CIA."

"Touché!" Higgins replied. "We've done our job. It was a horrible accident. That's all anyone needs to know."

"What about the judge?"

"His office was ransacked. Sounds like a burglary gone bad to me."

"Make it official." Nathan hung up.

Higgins put the receiver down and returned his attention to the television. The graphic images of the disaster sent a shiver through him—a good kind of shiver.

Chapter Ninety-Nine
A MILITARY POLICE ACTION

Colonel Fallon plunged a fork into his pancakes. An airman rushed into the Officers' Mess and switched on the TV. "Get a load of this, Sir."

As the newscaster talked about the murder of Judge Freeman, a sick feeling churned in Fallon's stomach. Marston had told him that Freeman had issued the warrant for Anderson. Now the judge was dead. How could that be? A coincidence? Not likely.

Just as he was digesting that information, news of a plane crash took center stage. He watched intently as a helicopter circled the crash scene.

Devin and Toothless bounded in. "What's all this?" Devin asked and sat down.

Toothless grabbed the Frosted Flakes and began eating them out of the box.

"I'm not sure." Fallon didn't take his eyes from the newscast. "A few minutes ago they were talking about Judge Freeman being murdered and then this plane crash came up. Got the news people busy, that's for sure."

"Wasn't Freeman…?"

"You see the connection, too?"

"But how could he wind up dead over that? Curtis isn't that powerful."

"Someone is." Fallon took a sip of coffee, thinking. "What if Curtis is just a pawn in a bigger game?"

Devin made a face as if he didn't agree.

"Marston and I figured that Curtis didn't have the resources to conduct a military assault on Atomtech. So he had to have a connection to a government source with a military agenda, whether he knew it or not. Marston was checking into that scenario."

"I wonder if he found something," Devin said and pointed to the TV set. A picture of a FBI jet appeared, offset in a window next to the newscaster.

"It has been confirmed," the reporter announced. "The plane that crashed into the Dreamland Mall was an FBI jet en route to Los Angeles. It had just taken off from Andrews Air Force Base when the pilot reported engine failure. On board, a task force from the Las Vegas bureau perished, along with an agent from the DC Office of Special Investigations. There were two crew members."

Colonel Fallon dropped his cup. It shattered and coffee splashed everywhere. The connection was solid. Curtis was the common element. But Curtis had a powerful protector. Who? Fallon looked at Devin. "I talked with Marston only an hour ago. It was all set." He made a fist. "Now this. I don't get it, Walter. What's going on?"

Devin didn't answer, just poured himself a cup of coffee.

"Do you realize that we're the only ones left?" Fallon said. "The only ones that know about Curtis and his 13th Power project? Everyone else is dead—the task force, the judge, agent Marston. My copy of the report was probably destroyed, too"

"Report?"

"A computer disk with all the evidence. Marston said it was safe on the plane. Hell—it's toast by now. We're in this thing alone."

"Except for the bastards that did that," Devin said, indicating the TV with a nod.

"You can bet someone else knows what's going on at Solartech Labs." Fallon rubbed his forehead. "Someone with enough clout to derail every attempt to intervene—someone who doesn't want any public attention and has a vested interest in Curtis' Simi Valley enterprise."

"Who?"

"I don't know but it's time we flush the snake out of its hole. God knows there's no one else left to do it." He threw his napkin on the coffee spill and stood.

"What are you going to do?"

"Take the Apaches in on an MPA."

"MPA?"

"Military Police Action."

"You can do that?"

"In an emergency, I can do that. And believe me—this *is* an emergency. Meet me in the com-center at 1100 hours. Be ready to go." He headed for the door.

Devin smiled.

Toothless chucked another handful of Frosted Flakes.

THE NEW FORMULA

Janis took off his glasses, tossed them on the console, and rubbed his aching eyeballs. He'd been working with Ray and Lo through the night reformulating the event program, feeding new formulas into the Supers and rerunning the CEI. The results were bizarre imitations of the possibilities of the 13th Power. The Higgs was elusive, always producing an error message. Then it was back to the drawing board.

Their only hope was the right calculations to achieve containment. Curtis would get his Higgs and let them go home.

"How long do we have?" Ray asked, frustrated with another error message.

"Maybe lucky, six hours," Lo said. "But time goes fast when we have fun."

Pushing the keyboard aside, Janis laid his face down on his arms. Fighting sleep, he feared for Lisa's horrible predicament. Seeing her tied up and tortured had made his heart ache. Tormented by her anguish, he had been pushing his skills to the limit, hoping beyond hope he could save her with a stroke of genius.

Janis shuddered. What an aberration, the Higgs, a particle existing on the edge of reality. The 13th Power negative equaled the 13th Power positive. Reciting that equation over and over in his mind, he understood why the Supers bleeped out the errors—they knew the answer was wrong. Janis flinched. The Supers knew? Hell no. Computers only knew what they were told.

"That's it!" He nearly toppled from his chair in excitement.

Ray stopped typing. "What?"

"We're going about this all wrong." Janis threw his glasses on. "The Supers know the formulas won't work because they've been programmed with the mathematics we know and use everyday. Positive and negative are never equal. But we're dealing with a realm that is beyond our reality. Our rules of physics don't work at the 13th Power. Remember our hypothesis in college? The rules of numbers don't work there either. Positive does equal negative."

"Oh, sure," Lo said. "If I program Supers that way, it'll make big mess of everything."

"Not exactly. We need the math to work by our rules up to the moment of laser firing. At that exact instant we need a reprogramming statement telling the Supers that negative and positive are equal, just before they clock out."

"But the space-time continuum will be mathematically impossible." Ray said. "Time will stop."

"Dead in its tracks," Janis said.

Lo squinted. "What time will stop? In MIGGS or in real world?"

Janis didn't know for sure but he had a theory—actually more of a hope? "Long enough to contain the Higgs and bail out before the void opens. Punch in the numbers at laser firing, then run it."

Lo typed and the CEI engaged. The monitors displayed the scheduler with the new formula, negative equals positive. At laser firing, no error message appeared.

"Yes!" Ray exclaimed, his face beaming under the stubble of a new beard. "Bring up *MOM* and the list of errors from the test fire. Delete the time sensitive ones. What are we left with?"

Punching the keyboard, Lo brought up the list.

"Get to work on those."

"We've got it, Janis," Ray said, patting him on the back.

Janis forced a smile. Had he been too hasty? He felt as though something was wrong with this approach but he couldn't put his pencil on it. Containment had to take place in the gravity simulator where the event horizon was critical. If positive equaled negative, would the escape velocity still be 186,000 miles per second? A lapse in the MIGGS would mean disaster. The Higgs and the void would not be contained. The thought of being sucked out of existence sent a chill down his back. He had to be sure that wouldn't happen.

After opening the scheduler, Ray deleted the fail-safe messages, giving the Supers total control over the sequencing of the MIGGS, ionizer, synchrotron and laser. With a few more keystrokes, the Supers tapped into the power station, too.

"You sure about that?" Janis said over his shoulder.

"Without a glitch."

Janis winced. The Supers controlling everything made his stomach hurt. He needed an insurance policy. "Lo—put a back door in both the scheduler and laser sequencer. If anything even looks like it's going wrong we'll be able to get in and shut the experiment down."

Lo went to work.

Janis saw Ted shuffle toward the coffeepot. It was time to have a little talk with the old man.

BREAK IN

"Ted—good morning." Janis grabbed a cup. "I'll take a splash of that." Ted poured but didn't seem talkative.

Janis waited while Ted filled a mug and set the pot on a burner. He began to walk away. Janis stopped him.

"The test fire yesterday, Ted—you kept saying you 'told us.' Told us what?"

Ted didn't answer.

"What were you afraid of?"

"Nothing." Ted turned toward his console.

Janis blocked his way. "Don't bullshit me. You were horrified. Why?"

Ted sidestepped but Janis quickly checked his move. "My guess is you know something."

"So vhat if I do?"

"Let's have it, Ted."

"I can't talk about it."

"Why not?"

Ted's eyes darted around the control room. "Where's Curtis?"

"He's not here."

Ted leaned to Janis' ear. "In Mother Russia…" he whispered, "…we discover 13th Power very dangerous." He took a swig of coffee and stared over the brim of his cup, looking as if he anticipated more questions he didn't want to answer.

Janis didn't make him wait long. "What did you think was going to happen?"

"Vhat we saw—the void. I think it might escape MIGGS. Maybe it could."

He limped to his station and Janis followed him, listening.

"Void open to vacuum of space, like back door to universe, suck out everything, maybe whole world." He set his cup down. "I tell Curtis—I tell CIA. Too dangerous I tell them both. Nobody listen."

Janis put a hand on the old man's shoulder. "If it's any consolation, we believe you, Ted."

"Boris," he said with a toothy smile. "Real name Boris."

Janis' heart skipped a beat. Tracy's verbal slip—when she had said Boris instead of Ted—came crashing back into his mind. In yesterday's confusion, he'd let it go. But today he knew better. Tracy knew more than she was letting on. He looked at the vacant chair at her station. What was she up to?

Sipping coffee, Janis walked back to his station. He saw Lo working through an error message. Leaning over his shoulder, Janis whispered, "Can you get into Tracy's database?"

"For what?"

"I need to find out what she's been doing at her terminal."

He stopped typing. "First I'll need her terminal access number, but guess what else. Can't do it in secret. The Worm will know we logged on and report to someone."

"Screw the Worm, Lo. If this thing goes bad this afternoon, the snoop program will be with us in oblivion anyway. Try to find her access number."

Lo resumed typing as Janis started pacing.

Matching his stride, Ray joined him. "Now what?"

"Nothing," Janis answered gruffly, reacting to lack of sleep. "Scheduling program set?"

"Yes."

"I've still got some problems to work out."

"What kind of problems?"

"When I figure it out—you'll be the first to know."

Ray went to his station and slumped in his chair, obviously exhausted.

Lo signaled Janis. "Access number."

"Let's see it."

The display opened a "Welcome" window and asked for a password. "What?" Lo said. "Damn! Now I need to find password." He returned to his hacking.

Janis stared at the monitor. "Why the double security on her terminal?"

Lo shrugged, his display changing windows as he worked his magic. "Ah ha!" he said with a grin. "She like Irish Tea."

"How do you know?"

"Password." Tracy's desktop appeared on Lo's screen, scrolling formulas and equations. Janis recognized those relating to the speed of light but the others he hadn't seen before. She'd programmed a spreadsheet of some kind, capable of running several scenarios simultaneously. Janis couldn't make any sense of it. But he was sure of one thing—Tracy had an agenda that had nothing to do with the 13th Power. "What is she looking for?"

"The particle beam," Tracy said over his shoulder.

Janis started, nearly spilling his coffee, the unexpected sound of her voice sending a shiver through him. Busted.

Lo sat upright. "So, this s-stuff yours," he stammered. "Just pop on screen—like magic."

"Like, hell." She looked Janis in the eyes. "All you had to do was ask. Day before yesterday I'd have told you nothing. But today is different. Since the test fire—I'm scared."

"Why?" Janis thought he'd start throwing questions at her.

"I'm not convinced the particle beam technology is worth the risks we're taking."

"What about the particle beam?"

She touched his hand. "It's too complicated to explain right now but listen to me. We've got to stop Curtis. You were right. A perfect test fire would have been a disaster."

Janis led her to the MIGGS window, away from the others. "I don't know how many agendas this project has but I can tell you I'm sick of them. Still, we can't stop now. The Supers are set to run the 13th Power experiment without the fail-safes. Curtis wants us to snatch the Higgs before the void opens and we believe we've made that possible."

Tracy's eyes widened. "N-no! You shouldn't have taken my advice. You know better."

"We had no choice. Curtis is holding Lisa hostage and he'll kill her if we don't cooperate."

"Lisa?"

"Ray's daughter." He left it at that.

"That doesn't surprise me. I've heard he's a man to be wary of." Her voice was almost a whisper.

Janis gave her a baleful glare. "You also know that Ted is really Boris."

Tracy gasped, her lips started trembling. Speechless, she turned away.

But Janis wasn't going to let her avoid him. He yanked her

around. "Right now I don't have time to give a damn about what you know or why you're here. We're in trouble and I need your help."

"What?"

"That lunatic Curtis expects us to contain the Higgs in a millisecond after the laser fires. We've been working all night trying to get the Supers to run the scheduler without error messages. Nothing worked until I added the formula, *negative equals positive*, at laser firing."

"You didn't."

"It fixed the error messages."

A look of panic came over Tracy's face. "But what about the MIGGS?"

"We may have a problem there."

"I can think of two problems right off the top. Did you cross-formulate it?"

"I can't come up with the equations to double check the programming statement against the escape velocity. The MIGGS is a simulator—mathematics makes it work. One wrong formula and it's nothing but an illusion. I'm afraid I've overlooked something."

"If the escape velocity is wrong, the MIGGS won't contain the 13th Power. It'll expand without restraint." Tracy looked around the control room. "You're talking goodbye Solartech Labs, California, and who knows what else. Stopping time was a tricky way to try to make it work."

"But there's a catch. Even if the new programming statement works, when time stops in the MIGGS, the rules of math and physics will be altered and the escape velocity will change as well. Poof. The MIGGS becomes an illusion, the 13th Power escapes, and the space-time continuum bridges the gap between the universe and the atom."

"Disintegration?"

"Total." Janis looked at the MIGGS window. "In the impossible mathematics of negative equals positive, the standard formulas won't work. Two plus two won't equal four, which it must to make the MIGGS work. It can't be cross-formulated with standard mathematics. We need new formulas." He squeezed her hand. "And Tracy, we have to know for sure. Nothing will survive."

"Then we better start working on those formulas." She headed for her station. "If this doesn't work, we're all going to die today."

Janis felt a chill.

Suddenly, the video monitors around the room flickered on and slowly came into focus. What—? Like a horror movie coming to life in the living room, a vivid image of Lisa appeared. She was struggling against shackles that anchored her arms and legs to a stone wall. Her body was wrapped in chains. She cursed at Judas who was quick to push the transmitter button. Blue sparks crackled. Her screams filled Tech-Com Control.

Tracy turned her head away.

Knowing he was on the air, Judas put his rat-gnawed face in front of the camera lens and pushed the button again. He laughed as if he were having the time of his life.

Janis couldn't breathe. Lisa's agonizing screams pierced his heart like arrows.

"You bastard!" Ray yelled and threw his sling to the floor. "I'll kill the son of a bitch!"

A light came on above the control room and Curtis emerged from his office. He leaned on the metal railing and tapped his staff on the landing. "I thought a little motivation might be in order here," Curtis bellowed. "Anybody screw up and Judas will kill her, right before your eyes. Not quickly mind you, but slowly. Painfully. He'll fry her, a little at a time."

"Curtis, you bastard!" Ray yelled. "You'll have your Higgs. I hope you choke on it."

"I'd better have it or you'll choke on Lisa's memory." He went back in his office.

Lo sat at his station staring at the video monitor, his face clouded with fear. "Poor Miss Lisa. Tiger claws slash deep."

Boris limped up to Janis and put a hand on his shoulder. "I not know vhat more dangerous, 13th Power or asshole up there. Sorry I ever met him. We now must do best we can to save the lady." He turned back to his console and picked up his coffee cup, his hand trembling.

Janis went back to Tracy's station where her monitor lit up with equations and formulas on a spreadsheet of lettered rows and numbered columns. "Try 47-D," he suggested.

She was intensely focused on her screen. Her pretty face and sexy hair didn't matter now. He needed her expertise with the spreadsheet she'd developed. Never before had he counted on a woman so much. There was no time for competition. They had to work together to get out of this mess. Her fingers danced over the keyboard.

The Supers made the calculations.

ERROR.

Lisa's screams pierced Tech-Com Control.

Ray rushed over. "We've got to start this experiment before they kill her, damn it! What's the problem now?"

"There's a good possibility the MIGGS won't work with my new formula," Janis said.

"It *has* to work—our lives depend on it."

"The escape velocity might be wrong," Tracy explained.

"Try 44-B," Janis said to Tracy, leaning on the back of her chair.

Tracy typed.

"How are we going to know?" Ray asked, looking at his daughter's horrible condition on the video screen.

"We're cross-formulating it..."

ERROR.

"Take out the new formula," Ray said. "It's too dangerous."

"It's our only hope to contain the Higgs before the void appears. We just need to prove it won't screw up the MIGGS."

"If it does—everything's gone."

"We have to keep trying," Tracy said. "There's no time to lose."

Janis returned his attention to the formulas. Somewhere in that jumble of numbers the answer lurked elusively. "Try 45-C."

Tracy typed.

Ray went back to Lo's station where his monitor scrolled the errors from *MOM*.

Tech-Com Control was silent, except for Lisa's bone-chilling screams.

Chapter One Hundred-Two
THE RESCUE

From the curb, Steve kissed Susan goodbye and waved to Tom. "Take care of her."

Tom gave him a two-fingered salute.

Susan held onto Steve's arm, not wanting to let him go. Doubts flooded her mind. Maybe she shouldn't have made such a big deal over leaving the others at Solartech Labs. Maybe she was sending him to his death in a valiant effort to appease her. Maybe she would never see him again. Steve gently pulled her grip from his arm. "Don't worry. I'll be back. Just stay here like we planned."

"But... "

Steve placed his fingers over her lips. "I know what I'm doing."

She stood helplessly, tears flowing down her cheeks as Steve's red Lebaron disappeared into traffic on Balboa Boulevard. An empty feeling enveloped her. What had she done?

Stopped at a traffic light, Steve checked the case on the seat. In it was the gadgetry he needed to circumvent Solartech Lab's security. It had worked before, when he breached the perimeter at South Gate. Though he wasn't looking forward to doing it again, he felt confident he could pull it off. As he double-checked his holstered .45, the light turned green. He accelerated toward the freeway and north to Simi Valley.

*   *   *

A squadron of Apache helicopters sat poised for flight on the tarmac at Nellis, the noise of roaring engines and thumping rotors filling the air. Devin, looking out the communications building's front door, watched twelve Hueys approaching from the north. Within moments they were hovering loudly overhead. He could see fifty-caliber machine guns, each armed with heavy ribbons of shiny ammunition, protruding from open side doors. Men seated inside wore white armbands with "SP" printed in bold blue letters. They were ready to put an end to the experiments at Solartech

Labs and arrest Curtis. Finally, the bastard was gonna pay.

Colonel Fallon ducked under the rotating blades of his Blackhawk helicopter and waved Devin and Toothless to climb aboard.

The pilot radioed the tower. "Mission Command One—ready at Alpha Bravo." A moment later, the shiny black chopper lifted off and headed west.

Cleared by the tower, the formation of Hueys followed the Blackhawk. Devin watched the Apaches rise from the tarmac in unison and join the armada now hammering over the city. From the north, he saw another squadron of Apaches flying an intercept course toward them. Dispatched twenty minutes earlier from Indian Springs, they were going to fortify the Nellis assault force. The Colonel nodded to his pilot who returned him a thumbs-up signal. They were right on schedule.

Over downtown Las Vegas, the squadrons merged and flew toward Simi Valley, their chopper blades beating to a rhythm unlike anything Devin had ever heard before.

*   *   *

Inside Tamarack Hall, Steve slapped dust off his jeans. After breaching the perimeter again, he thought he'd start his search for Janis and Lisa at their quarters. As he walked down the hallway, a scream came from a room up ahead. Sheila had just opened the door to Janis' room. Steve ran to her side. A wave of panic swept over him.

What a mess. He walked in and righted the couch. As he picked up the phone from the floor and placed the receiver back on its hook, he noticed the cord had been ripped from the wall. What happened here? The place looked like the aftermath of a barroom brawl. When he spotted a smear of blood on the bedroom door, he knew someone had put up one hell of a fight. He turned to Sheila. "Janis must be in big trouble."

"No, Señor. I don't think so," she said. "I saw him leave with Lo this morning. Lisa stayed here, still sleeping."

"Oh, damn!" Steve ran out. "Don't touch anything."

She shook her head and closed the door.

As Steve rushed through the lobby, he realized that Susan was right. He shouldn't have left without them.

Outside, he hailed a passing staff car. "Run me by the labs, will you?"

"Hop in."

At the entrance to the lab buildings, Steve thanked the driver and sprinted up the escalator to the lobby, where a guard sat watching the monitors on the wall.

"How may I help you?" he said evenly.

"I'm looking for Alex," Steve said, his eyes scanning the monitors. "Is he around here…?" He suddenly spotted Lisa on one of the screens, chained to a stone wall, struggling and screaming. What the—?

"He should be at C-Wing… "

Steve put his .45 in the guard's face.

"What the…?"

"Your gun. Give it to me. Slowly." The guard handed over the pistol—grip first. Steve tucked it under his belt.

"There—on monitor 27. Where is that video coming from?"

"D-Block—in the basement on the right." He pointed to a gold elevator door.

"Why is she in chains?"

"Mackey and Crawford tried to back out of the 13th Power experiment. Curtis is using her for leverage." The guard shook his head. "None of us are backing him on this but we have no choice. He's threatened to kill our families if we don't cooperate. The man is a tyrant—and so's his henchman there." He pointed to the monitor.

Steve looked again. "Judas!" Thoughts of revenge raced through his mind. "I'll be damned," he said, looking closer. "The rats damn near got him."

"He's really pissed-off, too."

"I'll bet." With a swift stroke of his .45, Steve knocked the guard unconscious. "About as pissed-off as you're going to be when you wake up with that knot on your head."

Rummaging through the drawers behind the counter, he found a roll of duct tape and a guest ID tag. He clipped the tag to his shirt, dragged the guard into a men's room, and taped him to a toilet—thankful no one was around.

As he placed tape over the guard's mouth, he suddenly

became aware of a noise outside. Faint at first, it was getting louder and louder. He had trouble placing the familiar sound, but finally it came to him. Choppers! Just great! He ran out of the men's room and headed for the gold elevator, his .45 and the guard's revolver in his hands.

WITHOUT BACKUP

Alex closed his office door and logged on to the CIA Web site, typing his password for *The Ark*. Things had gotten out of hand, way beyond his control. The instant message window came up with a flashing cursor. He typed *Apache assault choppers approaching from the north. Curtis is torturing a female hostage to force the scientists to continue the experiment. Due to fire within minutes. Request permission to terminate mission immediately. Mole.*

He waited. How could the military have gotten involved? It must have been Devin. The computer flashed a return message. *Arrest Melvin Anderson. That'll give the military credible evidence that the CIA was on top of this thing. Then eliminate the Russian and Dr. McClarence. They're the only ones that can implicate us. The Ark.*

Alex typed back: *Implicate us? In what?*

Never mind. You don't have much time so get on it.

From the top drawer of his desk, Alex picked up his Glock. The thought of using it on Tracy and Boris settled in his stomach like a rock. But he'd do it—such was his loyalty to *The Ark*. Though Alex wasn't looking forward to arresting Curtis without backup, he knew he had to, before the military arrived. Grabbing a pair of handcuffs, he closed the drawer. Melvin Anderson would be on a plane to Sumatra by morning.

*   *   *

Tracy sat at her station in Tech-Com Control. Her monitor scrolled formulas across the screen with error messages following each calculation. Janis had helped her program the spreadsheet, which now worked through the variables automatically. The escape velocity of the MIGGS eluded her. Over her shoulder she saw Janis pacing, occasionally glancing at the video monitor. Judas seemed to enjoy torturing Lisa, laughing every time she screamed. Tracy felt ill.

The technicians reported to their stations. They too appeared tense and uncomfortable with Lisa's situation. As if in shock, they went about their jobs in silence.

Boris stood at the main console, working the controls. With the whir of electric motors, the new titanium cylinder came down from the ceiling, its shiny chrome finish glistening in the blinking green light. With the joystick, Ray maneuvered the gun sight on his monitor. The titanium cylinder swiveled right and left until *Laser Locked* flashed on the screen. Janis and Ray looked at each other, their eyes red and puffy from lack of sleep. Tracy thought hers probably looked just as bad. How had she ever let *The Ark* talk her into this?

She glanced up to the office window where Curtis stood, a pleased look on his face. Her stomach felt sick. Then Alex walked in. He looked nervous, his golf shirt soaked with sweat. Without a word, he headed up the stairs. Curtis backed away from the window as Alex went into his office. She looked at Janis, who shrugged. It was almost noon.

*   *   *

Alex wasted no time. He pulled the Glock out of his waist-band and pointed it at Curtis, straight-armed. "CIA, Melvin. You're under arrest."

Curtis just stood upright, holding his golden staff and glaring from under the black brim of his hat. "You don't say."

"Drop the walking stick—hands up and turn around." With his left hand, Alex took the handcuffs from his back pocket. "Drop it, I said. And turn around!"

"You think you can just waltz in here and blow my deal behind a CIA smoke screen? Who the hell do you think you are anyway, a hero or something? You're a nobody—a nothing—a bug I'm going to crush under my shoe."

"Make it hard—make it easy, Melvin. It's your choice. Either way, you're going back to Sumatra. They'd love to know you're still available for immediate tenancy. Or maybe they'll just throw you a hanging party, right off. I'm sure they haven't forgotten about Fred Jenkins. Personally, I don't give a damn. Now assume the position and quit wasting my time. I've got two other fish to fry."

Curtis turned his back to Alex and outstretched his arms, raising the staff in the air. His coat spread open making him look twice his size.

"Don't be stupid, Melvin. Drop…"

Suddenly, the sound of a toilet flushing and a door opening jerked Alex's attention to Jonathan, coming out of the bathroom. "Okay, boss. I'm ready to… "

Alex pointed the gun at Jonathan. "Get over… " A sudden wrenching pain stung Alex's arm, the Glock slamming to the floor. He grabbed his arm, which Curtis had struck with his goddamned staff. In a heartbeat, Alex found himself pinned against the wall, the tip of the golden staff pressed hard into his throat. Grabbing the staff with both hands, Alex tried to wrench it away but it was caught under his Adam's apple, cutting of his air.

"CIA, my ass," Curtis said. With his thumb, he pressed the golden eagle's emerald eye. With a shrill sound, spring steel ejected a dagger into Alex's neck and, with a thunk, embedded in the wall behind him. Impaled with his eyes wide open, he could still see Curtis sneering at him. Alex tried to take a breath. It was no use. He tried to kick. His legs wouldn't obey. Lungs burning, he dropped the handcuffs. Darkness covered him in painless sleep.

Chapter One Hundred-Four
WHEN WORLDS COLLIDE

Curtis stepped out of his office, and brandishing Alex's Glock, yelled down to Tech-Com Control. "Proceed." It was noon.

Ray looked at Janis. Janis looked at Tracy.

"Not yet," she said. The escape velocity had still not been computed.

On the video monitor, Judas pushed the transmitter button. Lisa's cries grew more intense as he cranked up the power of his torture machine.

"Let her go first," Ray demanded.

"And ruin all the fun?" Curtis quipped.

"I'll do anything."

"Then start the firing sequence."

"Give us more time," Ray said.

"You've had enough time."

"But we're not ready."

Curtis grinned slyly. "I'll bring her to you."

Lisa screamed. Judas laughed.

"All right!" Ray shouted.

Janis yelled, "No!"

Lisa's torment pained Ray more than he could stand. If they were all going to die anyway, shouldn't they die together? He couldn't bear the thought of his daughter taking her last breath chained to a stone wall, Judas' face the last she would see. He felt faint with fear. The room spun around him. It was the only way— the only way— the only— He pressed the *Fire* button.

Instantly, the Supers began to run the scheduler. The digital clock above the windows showed 4:10 and began counting down each second.

"What have you done?" Janis yelled. "We're not ready!"

Ray turned to Janis, whose face was sour with anger. But Ray didn't care. It was time the hotshot mathematician earned his money. Ray pointed to the clock. "Then you better *get* ready, Janis. You have four minutes." Then Ray yelled at Curtis. "Are you happy now?"

Curtis just smiled.

"Let her go!"

Lisa screamed again.

Curtis leaned over the railing. "I think not. I like her just fine where she is."

"Bastard!"

The MIGGS began to rumble, to vibrate.

"Now you've done it," Janis said. "Look!"

A red glow emanated from the MIGGS window as the black swirling mist began to form. The monitor at Johnson's station displayed a swirling funnel of colors. All they could do now was watch and wait. The fail-safes were gone.

The clock hit 4:00 and the ionizer charged automatically. An electronic female voice announced *"Three minutes to synchrotron."*

"Get back or I'll kill her." Judas's voice echoed through Tech-Com Control, loud and agitated.

What—? Ray gaped at the video monitor. Judas had his back to the wall, holding the transmitter in front of him with both hands, like a gun. "You think I'm shittin' you?" Judas twisted the button on the transmitter to full power.

Steve Raven stepped into the picture. "Go straight to hell!" He opened fire on Judas with both guns blazing. The transmitter clunked on the floor. Judas keeled over. In the flash of an instant, he was on his way to eternity.

Steve frisked through the dead man's pockets, pulled out a key, and unlocked Lisa's chains. She collapsed in his arms. Steve put his face in the camera. "Choppers coming in, Janis. Let's blow this pop stand."

The clock hit 2:49.

"All right!" Ray cheered with a smile of relief. Lisa was safe. It was over. He rushed to his console and hit the Abort button. Another wave of terror rippled through him when *CHANGES LOCKED OUT* flashed on the monitor in bright red letters. "Damn it!" His elation turned to instant despair.

"Two minutes to synchrotron."

"What's wrong?" Janis asked.

"We're locked out! There's no stopping it!"

Janis just smiled and put his hand on Ray's shoulder. "Is that all?" He turned to Lo. "Shut her down, Lo." The clock hit 2:21.

"Put tiger in cage." Lo started typing.

"What's he doing?" asked Ray.

"Opening a back door to the scheduler."

Access Denied flashed on the screen in a window labeled *Worm Security*. "What the...?" Lo's face twisted in disbelief. "Worm took out back door. We're screwed."

Ray's pulse went off the scale. "Now what are we going to do?"

Janis turned to Tracy. "We may have to go through with this, after all. Where do we stand?"

"I don't know yet, Janis." She looked at the clock. 2:00

"One minute to synchrotron."

"Oh God, I just don't know." Her fingers worked the keyboard again.

Janis looked at Lo. "Try the back door to the laser sequencer."

Lo typed.

ACCESS DENIED.

"Shit!" Ray shouted. "There has to be a way to stop this damn thing."

"Shut down the power," Janis said. "Roger—pull the plug."

"I can't. The Supers have complete control. My panel is useless."

Johnson stood, pointing at the MIGGS monitor. "We've got a bright red event horizon, Ray. Escape velocity 186,000 miles per second. We'll be all right."

Ray asked Tracy, "Is it real or an illusion?"

"God—I'm trying...."

The targeting electromagnets switched on, their roar now shaking Tech-Com Control as the clock hit *1:00* and ionizer injected the nuclei into the synchrotron. The RMS microscopes focused on the electron target and the CEI engaged.

"One minute to laser firing."

The synchrotron began accelerating nuclei to their doom. They spun faster and faster in their magnetic sling, the meters rising higher and higher. Ray took a step back from his console. Everything was working perfectly. They'd be okay.

"It's wrong!" Tracy yelled, pointing at her monitor, *FAULT* flashing across the screen. "The MIGGS is just a swirling shadow."

"Everybody out!" Boris yelled and ran for the exit.

Ray hit the intercom mike. "Attention all personnel." His voice echoed through Solartech Labs. "Evacuate the building. Tech-Com Control is going to blow in forty-seven seconds."

An emergency horn resonated throughout the compound, sending workers scrambling for exits. Ray was headed for the door when Janis grabbed his arm.

"Where do you think you're going, damn it? You got us into this mess. What are we missing here?"

"We gotta get out of here." The clock flashed 0:25.

Tracy sat at her station, choosing to die at her terminal. "The damn Supers should know this isn't going to work," she said. "They're supposed to control everything."

Janis turned to Ray. "They're supposed to, but they don't. They don't control the titanium cylinder."

The clock showed fifteen seconds. "For Christ's sake, Janis—there's no time for this conversation."

"Do they, Ray?" Janis shook him.

"Taking the cylinder out of the MIGGS won't stop the particle beam."

Janis looked at the clock. —Nine seconds, 0:08, 0:07— "But we can sure as hell redirect it." He ran to Ray's station, grabbed the joystick, and yanked it to the left. The titanium cylinder rotated sideways in the MIGGS.

0:00. The laser fired.

From out of the synchrotron came a beam of intense light, buzzing with accelerated particles. The power of sunlight was fused and focused on a single point, which struck the shiny side of the titanium cylinder and reflected back into the particle accelerator, disintegrating the laser resonator and a large part of the synchrotron. The disintegration of atoms left a huge space devoid of matter, which atmospheric pressure reclaimed with a boom deep under Simi Valley.

Janis heard it coming, rumbling in the distance, getting louder and louder, closer and closer. The building started shaking.

"Jesus!" Ray spread his feet, steadying himself on the floor. "What's that?"

Clinging to a console, Janis shouted, "Sounds like the concussion coming back this way."

"Let's get out of here!" Ray ran out and didn't look back.

"Tracy!" Janis yelled, stumbling toward her station. Video screens crashed to the floor. Windows cracked. Terminals spewed popping sparks. Plaster rained down.

Hanging on to her trembling console, she stood staring, open-mouthed and wide-eyed at her screen. "It worked! I can't believe it—the particle beam worked!"

Janis grabbed her arm. "Run!" He pulled her out of Tech-Com Control.

Running through the glass-enclosed catwalk, he saw windows at the far end of the building explode and scatter glass down to the ramp. Like a tidal wave crashing toward them, windows blew out, one at a time, getting closer and closer, louder and louder, a deafening noise now thundering through the halls. "Hurry!"

Creaking, the floor suddenly twisted, the glass enclosure cracking around them, sending fracture lines hissing along the catwalk, as if racing them to the corridor. Janis pulled Tracy along, stumbling and tripping. They were almost to the building on the other side, almost to safety. With a horrendous bang, the catwalk buckled and fell.

"JUMP!"

Chapter One Hundred-Five
THE SURVIVORS

Janis and Tracy leaped just as the catwalk broke away. Hitting the corridor floor together, they slid on the tile and slammed to a stop against a wall. Breathing hard, he looked back. In a shower of glass and twisted steel, the catwalk crashed to the ramp below. Through a gaping hole left in the building, he could see the steel archway with its ominous greeting teetering back and forth. Creaking eerily, it twisted and plummeted to the ground. He wiped sweat from his forehead. That was too close.

Dust and smoke billowed from the debris and swirled into the corridor. Janis pulled Tracy to her feet. She held his hand so tight it hurt. But they were safe. Hand in hand, he led her toward the lobby. In silence, he turned to look at her. A light smile graced her lips and their eyes met. He felt warm inside. Could she be the one?

Suddenly, from a dark office, Jonathan leaped out, brandishing a Colt revolver and blocking their way. His eyes glittered with fury.

Janis pulled Tracy close as he calculated his next move. Jonathan wouldn't shoot them. Janis was sure of it. But his confidence changed abruptly when Curtis stepped from behind his aide. Janis tried to swallow a lump in his throat as Curtis walked forward, tapping his golden staff. His menacing glare escalated Janis' concern for their safety.

Curtis stood in front of him, the staff at his side, a gun tucked behind his belt. "We made a deal, Dr. Mackey," he said. "A deal we sealed with a handshake. In the performance of my part, I transferred the balance of the agreed-upon fee into your bank account."

"You shouldn't have."

"I didn't get my money's worth, Dr. Mackey. Where's my 13th Power?"

Janis released Tracy and went nose to nose with Curtis. "The 13th Power doesn't belong to you, *Mister* Curtis. It's not yours for the taking. It belongs to the cosmos, guarding the rules of physics and math that make our universe possible. Our galaxy is bound to the universe by those rules, the same rules our earth is bound to our sun and the tiniest atom's electron is bound to its nucleus.

Even you can't break those rules. Or has your lust for power made you think you have the right?"

Curtis didn't answer, just stared into Janis' eyes, looking like he could explode with anger. He clutched his golden staff so tightly his knuckles turned white.

But Janis held his ground. "Take the time to look up at the sky tonight. When you see the stars stretching across the heavens, be glad it's all still there." He pulled on Tracy's arm. "Come on. It smells bad in here."

Stepping in front of them, Curtis raised the golden staff, his thumb hovering over an emerald eye. "You're pathetic."

"You're the one who risked everything and gained nothing."

Suddenly, running footsteps and yelling voices echoed from somewhere down the corridor. Curtis whipped around. Devin and Colonel Fallon rounded the corner, followed by several SPs.

"That's him!" Devin yelled, pointing at Curtis.

A gunshot rang out.

Janis dove to the floor, pulling Tracy with him, shielding her with his body and looking back at Curtis. Gun in hand, he was watching Devin's blood pool on the floor. The round had struck him in the heart.

Curtis smiled. His gold tooth glinted.

"GOD DAMN YOU!" the Colonel yelled.

His men opened fire. Jonathan and Curtis fired back and dove into the dark office.

Janis sheltered Tracy in his arms, hoping a stray bullet wouldn't end their lives. When the gunfire stopped, he glanced up and saw SPs rushing the office doorway. But sensing a trap, they hesitated to go in after Curtis. "Throw down your weapons!" Fallon ordered. "Come out with your hands up!"

Silence.

The golden staff was lying on the hallway floor, alone.

Janis grabbed Tracy's hand. "Come on!"

Outside, he squinted against the hazy afternoon sunshine. Whining turbine engines filled the air. There were choppers everywhere—some hovering overhead. Others landed on lawns, streets, parking lots, and rooftops. The Air Force had invaded every part of Solartech Labs. SPs were posted all around, their rifles held at the ready. But there was no battle being waged with

Solartech Labs' security force. The incursion appeared to have been swift, without resistance.

Stepping over fire hoses, which were running every-which-way across the lawn, between fire trucks, hydrants, and the building, he led Tracy through a maze of men and machines, looking for the others. He saw a security guard kneeling on the grass, pulling stubborn duct tape off his clothes.

A team of medics emerged from the building, rolling a gurney. Janis stopped them. Carefully, he lifted the sheet covering a body. It was Alex, a golden dagger pierced through his throat. Tracy quickly turned away. Shaking his head, Janis dropped the sheet and motioned the medics to move on.

"Come on," he said to Tracy. "Let's keep moving."

They made their way to the fountain where Janis scooped up a handful of water and splashed it on his face and neck. Tracy patted water on her forehead. Boris found them.

"Dr. Janis. Dr. Tracy," he said. "You are very smart under pressure. I thank you." He shook their hands and smiled through ugly teeth. "I go now."

"Not so fast." Janis grabbed the old man's collar. "You and Tracy have some explaining to do."

They sat by the fountain as valves opened and water shot skyward. The cool spray was as refreshing as it was magnificent. Tracy and Boris explained their involvement with the CIA, the 13th Power project, and the President's Directive Number 119. The roar of the fountain overpowered their voices. No one else could hear what was said or the advice Janis gave them.

"Be careful where you tell this story. The CIA isn't going to want it made public. I think they'd sooner kill you." Just as he finished speaking, Ray found them.

"Brilliant, Janis," he said. "You guys all right?"

Janis nodded. "How about the others?"

"Shaken is all—thanks to you."

"And Lisa?"

"Steve took her to Tamarack Hall to get some clothes. Doc says she's okay, considering."

The Colonel and his men caught Janis' attention as they emerged from the building, toting Devin's body. Fallon carried the golden staff in one hand. He told his men to lay Devin on the grass.

The sight sent a shiver down Janis' spine. He and Ray ran to Colonel Fallon, who summoned a medic to bring a gurney. "And a clean sheet, too."

Toothless ran from a nearby chopper and kneeled beside his boss. "Why?" he wailed. "I should've gone in with him."

Janis lowered his head, not wanting to watch the big goon cry.

Ray stood stunned with his mouth hanging open, obviously distressed by the sight of Devin lying there dead. "Why couldn't he have just left us alone?"

The Colonel was quick to answer. "Because he cared—that's why. He was the only one who knew that Curtis was about to destroy the world. Even I didn't believe him at first."

"So where *is* Curtis?" Janis asked.

"Gone," the Colonel replied.

"He got away?"

"Disappeared down a stairway that led to hell for all we know. We found a maze of tunnels going every which way."

"Son of a bitch," Janis said. "The service access tunnels."

"We searched what we could, but it was obvious the snake had escaped into his hole. He's probably in Mexico by now."

"But he's no coward. He'll be back."

"And I'll be waiting," said the Colonel.

Disappointed, Janis headed toward the fountain.

Ray rubbed his stubbly chin as he walked alongside Janis. "You know what I'm thinking?"

"I can't imagine."

"This place needs someone like us to get it up and running again. I'm going to stay here—and Lisa, too. How about you? And let's ask Tracy and Boris. We make a great team."

"Sounds like a good idea, Ray. But count me out. I miss my quiet life in Colorado."

"Won't you even think about it? It'll be just like old times. Only better."

"When was the last time I heard that?"

"Janis." His name floated in the air with the sweetness of Lisa's voice. He whipped around and saw her running toward him from the open door of a staff car where Lo leaned against the fender and beamed a smile broad as his face.

"Janis," she called out as she ran. Golden hair flowed behind her like silk.

She threw her arms around his neck and hugged him. Her body felt warm.

"Don't ever let me go, darling," she whispered in his ear.

"Lisa. I'm going home."

"No," she said and hugged his neck tighter.

"My mother needs me and your place is here with your father. He risked the world for you. He needs you and you need him."

Her sparkling eyes met his. "It feels so good not to hate him anymore."

"I'm happy for both of you."

She hugged him one last time and whispered softly in his ear. "Thanks for the ride, cowboy."

He tipped an invisible hat. "You're welcome, ma'am."

As she ran to her father's side, Janis felt a sudden loss. He was going to miss being her cowboy.

A red Lebaron pulled up to the curb.

Janis walked toward Tracy. She was as smart and courageous as she was beautiful. He took her hand. Her eyes looked sad. "Goodbye," he said. "If you'd like to see the peaceful side of life, call me at the University of Colorado. We could use a brilliant scientist like you."

"I just might do that," she said with a warm smile that lit up her eyes.

Janis walked to the Lebaron without looking back.

As the car drove out of sight, Lisa waved goodbye. She knew Janis didn't see her but it made her feel better, just the same.

Chapter One Hundred-Six
OUT OF THE ASHES

In the CIA office of Chief Higgins, the red phone on the desk rang. He let it ring longer than he had to. "Higgins."

"What happened out there, Lawrence? My communications are down."

"Look, John—we've lost Alex. I've pulled the rest of my men out. It's over."

"Did we get the particle beam for the President?"

"No. The Worm's transmissions were cut off by an explosion."

"Damn it, Lawrence! What am I going to do now?"

"Guess it's back to old-fashioned diplomacy," Higgins said. "Now I'd like to get back to my guest list for the party."

"Party? What about our involvement in this thing? Are we covered?"

"Quit worrying, I tell you. There's no evidence left *anywhere* to link us to the 13th Power project, Atomtech, Judge Freeman or the Hawker crash. I've covered our tracks. So, relax. We're home free."

"What about the 'black box'?"

"I've got a team at the crash site," Higgins said, annoyed. "They're going to offer to expeditiously transport it for quick analysis. Nobody will ever see it again."

"And Tracy and Boris?"

"We'll get them."

"You sure?"

"It's all arranged."

"It better be." Nathan hung up.

Lawrence huffed. *The Ark* worried too damn much.

*   *   *

Joe Rose sat on a flatbed trailer hitched to a cab-over semi and scanned the black scene of the jet crash. Acrid smoke wisped from small pockets of smoldering debris, carrying with it that same rancid smell of every crash site he'd seen—a mix of charred flesh and burned jet fuel. The air stunk of death. And though he'd seen worse in his twelve years with the NTSB's crash investigating team, this crash fell into his one-size-fits-all category of air disasters. Bad.

Arching his back to relieve the stiffness in his muscles, he realized the endless hours of waiting were taking their toll. Affectionately known as "The Scrappers," his team had the last and hardest job to be done. It sometimes took hours, sometimes days. This mess didn't look too tough. Not much of it was over waist high.

For the past two hours, he had watched recovery teams scour through tangled aluminum and twisted metal. Their orange fire suits and helmets glowed in the blackness of the charred wreckage around them. With small yellow flags, they marked the locations of the grisly remains of passengers and crew. Large yellow body bags were laid out among the flags. He didn't understand how they knew which pieces went into which bags. Or did it really matter?

Flash bulbs popped, giving the crash site an eerie contrast of grays, blacks, and shadows. After the photographers finished, a coroner's team went in to do the gruesome task of body removal. While they worked their way through the rubble, filling their yellow bags, investigators stood off to one side, huddled in conversation. The I-team—with their neatly pressed white lab coats—looked too sterile for this bleak environment. Joe glanced down at his dusty blue jeans and black rubber boots. He was dressed for the dirty work.

Day turned to dusk by the time the investigators finished. Joe pulled a roast beef sandwich from his lunch box as the recovery team tagged mangled pieces of the wrecked Hawker—red for the scrap yard, green for the hanger for closer inspection. The red ones would go on his flatbed.

A sudden commotion near the twisted tail caught his attention. An I-team member was carrying something. Several others gathered around him. Joe raised his eyebrows. They'd found the prize, the "black box," containing the flight data and cockpit voice recorders, all vital clues to the demise of the Hawker.

A group of dark-suited men—Joe counted four of them—approached the I-team members. This was unusual—who were they? He ate the last of his sandwich and watched. After what appeared to be a lengthy discussion, the I-team gave the "black box" to the suits who rushed it away in a black sedan. Joe bit his lower lip. Must have been something really important about that flight.

A diesel generator rattled to life. With a thunk, huge floodlights came on, the brightness making him squint. He chucked a cookie and closed his lunch box. It was time.

"Let's go, boys," he said into his two-way.

His men worked through the night under floodlights. With blazing torches they cut up the jet and loaded his flatbed. A chunk of wing and the tail section were already secured with tie-downs. Joe thought the job was coming along just fine. As the early rays of dawn began to penetrate the sky, one of his men called him over.

"What is it, Al?"

"Look what I found." He yanked on a steel box, half covered by debris and scorched black. "Help me with this."

Working together, they freed it from the rubble.

"It's an air-safe, boss."

"And a heavy one." Joe groaned, rolling it over. The dial on the door was broken off but the hinges were still intact. "I've heard about these air-safes—they're fire, bomb, and impact proof. This one survived the crash."

Joe pulled a rag from his pocket and rubbed soot off the door, revealing a seal and inscription. "It's the FBI's all right."

Al rubbed his prickly chin. "Do you think there's any money in it?"

"I doubt it. These things are used to protect important documents, maybe critical evidence in their investigations, in files or on computer disks."

"Maybe they stashed somethin' in this one."

"Who knows." Joe stood and stuffed the rag in his back pocket.

Al gave the air-safe a kick. "What should we do, boss—scrap it?"

"No. Let's return it to the FBI. They'll know what to do with it."